Check out the latest about Genevra Bonati.
genevrabonati.com

Forgiven and Free, A Halted Heart

ISBN# 978-1-7363544-0-7
LCCN or CIP# 2020925244

Printed in Colorado.
United States of America.

Dedicated
to the
Life-Givers!
You…
Bring Life—
Bring Love—
Bring Hope—

FORGIVEN & FREE
BOOK I

A HALTED HEART

GENEVRA BONATI

CHAPTER ONE

If I speak in the tongues of men and of angels but have not love,
I am only a resounding gong or clanging cymbal.
1CORINTHIANS 13:1

Caitlynn Grant stood under a canopy of trees, flashing her best TV smile at the camera pointed toward her face. As it sometimes happened, things weren't going as planned, and she had to improvise. "Hold up a second," she said and handed the microphone to her cameraman, Ryan. "I have to get something from the van."

With each step, her hiking boots crushed pine needles on the ground, sending up a burst of scent like sudden droplets of rain. She popped open the van's rear door, rummaged through a box, and pulled out a small rainbow-colored bear with the station's logo on its paw. She held the stuffed animal behind her back and hurried to where a young girl was sitting on a blanket with her mother.

Ryan handed Caitlynn the microphone, then trained the camera on her and whispered, "Three, two, one…"

Caitlynn stared into the lens. "This is Caitlynn Grant with Channel Twelve news reporting from about three miles west of Rocky Mountain National Park. Sarah, the eight-year-old girl lost in the forest for almost twenty-four hours, was rescued just moments ago by the Rocky Mountain Search and Rescue team." She stooped low, eye level with the young girl." Sarah, you're a brave little girl to survive all night alone in the mountains."

Sarah's lips quivered. "Thank you." She hesitated. "I said a lot of prayers."

"Whatever you did, it worked! Now I have a surprise for you in honor of your bravery." She presented the bear to the little girl.

Sarah's face lit up. "He's so cute." She hugged him close. "I can't wait to show my friends." Her eyes sparkled with unshed tears. "Thanks."

Caitlynn caressed Sarah's golden-brown hair, thankful she didn't have to report a tragedy. Her voice sounded husky with emotion. "You're welcome—and you deserve so much more." She turned her attention to the girl's mother. "Ashley, I'm sure you will never forget this day. You're reunited with your daughter."

Ashley shivered. "I just turned away for a few minutes to pitch the tent and the next thing I knew. . ." Tears streaked her cheeks as they mixed with the grime of a long, sleepless night of searching.

Caitlynn glanced at the high mountains, dense with evergreens and aspens, their leaves shimmering like golden nuggets in the warm Indian summer. "The important thing is that Sarah's alive after spending the night in the forest." She shook her head in disbelief. "And she only sustained a few mosquito bites and dehydration."

A blanket hung loosely around Sarah's shoulders. Ashley reached over, wrapped it snug around her daughter, and said, "Thank God she had on a warm jacket." Her lips formed a thin line.

"Yes," Caitlynn said, "the temperature dropped to forty-four degrees last night."

"I'm never going camping in a remote area ever again. Next time, it'll be in a campground with a city of tents, campers, and recreation vehicles, crowded with people and dogs and campfires!" A fresh wave of tears erupted.

Caitlynn brushed her fingers across her neck, signaling for Ryan to cut the tape. She gently touched Ashley's hand. "We can finish up in the studio. I'm very sorry this happened. Our viewers will be so glad there's a happy ending." She turned off the mic. "What a coincidence—there's an actual rescue on the weekend I decide to follow the search and rescue team in a training run. What unbelievable luck!"

Ashley brushed a twig from Sarah's hair. "You can call it whatever you want—coincidence or luck." Her eyes shone like two headlights penetrating a dark night. "I'm calling it a miracle."

They quickly packed up—wires, sound equipment, microphones, and the camera, shoving them into bags and cases. With a quick goodbye to the rescue team, Caitlynn and Ryan hauled the items back to the van, loaded it up, and hightailed it out of the mountains. Caitlynn sat shotgun beside Ryan. He navigated around several large boulders until he maneuvered onto the dirt road and drove toward the highway.

He glanced her way and flashed a sheepish grin. "I probably should've mentioned this before we taped, but, uh, you might want to freshen up a bit before we get back to the station."

Caitlynn lowered the visor mirror. Her crystal blue eyes were bloodshot from lack of sleep paired nicely with the streak of dirt smudged on her left cheek. A smoky smell coated her Strawberry blond windblown hair. She frowned and snapped the visor shut. "I guess I didn't think about how I looked. I just wanted to report the story the moment we found Sarah."

Ryan gave a supportive nod. "You're not only a great reporter, but you're also a good person. Traipsing all over the forest, trying to find a lost little girl…"

"Puh-lease. Who wouldn't search for a lost child?"

"Okay." He shrugged. "I suppose most people might. But would they go without dinner? Sleep in a tent? And then search from sunup to sundown with no break?"

"Believe me; I'm no saint. I just happen to have a warm spot for kids." Her hand fell to her abdomen, rubbing it gently as she glanced out the side window, hiding the pain in her eyes.

Ryan grinned and said, half-jokingly, "I can be a great big kid if you want me to."

She landed a soft punch on his arm. "You had to say that, didn't you?"

"Sorry… couldn't resist." Ryan's smile faded. "By the way, did you hear the rumor about the station getting sold?"

Caitlynn searched her backpack and pulled out a hairbrush. She slipped off her fleece headband, raked the brush through her hair, sweeping away dust and loose dirt. "Why should it matter to us? It has happened before, remember? Seven years ago, and we kept our jobs."

"What if they want to make you a news anchor again?"

"I've declined so many offers from our news director that I think Ed's grown tired of asking." Caitlynn couldn't see herself sitting behind the desk, waiting for the news story. She always had to be the first person on the scene, scooping the news, not telling it. She majored in journalism in college, and thought she wanted to be a high-profile anchor, that all changed when at age twenty, and interning at the local news station, she was assigned to go out in the field.

She stuffed the brush back inside, pulled a single disposable wet wipe from the pocket, tore open the top, and washed away the remaining dirt off her face. "Besides, I didn't have the reputation back then that I do now. Hopefully, whoever buys the station will see I'm really good at my job."

She wadded up the wipe and shoved it into the empty package. "What about you, Ryan? What if they stick you in the studio behind a camera?" The last time the station sold, Ryan was working in film editing part-time, but for the last three years, he was out in the field with Caitlynn full-time.

He waved his hand in the air. "That's crazy. There's no way I would accept that position. Not if it meant working without you…" He joked. "I've finally mastered the best camera angle to show your good side."

"Ha-ha, very funny!" She pulled lip balm out of her makeup bag and swiped it across her lips. "Seriously, you're great to work with too." She shrugged. "I'm not worried. Station owners are always trying to buy more market share, but nothing ever changes."

Ryan frowned and switched on the radio. "I hope you're right."

Caitlynn leaned back against her seat. "We'll find out soon enough. The all-hands-on-deck meeting is right after the nightly news."

When they returned to the station, they made a beeline to the green room to edit and wrap up the story in time for tonight's broadcast.

###

The ten o'clock news story of Sarah's rescue and the joyful outcome wrapped up the broadcast. When the show ended, Caitlynn followed the evening news team to the conference room.

Ed Greene sidled up to Caitlynn and tapped her shoulder. He always wore a blue suit and a tie with some sort of pattern on it. Today it was green with circles. "Great story, as usual, Caitlynn. Leave it to you to be in the right place at the right time!"

Caitlynn smiled. "Thanks, Ed. I'm glad I could report something positive for a change."

"I'm sure our viewers are just as thankful," he added, shaking his head. "Poor Mom."

Ryan walked over, and together they filed into the conference room. The stale aroma of coffee hung in the air. A large mahogany table sat in the center, and every seat occupied with news anchors, office staff, and camera crews. Caitlynn and Ryan squeezed in and stood against the wall with the rest of the latecomers while Ed took a seat reserved for him at the end of the table.

The station manager, Russell Creighton, stood at the table's head. "I'm sure all of you have heard the rumor about the station selling. A bid was presented to buy partial ownership of the station to the board, and they've accepted the offer." He scanned the crowd. "Effective immediately, I will no longer be the station manager. I've accepted a job in Dallas. Your new manager—and part-owner—will begin on Monday."

Murmurs rumbled throughout the room. Caitlynn shrugged. The station had seen plenty of shakeups, but nothing much changed.

Ed stood and shook Russell's hand. "I think I can speak for all of us here. You've been great to work with, and we're going to miss you."

"Thanks, Ed. I appreciate your kind words. I've heard positive comments about the new manager, and I've talked to him several times this week. I think he should be a great fit for our team."

Caitlynn crossed her arms. *We'll see about that.* She liked Russ and his low-key approach to managing.

"Who is the new guy?" Ed asked. "Do any of us know him?"

"I don't think so," Russ answered. "He's from Chicago. A man by the name of Steven Preston Carr."

Caitlynn gasped, her hand covering her lips. Her body swayed. Clutching Ryan's arm, she inhaled deeply. *This can't be happening.* Small lights danced in her peripheral vision.

Ryan's eyes widened. "You're white as a sheet, Caitlynn." His voice lowered, "Are you going to pass out?"

He quickly grabbed her by the shoulders and forged his way through the crowd toward the exit. One step out into the hallway, and Caitlynn gulped in the fresh air. She desperately tried to regain her composure.

"Are you okay?" Ryan asked.

"I'm fine, I just needed…some…um…air." How fast could she get him to leave? "I, uh, I saw a huge cake for Russ in the kitchen. You're gonna want a piece."

He furrowed his brow. "You sure? I'll come back and check on you in a few minutes."

"Stop exaggerating. I'm good." She pushed him toward the conference room. "Go!"

"Okay, I'll go, but I don't like it. You still look like you might faint or something." He stared at her, concern in his eyes. "Catch up on your sleep. I'll see you Monday."

She flashed a pretend smile, knowing that sleep wouldn't be an option. Only one thought flooded her mind: this had to be a cruel joke.

She stormed down the hall and into her office to grab her bag and coat. Laughter from the meeting reached her ears, but nothing about this moment felt funny. Nauseous, her stomach lurched. *It's okay, just breathe.* After a few deep breaths, she gained her composure and made her way to the parking lot.

Caitlynn drove home with the convertible top down in her silver-blue Solara, hoping the familiar feel of the whipping wind and the sound of the cars whizzing past would help clear her head.

But all it seemed to do was mess up her hair. She rolled up the driver's side window, but neither the freedom of the wind against her skin nor the fresh autumn air helped to relieve this living nightmare. She glanced west of Denver and imagined the Rocky Mountain's panoramic view—too dark to see on this chilly night. On many mornings, a beautiful mist would hover over the mountaintops, and she always wanted to reach out and touch it. She scoffed at the thought. It would be nice if a mist would sweep in and engulf her. No, not a mist—she wanted to disappear into a fog so dense it would take a team of search and rescue volunteers to find her. She could just get off at the next exit and drive off…go somewhere, anywhere away from him.

As she exited the highway, a pang of anger hit hard. This news most certainly ruined her weekend. She just couldn't let herself be preoccupied with thoughts of *him.* But the reality was staring her in the face: she would think of nothing else, her mind consumed by the anticipation of seeing him on Monday morning. And after that, she'd actually have to work with him. She clenched and unclenched her fist while sucking in a deep breath. Nothing calmed her racing heart. Accepting the inevitable, she could only think of one strategy when she saw Steve.

"Defend my turf," she said into the night air.

Never again would she let the past repeat itself. Ever.

CHAPTER TWO

The building loomed twelve stories high, casting shadows on the pavement in the early morning light. Steven Preston Carr III swallowed a lump in his throat as he peered up at the brick building. For a moment, he questioned his choice to take on this job. Three months ago, it sounded like a good idea. Now, though, as he stood there in his gray suit and blue tie, his hand clutching an almost empty briefcase, he wondered how all of this would play out.

Steve liked to get to work early, but today he arrived forty minutes before his usual time. On his first day as station manager, he needed time to get comfortable with his new surroundings and prioritize his day. By 6:30 a.m., he'd organized his desk, written out his to-do list, and opened, *My Utmost for His Highest*, devotional to today's date, October 25th.

After reading the passage, he placed the book in the drawer and said a prayer for strength. He wasn't looking forward to seeing Caitlynn. He couldn't be sure how he would feel when they met again. It had been twelve years since they last saw each other. He knew he'd hurt her in the past, but hopefully, she'd moved on. He remembered Caitlynn as beautiful, vibrant, and warm-hearted. She was probably married, busy with a family, and by now, he was nothing more than a bad relationship, as forgotten as the college exams they'd both crammed for until they were all blurry-eyed.

He glanced at his watch and sighed. So far, he'd been shown to his office by a young intern, but no one had come in to say hello or introduce themselves, which seemed a little odd. Maybe he'd gotten here too early; however, there was a meeting request to acquaint himself to the staff in one hour.

Steve left his office and walked to the break room to refill his cup of coffee. A few employees lingering near the coffee station paused to introduce themselves, then promptly left the room. The station hummed with the sound of keyboard strikes from reporters writing today's top stories while competing with the muted hum of television broadcasts from various networks. He smiled at one of the staff writers and introduced himself. Several others in the room made their way over.

Energized by their brief welcome, he strode down the hall and froze in his steps. His heart raced uncontrollably. *Caitlynn.* Her high heels struck the tile floor in quick succession as her arms swung back and forth in time with the sound. Dressed in a royal blue blazer, white silk top, dark tailored pants, and a grim expression. Twelve years ago, her long blonde hair was perpetually in a ponytail. Now it was a warm strawberry blonde and brushed her shoulders. After all these years, she was still beautiful.

He stepped forward and stretched out his hand in greeting but quickly hid his disappointment and pulled his hand to his side when he saw the grimace on her face.

"What are you doing here," she spat.

"That's such a rhetorical question for a reporter," he joked.

Caitlynn crossed her arms, her glare locked in on his face.

"The years have been kind to you. You've hardly changed." Except that he could barely make out the freckles that graced her cheeks and nose. Why would she cover them with makeup? He had loved those freckles…

The hard look in her eyes softened, "If that's a compliment, I'll take it."

Steve grinned. "It is, and you're welcome."

Caitlynn reached up and twisted a loose strand of hair behind her ear. "You haven't answered my question."

Steve had forgotten the nervous habit she had of messing with her hair. The memories of their past crept into his mind. They were both twenty-two the last time he saw her twisting a strand of hair, tears in her eyes, while he hurried to move out of their apartment near the campus of the University of Colorado. So many regrets. He shut out the imagery. "I've been busy developing my career, which in a way has gone full circle—here I am with you again.

Caitlynn's grimace deepened. "How long is your contract for at the station?"

"Wow," he said, "you must be a great reporter the way you're hammering me with the what, where, when, why, and how."

"You haven't answered the question," she said.

I should've prayer harder. What was I thinking? That she'd bury the past? "You amaze me." He shook his head slightly. "You stand here with a frozen smile—no, a scowl—plastered on your face like you honestly don't know how long my contract is. You must know I'm here indefinitely. I'm part-owner of the station."

She bit her lip. "I heard rumors, but I like to get my information straight from the source." She crossed her arms again and glared. "It's a lesson I learned the hard way." Her forced smile faded to a frown. "All I can say is…with you as my new boss, my life has just gone from bad to worse." She stomped off as if she were running from a ghost.

He walked slowly back to his office, trying to soak it all in. Caitlynn still looked beautiful and vibrant, but what had happened to her warm heart?

CHAPTER THREE

Caitlynn stood just outside Steve's door; her chest tight as if an elephant stood atop—crushing down with all its might. Except for the weekly staff meeting on Tuesdays, she'd successfully avoided him. Thankful was the only word she could use to describe the fact that today was Friday. Forcing herself to breathe, she tapped on the door and walked inside.

Steve looked up, dropped his pen, furrowed his brow. Was it worry? Concern? Or her imagination? "What can I do for you, Caitlynn? You look a bit—frazzled."

Sitting in the chair opposite his, Caitlynn replied, "I want you to know I'm scheduled for surgery in a few weeks. I'll need to schedule medical leave." Her eyes were gritty. *Stay strong. Don't cry.*

His chair scraped across the floor as he scooted in closer to the desk.

On the credenza next to his desk, Caitlynn glared at the picture of Steve sitting at the Cubs baseball stadium next to his son—a cute kid –around seven years old, grinning ear to ear, wearing a baseball glove with a baseball nestled in the pocket of the glove. Where Steve had dark wavy brown hair and deep blue eyes, his son had sandy brown hair, the same blue eyes, plus a scattering of freckles across his cheeks and nose. She frowned and clenched her fist. "You should get Tina to fill in for me . . . she's dying to replace me." If only she could run out of the room.

He raised his brows. "Surgery?" he repeated in a worried tone. "How long will you be out?"

She kept her voice as neutral as possible. She went to great lengths to keep all inflection out of her voice when reporting a tragic or emotionally draining story, and she relied on that training now. "I have a doctor's appointment on Monday to discuss the exact timeline for my procedure. I'm scheduled the day before Thanksgiving." She bit her lip to keep it from trembling. "My best guess is that it's about a three-week recovery time."

He pushed his chair back like a caged tiger ready to spring at any second. "That's just great. Thanks for telling me this now." He glanced at the calendar, drumming his fingers on the desk. "Thanksgiving is a month away. I feel like a complete jerk. Why did you say you would do the story at our staff meeting?"

"I don't recall you offering me the option of choosing to do the story. In fact, I believe you said—and I quote—'I want you to do a story on teenage girls who keep their babies.' Don't worry, Steve; you'll get your story."

"Caitlynn, I can't ask this as your boss, but as an old friend, I have to ask. What kind of surgery are you having?"

This is exactly the conversation she dreaded, and why she didn't want to see him alone in his office. She didn't want to go down memory lane—it was too painful. She focused on the panoramic picture of Maroon Bells above the credenza, desperately trying to calm her temper.

Old friends? That's how he see us as old friends? We were in love…college sweethearts for three years. *We lived together.*

She squirmed in her seat. "Is that what you thought we were in college—just *friends?*" Caitlynn spoke through gritted teeth. "You'll find out soon enough; nothing stays a secret in our office. But for now, I'd like to keep it private."

"I'm sorry." He cleared his throat. "Of course, I'll arrange for your fill-in. Tina can pinch-hit for you… I had no idea." Steve stared at her with another look of sympathy she didn't need nor want. After a moment, he said, "Caitlynn, I'm not as insensitive as you seem to think. If there's anything I can do, I'd like to help. Maybe you could give me a second chance. I'm not the person you knew twelve years ago."

Is he serious? He had a lot of nerve sitting there all high and mighty and acting like he cared. Her cheeks burned. "You know what? I'm sick to death of men and their second chances." Without another word, she bolted out of the room.

On the ride home, Caitlynn gripped the steering wheel until her hands hurt. She was angry, but there was also a layer of sadness, buried deep, that was threatening to surface.

Acting more like a broken-hearted teenager—not that of a woman thirty-four years old. Embarrassed recalling how she handled her frustration, a tell-tale burn surfaced, and she knew her face flamed red.

When she turned down her street, she forced herself to calm down. But then she saw Jake's chrome and leather Harley Davidson taking up one whole side of the driveway. Caitlynn pressed the remote and pulled into the garage of her townhome. She gathered her stuff, then opened the door that led to the foyer and dumped her tote bag and laptop case on the table.

Jake met her in the hall and hugged her. "Hey, you're late. What took you so long?"

They'd dated now nine months, and during that time, Jake had made her laugh and forget about all the things that bothered her. He was handsome, carefree, and athletic. Always up for the two of them to go running. At one point, she thought he might actually be "the one," but as time wore on, the luster had worn off, and these last few months, it had even grown dull. Their connection lacked oomph. At first, she chided herself, wondering if perhaps she was doing something wrong. And was it something she could fix? But then realization dawned, she was doing what she always did with all the other "Jakes," merely settling. Why couldn't she find real love? And did it even exist?

Caitlynn shrugged from his embrace. "Don't you remember? I talked to my boss today."

"Oh. Yeah. How did that go?"

"I could've handled it better." A deep sigh of regret escaped. "I said some things I wish I could take back."

He shrugged. "It's Friday. My bet is he'll be too busy this weekend to think about you. Right now, you need to get ready. We want to make it to Estes Park before it gets too late."

They had booked a cabin rental three weeks ago for the weekend—a quaint mountain town near Rocky Mountain National Park. But now the idea of a weekend getaway and hiking held little appeal.

"Could we cancel?" She rubbed her eyes. "I'm wiped out."

"Are you sure?" Jake brushed up against her as he caressed her back.

She grabbed his hand, stopped it from venturing lower.

Jake frowned. "I had other plans." He wrapped his arms around her waist and pulled her close.

She twisted out of his grip and stepped away. "I'm sorry. Maybe we can stay here? Get take out. Watch a movie and relax?"

He waved his hands through the air. "Look, if you don't want to go away for the weekend, that's fine. We can stay here or go to my place."

Caitlynn retrieved her laptop from her bag and placed it on the table in the foyer. A mirror hung above the table, and she caught a glimpse of her pinched lips, her face a ghostly pale. It wasn't hard to see the exhaustion etched in the lines around her eyes.

"What do you want to do if we stay here?" She shut her eyes, knowing his answer was a far cry from a caring, thoughtful, and loving relationship she craved.

He slid his hands around her waist and brought her in close. Kissing the nape of her neck, he said, "You have to ask?"

She spun around and scowled. "Why is it my boss can comment on my frazzled appearance, but my boyfriend doesn't see it? Can't you see how worn out I am? Do I look like I want to fool around? This is not what I'm looking for! I shouldn't have to tell you how tired I am. I want you to see it! Isn't it obvious? Just look at me!" She took a deep breath and mumbled, "There has to be more to life than dead-end relationships that only want one thing."

Jake stepped back as if slapped across the face. "What are you saying, Caitlynn?"

"I'm saying it's over." She walked over to his packed duffel bag, snatched it up, and hurled it at him. "You just don't get it, and I'm too tired to explain. We're through."

Jake stood still; eyes wide. "What?"

She sighed. "As usual, I'm wrong. I thought you might be the one, but it's become crystal clear you don't want to move into a serious relationship. Every time I try to have any kind of meaningful dialogue—you cut me off. I'm nothing more to you than a casual relationship. I want more…I deserve more."

An image of Steve suddenly flashed in her mind. *Why is he here? Has he come back to torment me?*

Jake rubbed his temples as if trying to rid himself of her. "And I thought we were two consenting adults. We both knew coming into this relationship what we both wanted. Sex—no strings attached. Why the change in your attitude? I thought that's what you wanted when you gave out all the no-long-term-commitment signals."

Signals? What signals? "You need to leave."

He slammed the door on his way out.

CHAPTER FOUR

Steve parked the car at the Land Rover dealership and stepped out.

Tyler, wearing a red t-shirt, jeans, and blue tennis shoes, shut the passenger side door and pointed. "Hey, Dad, look at all the cool SUVs!"

"Listen to you, calling them SUVs. How do you know what they're called?"

"Daddy." Tyler rolled his eyes. "I'm smart. I'll be eight soon, and then I'll be nine, and that's when I'll be even more smarter!"

Steve laughed. "Hopefully, you'll learn about English grammar too." He grabbed his son's hand and headed toward the showroom. "I have a big surprise for you."

Tyler swung their hands back and forth like a pendulum. "What is it?"

"I'll get to it in a moment. I'm curious—you've been to see me a few times now. So far, how do you like Colorado?"

Staring at the ground, he answered, "It's okay, but I wish you still lived in Chicago near me and Mom."

Steve's shoulders slumped. He was certain his heart would tear apart from guilt. "I wish I could be close to you too." He patted his son on the head. "But at least I'll get to see you for the entire weekend, twice a month!"

When Steve bought partial ownership of the station, the board asked if he wanted the position as station manager on site in Colorado. At the time, he wasn't open to it, but then he took a long, hard look at his life. Why live in a high-end two-bedroom apartment in Chicago, commuting an hour away from Tyler? He hated divorce, especially what it did to the family. He tried everything to save his marriage, but after eight years together and two years of separation, he knew Brenda would never have a change of heart and try to work it out. His toughest decision by far was moving to another state away from Tyler.

Tyler flew out Friday evening all by himself. Always nervous about his son flying alone, Steve barely slept the night before, and while waiting at the airport, he paced like a nervous cat. When Tyler exited the tarmac, his heart almost burst. He'd hug his son long and hard, his heart heavy with guilt not wanting to let him go. Tyler was tired and cranky but also excited.

The very first time he'd brought Tyler to the home, Tyler practically flew up the stairs to see his bedroom. He let out a happy yell and jumped up and down when he saw his bedroom—the exact replica of his room in Chicago, complete with the Cubs dugout Steve had made for him where his bed nestled. Same dresser and desk and toys. A baseball glove and ball on the ready.

He focused his attention back to Tyler, and bent down, eye level with his son. "Are you ready for the surprise?"

Tyler eagerly nodded his head.

"When the mountains get snow, we'll hit the slopes. But I want to be safe, so I want a vehicle that can go through piles of snow with no problem."

"I love to ski!"

Steve squeezed his son's shoulder. "So, how about you help me pick one out?"

Tyler let out a squeal. "Really? You're going to let me help? Awesome!"

Row upon row Ty carefully studied each SUV, looking them over before dismissing it with a shake of his head. Steve expected Tyler to pick the first one, but after going through four aisles of cars, he realized this was going to take longer than he expected.

"We've passed perfectly good vehicles," Steve said. "What is it you're holding out for? Maybe I can help."

Tyler huffed, "I'll know it when I see it." He scanned the next row over and then he shouted, "Oh…look!" He yanked Steve's hand as he ran over to a car near the back. "Wow! This is the best SUV ever!"

"Ty, are you sure? It's very…noticeable."

Tyler jumped up and down with excitement. "Yeah, Daddy, this is perfect! This is the one!" he exclaimed.

Steve burst out laughing and turned to the salesman who hovered like a hawk. "Andy, what do you call this color? Canary yellow?"

"No, we call it Borrego yellow. One of the color choices in our Discovery series model."

Steve turned to Tyler. "Why do you like this vehicle so much?"

Tyler's infectious smile appeared again, "My favorite Hot Wheels SUV is exactly the same color! How awesome is that?"

Steve ruffled his son's hair as he shrugged his shoulders and chuckled. "Okay. I guess I should be grateful you don't own one in purple! And, you're also lucky I happen to like the color yellow."

Andy spoke up. "I'll grab the keys, and we'll go for a test drive."

###

Steve maneuvered the SUV into a parking spot at Vista View Church. It was a large stone building with a beautiful large wooden cross front and center above the etched glass doors.

"Let's go. We're running late, and I need to check you in at children's church."

Tyler slammed his door shut. "I never go to church with Mom. She says Sunday is fun-day."

Steve gritted his teeth, trying to stop his irritation from spilling out. "Ty, we went over this last night. Don't you remember going to Willow Creek Church when you spent the night at my apartment? You loved it!"

"Yeah," Tyler whined. "I remember, but I don't know anybody." He stopped on the sidewalk, crossed his arms, and refused to budge. "I don't wanna go."

"You're trying my patience," Steve muttered and grabbed Tyler's hand, continuing to walk toward the entrance. "I don't know anybody either, and you don't see me about to cry. You didn't have any friends at our old church when you first went, but by the end, you had a bunch, remember? You can make new friends again. You'll see."

They entered the children's area and stepped up to the check-in counter.

"Hi, I'm Lee Yamagucci," He said as he shook Steve's hand. "I'm the children's pastor."

"Hello, I'm Steve, and this is my son Tyler, who isn't too sure about all this."

Lee glanced at Tyler and pretended to pout. "Hmm, that's too bad. We're going to have a puppet show. Then we're going to play after the children's service, eat popcorn, drink apple juice, and take turns on the indoor slide that's two-stories-high."

Tyler dried his eyes with the back of his sleeve.

Filling out the paperwork, Steve nonchalantly asked, "What do you think, Ty? You want to try the slide?"

Tyler nodded.

Lee studied the paperwork. "How long have you been in Littleton?"

"About four months. Moved here for a new job. Ty lives with me every other weekend, and the rest of the time in Chicago with his mother."

Lee came around the corner and bent down to Tyler's level. "Wow! I never get to go anywhere! I'd like to go to Chicago sometime." Lee stood. "Right now, I want to show you around and give you a tour of the children's wing. You might miss some of the worship time, but I'll try to finish quickly."

They made their way down a long hallway and approached a room to the right. Lee opened a door and stepped inside. "This is our gym that converts into our children's chapel. Kids check-in at their classroom for the first fifteen minutes, and then all the children from ages 5 to 12 gather here for worship and a message."

Any free time we have leftover, the kids get to play on the two-story slide." Lee opened another door and motioned them inside.

"Dad!" Tyler squealed. "Look!"

A replica of Noah's ark, animals painted on the walls, as if they were headed inside two by two. The giant structure towered up from one landing to another to the top of the long slide.

Lee smiled at Tyler. "I bet you can't wait to try out this slide!" Tyler nodded. A popcorn machine shot out the popped corn, filling the room with its tantalizing scent. Lee scooped up a portion and offered some to Tyler. "You're the first to get popcorn today."

Steve asked, "Ty, you want to give it a go?"

Tyler took a bite of popcorn. "I guess so."

Steve found his way to the sanctuary, and took a seat toward the back. During the sermon, his mind flashed to Caitlynn, her surgery…hopefully, not serious. He sent up a prayer for her and stuffed down the disturbing thoughts buzzing about like a bee to honey. How he'd left her all those years ago, ditched her like an old pair of shoes, running away from his part in their break up like a thief in the night. He prayed again for forgiveness, just in case God didn't hear him the first time. He refocused and listened to the inspiring service, then sent a prayer of thanks that he'd finally found a church home. Afterward, the congregation spilled out into the corridors, and the children came running out from down the hall.

Lee spotted Steve and walked over. "Tyler did great! He ran up those stairs and down the slide at least a dozen times with his new friend Hunter. I think they might end up really good friends."

"That's a relief. It's been tough for Ty with all the change in the last few months. At least now he has a friend."

"Do you like basketball?" Lee asked. "Our gym is open on Fridays, from four to seven. Why don't you come by next week? It's a pick-up game, so you can come whenever you can get here. We'll rotate you in."

Tyler ran over and jumped into Steve's arms. Giving Tyler a quick hug, Steve set him down. He looked up at Lee and said, "That sounds great. I should be able to make it next week."

CHAPTER FIVE

Caitlynn fidgeted on the exam table. The sterile white paper crinkled with each movement. Monday mornings were a struggle, but adding an early doctor's appointment made her all the more irritable. She tapped her foot in triple time.

A light rap sounded against the door and in walked Dr. Gregory Plummer with her chart. "Hello, Caitlynn. How are you feeling?"

"I'm tired of being in pain, and ready to get on with this. Just wish there were another way other than a hysterectomy…"

His gaze softened. "The Laparoscopy procedure we did three years ago helped—but it didn't completely rid you of the endometriosis. I suspect you have lesions growing as well. That's why the hysterectomy, though we won't know until the surgery if the scar tissue has attached to other areas of your body, such as your bowel and intestines."

Her heart pounded. "How long will it take to recover?"

"If it all goes as planned, and you don't have any complications, you should be back to work anywhere from three weeks to a month."

She closed her eyes and tried to soak in the doctor's words. Realizing he was still speaking, she opened her eyes and refocused her attention.

"You've tried everything from hormone therapy to various treatments, and nothing has worked. If we delay the hysterectomy, it will only cause you more pain. It's the best option and the last option if you want to get rid of your pain. Does scheduling the day before Thanksgiving still work?"

Unable to speak, Caitlynn nodded her agreement.

He patted her arm. "I'll have the nurse come fill out the necessary paperwork and give you the information you need for the post-surgery instructions."

"Dr. Plummer? Is there anything I could've done to cause this condition?"

He rolled the chair closer. "There's no solid scientific evidence as to what causes endometriosis. The human body is complex, and every individual is different. Several theories exist regarding the development of the condition. Hormone imbalances, or Pelvic Inflammatory Disease which is caused by an infection-for example microscopic tears after a pregnancy. Or bacteria that enter the uterus following an abortion procedure." He shrugged, "And in some patients, it just happens. No one knows why."

Smiling sympathetically, he stood and whisked the door open. Cool air wafted inside, chilling the room. "I'll see you in two weeks. Don't forget; you can't drive for a few weeks or lift anything heavy after the procedure. And you're going to need help during the recovery." His voice faded as he closed the door.

Caitlynn let out a sigh of frustration mixed with fear. Sharp tingles ran down from the top of her scalp to the tip of her toes. The last time she needed help after a medical procedure resulted in a fever of 102 degrees, a raging infection, and not a single soul to help.

She needed help again—and now, after all these years, and she still had nobody. *What should I do?* Hire someone from a home health care company? The idea of a complete stranger coming to care for her seemed far from comforting, but there were no other options. Her mom lived in Phoenix and suffered from Rheumatoid arthritis. Ryan? A single guy with a girlfriend? Too embarrassing. Becky was her only friend, but she worked twelve-hour shifts, and when she wasn't working, she cared for her family. Loneliness smothered her, and she gasped for breath. She should've taken the time on her career climb to make some friends who would go the extra mile.

###

That night, Caitlynn sat on the couch with the TV on in the background, but she could barely focus. Her mind kept drifting back to her appointment, hearing the doctor's words play over and over in her head.

When her gynecologist diagnosed her with endometriosis—a painful chronic condition where the tissue grows outside of the uterus—she was both scared and relieved. Relieved because she had an answer to her pain, but scared because it meant a lifetime of treatment and discomfort. The reality of her endometriosis could be pinpointed to an exact time in her life, immediately after college. Listening to Dr. Plummer talk about the ways endometriosis could attack was as if a light bulb flashed, and she knew, without a doubt, her endometriosis was caused by Pelvic Inflammatory Disease. The high fever, the infection, several rounds of antibiotics. Now, years later, the reality stared her in the face: another surgery would be necessary to ease the pain. A complete hysterectomy—uterus, ovaries, fallopian tubes, and cervix couldn't be ruled out…

Caitlynn was overwhelmed with her personal life, so she did what she always did in this situation: focus on work. Her mind raced, thinking about possible news stories to cover. And then out of nowhere, she started crying. What was she grieving? The lack of family? No husband? No children? What if she never got married? Would she still try to have a baby through adoption? What would being a single parent look like?

"Stop it!" she shouted to the empty living room. I have to deal with the root of this. Endometriosis. It took away her ability to have children naturally. And that was what she longed for her entire life. And now…a vast emptiness sucked her down so low, forcing her to gasp for breath.

"Calm down," she whispered. She grabbed her notepad and stared at her scribblings of potential news stories. Working always made her feel better. Ever since Steve showed up, she'd been even more determined to find the right story to showcase. She wanted it to be her segment, an important piece that spoke to people in a very raw and human way.

And then it hit her. She'd find a pregnant teenager and follow along as she prepared for her baby's birth. Interview the girl at each milestone from the pregnancy to the delivery, then air a three-night special on the teenage pregnancy epidemic. Other news programs talked about the rising number of teenagers giving birth, but so far, there's never been a human-interest piece on what impact this decision had on them. Or their babies. She thought about her mom, raising her without a father. He was out of the picture by the time she was eight years old. Her mom said after he returned from the war in Iraq, he couldn't cope. PTSD. They divorced—and he disappeared.

She doodled a question mark on the page. How to find a pregnant teenager? Call the local high school? Visit a pregnancy crisis center? All those would work, but an idea formed. She jotted it down and flung the notepad on the other end of the couch. Ugh! How was she going to handle a story like this without going crazy with jealousy?

CHAPTER SIX

The Avondale Adoption Agency was located a short ten-minute drive from the TV station in a 1930's Bungalow style home. Stone cherubs flanking each side of the wide steps leading up the porch to the purple door; stood mischievously.

Caitlynn reached for the door handle and paused, her hand feeling sweaty. Something inside her felt jittery. Nervous. Anxious. She waved it off and rubbed her palms on her pants and then stepped inside.

The waiting room was thankfully empty. Caitlynn strode up to the receptionist. *Good. I can get in and out quickly.* "Hello, I'm Caitlynn Grant from Channel 12. I wondered if I might speak to the president of the agency."

"Ms. Amber Wright?"

"Yes. Is she available?"

"She has a meeting in about ten minutes, but if you don't mind waiting, we could fit you in afterward."

"How long is the appointment ahead of me?"

"It depends. It could be anywhere from 15 minutes to one hour. I have an hour blocked out. You can come back in an hour, or you can wait."

Caitlynn twirled a strand of hair. Her stomach growled, reminding her breakfast was hours ago. She crossed her fingers, hoping for the fast fifteen minutes time slot. "I'll wait."

Caitlynn took a seat, sinking comfortably into one of the leather chairs. In walked an attractive teenage girl with light brown hair and pretty light blue eyes. Following her was an older version of the girl, trudging behind in sullen silence. Their eyes appeared bloodshot from crying. Caitlynn stole a glance. Sure enough—a baby bump, barely discernable.

The teen approached the receptionist hesitantly. "Hi, I'm…um, Jillian, and I have an appointment in a few minutes."

"Yes, of course. Ms. Wright is expecting you."

The mother stood a few feet away from the desk and continued to blot her swollen eyes with a tissue.

"I'm sorry," Jillian blurted out. "I've made a mistake!" She took a step forward. "I've decided to keep my baby." She rubbed her stomach. "I only came here because my mother"—she gave a slight nod toward the older woman—"wants me to give my baby up for adoption. I want to keep the baby, but she insisted I come and talk to Ms. Wright."

The receptionist nodded in sympathy. "This is the biggest decision you will ever make because it involves the life of your child. And while we take pride in our agency's ability to match each child to a wonderful adoptive parent, you have every right to change your mind. Thank you for coming in today. We appreciate the effort it took to speak to us in person and tell us your decision."

The receptionist directed her gaze at Jillian's mom. "If there's anything we can do, please let us know, and if your daughter changes her mind, you know where to reach us."

The mother let out a soft sob and dabbed her eyes, nodding slightly. Caitlynn glanced away, swallowing a lump in her throat.

Jillian grabbed her mother's arm. "Come on, Mom. It'll be okay. You'll see."

They shuffled out of the waiting room, and Caitlynn felt rooted to her seat. A young pregnant teen, faced with a big decision—was precisely why she'd thought of this place.

Caitlynn darted after them. "Excuse me."

"Yes?" Jillian stopped and turned. Her mother continued down the stairs toward the car.

"I'm Caitlynn Grant from Channel 12 News. I'm covering a story on teenage girls who keep their babies, and I was hoping you could help me."

Jillian's eyes narrowed. "Depends."

Following her down the stairs toward the driveway, Caitlynn said, "I want to delve into the reasons why more teenage girls are now keeping their babies. I'd like to contact you, once a month, let's say, and find out how you're coping. And then interview you again after the birth of your baby. The story will air in our human-interest spot. What do you think?"

Jillian stared a moment with her piercing blue eyes; a smirk played at the corner of her lips. "I like the idea. It will make Marcus sick with jealousy." She turned to her mother. "Did you hear? I'm going to be on TV."

Her mother scowled. "The last thing you need in your life is public disgrace." She stepped into the car and slammed the door.

"Mom?" Jillian's eyes turned to slits as she yelled through the car window, "Are you talking about me? Or you, Mom?"

Caitlynn's cheeks flamed. She quickly fished the notepad from her purse. "I . . . uh, just need your contact information, and I'll get in touch soon."

Jillian wrote down her phone number and tilted her head toward her mother. "Don't worry… she'll come around. She fought me the whole way over here. She thinks I'm making the worst mistake of my life, because Denver University offered me a full-ride academic scholarship—and, of course, I won't have that opportunity now." Jillian opened the car door, slid into the driver's seat and started the engine. "I'll talk to you soon."

They drove away, as Caitlynn's heart hammered in her chest. She touched her belly and felt a pang of sadness and longing. She questioned if she was making a mistake with this story, but something told her that she needed to do this. She slowly walked back into the agency. "It looks like you lost a client, I guess," she said to the receptionist.

The receptionist nodded in agreement. Sighing deeply, she pursed her lips. "It's the trend. Yet there are so many families who would love to have a child but can't."

Caitlynn's stomach tightened into a knot. *Including me.* She looked away, hiding the pain, wondering for the hundredth time, why she agreed to do this story? Stubborn pride?

"Not everyone can afford to go overseas to adopt." The receptionist continued. "It breaks my heart when we have to tell our clients the wait to adopt a baby could be up to three years."

Just then, a tall, slender African American, woman dressed in a soft blue skirt and an ivory silk blouse, entered the reception area. Her neatly short hair accentuated her high cheekbones and green eyes. "Is my next appointment here?"

"The young woman showed up but canceled. She decided to keep her baby." The receptionist motioned toward Caitlynn. "This is Ms. Grant from Channel 12. She wanted to see you if you have time."

"It appears I do now. I'm Amber Wright." She shook Caitlynn's hand and gestured toward her office. "Come in." She motioned Caitlynn over to one of the two chairs across from her desk, walked around to her office chair, sat down, and smiled. "How can I help you?"

Something about her warm smile helped Caitlynn relax. "You lost a client today. Does that happen often?"

"More than I'd like." Ms. Wright sighed. "The birth mother has the right to change her mind and back out of the adoption process at any point along the way."

"But you never even had the opportunity to discuss adoption with Jillian."

Ms. Wright arched an eyebrow. "You met her?"

Time to 'fess up. "I wanted to meet with you today to see if you knew of a pregnant teen who decided against adoption and planned to keep her baby. I'm doing a special report on teen pregnancy and why some girls choose to keep their babies. I was in the waiting room when Jillian canceled her appointment, so I asked her if I could interview her."

"Some women want to know all of their options before making a decision regarding their child. Others know right away that adoption is the right solution."

"Have you seen a rise in mothers deciding against adoption?"

Ms. Wright pulled a binder from a drawer in her desk. "Those statistics are difficult to determine because many pregnant teens never enter into the adoption route. They decide right away to keep their babies." She opened the cover and flipped to a particular page. "From my office, I can tell you that last week two teenage girls decided against adoption." She pointed to a photo of an infant and the mother on another page. "I had one girl come in five months ago with a three-month-old, who decided to give her baby up because she realized she couldn't take care of her child the way she wanted."

"Did she go through with the adoption?"

"Yes. A wonderful couple from our database and the interview went very well. We expedited the adoption in four weeks, and now the baby has a new family."

"That must've been difficult."

"We have a post-adoption counselor. She guides the birth mom through the grieving process."

"I really appreciate your time. I came here today to scope out information, and I found it." She shook her head in amazement. "I had a bit of a hunch, really, and decided to run with it." She smiled broadly and stood to leave. "It's been great meeting you, Ms. Wright."

"I feel the same way—I watch you on the news. Do you know when your story will air?"

"I'm not sure. The plan is to interview her throughout the pregnancy and birth then air the final piece."

They walked to the front door. Amber shook Caitlynn's hand. "I look forward to viewing the story."

Caitlynn opened the car door and collapsed on the seat. These conversations, first with Jillian and then with Amber, had upset her. Both of them wanted what they thought was best for the child, but they each had a very different agenda. *Adopt or keep?* A deep pain pierced her heart, and a heavy sadness washed over her—*a Hysterectomy.* There would be no baby for her—ever—unless she adopted—and who would choose a single parent to raise her baby when the child could have a loving home with both a mother and a father?

It was late in the afternoon. Caitlynn's head pounded from hunger. She clutched the steering wheel as a wave of dizziness swept over her. The idea of sitting down to eat a sandwich while pretending that she wasn't angry about her upcoming surgery turned her stomach into a hard knot. She started the engine, pulled out of the parking lot, ignored the hunger pains, and pressed hard on the accelerator.

CHAPTER SEVEN

Steve sat and drummed his pen against his desk, anxiously thinking about Caitlynn. He didn't see her at all yesterday, and now, knowing they'd meet up today at the Tuesday afternoon staff meeting, he couldn't focus on his notes.

He stood, pacing, his hands stuffed in his pockets. He figured if he and Caitlynn were going to work together, it was up to him to take charge of the problem. Establish boundaries. After the painful confrontation in the hall, and then learning of her impending surgery, he realized he'd better stay strong in his convictions if there were any chance at all to show Caitlynn the man he'd become.

He was a new creature in Christ.

Born again.

Forgiven.

He lowered his head and massaged his forehead, remembering his college years. Some of his best memories of his life were spent with Caitlynn—sharing a class, studying together in the library, and watching the street performers at Pearl Street Mall, holding her close on the couch. But then he walked out on her. Caring more about himself and his career than he ever did about her welfare. He was such a self-absorbed fool back then.

He ambled back to his desk and sat, sinking low in his chair. Nor was he better with his ex-wife. His failure to keep his marriage healthy ate at him until his gut burned from the loss. Failure was just one of many regrets. More than anything, he wrestled with the deep sorrow that his son was the innocent victim. Steve knew he'd been as much to blame as Brenda. In fact, he blamed himself more for being blind to the signs of her affair. Why didn't he fight for what they had? Deep down, he knew: he had never loved her the way he should have. What he didn't know was why?

Aside from Tyler, the only good thing sifted from the ruins was his reaching out for help and finding his answer in Jesus Christ. If not for God's grace and the unconditional love he'd experienced this past year, he would have given up and become a working machine: get up, eat, work, sleep, repeat. Living out his faith with God's generous gift of grace and mercy gave him the freedom to push past the mistakes and look to the future with renewed hope.

Steve forced his mind back to the job at hand and finished up a few of the discussion items for the staff meeting. Breaking for lunch, he went downstairs to the cafeteria, grabbed a sandwich, and noticed Caitlynn sitting alone at a small round table. "Do you mind if I join you?"

She motioned to the chair across from her. "Go ahead."

Steve put his tray on the table, sat, then bowed his head for a quick prayer over his lunch.

"You pray?" Caitlynn stared in disbelief.

"I do now." He tilted his head to one side. "You probably remember all the times we made fun of the Campus Crusade for Christ students."

"Yeah, I do. That's why I can't believe it. Steven Carr, a praying man."

"If it makes you feel any better, I'm pretty new at all this. I went to church after 9/11, searching for answers to so many questions."

"And you found them in Jesus Christ, right?" She took a sip from her bottled water.

Steve's eyes brightened. "Caitlynn, are you a believer?"

She scowled. "No. I believe there's a God, but I've never seen him do anything for me. At least nothing that would make me pray to him over my lunch."

He prayed silently for guidance. Jesus? *What should I do? Change the subject*

"What do you do in Denver for fun? I never ran out of things to do in Chicago."

Caitlynn pushed her fork around the salad. "For most Denverites, the Rocky Mountains are their playground."

He took a bite of his sandwich. "What kind of things can I do with my son, Tyler?"

Her jaw dropped for a second before she snapped it shut. "How old is he?"

"Seven. Ty lives with his mother in Chicago, but he visits me two weekends a month."

Caitlynn's eyebrows arched. "You mentioned earlier that you were divorced. How long has it been?"

"Two years."

"When do you see your son again?"

"Next weekend."

Caitlynn ate a bite of salad. "I have an idea. It's supposed to be warm, so why don't you take him hiking. Take him to Castlewood Canyon. They have trails and a museum about the area wildlife and some historical facts about the canyon's history."

He could apologize for his part in the breakup, and hopefully, they could come to some kind of a truce. He stepped out on a very flimsy limb. "So, do you like to hike?"

"Yes." She hesitated. "I do."

"Why don't you come? We could use an experienced trail guide to show us the way," he joked. "The last time I hiked, I walked on a paved path through a forest preserve in Chicago."

Caitlynn smirked. "When did you become such a city boy. I thought your Mom owned a 'horse farm'? What happened to you?" She pushed away from the table, her food untouched, and stood.

Her smile didn't reach her eyes. "How can I pass up such an invitation? I would love to meet your son. Let me know what time and I'll be there." She turned and walked away.

Was that a smile or a scowl? If she didn't want to go, why didn't she just say so? Steve finished the last bite of his roast beef sandwich, wondering if he'd said something to make her want to get up and leave her lunch unfinished. Or if she did that all the time and no one ever bothered to notice.

By Thursday, Steve was looking forward to playing basketball tomorrow to relieve some pent-up stress. He leaned back in his chair and stared out the office window. Not the best of views—barely able to see the mountains in the distance, but mostly staring at another high rise. He checked the clock on his laptop. Brett Tanner would be here soon.

When Steve bought part ownership of the station, he was motivated to make the business higher profits. He didn't want to take over the station the way his father always did—"clean house," his father called it, but to Steve, it was more like purging. If he had to let go of an employee, there had better be just cause—and Steve tried to avoid doing so—fortunately, he only had one person to place on a performance plan—the sportscaster, Brett.

A knock sounded. He silently prayed for wisdom. "Come in."

Brett walked in, wearing a white dress shirt and a grey athletic cut suit that accentuated his broad shoulders. Tightening his purple paisley tie, he took the seat opposite. "You wanted to see me?" His dark brown eyes darted from the floor to Steve.

"Yes. I've been going over our viewer comments to see how we can improve our market share, and I've noticed that most of our negative letters are directed toward the sports segment of the show. Do you know why?"

Brett pulled his shoulders back and straightened his spine. "My guess is they can't take a little bit of criticism about their players. The fans in Denver are biased, especially if I'm slamming their beloved Broncos. They're such wimps. If I see something I don't like, then I expose the issue." He shrugged. "I don't see why I can't speak the truth."

"The problem is, what you believe is truth, other sportscasters covering the same story see differently," He leaned forward, "and evidently, so do our viewers."

Brett glared at him. "Do you have an example?"

"The Denver Nuggets held a press conference to talk about the start of their season and the changes they're making. Carmelo Anthony talked about how he had considered himself an offensive player in the past, but now fans are going to see aggressive defense in addition to stealing the ball from his opponents. The other stations talked about Carmelo Anthony turning over a new leaf and becoming a more balanced ballplayer. Your viewpoint is that he's never going to change, so why should anyone believe him?"

"So?"

Steve stared into Brett's eyes; his gaze steady. "That's putting a negative spin on an interview, and if I was Carmelo and I heard this broadcast, I would never allow you to interview me again."

Brett loosened his tie. "What are you saying? Are you firing me?"

"No. I'm not. But I am placing you on a plan. I'm giving you three months to improve your performance. After that, we'll meet again and see where you stand. I want to see a better outlook from you and some positive letters coming in."

Brett frowned and pointed across the desk. "I did a bit of research on you when we were told you'd be our new boss. You're from Chicago. Your father owns Carr Communications, which owns all the major stations from New York to Los Angeles." He smirked. "So, tell me… did your daddy pay for this one too? Or maybe this market's too small potatoes for him to bother with, so he gave you his leftovers?" Brett stood, scraping the chair legs against the floor.

Steve was speechless. Why did doing the right thing always turn out to be difficult? Would the unfair comparisons to his father ever stop? Growing up, he rarely saw his father. Steven Preston Car II, although he went by Preston, had a reputation for being a ruthless cutthroat in business. His father would've come in day one and fired Brett without a second thought.

Steve drummed his fingers on his desk. "Careful, Brett. Think before you speak."

"You know what? Don't bother working out a plan." Brett leaned over the desk, shaking his finger in Steve's face. "I could walk out right now, but I don't want the station, or my reputation, to suffer because of you. So, consider this my two-week notice. I pride myself on being real. If I think it, then I say it, and I don't care if I step on some toes along the way." His eyes sliced into Steve like daggers. "You can find someone else to play the part of Goody Two-shoes." He stalked out.

Steve sighed deeply and closed his laptop. He should fire Bret this second, but what would lashing out in anger do? He still had to find another sports anchor. He closed his eyes and prayed, "Help, Lord!" As he spoke those two words, he wondered if God ever tired of SOS prayers.

Steve hustled out of the office, trying to make the Friday evening basketball game. Yesterday's conversation with Brett still rankled him. He parked near the church gym entrance, grabbed his duffel bag, and jogged to the door. The pickup game was in full force. He didn't have to look long for Lee.

Lee nodded at Steve and trotted over. "Hey, I'm glad you made it. The bathrooms are around the corner. When you've changed, come join in."

Steve quickly changed, then stepped onto the court, covering Lee—confident he could take the guy on—no problem; since Lee had to be about 5'8" to his 6'1". Lee outmaneuvered him, and laughed as he went up for the shot.

Game on. Steve ran to the half-court line as his teammate, Troy, threw the ball inbounds to him. He saw the break and made his move before his opponents could reach him, executing a perfect layup.

"Woo-hoo!" Troy yelled. "That was textbook, baby! We got us a white man who can jump!" Troy reached out his hand, and the two men bumped fists. "I thought I was the only brother here, but now we got us another, even if you are white." Troy sized him up. "And are you ever white! Look at those legs—they're scarin' me!" he chuckled.

Steve pretended to look insulted and passed him the ball. "Hey! I worked hard on this tan!"

Lee faked a frown and crossed his arms over his heart. "Troy, I'm hurt. I thought I was your brother!"

Troy threw the ball at Lee's chest. "You were before this guy showed up. Now you're gonna have to settle for being my bro' in Christ."

Lee laughed, dribbled the ball to his side of the court, and landed a two-pointer.

Troy sobered. "Okay. Point taken."

A half-hour flew past, the men driving the ball back and forth across the court. Steve was sweating, his legs and arms burning. But he felt so alive. They finally called it, and Steve was secretly grateful. He fist bumped with the guys when they departed, then took a seat on the floor next to Lee.

He hadn't played basketball in a while, and his lack of training showed in his inability to catch a breath in the mile-high altitude. Leaning heavily against the wall, he made a mental note to run more, he toweled off the beads of sweat on his brow.

Lee leaned over and stretched his hamstrings. "Does Tyler come back next weekend?"

Yes. It's supposed to be a nice weekend, and I told him I'd take him hiking—although now I'm not so sure if that's a good idea." Steve reached for his toes, feeling his hamstrings ache in protest.

"Why?"

"Well, I asked this woman from work if she wanted to join us, and she said yes. Now I'm second-guessing myself."

"Seems innocent enough to me. You're only going hiking. And you've only just met her, so I don't see how it would be that threatening."

How much should I confide in Lee? The first time he met the man, Lee had seemed like someone he would want to know better—especially when Lee went out of his way to help Tyler get comfortable at church.

Deciding to take a chance, he blurted, "That's the problem. I didn't just meet her. We were an item in college. Things were pretty serious between us."

Lee was silent for a moment. "I see why you might have second thoughts. It sounds like you two were more than 'just an item'." He stood up. "Did you know you were going to be working together when you took the job?"

Steve hefted himself off the floor and twisted his torso from side to side feeling his tight back muscles loosen up slightly. "Not at first. I found out she worked here when I looked over the employee list. I never planned on seeing her again, but I think God must've put her in my path. I know I need to make some things right between us." His voice lowered. "I should apologize to her for so many things."

Lee leaned over and stuffed his gear into his bag. "That makes it easy then. You're supposed to be back in her life. You have to figure out when the timing is right to ask for forgiveness." Lee stood and looked him in the eye. "You're brave. So many Christians out there, including myself, have an 'I'm sorry' or two to deliver but haven't done it yet." He picked up his bag. "Let me know how it goes; maybe you'll give me the courage to 'fess up to a few.'"

Steve grabbed his bag and they walked toward the exit. "Will do."

Lee squeezed Steve on the shoulder. "I'm glad you came."

CHAPTER EIGHT

Steve parked his SUV at Starbucks in Castle Rock and snatched up his ringing cell phone. A glint of sunlight highlighted the caller's number. *Is Caitlynn canceling*? Other than the lunch in the cafeteria last week, the only time he ever saw her was at Tuesday's staff meeting when she did everything in her power to avoid him. He practically had to chase her down after the meeting to remind her about their weekend plans. That she had said yes to the hike had been an unexpected surprise. They agreed to meet at Starbucks and take one car to the canyon.

"I'm running late, but I'll be there in about ten," Caitlynn said.

"Great! Tyler and I are looking forward to seeing you," he said, and then felt silly.

Once inside, Steve ordered a black coffee, and chocolate milk and a blueberry scone, for Tyler. They sat at a table next to the window. "Ty, I need you to be really good today, and be very nice to Caitlynn."

Tyler slurped from a straw and nodded. "Yep."

The glass door swished open, and a blast of brisk air blew inside as Caitlynn approached. In a long-sleeved powder blue T-shirt, khaki shorts, and tan hiking boots, she exuded a confidence he found appealing. Sunglasses rested on top of her hair, and she held a baseball cap, a windbreaker, and a backpack. He was no expert, but it seemed she only wore lipstick and mascara. Heads turned, and eyes stared as Caitlynn glided through the coffee shop utterly unaware that her beauty drew an audience.

"Hey." Steve waved her over.

"Hi." She dumped her things on an empty chair and sat down. "What a gorgeous day for a hike."

"Caitlynn, I'd like you to meet my son Tyler." Steve cracked a smile. "Tyler, this is Ms. Caitlynn."

"Nice to meet you." Tyler stuck out his hand.

She clutched his hand in a firm handshake and smiled slightly. "Nice to meet you too. Are you ready to beat your dad at hiking? With you as my sidekick, I'm sure we could take him on together."

Tyler's grin exposed one adult tooth and a gap where another tooth would come in soon. "Yeah, we're gonna beat Daddy!"

Steve watched the two connive. "It's going to take more than the two of you." Pointedly, he glanced around the store. "Who else is coming?"

Caitlynn laughed. "Let me get some tea and we'll get going."

"You're a tea drinker now? I remember how much coffee you used to drink."

She paused for a moment. "Things change. I love coffee, especially its smell, but unfortunately, I can't drink the stuff anymore without getting major stomachaches."

After Caitlynn ordered a chai tea, she gathered her belongings and they went out into the parking lot. Steve pressed the keyless remote to unlock the SUV.

"Whoa. Is this yours?"

Steve hid a smile. "Yes, it is. Get in."

A giggle escaped, her eyes sparkled, and he could tell she was about to tease him. "Okay, but I never took you for a yellow kind of guy. Are you going to start wearing pink at the office now too?"

Tyler squealed with delight. "I picked out the SUV. Do you like it?"

Caitlynn ruffled his hair and opened the door. Breathing in the scent of the new car smell, she said, "I like yellow and pink."

They rode the first few miles in a comfortable silence. Then Caitlynn remarked, "Don't you love the blue sky in Colorado?"

The warmth of the sun reflected off the windshield. "Coming from the dull gray sky of Chicago, I don't think I'll ever grow tired of it."

Tyler squirmed. "Dad? How much longer?"

"About ten minutes." Steve responded.

Tyler unbuckled his seatbelt and scooted to the middle.

"Tyler, get back in your seatbelt."

Ty jumped up and down, his head almost bumping the ceiling.

Steve looked in the rearview mirror and fought to control his anger. This behavior was new. Did he act out like this with Brenda? Is this a byproduct of divorce, or is it typical behavior of a seven-year-old? "Ty, get back in your seatbelt now. Remember what we talked about in Starbucks?" He arched his brow.

Tyler huffed and went back to his seat and clicked the seat belt into place. Then he pulled out the blueberry scone, stuffing it into his face and spilling crumbs everywhere while he kicked Caitlynn's seat.

A quick glance showed Caitlynn suddenly engrossed in the view out the side window, obviously embarrassed for him. *What is it about kids that they're always at their worst behavior when you want to make a good impression?* The need to discipline his son won out.

Steve eyed Tyler through the rearview mirror. "Tyler." He spoke firmly. "Knock it off, or we're turning around and canceling the hike."

Tyler's eyes popped open. "Sorry, Daddy," he whined. "I want to go hiking." He wiped his face and then bit his bottom lip. "I'll be good, I promise. Can I have a do-over?"

"Ty, you were told to be good, and you weren't. Why do you think you deserve a do-over?"

"Daddy, I'm really sorry." He pleaded. "I'll be good. I promise."

Steve stood firm. "I'll give you a do-over, but you need to apologize to someone else in the car, and you need to keep your promise."

Tyler reached across and softly poked Caitlynn's arm. "Ms. Caitlynn, I'm really sorry. I promise I'll be good. Do you forgive me?"

Caitlynn twisted around and patted his knee. "Of course, I will," she said with a smile.

Once parked, Steve opened a small cooler from the trunk filled with snacks, soft drinks, sandwiches, fruit, and chips for a picnic.

"I'm going to put a bottle of water in the pocket of your backpack so you'll have it when you get thirsty," Steve said to Tyler.

"Can I take some chips with me? I might get hungry."

Steve tossed the chip bag to Tyler. "Here you go. Put them where you know you'll find them, and these peanut butter crackers."

Caitlynn asked, "Do you two have a hole somewhere? Didn't you just eat?"

"Yeah? So what? We're growing boys—isn't that right, Ty?"

"Yep, I'm growing tall, and Daddy's growing a tummy."

Steve hoisted Tyler up and tickled him. "You better take that back!" Tyler giggled and squealed. Steve put him down. "Okay, are we ready?"

Ty nodded. "Are you Ms. Caitlynn?" he asked.

Steve shut the cooler, locked the car, and stepped beside Caitlynn, hiking the winding trail's uphill incline. Tyler ran ahead. Steve tried to keep an eye on him, but each time Ty rounded a bend, the Ponderosa pine trees and scrub oak blocked his view and his son dropped from sight. Finally, Tyler stopped at a sign. It had a picture of a snake. "Dad, is that a rattlesnake sign?"

Steve read aloud. "Stay on the trail, dogs must be on a leash, and if you see a snake, back up and give it some distance. That's a sign you won't find in Chicago."

Tyler's voice rose excitedly. "Nope. I hope I see a snake! I'll tell all my friends in Chicago!" He scampered ahead.

Caitlynn shivered. "I hate snakes. Remember the scene in Indiana Jones when he was in the pit with the snakes? Just thinking about that scene still gives me the chills."

He shrugged. "I wouldn't worry. Probably enough people have hiked this trail that the snakes stay as far away from humans as possible."

"I grew up in Colorado. Watch out for other predators like mountain lions and coyotes." Caitlynn peered into the bush. "They could be lurking Ty, so stay close."

Slowly, they meandered down the trail. Tyler stopped impatiently and waited for them to catch up.

Caitlynn breathed deep. "It feels peaceful out here. Can you smell the pine trees?" She pointed at the sky. "Whoa! Take a look at their wingspan. Have you ever seen birds that big?"

Tyler raised his hand to his forehead shielding his eyes. "Dad, they're circling. Does that mean they found a dead animal? Are they going to eat it?" He said in a rush. "Can we go and look?"

"I'm sure you're right, but their vision is so much stronger than ours. It could be a long way away. Let's keep walking."

Caitlynn watched Tyler kick a rock down the path. She turned to Steve. "I can tell you're a great dad…you're so patient with him."

His eyes widened in surprise. "Thanks, but I wasn't always patient. I was way too consumed with my career to do much with him other than watch him play whatever sport he was doing—when I had the time." He stared at the ground. "I'm ashamed to say; I was a spectator dad."

"Let me guess," she said sarcastically, "once you had your son every other weekend you were forced to be a hands-on dad. Am I right?"

"Yes and no. Do you remember my father?"

"Barely. I remember a handsome older man who was fond of wearing a navy blazer with a starched white shirt, khaki pants, and deck shoes. You used to make fun of your dad. You'd say, 'All he needs is a captain's hat and he could sail a cruise ship.'"

He grinned sheepishly. "I forgot about that." He kicked a stone. "My father controlled my life for so long. And I let him. He kept buying up failing television stations in all the large cities, and then demanded I turn the stations around." He shook his head. "I was gone every week. I came home on weekends emotionally empty and physically exhausted. I had nothing left to give Brenda or my son."

Steve sighed. "By the time I left again on Monday, I'd be running out the door." He stared into the horizon. "We fought constantly. She asked me to find a job that didn't require so much travel, but I didn't listen. Honestly, I can't blame her for divorcing me. *I wanted to divorce me.* Talk about miserable—but I didn't know any other way but to become a workaholic like my father."

"What happened?"

"It all happened on 9/11."

Steve's eyes cut to her. "I was in Manhattan that day, busy trying to buy out one of my competitors. We were having a heated discussion. The owner thought the station was worth more on the dollar than I wanted to give him . . . or I should say, more than what my father wanted to offer," Steve said bitterly. His chest tightened. "We heard the impact of the jets. We rushed to the window and saw smoke coming from the tower. The elevator couldn't get down fast enough. We ran out into the street." His breath quickened. "All we could see was smoke and dust. The stench of fire and jet fuel filled the air. We couldn't breathe. People were running up the street trying to escape. Men were carrying out those who couldn't run. We were the first station to televise the disaster."

He shook his head. "One minute we were fighting over money, the next we were ushering people into the building and handing out food and water from the cafeteria. We couldn't leave the station. I stayed and helped for as long as I could." He sighed deeply. "When I returned to Chicago, I couldn't get it out of my mind. Like many people searching for answers, I went to church and felt peace for the first time in my life. I resolved that I would never let anyone control me again the way my father had. I walked away from the job and started to work on saving my family. But by then, it was too late. She left me for someone else."

Caitlynn had a sincere look on her face. "You really went through a rough time. I don't know what to say." She twirled a strand of hair. "I could tell you how my life has been the last twelve years, but you wouldn't want to hear the sorry details."

This wasn't the response he expected. He stopped on the trail. "Why are you so angry?"

Her eyes narrowed to slits. "Why do you have to ask? You should know." She glared at him. "You were the one who dumped me. Remember? You said you were going to work at your father's station, get settled, and then get me a job working with you." She crossed her arms. "I vowed never to be that vulnerable again. And I've succeeded…until now. Do you know why I came today?"

"To meet my son?"

"That part is true, but the other reason was to convince you to leave." Her eyes narrowed. "Why are you here in Denver anyway? You should move back to Chicago. It would make it easier on your son."

It was logical questioning. He swallowed, trying to find the right words. Tyler was about to round the bend ahead, so Steve quickened his pace. Tyler was too far ahead of them. *Okay, God, I could use some help here—and some patience.* An immediate peace flowed into his heart. He blurted, "I believe God brought me to Denver for a reason."

"God? Are you sure it wasn't your own desire to start fresh? A new beginning?"

"Caitlynn, look around. What do you see?"

She shrugged. "I see a path ahead." Her tone softening. "But we have no idea where it's going." She inhaled deeply. "I smell the heavenly scent of ponderosas."

Steve gazed at her. "Hmm, heavenly describes it perfectly. What else?"

She scanned the trail. "I hear birds, and cute little chipmunks are darting past us for safety in the scrub oak. Pikes Peak looks perfect against the deep blue sky. It's beautiful."

They were twenty minutes or so into the hike, and he hadn't seen Tyler for several minutes. If he was going to apologize, he'd better do it now before Tyler came running back. "You're right." Steve stole a quick glance at her. "What I'm looking at is beautiful." He turned and scanned the mountains in the distance. Standing at over fourteen thousand feet, Pikes Peak was magnificent. Its snowcapped peak glistened like diamonds against the backdrop of the blue sky.

"What about God? He asked. "He created all the beauty that surrounds us. When you speak of creation's beauty, you're actually telling God thanks for making it all so exceptional. Maybe next time you have the opportunity, you can tell God."

Caitlynn stared at Pikes Peak and whispered, "I wonder what it would be like to believe in a divine force."

Guilt flooded his soul. He'd asked her here for a reason. "Since we're being honest, here's why I asked you to come. About the past . . . there's something I need to tell you . . ."

Steve stopped dead in his tracks. He could feel the blood drain from his face. "Do you see Tyler?" he whispered.

Her eyes widened. She darted a few feet ahead and looked around. "No."

A chill ran down his spine. He lunged forward and grabbed her arm, stopping Caitlynn from taking another step as he heard the distinct sound of a rattler reverberate nearby.

Steve ran toward the sound. "Tyler!"

"Tyler? Where are you?" Caitlynn shouted.

Steve stopped to listen. *This is my fault.* The only thing he saw were bushes on both sides of the path as it wound down the trail. *Why did he let Ty go so far ahead?* They had to have walked at least three miles from the trailhead. What was he thinking? He wasn't in Chicago. He was so far removed from his comfort zone; he had no idea how to find his son.

His heart pounded like a jackhammer. A recent article in the paper had mentioned that a mountain lion had been spotted not far from here, in a subdivision in Castle Rock. He wiped the sweat from his brow. How was he going to explain this to Brenda?

Steve stopped and faced Caitlynn. Adrenalin shot through his body like an electric current. His chest tightened, squeezing his heart until it hurt. "Caitlynn," he spoke in a rush. "The Bible teaches that we have not, because we ask not. Will you pray with me that we find Tyler?"

Caitlynn nodded. The way her bottom lip quivered; he could tell she was trying hard not to cry. He reached out and held her hands.

"You feel as helpless as I do, don't you?"

Steve leaned in close so he could hear her. "I keep thinking about that rattlesnake we heard...I'll do anything to help find Tyler. If you think it's going to help, then pray!"

Steve closed his eyes. She did the same as his voice cracked from pent-up emotion. "God, we can't find Tyler. We desperately need your help. Please show me where he is." He ended in a whisper, "I can't do this without you. Amen."

Steve released one of Caitlynn's hands but held tightly to the other as they walked on searching for his son. Vultures circled closer toward the ground, narrowing in on their prey. They came to a dirt path that branched off from the main trail.

Follow it.

Steve let go of Caitlynn's hand as they walked the narrow path in single file. They screamed Tyler's name, but there was no response. *Please, God, let Tyler be okay.*

And then he heard his son's loud cry. "Daddy help!"

He quickened his pace, when he rounded the corner, he spotted Tyler kneeling down on the ground holding a long stick. He rushed over and embraced his son. He frantically scanned for injuries. Tyler's knee was bleeding through a tear in his jeans. Tears streamed down Tyler's dirt-stained face.

"Daddy, I saw the birds swoop down, so I ran as fast as I could to see what they were looking for. I saw this path and I followed it." Tyler shook with the force of his crying. He pointed above the trail. "Look over there, Dad. I smelled something funny and I went to see what it was. I didn't get very close because I got so scared, so I started running back toward you, but I fell over this stick."

Next to the path, a deer lay on its side. Flies buzzed around the dead carcass; the flesh torn. Pieces of meat ripped from its body, and the smell of rotten flesh hung in the air. Deep claw marks swept across its fur, a reminder of what killed the animal.

Steve wanted to protect his son, but instead, he'd lost him. He'd failed . . . again. He did the only thing he could think of doing; he scooped Tyler up and held on tightly to his son.

Caitlynn shivered as she covered her mouth and nose. "It may be a mountain lion kill." She looked terrified. He wanted to reach out and comfort her too, but his son was his first priority.

The hair on the back of Steve's head tingled. They needed to get out of here. The kill looked fresh. Could the animal that killed the deer be watching? "How fast can you move?" he asked Caitlynn.

"Right now, I think I could fly out of here. Let's go."

Steve charged down the trail holding Tyler firmly against his chest. Caitlynn followed close behind. Within minutes, they were at the parking lot, and inside the car.

Tyler climbed into the backseat. Caitlynn slammed the passenger door shut while Steve guzzled his water, trying to catch his breath and slow down his racing heart. Once he felt in control, he drove out of the park. A quick glance back at Tyler a few minutes later showed he was fast asleep. Caitlynn's eyes were closed. She probably couldn't bear to talk or look at him. How did a father lose his son? He drove in silence to Starbucks.

When they pulled up next to Caitlynn's car, Steve turned to her and said, "I'm sorry how things ended today." He frowned and shook his head in disgust. "I wanted to tell you something, but I guess it will have to wait."

She held his gaze. "Whatever it is, it can't be more important than finding your son." She tilted her head to one side. "You know when I told you I thought you were a great father?"

"Yeah?" Steve said hesitantly. *Here goes.* She's going to tell me exactly what I've been saying to myself the entire way back. How could you be such a lousy dad?

"I think you're an amazing father. You took such control out there. You even prayed for your son. I don't know what to say, so I'll just say it again. You're an amazing dad."

Steve's eyes were gritty and dangerously close to spilling out tears. *Don't lose it now!* "Thanks." He looked away quickly. "I'm sure I did what any father would do. *Except that another father wouldn't lose his son in the first place.* "See you Monday."

She shut the door quietly behind her.

As he watched her walk to her car, he swiped the tears from the corner of his eyes. Then looked over his shoulder at his sleeping son. His face stained from dirt-mingled tears, his pants torn, his shirt filthy. His son was safe. *Thank you, Jesus.* Tyler's favorite place was Chuck E. Cheese. There had to be one somewhere in this city. He would take Tyler there for dinner. He watched his son's rhythmic breathing and prayed another round of thanks to Jesus. Then he started the engine. They were going home.

CHAPTER NINE

*If I have the gift of prophecy and can fathom all mysteries and all
knowledge, and if I have a faith that can move mountains, but
have not love, I am nothing.*
1 CORINTHIANS 13:2

With her fleece-lined throw draped loosely around her
shoulders, Caitlynn opened the balcony door and reclined on a
chaise lounge in the cool of the evening. The heat from a cup of
herbal tea warmed her hands as she breathed in fragrant mint and
chamomile. The sunset of fiery reds and oranges against the
mountain's panoramic backdrop was breathtaking. Still, none of the
surrounding splendor could stop her onslaught of thoughts about
yesterday's hike.

The hike had revealed that other than where they work, she
and Steve didn't share one thing in common anymore. In college,
they were inseparable. Never once did Steve ever act interested in
spiritual matters. Yes, they'd made fun of the "Jesus Freaks"
commenting how they lacked the strength to rely on themselves.
That was about the extent. He was a Christian now. That was
blatantly obvious on the trail. She didn't know what to think when
he'd asked her to pray with him, but she went along with it. Was he
going to throw his religion in her face?

Caitlynn scoffed as she relived memories, not all of them
pleasant. As a child, her mom and dad took her to church, and her
parents could've won an Oscar, pretending they were a happy
family. The façade ended when her Dad walked out of their life
when she was eight years old. The pastor came by and urged her
Mom to continue attending but she was too embarrassed. That was

the end of Sunday School. Her father abandoned her, and somehow, she always blamed God for not coming to her aid. The anger and hurt over her past are why she didn't particularly like Christians. She always thought of Christians as being "high and mighty." They acted as if they were all invited into a private club that excluded her. They talked about God's love, prayed over their meals, and read the Bible or self-help books to become a better Christian. She didn't have time for that.

She was firm in her belief that if you were kind to your fellow humans and the earth, you were putting some good out into the world. A pang of guilt sprang up when she thought back a few years ago of Daniel, a Christian coworker. Everyone at the station made fun of him because he'd make a lame excuse up why he couldn't make it to happy hour; had invited her to his church. "Do I look like a charity case? I don't need whatever crutch you do to get through life. I don't need your religion. I create my own destiny." She felt sorry at how she'd snapped at him. Truth be told, he'd caught her on a particularly bad day, but she did mean every word. Needless to say, Daniel didn't last long at the station.

She took a sip of tea. *This shouldn't be happening.* Steve…back in her life again. True, she had wanted to meet his son, but the main reason had been to convince Steve to hightail it back to Chicago. His very presence made her feel uncomfortable. Her job was the only thing in her life that she found satisfying, and instead of looking forward to what the day would bring at work, she had to worry about how she could avoid *him.*

The instant she set eyes on Tyler she was smitten. Thinking about how close they came to losing Tyler, the helplessness and despair still overwhelmed her a day later…who wouldn't love that kid? With those gorgeous blue eyes and freckles across his nose and cheeks, and his haircut spiked in the front, courtesy of too much hair gel.

The smart decision would've been to stay as far away from Steve as possible. She wanted to hurt Steve the way he'd hurt her. He walked out on her just like her father. Steve's family obligations, his career, every important life decision took precedence over their relationship. She was deeply in love with him in college. They lived together for two years. Her plan to marry him and live happily ever after backfired, leaving her heartbroken. Every relationship since then never lasted, always ending badly. And always, her fault. She bit her lip. At least he'd been married. He all but admitted it was his fault his marriage ended in divorce. Nevertheless, he had a beautiful child to love. She could've had a boy just like Tyler. *What if?*

She closed her eyes and rubbed her belly, trying to shut out the pain. The hysterectomy was the last straw. No husband. No children . . . ever. She supposed she should have listened to the doctor when he suggested counseling. She sighed deeply. It was probably overdue. The surgery didn't bother her so much at first, but now watching Steve and Tyler left her feeling robbed. Everything lay heavy on her mind—the story deadline, the impending hysterectomy, break-up with Jake, and worst of all, Steve's reappearance in her life. As darkness fell, cold reality began to surface.

Steve had ruined her only chance of happiness.

A rush of intense anger gripped her heart and filled her being. Her chest tightened, and her breath came out in tiny gasps. He can't be trusted. If he could leave her then, what was stopping him from doing it again? As her boss, he had the power to demote her—or worse, fire her and find a replacement. She couldn't let him destroy everything she loved and had worked so hard over the years to build.

She was determined to fight. She had to! Her job, her career— this was her life. All she needed was a plan...

That's it! Her heart raced. The simplicity was so beautiful— she had to laugh. What one thing, above all others, did he value? *Christ.* If she knew anything at all, she knew most men were susceptible to a woman's charm, and there she had the advantage. He desired her. There was no better way to destroy a man's faith than by temptation. It didn't get past her yesterday when Steve looked at her and said, "What I'm looking at is beautiful."

Engulfed in darkness, her tea now cold, she shivered and tightened the throw around her shoulders as a chill crept deep into her soul. Her eyes narrowed. Tomorrow, she would set into motion her plan to weaken Steve's supposed newfound faith… and send him back to Chicago—and out of her life for good.

Early Monday morning, Caitlynn rapped on Steve's office door.

"Come in." Steve's eyes widened when she walked in. "Do you have a hot date tonight after work tonight?"

She eased into the leather chair and crossed her leg, revealing a glimpse of thigh. "No." She blinked rapidly and flirted. "A girl's allowed to dress up once in a while. I thought you might want to join me for dinner."

His gaze traveled the length of her legs… and lingered for a brief moment. His eyes lit up and his brow arched. "I'd say you're trying to hit on me." His laughter echoed in the small room. "I'm trying to imagine what you're up to. Are you asking me out?"

Why had she thought this plan would be easy? A hot, tingling sensation on her cheeks meant she was turning bright pink. She wanted Steve to pay and get out of her life once and for all, but thinking up the plan and executing it were two different things. She was so out of her comfort zone that she wanted to turn and bolt out the door. Instead, she straightened her spine and plowed ahead like a ship tossed on a stormy sea. "No strings, just dinner. You have to eat, and so do I, so we might as well eat together." Her eyes met his. "That's what people do you know." She leaned forward, licking her lips. "They eat together."

He cocked his head to one side. "Okay, Caitlynn, I'll play your little game. What night would you like to have dinner on our non-date, and should I pick you up at your house? Oops, it's not a date—I-I forgot. Where do you want to meet and what time?"

"How about the Fish House? I know you like seafood." She spoke through gritted teeth.

"That's fine. Name the day and time."

"Do I have to do everything?" She clenched her fists in frustration. "Can't you pick the day and time?"

He smiled slowly. "I'm not the one planning this event," he said with a familiar glint in his eye. "You are."

His teasing irked her. "How about Friday night at seven?" she suggested. Playing the femme fatale was so much harder than she'd imagined. She pressed her lips together. "Will that work for you?"

He looked thoughtful. "That should work, but I think you should know—"

Her heart thumped in her chest as she interrupted. "N-no conditions." She stumbled over her words. "Either yes or no."

"Yes." His tone changed into his best news reporter voice. "Yes, of course, that will be perfect." He hid a grin. "I'll meet you this coming Friday night at seven at the Fish House for dinner on our non-date." His tone turned serious. "Just remember, Caitlynn…I didn't suggest this. You did."

"Fine," she said sharply. "I'll take full responsibility." Caitlynn stood, heading for the exit. "See you Friday."

"Hold up a second." He rocked back in his chair. "I know you're up to something. I should care, but I want to see just how far you'll go." He breathed in, then exhaled slowly. "I have faith that whatever you're up to will soon be brought to light."

She clutched the doorknob, hoping the smile she plastered on her face was seductive. "I guess you'll have to wait for Friday," she purred. "Until then, I'll see you tomorrow at the staff meeting." She clicked the door shut.

CHAPTER TEN

Steve wheeled the car into his private drive, pressed the remote to open the security gate, and drove a hundred yards or so down the long tree-lined driveway. Another button opened the garage door. This is ridiculous. Am I living in the White House? He made a mental note to keep the gate open from now on.

Once inside, he padded into the large kitchen that opened into the great room. The only sound he heard came from the hum of the refrigerator. In four days, he'd see Tyler again. Tyler brought nonstop energy and a curiosity for life that warmed Steve's heart. As he heated some leftovers for dinner, he picked up his cell phone and dialed.

"Hi, Tiger, how was practice?"

"The coach did a few drills, but mainly we worked on our backhand stroke."

"I suppose you're going to want to play some tennis while you're here."

"I guess..."

He sounded like he wanted to throw in the towel. "What's up, Ty? Why are you so down?"

"The last twenty minutes we paired up and I had to play Trevor. I can't beat him no matter how bad I want to." Tyler sighed.

Steve switched his phone to his other ear and tried to think of something encouraging. He opted for the hard truth. "You can't win every game. Sometimes you can learn more from a loss than a win. What did Trevor do that you couldn't beat him at?"

"He has a drop shot and I don't," Tyler mumbled.

"See? Now you know you need to learn a drop shot. Don't worry; you'll get the shot. It just takes time and practice."

"Can you teach me a drop shot this weekend?" His voice rose in excitement. "Can we go on Friday night? My flight arrives at four. We could go to the health club on the way home."

"We can't go on Friday. Besides, you're going to be here all week for fall break. We'll go Sunday after church."

"Why can't we go Friday?" he whined.

"Ms. Caitlynn invited me to dinner on Friday. So, I guess we're both going to dinner Friday night."

Tyler's voice grew excited. "Is this a date, Dad?"

For the last two days, Steve tried not to think of Caitlynn, but he'd failed miserably. The image of her sitting across from him, showing off her sexy legs was etched in his mind. "Um . . . no, she's just trying to be friendly, I guess. I'm sure she'll be happy to see you."

"I like her; she's nice to me. Just a sec, Dad… Mom's saying something." There was some scuffling on the phone, then Tyler shouted, "Okay, Mom!"

"Oh, man, Ty… I think my eardrum just burst."

"Sorry, Dad," Tyler said hurriedly. "I gotta go. Mom's calling me to dinner."

"See you Friday." He paused a second. "Ty, make sure you wear something decent on the plane so we won't have to stop to change."

Steve leaned back on the couch. His conversation with Tyler made him pause twice. Was this a date? He didn't think so. It seemed like Caitlynn was testing him. Something in the back of his mind told him to pray for strength—he had a feeling he'd need any help he could get.

###

Steve glanced impatiently at his watch, drumming his fingers on the crisp white tablecloth. Tyler excused himself to use the restroom while Steve sat at their table waiting for Caitlynn.

And then she showed up. Steve did a double-take when she waved—and his breath quickened. Caitlynn strutted toward him wearing a sexy, black halter dress with a neckline that plunged so low it didn't leave much to the imagination.

His stomach flipped like an acrobat at the vision she created. The dress ended above the knee and clung everywhere else like an extra layer of skin. Black heels accented her shapely legs and delicate ankles.

His stomach fell and stayed there. *I should've prayed harder.*

She kept her eyes focused on his like a laser locked on a target. Her face was a vision of perfection. How did the Creator make eyes the crystal-clear blue of the Caribbean? Her high cheekbones had a sweep of color, and her red lips looked soft and shined like a mirror. Her strawberry-blonde hair flowed in soft curls around her face. He stood and slid her chair out.

Seated, she continued to focus on him. "I see you still have manners. Thank you."

"Some things are never forgotten; he took a seat and murmured. "I was under the impression this was a non-date, but you're all dressed up. Why?"

Her lips curved into a slight smile. "I thought you might like to see what you missed in the past twelve years."

"Not only do I know what I'm missing, but so does the entire male population in this restaurant." He tore his glance away and panned the room. "I believe every eye in this place turned to look when you made your grand entrance."

She laughed and shrugged a bare shoulder. "I wanted you to know I saw you sitting in the corner—that's all... Besides, who cares if the men stare? I don't remember you as the jealous type."

Tyler hurried back and took the chair across from Caitlynn.

Steve's first impulse was to lean over and cover his son's eyes. "Tyler, you remember Ms. Caitlynn?"

"Uh-huh. You sure look different. You look pretty. Are you a movie star?"

A trace of pink washed over her face. On the walk over to their table, she'd honed in on Steve like she was a hunter and he the prey. Seeing her obvious discomfort, Steve hid a smile.

Caitlynn quickly grabbed a goblet of water and took a sip. "N–no, Tyler, I'm not, but thanks for the compliment." She looked over at Steve and arched a brow. "You didn't tell me your son would be joining?"

This time he couldn't stop. Steve grinned mischievously. "I tried, but you interrupted me, remember?" He chuckled. "You said—and I quote— 'Everyone needs to eat.'" Caitlynn ignored Steve's last remark, which only caused him to grin wider. "You look amazing." He couldn't stop staring.

She cast her eyes down, ignoring his comment.

She grabbed her napkin, placed it on her lap, and smiled at Tyler. "I hope you're as hungry as I am."

"Yep. I'm starving. I couldn't even eat a roll! Can I have one now?"

"Sure. Do you need any help?"

Ty grabbed a roll and reached for the knife. "Naw, I'm good," he answered just as the utensil slipped from his hand and clattered to the floor. "Oops."

Caitlynn reached for the plate. "Do you like butter?"

Tyler nodded.

"Here." She snatched up her knife. "Let me have your roll and I'll make it for you—but you have to tell me exactly how you like it." Her voice shook.

"Thanks!" Tyler exclaimed. "Can you cut it in half and put the butter in the middle?"

"Sure can. Do you want me to put the other half on top?"

"Yeah, and smash it down real good, so the butter gets on the top too."

"Mmm, that's just how I like mine. I think I'll have one too. How about you, Steve? Would you care to join us?"

Although he liked what he saw, Steve looked at her in sympathy. Her flushed cheeks and her shaky voice—revealed her act. Obviously, wearing evening cocktail fashion wasn't commonplace for her. She was failing miserably. Trying to reassure her, he held out the bread plate, and said, "Absolutely, I'll have what he's having."

Caitlynn placed a roll upon Steve's plate, and with a nervous jerk, she reached inside for another. "Tyler, I assumed you were in

Chicago this weekend because you were at your dad's last weekend." She placed the roll on her plate. Steve pretended not to notice when she attempted to discreetly push together a bit of the fabric on her low-cut dress.

Tyler tore off a piece. "I have fall break this week, so I get to spend it with my dad." He stuffed the morsel into his mouth. "My friend Hunter is on break too. We want to see a movie."

"You met a friend? Already? Does he live in your neighborhood?" she asked.

"We met at church."

The waiter came and Caitlynn ordered grilled mahi-mahi. Tyler wanted chicken fingers, as usual. Steve decided to go for broke. "Lobster tail for me—with lots of melted butter on the side."

As the server hurried off, Caitlynn turned to Steve. "What about work? Are you coming in this week?"

Steve couldn't stop staring. *What was the question?* He swallowed hard and focused. "Y–yes. Hunter's mom recommended her daycare. I've arranged for Ty to go this week, and then I'll work from home on Friday."

Caitlynn turned to Tyler. "I bet you didn't know this, but I can tell you both came from Chicago because of your accents?"

Steve stole a glance at Caitlynn, glad that she finally looked somewhat comfortable talking to Tyler.

Tyler's smile revealed a tiny dimple on one cheek. "Really?"

"Yep. I can tell you don't live in Denver because of how you pronounce your words. When I first met your dad, I laughed at him because he talked so fast and when he said 'hot,' I thought he was saying 'hat.'"

Steve whispered loud enough for Caitlynn to hear as he pointed to her. "Tyler, we don't sound funny. She sounds funny."

Tyler laughed and fired back. "Yeah. You're the one that doesn't talk right."

"No fair." She grinned happily. "It's two against one!"

Watching Caitlynn smile genuinely for the first time that night, Steve sucked in his breath, admiring the way her hair glowed like fire against the backdrop of her black dress, and her bare shoulders sprinkled lightly with freckles. Caitlynn looked to be enjoying their company. Steve joked, "You probably should've thought about that beforehand. The Carr team sticks together." He joked.

The waiter arrived and swiftly placed their food on the table. "Is there anything else I can get for you?"

"No, we're great, thanks." Steve speared a piece of lobster and savored the mild flavor. He watched Caitlynn and Ty enjoy their food.

"Are chicken fingers your favorite?" she asked.

"I have lots of favorites. For breakfast, I like pancakes or waffles. For lunch, I like macaroni and cheese, and my favorite dinner is chili cheese dogs and tater tots."

"Yum. Sounds like the perfect kid menu. There's not a veggie or quality food group anywhere."

Steve listened to the banter between Tyler and Caitlynn. He couldn't remember the last time his son engaged in this type of fun around a table. He watched the two of them together. Caitlynn looked to be having a good time. In fact, she looked stunning. His heart pounded. The soft candlelight from the table softened her features, and for a moment he was transported back to Freshmen year when they'd first met. "Cat, could you pass me a roll?"

Caitlynn's hand froze in mid-air. Her eyes glazed over, and she quietly placed her fork on the plate. "Don't ever call me that again," she said sharply. "That person doesn't exist anymore." Her face paled and she stood abruptly, almost tipping the chair. "If you'll excuse me, I need to use the ladies' room."

Steve rose quickly and reached out to steady her rocking chair. "Caitlynn, I'm sorry. I didn't mean to upset you."

She stared at him for a brief moment, pressed her trembling lips together, then turned and walked toward the restroom.

He sat down hard and frowned down at his plate. The lobster was succulent and moist. The rice pilaf had just the right touch of seasonings. The vegetables were crisp yet tender, with a hint of garlic and butter for flavor. But his stomach twisted in knots.

Five minutes went by, and still no sign of Caitlynn. Should he go after her? Call her cell phone and apologize again? He was an idiot. What was he thinking? That was the problem. If he'd been thinking, he would've known not to call her by that name.

Tyler shook his arm. "Is Ms. Caitlynn coming back from the restroom?" He wore a worried expression.

"I don't think so. She's probably on the way home. I screwed up and made her mad. If you're finished eating, we'll go, and I'll call her later and tell her I'm sorry."

"She's nice. I'm sure if you say sorry, she'll forgive you and give you another chance." Tyler still had the youthful innocence to believe that saying "I'm sorry" was all that was needed to forgive and forget.

In her haste to reach her car, Caitlynn strode almost at a run in her high heels. Rummaging in her handbag, she fished out her keys and clicked the remote. Opening the door, she slid into her car and then slammed the door shut. She leaned against the headrest and closed her eyes. Everything she had hoped would happen tonight was a bust. He couldn't stop staring at her, but with Tyler at the table, she'd had to scratch her plan of seduction.

The first few minutes of dinner had proved embarrassing and awkward. If a blanket had magically appeared at the table, she would've thrown it around herself like a shawl. Luckily, Tyler was so cute it didn't take long to focus on him and tolerate his father. She'd delighted in teasing Tyler and watching his face light up. *How did kids do that?* Their faces, cheeks, eyes, smiles— everything all lights up at once when they laugh.

But then he dared to call her Cat, her nickname she esteemed only for those close to her…he lost that privilege many years ago. She scowled. Memories of the two of them together filled her mind, a collage of photos suspended in time. All those times he called her Cat when they were together and in love. She felt like a fool running away, but there was no way she'd go back. Her pride wouldn't let her. Why go back and pretend everything was okay? What they had twelve years meant nothing to her now…so what did it matter what nickname he called her?

From the moment her eyes had rested on Tyler, she'd known she didn't have the nerve to go through with tempting Steve. There had to be another way to get back at him—and get him out of her life—without hurting Tyler.

Caitlynn started the car and drove away, never once glancing back.

CHAPTER ELEVEN

Caitlynn flashed her volunteer badge to the security guard working at Children's Hospital. Two years of volunteering every other Saturday earned her quick entrance and a friendly smile. She exited the elevator on the third floor and tapped softly on the neonatal ICU's glass door. Her friend, Becky—who was, in Caitlynn's opinion, the best pediatric nurse at Children's, grinned widely, and pressed the button to unlock the door.

Tiptoeing, Caitlynn washed her hands and donned a sterile gown, face mask, and gloves. The low-pitched whir of life-saving machinery hummed, and the smell of antiseptic filled the air.

Tiny infants' soft cries tugged at Caitlynn's heart. She wanted to reach out and hold every single one. A baby around four months old, with oxygen tubes taped to his face and around his nostrils, was nestled in Becky's arms. "Hi, Caitlynn," she whispered, "I haven't seen you in a while. Would you like to rock little Ethan?"

Caitlynn quietly scooted a rocking chair close to Becky's and sat. Becky gingerly deposited Ethan into her arms.

"I was here two weeks ago last Saturday." Caitlynn whispered. "It must've been your weekend off."

The baby rested peacefully, snuggled in the blanket wrapped tightly around his body. As Caitlynn caressed his little cheek and rocked him softly, she asked, "What's wrong with him?"

"The little guy caught bronchitis from his older brother, but then it developed into pneumonia. He's doing so much better. His color has improved and he should get off the oxygen today. He could be back home by Monday." Becky stroked his cheek; his lips quivered into a smile. "I have to go do my rounds. My lunch break is in an hour. Do you want to join me?"

Caitlynn looked down at the sleeping child. She hated to think of leaving him, but she needed to talk. "Sure. I have so much to tell you. Come and get me when you're ready."

Becky walked away.

Smiling at Ethan, Caitlynn snuggled as close as the oxygen tube and I.V. would allow, rocked in a steady rhythm, and softly sang *Hush Little Baby*.

Caitlynn stood in the cafeteria line watching Becky load her tray with a turkey wrap, an orange, and a soft drink. Becky looking over at Caitlynn, "That's your lunch? A cup of chicken noodle soup?" Becky asked.

"I'm not hungry. I ate a big breakfast."

Becky looked doubtful. "What was that? A meal-replacement bar? You need to put some meat on your bones. You have to add one more item to your tray. Pick something."

"Fine." She put an apple on her tray.

"Oh, no, you don't." Becky put the fruit back. I remember the last time you picked an apple—you said it was mushy and threw it away. Now go on and pick something else."

"You act like you're my mama."

"Well, someone better! Girl, you're gonna blow away if you don't eat more. If I knew your mama's number, I'd call her and tattle on you. Now pick something else!"

Caitlynn added a banana and a bottle of water and went to pay. "I'm paying for hers too," she said to the cashier, tilting her head at Becky.

"You make me crazy… you know that?" Becky flashed a smile.

"It's the least I can do for my mama." She teased.

They found an empty seat. Caitlynn had a taste of her soup, pursed her lips, and quickly drank a sip of water.

Becky's eyes widened. What's wrong with the soup?"

"It's salty."

"Then add some pepper. Spice it up some. You can wash it down with your water."

Caitlynn reached for the pepper. "I don't know why I put up with you."

"Because I'm your friend, that's why. I'm never going to stop hounding you about your—uh...diet. Now, what's your big news? Lay it on me."

You're my only friend. The girls at the station were nice enough, and she'd go out for happy hour occasionally, but the friends she'd made early on worked for different networks now. Trying to make friends seemed pointless. Most of them were either vying for her job or on their way to other career opportunities. Caitlynn knew Becky would help her after her surgery, but she hated to ask because Becky worked long hours at the hospital. No way could she take the precious little time Becky had with her family. Caitlynn took a swig of her water, swallowed and sighed. "Steve works at the station."

Becky almost choked on her food. "The infamous Steve? The one who broke up with you the day you graduated from college? That Steve?"

"He didn't break up with me. He took the job his father offered him. The distance between us did the rest."

"Don't defend him! He left you. Remember? And if I recall correctly, the jerk broke your heart. Am I right?"

"That was a long time ago. Can we change the subject?"

"I don't think so," Becky said in a singsong tone. "You're the one who brought it up in the first place. Tell me more."

Caitlynn crossed her arms. "He's divorced and has a seven-year-old boy named Tyler." Her tone softened. "Tyler's a miniature Steve, but instead of wavy dark brown hair, he has sandy brown hair. He spikes it in the front with so much gel it stands straight up. Unlike his father, his nose is brushed with freckles; but he shares the same deep blue eyes and dark lashes. I'm sure Tyler will break hearts too someday. Anyway, he travels from Chicago to Denver to visit his father twice a month and on holidays."

"Wow. That has to be difficult. Why would a father move so far from his son?"

"He said God told him to move and that it would be okay."

"Well, you know, the good Lord does work in mysterious ways, but that makes no sense at all. The kid must be a mess."

Caitlynn smiled. "He's so cute. He has a good attitude about the whole thing."

Becky's eyes widened. "And when did you meet his son?"

"Um, I went hiking with them, and we ate dinner together yesterday."

"You went hiking! You ate dinner? Oh no! You're falling for him, aren't you? I can see the whole sorry mess happening all over again."

"Nothing's happening. I like his son—he's adorable—but unfortunately, I have to work with his father." She looked down and frowned. "Hopefully, not for long."

"Whatever you say, Caitlynn. But I know better. You're in deep, and the person who's gonna get hurt is you."

Just then, Caitlynn's phone vibrated, and when she pulled it out of her purse, her stomach dropped. "It's Steve," she whispered, and Becky shook her head. She quickly answered the phone.

"I'm sure you heard the apology I left on your voicemail," Steve said, "but I wanted to apologize again. I wasn't thinking. Tyler hopes you're not mad at him. The hike didn't end well and neither did uh, last night." He, um, wants to know if you'd like to come over for chili cheese dogs sometime this week."

Caught off guard, she frowned. His sincere apology had come through loud and clear in his message. She'd even listened twice before deleting it. And now he was apologizing again. This was definitely not the Steve she used to know; the Steve who stubbornly refused to say sorry for any wrongdoing.

She brushed a strand of hair away and tried to think of how to decline the invite. Her first reaction was to refuse, but Tyler was right. Each time she was with him, something happened to ruin it. Flat out refusing would hurt Tyler's feelings—so she gave in. "I'm only doing this for Tyler, understand?" She bit her bottom lip and said, "What day works for you?"

"How about Thursday?"

"That's fine." She held her breath. "Let Ty know I'll be there." Caitlynn ended the call, sighed deeply, and put the cell phone into her handbag.

Becky crooked a half-smile. "Like I said, in over your head."

Her throat suddenly dry, Caitlynn swallowed. "I know what I'm doing. I'm curious though. Why did Steve care so much to apologize? I never remember him apologizing before. It seems so out of character."

"I have to get back to work." Becky squeezed Caitlynn's hand. "If you need a shoulder to cry on when this falls apart, you know where to find me."

Caitlynn stared at the memo pad on her desk, doodling tiny circles, triangles, and squares in the margin as she thought about her surgery and upcoming assignment. She'd jotted Jillian's home phone number on the top of the page. Jillian wanted to keep her baby. It was also obvious her mom didn't agree. There was a conflict of interest. Legally, as a minor, Caitlynn needed Peggy's permission to move forward. She dialed the number.

"Hello, this is Caitlynn Grant from Channel Twelve. I spoke with your daughter—"

"Yes. I remember," Jillian's mother interrupted.

"I'd like to get started on this assignment," Caitlynn said, hoping this would go well. "There are a few legal details to discuss. I need parental permission, and I would also like to get your side of the story."

The woman sucked in a sharp breath. "First of all, we are not an *assignment*," she said tartly. "We are in the middle of a family crisis. Most people handle these things privately; they don't have the entire Denver metro area watching their life fall apart on the ten o'clock news."

Caitlynn closed her eyes and shook her head. "I'm sorry." She needed to start over. She flipped to a new page on her notepad. "I didn't get your name the other day."

"Peggy Walker."

She printed the name on the top of the new page. "Peggy, I know you think you're alone, but you're not. Research states that for every 1000 adolescent females, ages fifteen to nineteen, there were forty-two births. Thirty-four percent of teen girls in the United States end up pregnant. One-third of teen pregnancies end in abortion. I want to tell Jillian's story because it could make a difference to other teenagers and their parents. I promise to handle this carefully, with your family's feelings in mind, and I'll let you and your daughter know what I plan to say every step of the way. I respect your privacy, and if there's a topic we cover that you feel too sensitive to air, I'll remove it from the story."

There was a long silence. "That sounds good, I guess. I know my daughter wants to do this." She blew out a breath. "Come over, and I'll give you whatever permission you need."

"What time would be good for you? I also need Jillian to sign the documents."

"Why don't you come by around five o'clock in the afternoon this Thursday."

Caitlynn closed her eyes and crossed her fingers. "Is there another time this week? I have an engagement that day."

"You could come by Friday, but I work late and won't get off until seven."

"Will eight o'clock work for you?"

Peggy sighed again. "I guess so. Let's get this over with."

Caitlynn ended the call and drew a smiling face, happy that she could change the meeting to Friday. It would be another long week, but she didn't mind. Now she had two things to look forward to.

CHAPTER TWELVE

Steve skimmed through the pile of résumés. He had two weeks to find a sports anchor. Most of the candidates were experienced, but he was looking for a fresh face who didn't view Denver as a steppingstone to broader markets. Then an idea surfaced. If he hurried, he could be at the University of Colorado within the hour.

Forty minutes later, he was strolling toward the commons area on campus in Boulder. He'd walked down these same sidewalks nearly twelve years ago. It felt like déjà vu. Students wearing jeans and T-shirts rushed past him under the burden of heavy backpacks. He glanced down at his dress slacks and white button-down dress shirt and felt out of place.

Steve took a deep breath as he entered the School of Journalism and Mass Communication building. A janitor swished a stringy mop back and forth across the tiled floor. The potent smell of the industrial cleaner transported him back to the first time he stepped foot in this building full of fresh ideas and ready to tackle the world. Memories swirling, he yanked off his tie, shoved it into the pocket of his blazer, which he then peeled off and slung over his shoulder. He walked down the hallway until he found the room and entered.

A young man and woman were seated behind a large desk in the campus news studio, complete with a detailed weather map, camera crew, and several monitors. He found a seat toward the back. The professor put his finger to his mouth. "Audience, quiet please." He held up three fingers. "We are on the air in 3 . . . 2 . . . 1 . . ."

The news anchors read the monitor well, projecting the correct inflection in their tone. Steve could tell they were comfortable with the camera angles and they looked professional. At the break, a young man entered, sat down, and faced the camera. He had dark blond hair and green eyes, with an athletic build and youthful look. Steve viewed him on the monitor. The camera loved him. Good so far, but could he bring a fresh perspective to sports?

"This is Connor Jackson. The Broncos ended their four-game losing streak with a win over the Falcons. The Falcons were indeed in last place in their league, and the Broncos barely won by a field goal. But, hey, they won! Let's hope this victory will give the team the confidence they need to beat the New England Patriots next Sunday at Invesco Field. In other news, the Denver Nuggets have yet to lose. They won against the Utah Jazz, 103-92. You may remember that after his Olympic win, Carmelo Anthony vowed to step up his defensive game—and he didn't disappoint! His new attitude toward defense hasn't gone unnoticed. The coach had this to say . . ."

Steve had heard enough. He liked the guy. He tuned out the rest of the newscast and waited until the end before he began introductions. Holding out his hand, he said, "Hi, I'm Steven Carr, the station manager for Channel 12."

"Connor Jackson."

"I'd like to talk to you about a job opportunity as a sports anchor if you're interested."

Connor's brows shot up. "Definitely. It would be great to move back to Denver. I grew up there, and my fiancé and I would love to live close to our families."

Steve handed his business card to Connor. "E-mail me your résumé. If I like what I see, I'll give you a call to set up a time for an interview. When do you graduate?"

"I graduated four years ago. I'm just doing a favor for my professor—he was taping the show for the first-year class to critique our performances."

"Where are you working?"

"At KGJC, Grand Junction. I'm the sports anchor."

Hopefully, the station in Grand Junction would soon have to find a new sports anchor. Steve shook Connor's hand again and said, "I look forward to hearing from you."

Excited his hunch paid off, he walked to his SUV with a spring in his step and drove out of the campus toward Highway 36. He knew that once Ed met Connor, he'd be impressed too.

Just then his cell phone beeped. It was his father. He stiffened. Trying to talk to his father was another stress he'd prefer to ignore, but unfortunately, he couldn't put it off any longer. "Hello."

"I'm calling to see how you're holding up at your new job?"

"So far, things are going as expected, with only a few issues. I have to replace the sports anchor, and I'm trying to increase the ratings with a new marketing campaign. I'm calling it *Community First*. Our ratings are slowly rising plus it's generating positive news for a change." He steered the car into the slow lane. "I'm trying not to force too many changes. I don't want anyone to feel threatened and quit."

"Speaking of surprises, I looked up the station's website, and I see that Caitlynn Grant works for you."

"Sure does. She's a field reporter—specializing in human interest stories."

"The last time I saw her, you were both graduating. I bet she's married by now with kids?"

"No to both."

"Son, you'd better be careful. She wanted to marry you, and if I hadn't intervened, who knows what would've happened."

"That's right, Father." Steve's voice tightened. "You sure did your best to save me from her, didn't you?"

"Steve, you know she's not our caliber. Nice girl. Poor, raised by a single mom. Hardly the standard I have in mind for my only son."

"Yeah…and look where I am today: divorced with an ex-wife involved with a Grand Prix racecar driver from France. Not to mention, a son who travels back and forth from Chicago."

"I didn't call to argue with you. Just listen to me and stay away from her."

"Thanks for your concern," he muttered through gritted teeth. "I'm hanging up now."

He chucked the phone onto the passenger seat. All this time he thought his father didn't like Caitlynn because they were living together. The real reason was that she didn't come from the right side of the tracks.

Twelve years ago, he'd wanted to be just like his father, and he had allowed his father to manipulate him. He worked for him and did whatever his father asked without ever questioning his father's motives. It was evident now: he desired money and power—and according to his father, there could never be too much of either.

Past decisions made in the pursuit of money and power, filled Steve's soul with regret. Years and years of traveling across the country, buying out stations for his father's media empire, hardly ever home to see his son. His belief system had changed the moment he became a Christian. No longer was he ruled by those dominions. A commitment to faith and family replaced the empty pursuits of money and power.

His father's voice warning him to stay away from Caitlynn fueled him into action. He snatched up the phone again.

"Hello?"

"Hi, Caitlynn, I'm calling to find out when your surgery is scheduled."

"It's the day before Thanksgiving."

Steve frowned. "Can you do me a favor and put your request on my calendar?"

"No problem. I was going to do it this week; I just haven't gotten around to it yet."

"I hope I'm not out of line, but is it anything serious?"

Caitlynn paused as if deciding whether to tell him. Then she blurted, "It's a female issue."

"Oh. Are you going to be okay?"

"It's not a life-or-death issue if that's what you're asking. Although I guess it is in a roundabout way—I'm having a hysterectomy." Her voice dripped with sarcasm.

Steve sucked in a breath.

"Are you still there?" Caitlynn asked.

His stomach churned as if sucker-punched in the gut. "Yes, I'm here." He gripped the steering wheel until his knuckles turned white. "I don't know what to say. I'm sorry."

"You don't have to say anything," she quipped. "It is what it is. There's nothing I can do now to change the outcome." She paused a moment. "I can't rewrite history."

Anger filled him. *A hysterectomy? This isn't fair, God.* He smacked the steering wheel. He was a child when his mother had a hysterectomy and could still conjure up the feelings of helplessness. He hated seeing his mom in pain.

He wanted to say a comforting word but knew that Caitlynn wouldn't want his sympathy. He changed the subject. "Are you coming to dinner on Thursday?"

"Yes—but as I told you, I'm only doing this for Tyler. Don't expect anything more."

"Understood. I'll email you directions to our house."

Steve hung up the phone. *She's too young. Why God?* He vowed right then to help her through her recovery. It could be an excellent opportunity to show her how much he'd changed.

After work, when Steve picked up Tyler at daycare, he noticed Tyler's face was flushed, and he had the sniffles. Steve rolled his eyes. He hated daycare centers—they were just a commune for bacteria. Brenda had hired a young woman named Alexis to stay with Tyler. At the time, he hadn't liked the nanny idea, but looking back, it was a better option than having Tyler spend all day stuck around an army of germs.

As soon as they came home, Steve fixed tacos for dinner and played a video game with Tyler. Before long, Tyler had dark circles underneath his eyes, and yawning.

"Okay, buddy, you need to get your pj's on and get ready for bed. I'll be up in a few minutes."

Tyler hardly put up a fight as he rubbed his eyes and headed toward the bathroom to brush his teeth. After a few moments, Steve went upstairs and peered into the bedroom. Tyler was in his pajamas and kneeling by his bed with his hands clasped together.

"God, please bless Mommy and help her not to be sad. God, please bless Daddy who I miss so much when I go home to Chicago. God, please bless my new friend Hunter, and help me to be extra good when Ms. Caitlynn comes over so she'll want to visit again. Amen."

Steve walked over to the bed.

"Can we get chocolate pudding for dessert when Ms. Caitlynn comes?" Tyler asked. His nose was running, so Steve wiped it with a tissue.

"Great idea, Tiger, I'll stop at the store tomorrow. Love you." He tucked his son into bed, kissed him on the forehead, and thought of Caitlynn.

Steve went downstairs, sprawled out on the couch. She was crystal clear that she was only coming over because of Tyler. But he wondered what her real motivation was. At dinner, she'd dressed to the nines, and while she looked knock-out gorgeous, it seemed so out of character. He didn't mean to call her Cat—it had just rolled off his tongue.

He hit the TV remote power button. There was no way he was going to disappoint his son. *Lord, help me to be patient with Caitlynn and keep Tyler from getting hurt.*

CHAPTER THIRTEEN

For three hours, Steve was on the phone with various people regarding the upcoming marketing meeting. His assistant, Paula, was racing frantically back and forth from the copier to her desk organizing the document and highlighting the details. The phone rang again; he ignored the call. A minute later, Paula chimed in on the intercom, "It's your son's daycare on line one."

"Steve speaking."

"Hi, this is Kelly Gardner from Discovery Daycare. Tyler isn't feeling well. He has a fever, and he says his stomach hurts. Might be the virus that's going around. You'd better come pick him up."

Tyler had complained of a stomachache this morning, but Steve didn't think much of it. Just another thing to feel guilty about. He grabbed his coat and told Paula he was leaving for the rest of the day. When Steve arrived, Tyler trudged toward him. His cheeks were bright red.

"Hey." He stooped down and hugged his son. "You don't look so good."

"I don't feel so good either," Tyler mumbled.

"Come on, let's get you home." He grabbed Tyler's backpack and they exited the daycare.

Once they arrived, Steve settled Tyler on the couch, put on his favorite cartoon, and wrapped a throw around his body. He touched his forehead; it was on fire.

"Tyler, what does your mom do when you have a fever?"

"She gives me medicine to help my fever go away."

"Anything else?"

"She makes chicken soup and toast."

"Sounds good. I should have a few cans in the pantry. And some liquid Tylenol too. Why don't you rest and watch cartoons? I'm going to make the soup and find the medicine. If you need me just yell."

He located the items, grabbed the fever reducer and a teaspoon from the drawer, and found Tyler asleep on the sofa. He shut off the television and touched Tyler's head and cheeks. He was burning up. Steve knelt next to the sofa and poured the liquid into the spoon. "Tyler?" Steve gently shook him. "Wake up; you need to take this medicine."

Tyler rubbed his eyes and grabbed Steve's arm to help him sit up. As if in slow motion, the spoon tilted sideways, and bright red liquid spilled, dribbling down the side of the couch. Steve watched helplessly as the syrup hit his Persian rug.

Tyler whimpered at first and then cried. Tears streamed down his cheeks. "I'm sorry, Daddy, I didn't mean to spill."

"Don't worry about it, Son." Irritated now at the slow "drip, drip, drip" seeping into the rug, he wondered, *does cherry-flavored red-dye come out of carpets?* "Let's have another go at this, Tiger."

This time, the attempt was successful. After that, he wiped up the medicine's sticky residue from the leather sofa cushions and tried to clean the red stain from the rug, which left a faint trace of pink. "I'm going to dish up your soup now."

He warmed the soup on the stove and was about to let Tyler sit on the couch to eat, but then reconsidered. "Come eat at the table. I don't want any more accidental spills."

Tyler slowly got up and wrapped the blanket around him. On his way to the table, he tripped, falling on the floor and burst into tears.

Steve heard more crying and banged the serving spoon hard against the pot. "Ty, I know you don't feel well, but you've got to stop crying about every little thing." He raked his fingers through his hair. "You're sick, but crying isn't going to help! Now stop it, and come eat your soup."

Tyler wiped his eyes and made his way over to the table. Steve grabbed the blanket and flung it over a chair. He set the soup on the table, kissed the top of Tyler's head, and sighed deeply. "I'm not so good at this, am I?"

"No." Tyler pouted as he sat down. "Mommy is much better when I'm sick. She knows what to do, and you don't." He wiped his nose with his sleeve.

Steve ruffled Tyler's hair, grinning slightly. "You're right—but I won't know how unless I try. How 'bout we call your mom and you can talk to her after you eat? Maybe that will help."

Tyler brushed a tear off his cheek. "I'd like that."

The following morning, Steve was worried. Tyler's cheeks were fire red and burning. "I guess you won't be going to daycare," he said. "I'm going to make you something to eat so you can have more medicine. You'll need to rest."

Steve made Tyler toast. He carefully measured out the liquid Tylenol and handed it to Tyler to swallow. "Good job." He said, in relief. "No spilling this time. I think we're gettin' the hang of this!"

"You did good," Tyler said with a glimmer in his eyes. But you have a long way to go to be as good as Mommy."

"That's why we have mommies." Steve squeezed Ty's shoulder. "They're good at lots of things." He handed Tyler his blanket. "You watch TV while I make a few phone calls."

He set up Tyler on the couch, then went into his office. He quickly called Paula to tell her he'd be working from home, leaned back in his leather chair and stared out the window, exhausted.

Thirty minutes later, he checked in on Tyler, who was lying comfortably on the couch. Steve sat next to him and placed the thermometer in Tyler's mouth. "Your temp is lower, but it's still above normal."

Tyler rubbed his growling stomach. "I'm hungry. Can I have some more soup for lunch?"

"Is your tummy still hurting?"

"It's better."

"All you've had is soup and toast. Do you think you could get down a grilled cheese?"

Tyler nodded. "I think so."

"You're not going to like this, but we have to call Caitlynn and tell her not to come." He patted Tyler's shoulder.

"Why?" Tyler asked, as his eyes widened. "I'm feeling better!"

"You caught a virus, and you've been running a fever—that means you're contagious and you could pass this on to Caitlynn and get her sick."

"You've been near me, and you're not sick." Tyler jutted out his lip.

"That's true, but I don't want to take a chance." Steve stared into his son's eyes. "She has to go in for an operation soon, and it's just not a good idea to be around sick people."

"Oh," he frowned. "I really wanted Ms. Caitlynn to come over. I wanted to show her my room, play video games, and eat dinner with her."

Steve wished he could fix this for Tyler, but some things couldn't be changed. He was more than willing to overlook his strained relationship with Caitlynn for his son, but he knew something Tyler didn't. *God's ways are not our ways.*

"I know you're upset, Ty, but sometimes things happen, and we don't know why. I don't know why you got sick, forcing us to have to cancel. We just have to accept that there's a good reason for this and make the best of the situation. Hopefully, we can have Ms. Caitlynn over another time."

Tyler pulled the blanket to his chin. "All right," he scowled, turning away abruptly. In a fit of anger, he snatched the remote and flipped through the television channels as fast as possible.

CHAPTER FOURTEEN

After lunch, Caitlynn strolled past Steve's darkened office. She figured he was probably working from home. She closed her office door and sat in front of her computer, scrolling through her emails to find Steve's email with the directions—but it wasn't there.

The games and snacks she'd bought were already packed in the car.

The phone rang. Caller I.D flashed Steve's name. *I bet he's calling about the directions.*

"Hi, are you working from home today?" she said.

"Yes. Tyler's home sick. He has a fever and isn't feeling well. I hoped he'd be better by today, but he's not."

"Poor kid. That's terrible."

"We need to cancel dinner. I don't think it's a good idea for you to be around a sick kid. I would hate to see you get this virus."

Trying to hide her disappointment, Caitlynn replied softly, "Yeah. I'm sure you're right."

"Tyler's upset. He had big plans for tonight. I hope we can reschedule when he's feeling better."

Caitlynn forced a light tone into her voice. "Tell Tyler I hope he feels better soon. Doesn't he leave tomorrow for Chicago?"

"He's supposed to. I'm not putting him on the plane if he still has a fever." He paused. "I don't know yet..."

"I'm sure you'll do the right thing," Caitlynn said goodbye and hung up. *What am I thinking?* It's probably better not to invest in any kind of interaction—especially if it could possibly hurt Tyler. Plus, it will only make things more complicated with Steve. A little voice whispered; you can't trust him. Remember how he broke your heart? *Stick to the plan to get him out of my life and back to Chicago.*

She swiveled in her chair and stared out the window. Sighing, she dialed Peggy Walker.

"Peggy, this is Caitlynn. Sorry to call you at work, but I've had a change in my schedule. I can come over tonight if it works better for you and Jillian."

"Yeah, great, I'll call Jillian and let her know you're coming over this evening."

Caitlynn pulled up to the Walker home and felt a pang of nostalgia. It was a ranch house with gray vinyl siding and red shutters. She grew up in a ranch, and there was something about this style of home that always made her feel a certain way. She could almost visualize the layout—an L shaped living room, and dining room, galley kitchen with two bedrooms and a bathroom down the hallway. She walked up to the door and heard shouting. She wondered if she should knock or go back to the car and call to let them know she'd arrived. Whatever was happening was probably because of her. She rapped hard on the door. The yelling abruptly stopped.

Jillian opened the door wide. "Come in." Her cheeks were red and blotchy.

Caitlynn stepped into the living room. It was stuffy and smelled of leftover dinner. The room was almost swallowed up by an oversized brown leather couch, and matching chair, a coffee table in the center.

Peggy sat slumped on the couch. "I'm sorry you had to witness this family bonding time." Sarcasm dripped from her voice.

"Is that what you call it?" Jillian laughed with contempt. "My mom's so pessimistic! The only thing she can talk to me about is the scholarship I'm forfeiting and the hardship I'll face and how I should get rid of it."

Peggy sighed. "Jillian, I didn't say *get rid of it*. You know my stance on abortion. I said to give the baby up for adoption to a family who's in the position to love and support the child."

The tension in the room flared like dynamite about to explode. Caitlynn spoke in a calm voice. "You're both coming from different viewpoints. Jillian, I'm sure your mom loves you and only wants the best for you. I think this might be an ongoing conflict between you two. Why don't we get to the reason why I'm here?"

"That's fine," Jillian quipped, "but I'm not changing my mind, Mom. I'm keeping my baby with or without your help."

Peggy stood, ignoring her daughter's last remark, and led the way to the dining room. "Let's sit here." She collapsed into a chair.

Caitlynn sat in the chair opposite from Jillian. Unopened mail lay piled up at one end, and a bowl of fruit with three apples sat in the center. She reached into her bag and passed out the documents to Jillian and Peggy. "I plan to interview Jillian every month until you deliver. The last meeting will be after the birth of the baby. How many weeks are you now, Jillian?"

Jillian's eyes sparkled. "Twelve weeks." She rubbed her stomach. "Where will the interviews take place?"

"You can pick the place and time. I'll be in contact, and we'll make the arrangement a few days before each interview." Caitlynn handed out a schedule. "These dates are only a starting point, and, of course, they're flexible—but at least this gives you an idea of what you can expect over the next six months."

After giving Jillian and Peggy a few minutes to glance at the details, Caitlynn said, "Jillian, I want to show the viewer what it's like to be pregnant as a teenager. I'm sure it won't be easy for you. After the delivery, I'd like to film you and the baby together when you're settled at home."

"I'm not worried. I know this girl from school who had a baby and they're doing fine." Jillian smiled brightly. "My mom said there were legal papers you wanted me to sign?"

Peggy glanced over the documents and then looked at Caitlynn. "We get final approval before the story is aired, right?"

"Yes, because of the sensitive nature of the story, I promise you'll get final approval before it's aired." She handed them a pen and told them where to sign. She breathed a sigh of relief when they gave her back the document.

With only a week away from her hysterectomy, she could cross off one item from her list—she found a pregnant girl willing to share her story.

CHAPTER FIFTEEN

Friday rolled around. Tyler felt better, just in time for his flight back to Chicago. The airport was packed. This always added to Steve's nerves when sending off his son. He missed Ty already and he hadn't even left…

"The next time you'll see me will be Thanksgiving break," Steve said as he pulled out Tyler's roller bag from the back seat.

"Are you staying at Grandma's house?"

"Yes. You know the drill by now."

Tyler's imitation of big puppy dog eyes expressed hope. "You could stay with Mommy and me."

With a heavy heart, Steve resolved to stand firm. "We've had this discussion before, Tyler, and I don't want you to ask me again."

Tyler crossed his arms in defiance. "Fine."

Steve hated travel days to Chicago as much as Tyler did. Knowing their only communication would be by telephone until Tyler returned upset them both so much that they always seemed to be at odds before Tyler left. Even two years after the divorce, Tyler chose to believe that they'd miraculously reconcile. From the multiple self-help divorce books Steve had read, he knew this wasn't uncommon, but it was a small consolation. That his son had to travel back and forth also grated on him. Tyler took it all in stride. But still…

Steve bent over and made a point to hold Tyler's hand. "I have to give you credit for the attempt. You're very persistent."

Tyler looked up and smiled. "A kid has to try!"

Steve laughed and kissed the top of his head. "Truce?" he said, and Tyler nodded. On a more serious note, Steve said, "At some point, you'll have to accept that Mommy and Daddy are not getting back together. We both love you, and that's all that matters. Don't forget, I'll see you soon. We'll eat lots of turkey and play football."

"Is Mom gonna come too?"

"Mom can come and eat dinner at Me-ma's house if she wants to. I'll call and ask her."

"And her friend Antoine?"

Inwardly, Steve sighed. He'd better take his advice and accept a few changes too. While it didn't bother him that Brenda had moved on, per se, it still felt awkward. Tyler was his only focus now, and if that's what Ty wanted, then he'd try and come to terms with this awkward invite.

"Yes. If he's in town, he's welcome too."

"Mom says he's here for a month. Antoine is trying out his new car on a track near Chicago. He said I could ride with him at one of his practice runs."

How could he compete with a Grand Prix driver from France? "You should have a great time. I'm jealous, Tyler. I'd love to race a car that fast. You'll have to tell me all about it."

They made their way into the airport and waited in line. When it was their turn at the ticket counter, Steve handed over the flight confirmation and identification and checked Tyler's bag. The ticket agent handed Steve his security pass to accompany a minor to the gate. Then Steve helped Tyler through security and found the gate for departure.

The time they both dreaded was here. Tyler whimpered, "I don't want to leave you, Daddy."

Could a heart break over and over? Steve hugged his son. "I know, but we'll see each other before you know it. Your mom can't wait for you to get home. She's worried because you were sick. She'll be relieved to know you're all better." Steve grabbed the stuffed sock monkey out of his backpack and handed it to Tyler. He kissed and hugged his son. "I love you, Tiger. I'll see you soon."

A flight attendant approached. "You must be Tyler," she said. She looked happy to see the monkey. "I see you've brought a friend."

Tyler held him up for inspection. "He likes to travel."

She perused the unaccompanied minor document and boarding pass. "Dad, I'll take care of Tyler from here. We're ready to board."

Steve hugged his son again. "Call me when you land."

The flight attendant took Tyler's hand and they walked toward the jetway. "You know, I have a grandson about your age. How old are you?"

Steve stood at the gate until the plane took off, oblivious to the rush of people who scurried past him as if he were a statue. He swallowed hard and blinked a few times. He would never get used to this.

On Monday morning, Steve double-checked his presentation scheduled this afternoon to the board members. A knock on the door interrupted his concentration. Before he could even respond, Caitlynn walked in.

"Do you have a minute?" she asked.

"Of course. Take a seat."

"You're not in Chicago, so I guess Tyler felt well enough to fly on his own?"

"Kids are amazing; I'm sure if I'd gotten whatever bug he had, I'd be laid out on the couch for the week."

"I'm glad he's feeling better. The reason I stopped in is to make sure you finalized my sick leave."

"You're all set. I authorized your request. It looks like your last day is tomorrow. Is your mom coming to help?"

Her leg jiggled so fast he wanted to reach out and stop her frantic pace. "No. My mom suffers from rheumatoid arthritis. Most of the day, she uses a wheelchair. She will try to walk a few hours with the aid of a walker to keep some strength in her legs."

He was sorry to hear that. Caitlynn's mom was always nice and polite to him. "Who's coming to help you? I was just a kid when my mom had a hysterectomy, but I remember she couldn't lift anything or drive for several weeks."

Caitlynn glanced down. "I'll figure something out. Don't worry. I've taken care of myself without any help for a long time, so I think I can get through this okay."

Steve frowned. Was she trying to minimize what was happening? "You've obviously never had surgery before. How long will you be in the hospital?"

"Knowing hospital policy, they'll probably kick me out as soon as the anesthesia wears off." She bit her lip. "I hope to be home quickly. I'd rather be at home than in the hospital."

"I'm sure you're right." He drummed his fingers on the table, then offered up the standard line: "Whatever you do, I don't want you to worry about things here. It'll all be here when you come back. Just get better."

Caitlynn brushed her hair behind her ear and sighed. "Thanks, I'll see you when I get back." She left the office.

Steve watched Caitlynn shuffle down the hall. A moment later, he'd located the company directory on the station's website and jotted down her address. To himself, he muttered, "I may be overstepping my boundaries, but you're crazy if you think I'm going to sit back and let you go through this without any help."

CHAPTER SIXTEEN

If I give all I possess to the poor and surrender my body to the
flames,
but have not love, I am nothing.
1 CORINTHIANS 13:3

Her last day at work, Caitlynn tried hard not to resort to a self-inflicted panic attack trying to tie up loose ends before her surgery. She still needed to go over the news assignments for Tina to complete while she was away. She didn't ask for help with the story about Jillian. It was important to keep Jillian's confidence. She walked over to the break room and grabbed a bottle of water from the refrigerator.

Brett walked in as she loosened the cap. "Need some help with that?"

She smirked at his joke. "I think I can manage to open a water bottle."

"Okay, but if you need help with anything,"—his gaze roamed from her head to her toes— "and I mean anything, you let me know."

She rolled her eyes. "You're such a flirt. We've been through this so many times. I don't date men from work."

"Is that so? That's not what I heard. Didn't you go hiking with Steve a few weeks ago? That's a date."

Caitlynn scoffed. "Are you having him followed? I only went hiking so I could try to get some information." She frowned thinking about Tyler; lost on the trail. "But it didn't work out. Why do you care?"

Brett's eyes darted around the room. "I'll tell you if you go out with me."

"Did you forget what I said? I don't—"

Brett interrupted. "Yeah, I heard, but your rule is null now," Brett said, his tone serious. "I'm leaving right after Thanksgiving, so technically, I don't work with you."

She tilted her head sideways. "This is news."

Brett tantalized her by adding, "If you want to hear more, you'll have to say yes."

What harm could come from one date? Caitlynn thought. "You're incorrigible. Okay, it's a yes."

He pumped a fist. "Yes! I thought this day would never happen. How does tonight after work sound?"

Steve walked into the break room. "How does tonight sound for what?" he chimed in.

Brett pivoted toward the door. "None of your business." He spat as he rushed off.

"Whoa. What was that all about? It wasn't as if the two of you were whispering in a corner."

"Nothing for you to worry over," Caitlynn shrugged. "He asked me out. I accepted." She could feel his eyes practically boring into her as she walked away.

"Caitlynn, hold up a minute."

She turned around and sighed loudly. "What?"

"I just wanted to tell you to be careful. How well do you know—"

She burst out a laugh. "Steve, who made you my guardian? I'm just going out with him. It's not as if we're *moving in together.*"

He sucked in a breath and stepped back.

A look of satisfaction crossed her face; she sauntered away.

###

Caitlynn frantically pulled multiple items from her closet. Three discarded outfits later, she settled on a black sheath dress with black patent leather heels, pulled her hair into a loose bun, and completed the outfit with diamond and pearl teardrop earrings. The only reason she'd agreed to go out with him was to get her mind off the surgery tomorrow.

Steve was right. She worked with Brett, but how well did she know him? There were office rumors of a cruel streak, but she chose to ignore the gossip. She twirled a loose strand of her hair, trying to calm the nerves that suddenly surfaced. What was she thinking? His joking and harmless flirting was one thing, but a dinner out? Why hadn't she done her usual first date routine and arranged to meet him at a coffee shop? She was committed now, and to make matters worse, she had no idea where they were going. She double-checked that her cell phone was charged and counted her cash. *Sixty dollars.* Hopefully, there wouldn't be a reason to need it.

The doorbell chimed. Caitlynn flipped on the porch light and opened the door. "Come in."

Brett whistled low and ogled her as if she was today's special at the meat market. "You look fantastic."

Caitlynn cringed inwardly and motioned for him to step inside. "Um, thanks. Let me grab my jacket." Turning her back to him, she closed her eyes. *He whistled. Am I supposed to feel flattered?* Why hadn't she paid more attention to the girls in the office who'd gone out with him?

Jacket in hand, she pivoted back around, and caught him staring at his reflection in the mirror. Her stomach churned as if she'd just spewed out sour milk. She wasn't looking forward to the car ride with him. Let alone dinner. She locked the door and followed him to the car.

After fifteen minutes of small talk, they pulled into the parking lot. The Hearth Restaurant, nestled in the foothills west of Denver, had a reputation as an upscale dining experience. Semicircular booths were arranged so that no matter where you sat, you had a view of the towering stone fireplace in the center of the room. A crackling fire blazed within the hearth and complemented the spectacular mountain vista highlighted by the floor-to-ceiling windows. The hostess led them to a booth closest to the fireplace.

Brett motioned outside. "The lights from the stars look nice, but I hoped we'd get here before sunset to enjoy the view."

The windows magnified the bright glow of the moon against the backdrop of the stars. "They look close enough to reach out and touch." Caitlynn stared in appreciation before looking over the menu.

A few minutes later, the server introduced herself and poured water into their glasses. Suddenly, her eyes widened, "Aren't you from Channel 12 News?"

Brett flashed a confident smile and answered loudly enough for the next table over to hear. "We are. I'm the sports anchor."

She turned and warmly addressed Caitlynn. "I remember the story you did on the girl who was lost in the mountains. I'm glad she survived. It must be fun working at a news station. You get to know all the stories before the rest of us do." She took out her pad and pen. "What can I get you?"

Before Caitlynn had a chance to reply, Brett smirked and spoke sharply, "I'd like the potato leek soup, and for the main course, the filet cooked medium with the au-gratin potatoes. He glanced over. "What about you?"

Caitlynn's lips tightened. *Wow.* Hasn't he heard of; ladies first? Why was he playing Mr. Big Shot? "The soup sounds good. I'll take the cedar plank-grilled salmon with roasted potatoes and sautéed vegetables."

"Any appetizers, wine, or cocktails?"

"I'd like to order a glass of your house Merlot for each of us," he said, then glanced at Caitlynn. "Did you want an appetizer?"

And now, a drink? Without asking. "No," she snapped and looked away.

When the server left, Brett asked "So, what do you think of our new station manager?"

"He seems to be competent at his job if that's what you're asking."

"Seriously? Are you always so politically correct? Lighten up a little."

She nodded slightly at the server who'd returned with their wine.

Brett held up his glass. "Here's to an evening full of promise."

He clinked his glass with hers.

His remark made her uneasy. Her hands clenched the glass. "Promise? It's just dinner—now you need to lighten up." She set the glass down and wiped her palms on her napkin.

Brett looked irritated. "Point taken."

She watched him guzzle the wine. A red flag waved frantically in her mind, *Big mistake, big mistake, big mistake!* When he finally set his glass down, only a few sips remained.

"How much do you know about Steve Carr?" He said.

"Why do you ask?"

"I did a bit of research on him. His father owns stations in New York, Los Angeles, Phoenix, Houston, and Chicago. He grew up in Barrington Hills, Illinois, where his mother raises racehorses."

The server brought their soup. Caitlynn sipped a spoonful and listened as Brett continued. "His father has two hobbies—horse racing and boats. He lives in Grand Cayman part of the year on their multi-million-dollar yacht, while Steve's mother runs the horse racing business."

Caitlynn raised a brow. "You did do your homework. Why was that? Were you feeling threatened?"

Brett slurped his soup. "It's always smart to know who the new guy is, especially when he's part-owner. Must be nice to have Daddy's money to help finance your business ventures."

The soup was delicious—the one bite she'd had of it. But listening to him slurp and scrape his teeth against the spoon, made her appetite disappear. "You don't know if that's the case. For all we know, he could've used his own money—"

"Why are you defending him?" His voice rose. "We both worked hard to get where we are today. I didn't see any handouts along the way. Did you?"

Still clutching her spoon, she squeezed it hard. "No."

"Exactly right. I'm not finished digging into his life. I'm onto him. Just wait and see." His face turned an angry shade of red. "I'm glad I'm leaving. I couldn't work for him. He didn't earn it. I took a sports anchor job in New Orleans when I found out he was coming here."

The server brought out the food. "Is there anything else I can get you right now? More wine?"

Caitlynn would have easily traded places with her if it meant escaping Brett's tirade. "Nothing for me."

Brett held up his empty wine and then eyed her glass. "You haven't even touched yours. What's wrong with it?"

"Nothing's wrong." The surgery was tomorrow, and she didn't want to drink. "I'm just not in the mood for wine."

"Such a waste." He looked up at the server. "I'll have another one."

"Here, take this." She slid her glass across the table.

The server stepped back and said, "I'll check on you later." She hurried away.

Brett frowned. "I was hoping you'd drink with me. I hate to drink alone."

"You seem to be handling it fine." At least her food was excellent. The smoky flavor of the fish complemented the rustic taste of the potatoes. The crackling fire created a beautiful ambiance, an old-world charm. She should be enjoying herself more, but she couldn't wait for the evening to end. Nor ignore what Brett had said regarding Steve.

She looked down at her plate and blurted, "Steve and I dated in college."

Brett's eyes widened. "What?"

She looked up at him. "His father made sure to put distance between us because he thought I wasn't good enough for his son. It worked. No love lost now. I'd like to see him as far away from me as possible."

In four gulps, only a sip or two remained of his wine and he motioned to the server to bring another. He chewed noisily as he shoved his food in his mouth. With his fork in the air, he pointed the tines at her and talked with his mouth full. "What if I told you I know a way to get Mr. High and Mighty as far away from you as possible, dragging his tail all the way back to Chicago? What would you say to that?"

"I'm listening," she said. His sloppy eating made her grimace. She'd eaten at business functions with him, and he'd always had impeccable manners.

"The station has a zero-tolerance policy regarding pornography. I know a hacker who can break into Steve's laptop and corrupt it with various . . . shall we say, unsavory websites."

She gasped. "I want him out of my life, but that is drastic. Isn't putting porn of women on another person's computer considered a felony?" She pushed the food around on her plate, took a sip of water. "Besides, don't you need his security password?" She wanted Steve out of her life—she wanted to hurt him as much as he had hurt her—but it wasn't worth going to jail to accomplish it.

"No." His eyes glinted. "There are other ways to gain entry."

She swallowed a bite of salmon. "How much does he charge?"

"It depends on the job." He scooped a large portion of potatoes into his mouth and chewed noisily. "Since it's a personal request from me, I'll see if he'll honor the 'friends and family' discount. All I need is the go-ahead." He laughed sarcastically and took another drink. "And money."

Caitlynn was silent. She swallowed hard and mentally visualized Steve trying to explain pornography away in an interview. Then she imagined Tyler's innocent eyes looking at her with contempt. Her dinner threatened to come back up. She stared at Brett in shock. And half-expected food to fall from his mouth.

"I'm not sure I want to jeopardize his entire career." Or mine. "What happens when people get fired for justifiable cause? It's hard to find another job, isn't it?"

Brett shrugged. "He can coast on his daddy's coattails. He's the only heir. I wouldn't worry about it."

The server set the new glass down.

Brett hiccoughed. "'Scuse me."

Realization dawned. *He's drunk.* The poor table manners, the angry remarks about Steve, and the crazy pornography computer-hacking scheme. "Brett, you've only had two glasses of wine, and you're drunk?"

He laughed. "Sherves you right. You wouldn't drink with me." He held the full glass to his lips, then set it down, pushing back his chair. "I'll be back in a moment." He swayed, reached out to steady himself with his hand, and knocked over the wine. Shaking his head, he frowned. "What a shame."

In one quick motion, Caitlynn grabbed her napkin and wiped at the stain. "I'll take care of this. Go." Brett stumbled into the next table on his way to the restroom. She covered the spot with his napkin, pressing the liquid to stop the spill from spreading. The tips of her fingers were stained red.

She was livid. When he returned to his seat, he plopped down and mumbled, "Shorry 'bout that."

Caitlynn couldn't keep the irritation out of her voice. "You were drinking before you picked me up, weren't you?"

"I may have had a couple of vodka tonics earlier." He shrugged. "What's the big deal?"

"*The big deal?*" she tried to keep her voice down to a whisper. "You're drunk, and I refuse to get in the car with you. I'm driving you home."

"No, you won't! That's crazy, Caitlynn, you're wiggin' out over nothing."

Caitlynn motioned the server over.

She hurried to the table. "Sorry, I didn't realize you had an accident. I'll get someone to clean it up."

"No need. We'll take the check."

The waitress directed the bill to Brett. "It was a pleasure serving you."

Brett threw cash on the table. "You're not driving, Caitlynn, and that's final."

"If you don't hand over the keys to me right now, I'm going to call the maître d' over and order a cab to take us home." Caitlynn stood up and held out her hand, ready for the keys to Brett's car. She was prepared to wrestle them from him if that is what it took. "Do you really want this kind of negative publicity? It wouldn't look good to start your new job with that kind of press."

Finally, Brett surrendered the keys. "What a way to ruin an evening, not to mention a perfectly good glass of wine."

Caitlynn sighed. The prospect of getting a drunk home and calling a cab to take her home was daunting. She turned away in disgust. "Let's go."

CHAPTER SEVENTEEN

With less than twenty minutes to eat, Jillian tossed her books inside her locker, grabbed her lunch sack, and headed down the hallway. Out of nowhere, little black dots swam before her eyes. She stopped abruptly and leaned against the wall as the dizziness overwhelmed her . . . again. Two guys slowed down as they passed. They gawked at her like she was a space alien. She glared back, wished for the hundredth time for someone that could relate—none of her friends understood what it felt like to be pregnant. She took three deep breaths, and focused in on making it to the cafeteria, without some kind of humiliating scene.

A sigh of relief escaped. She scanned the sea of faces, searching for her best friend, Tori Butler. They'd been friends since sixth grade when they met in Science class, trying their best not to puke at the frog they had to dissect. Then she spied her sitting alone at a table in the corner; her long dark brown hair pulled back in a ponytail. She was easy to spot because she always wore her favorite color—black. Jillian made her way past the maze of tables where her classmates talked in loud voices, making it impossible to ignore the room's pent-up energy. She sat and pulled out a peanut butter and jelly sandwich.

"I'm so glad you can't stomach the disgusting chicken tenders the lunch lady cooks either," Jillian said as she wrinkled her nose. "The deep-fried oil reeks. Disgusting. How'd you manage to find an empty bench?"

"Lucky, I guess." Her brown eyes covered with way too much bright blue eye shadow lit up her round-shaped face and glowing cheeks. She stared at Jillian's belly and took a bite of her sandwich. "You're really starting to show. You have a baby bump."

Jillian stifled a giggle. "I know." She looked over her shoulder to make sure no one was staring. Then she pulled up her shirt and revealed her jeans. "I've had to loop a hairband around the buttonhole of my jeans so I can breathe when I sit down."

Tori leaned across the table for a closer look. "You better buy some maternity clothes. Is it good for the baby to wear your clothes so tight you can't breathe?"

She rolled her eyes and took a bite. "The baby's fine. I go to the doctor on Friday. I'll ask what he thinks. After this checkup I get to see what I'm having, and if the heartbeat is strong, and all that stuff." Jillian flashed a smile. "I can't wait to see what I'm going to have." She swallowed her food and took a sip of her bottled water. "I hope I have a girl so that I can dress her in frilly dresses, pink tights, and black patent leather shoes."

"I'll throw you a baby shower. It will be fun! I can't wait to pick out a tiny baby girl outfit." Then Tori got serious. "But what if it's a boy, and it looks just like Marcus?"

"I was so in love with him, but now, I don't want to think about *him*. You're supposed to be my BF—why would you bring up that loser's name?"

Tori swallowed a bite of her sandwich. "Have you seen him hanging out with Marcy? She's such a tramp to go out with him when the whole school knows he's your baby daddy."

"She can have him. They sound perfect for each other. What a lowlife to break up with me when he found out I was preggers." Another wave of dizziness hit. Jillian dropped her sandwich on the table and closed her eyes.

Tori rushed to her side. "Jilly, your face is pale. I'm sorry I won't mention his name again." She grabbed the bottle of water. "Here—take a sip."

Some of the students were staring and whispering. Tori looked away.

Her cheeks flamed bright pink. The dizzy feeling passed, followed by a deep sense of embarrassment. "I'm good. Please go back to your seat. Everyone's gawking."

Her best friend walked around the table and plopped on the bench. "Hey, I was just trying to help. You looked like you were going to pass out."

"I'm sure this is normal." A frown creased her brow. "I guess I have another question to ask the doctor." She shook her head to shrug off the humiliating situation. "Did I tell you I'm going to be on television?"

"You're the only person I know who is lucky enough to be on television." She munched on a chip. "What are you going to do?"

"A reporter for Channel 12 is doing a story on teen pregnancy and asked if I'd be interested in scheduling several interviews. Jillian squeezed Tori's hand. "Hey, you can be on television too. I'll invite you sometime. We can talk about the baby shower!"

"Cool!" Tori grabbed their lunch sacks and tossed them into the garbage. "I'll walk with you to the lockers.

"Do you want to hang out tonight?" Jillian asked.

"I can't. I . . . um . . . have to work." Tori glanced down at her feet.

Walking out the double door of the cafeteria with Tori, Jillian tried again, "Do you want to go shopping for maternity clothes on Friday?"

Tori glanced at her cell phone. "I wish I could, but I promised Cara I'd go with her to find a homecoming dress. Her boyfriend's school is having it late this year. There's some kind of schedule conflict between football and soccer."

"What about Saturday? We could go then?"

Tori's eyes darted to the ceiling and then back to Jillian. "You go ahead and go. Maybe your mom would want to help?" The two-minute bell sounded. "Talk to you later," Tori called as she rushed off.

Jillian strolled on autopilot to her locker. She stood there in a daze as she grabbed her chemistry book. *Tori always shops with me. Why would she think my mother should come? Mom hasn't gone with me since seventh grade.* Jillian entered the classroom, slid into her desk, and drowned out her teacher's monotone voice. *Am I losing my best friend? I know! I'll go shopping and find a great-*

looking maternity outfit, and then I'll call Caitlynn to schedule an appointment for an interview. And I won't call Tori to tell her until afterward. She'll be so excited for me she'll come running over to find out all the juicy details.

CHAPTER EIGHTEEN

Gray clouds drifting past Steve's window as the plane flew toward Chicago matched his gloomy mood. Hardly focusing, his mind replayed yesterday afternoon's pick-up game at the church…

Lee hustled over. "You haven't been here in a while. I figured our prowess on the court scared you off."

Steve raised a challenging brow. "It's gonna take more than that."

Lee laughed. "We're glad you're here. Jump in when you've warmed up. A few of the guys can't make it, so it should be a good workout."

After a five-minute warmup, Steve joined the game tracking his opponent Dave's, every move. As he took a shot, Steve jumped up and smashed the ball, both crashing to the floor. "Sorry, man," Steve said as he helped Dave up and retrieved the ball. But he wasn't sorry. It felt good to let out some pent-up tension.

The game continued, but Steve kept playing aggressive defense, and they lost the game. He toweled off.

Lee walked over and patted his shoulder. "You seem wired. What's up?"

He wadded the towel and tossed it in his bag. "I've had a rough couple of weeks."

"Rough in what way?"

"Let's see . . . my son was ill last week, and I found out I'm no good at even taking care of my own sick kid. And he wants me to invite my ex—and her new boyfriend over for Thanksgiving—and then there's Caitlynn."

"What's going on with Caitlynn?"

Steve labored to keep his voice calm. "I thought God put me back into Caitlynn's life to mend our relationship, but I'm not so sure now."

"Why?"

"She knows how to hit every button to rattle me." He paused. He had enough in his life with Tyler and Brenda and work to keep him more than busy rushing to God for guidance. Maybe he should worry more about his own life and stay out of Caitlynn's. He shrugged. "She goes on the defense whenever I try talking to her. I'm pretty sure she says things she doesn't mean. She's very closed off." He paused for a moment. "I hurt her in the past, and it's clear she's not over it."

"Caitlynn sounds like she could use a friend," Lee said. "Do you know what she does when she's not working?"

"No." He grabbed his bag and looped it over his shoulder. "She doesn't make it easy. She has so many walls up. I need to be a high jumper to hurdle over them."

Suddenly, a thought popped into his head, his eyes widened. "I know what I'm going to do. I hope Caitlynn won't put up too much of a fight."

Lee picked up his backpack and escorted Steve toward the exit. "From what you've told me so far—whatever you're planning—you better be ready for the challenge she's gonna throw your way."

"So true. But this time, I'm not going to take no for an answer. I'm helping her whether she likes it or not."

Lee threw his bag in the back seat. "I'll be praying for you— and Caitlynn."

Prayer. He could use a double portion.

The aircraft hit turbulence jostling him in his seat and out of his reverie. The pilot announced touch down would be in thirty minutes. Steve was pleased at the plans he'd made for Caitlynn. Before departing to the airport, he'd searched the Internet for a reputable meal service delivery and ordered enough pre-made meals to be delivered to her home for two weeks. He was in a good mood because he could finally help Caitlynn, and there was nothing she could do short of throwing away the food. The real worry was his father. Their last conversation did not end on a high note.

The plane touched down and stopped at the gate. He unlatched the safety belt and stood. Face time with his father. His heart raced in triple time.

The limo service his family used was waiting curbside with his favorite driver, Logan, holding the door open.

Logan greeted him with a welcoming smile. "Great to see you. It's been a while."

"True." They shook hands. "Thanks for picking me up!"

Steve's mobile phone rang, flashing Tyler's home number.

"Hey, kiddo. Are you excited? Tomorrow's Thanksgiving."

Tyler's young voice raised an octave higher, "Yep, Mommy is bringing Antoine. I can't wait to see Me-ma."

Steve pressed his lips together. *Stay positive.*

"I'm sure she can't either. She'll probably cook all your favorites just for you."

"Yumm-o. What are you doing?"

"I just landed, and I ordered some online meals for Miss Caitlynn, her surgery is today, so hopefully she won't have to worry about cooking when she gets home from the hospital."

"That's terrible! She won't be able to eat any turkey or pumpkin pie tomorrow?"

"I'm sure there's some sort of Thanksgiving meal, but probably not. I bet she won't be up to eating much tomorrow."

Tyler's voice bubbled with excitement. "Daddy, I have an idea! When she gets better, let's make a turkey dinner and surprise her."

Steve shook his head, always amazed at the generosity of a kid. Didn't Jesus say, unless you change and become like little children, you will never enter the kingdom of heaven? "You're always full of good ideas. Why don't we surprise her when you're out here over Christmas break?

"Awesome." Tyler chirped.

Steve chuckled. "See you tomorrow. Love you." He pressed the end call button.

After exiting the highway, they turned onto a tree-lined street bordering with white split-rail fences on both sides, marking the acreage of his family's horse farm. Logan turned the limo into the drive. On each side of the drive stood bronze life-sized iron Stallion's rearing up like Centurions guarding the Castle. A steel security gate, usually locked, was open and ready to receive his visit, thanks to his mom's thoughtfulness, he was sure. They drove past two whitewashed barns with high-pitched green roofs, complete with a weather vane atop the highest point, paddock, and corral and approached the sprawling seven-bedroom and eight baths two-story Tudor home. His gaze went to the east wing where his room was located. A light shone through the window. Comforting him somehow. He pictured Tyler's bedroom right across the hall.

Logan stopped the Lincoln town car in front of the circle drive close to the entrance. Steve thanked Logan, tipped him, and turned the handle surprised the front door wasn't locked. His mom thought of everything. He set his roller bag by the door. The smooth marble floor accentuated his footsteps as he neared the kitchen. "Any one home?"

"I'm in the kitchen."

He followed the sound of his mother's voice. When he reached the kitchen, his eyes widened. "Whoa!" he exclaimed. A brand-new sub-zero refrigerator and a professional-grade six-burner stove with double ovens gleamed against the backdrop of the new cherry wood cabinets and with white granite countertops.

A fire crackled in the fireplace. Two cozy-looking light beige leather wingback chairs next to the fireplace looked so inviting.

He reached out and kissed his mom's cheek, holding her in a quick embrace. "Wow, Mom. The only thing that's still the same is the stone wall and wood beams."

"Isn't it spectacular?" Her hazel eyes sparkled. Auburn hair cascaded in soft curls around her shoulders, and the gold hoop earrings in her ears glistened. She wore a chef apron over her green sweater and black jeans that said, *Kiss the cook.* "I love cooking in my new kitchen."

Steve sniffed the air. "Something smells delicious. What are you cooking?"

"I'm making pies for tomorrow—as well as Tyler's favorite: a pumpkin roll."

"Where's Father?"

"He's in the library. He's been asking for you."

Steve frowned, clenching his hand in a fist. "Probably wants to know how much money I've lost the news station."

"Don't start." She took the pies out of the oven to cool. "Let's declare a green zone for a few days."

"Okay, Mom." He stared into his mother's eyes and nodded. "I will for you. But when are you going to stop protecting him?"

He left the room with a heavy heart, trudging down the hall, stopping in front of the double doors to the library. *Lord, I want to restore my relationship with my father, but I don't know how. Give me the strength and wisdom to see past our differences.*

Steve opened the door and peered inside. The flames from the fireplace cast an eerie shadow as they danced across the kindling, sending sparks up into the chimney.

His father spoke from the chair nearest to the fire. "You're not stepping into the lion's den. Come in."

Steve stepped into the overly hot and stuffy room, plastered on a smile, and sat down in the chair opposite his father. "Happy Thanksgiving, a day early."

"Is that all you have to say to your ol' man, a casual greeting you'd say to the neighbor?"

His dad looked more gaunt than usual, but the familiar scowl was in place. "Dad, I didn't come to fight. I'm here to enjoy the holiday with my son and my family."

"The last time we spoke, you hung up on me. Am I supposed to forget that happened?"

Steve sighed. "I could've handled our conversation better, I'm sorry." He drummed his fingers on his thigh.

His father shot back. "You think we could talk about it now, or are you going to walk out?"

Steve slumped in his chair. "Can we enjoy the brief time we have together in peace? Why don't we take a raincheck and bring out the gloves after Thanksgiving?"

To Steve's surprise, his father changed the subject. "Fine. Why don't you tell me how work is going? What changes have you made at the station to add to the profit margin?"

Fatigue washed over him. "Dad, I want to relax before I go back on Monday. I'd rather not talk about my work either. I worked on the flight over, and I need a break. If you're concerned for me, don't be. The board is happy with what I've done so far."

"I bet your board members aren't the only one happy." He snickered.

"Do you mean Caitlynn? I thought we agreed not to talk about it tonight."

His father struck his hand against the armchair. "Okay, okay. But I just want what's best for you. I want to see you succeed in every aspect of your life."

Steve combed his fingers through his hair. "I don't measure my success anymore by how well I do in work or financially —"

"If it's not how much money you have or what you've accomplished in your life, what's left?"

He looked at his father as if seeing him for the first time. Steve's voice lowered with a raw emotion he rarely acknowledged. "Dad, you know I've tried hard to make you proud. A few years ago, I did everything you asked of me, and I respect you for what you've accomplished. And I measured my success just like you..."

He held his father's gaze. "But I've changed. Before I left, I started going to church. I'm learning that success isn't measured by what we have or don't have. It's based on our relationship with people and with God. I want to invest in other people's lives, and I want to make a difference—"

His father scoffed. "Are you saying I don't invest in the community? You know how much I give to charities."

"Not at all. I'm saying that even though I strove to be successful, something was missing. I still try to be the best, but my focus has changed."

His father stood. "I hope this new direction you're going in pays your bills and puts food on your table," he said harshly.

This time it was his father who walked out.

CHAPTER NINETEEN

Caitlynn wanted to scream, *"Stop the train!"* when early Wednesday morning, the automatic double doors opened. Upon check-in, she was whisked over to the hospital registration and issued an identification bracelet. A volunteer wearing bright red horn-rimmed glasses escorted her to a room that would be hers for the duration. "Normally, I take incoming patients to the pre-surgery area, but you're considered a VIP. This is a private room, so you won't have to answer to a roommate nosing into your business." They stopped at room 322.

"Here you are. The gown is on the bed. Once you've changed, get comfortable under the covers. A nurse will be in soon." The door clicked shut.

Caitlynn glanced around—a white tiled floor with a bed in the center of the room. A cream-colored vinyl rocking chair sat near the bed. On one side of the wall stood a stark white cabinet for her clothes and personal items. Sterile and cold, but at least she was alone. She changed in the bathroom, placed her clothes in the closet, covered up, and waited. She wasn't alone for long.

As if in some sort of strange daydream, she watched as healthcare workers paraded past. First, a nurse introduced herself and discussed what procedure would be performed. Then the anesthesiologist came in and told her what to expect during the surgery. He left, and a different nurse came in minutes later. Blood was drawn, medication given. She gripped the sheet when the nurse inserted the IV. Finally, Dr. Plummer arrived.

He stood next to her and grasped her hand. "How are you feeling?"

"I'm so nervous my stomach is churning like a blender on high speed."

Dr. Plummer patted her hand. "You'll be fine."

Caitlynn tried to be brave, but she could feel her eyes prickle. "You're right. Let's get this over with."

"Sounds like a plan." He patted her hand one last time. "See you in a few minutes." The door shut behind him. She closed her eyes. The room once teemed with nurses and doctors; now felt empty and deadly silent.

When the attendant came to wheel her down the hall to the operating room, she held tightly to the bedrail, looked around wildly. What if she had the surgery and still had the pain?

The attendant reached over and held her hand. "I know you're nervous," he said in a calm voice. "It's a perfectly normal feeling."

The double doors opened to blinding lights. Nurses lurked in every corner. *What's going on?* Why do they need so many people attending me? *The last time I was on a gurney with a bright light, it was just the nurse and doctor.*

Hot tears ran down the side of her face and dripped onto the sheet. She closed her eyes, willing herself to forget the past. Dr. Plummer stood by her side, nodded to the anesthesiologist, and stared at her with sympathetic eyes. "Caitlynn, you'll be fine, trust me…" He spoke in a reassuring tone.

She twisted away.

The anesthesiologist put a mask over her nose and mouth. "I want you to breathe in slow breaths, count backward from ten, and think of something pleasant like walking on the beach, going on a special vacation, or enjoying a perfect outing with someone you love."

As Caitlynn counted down from ten, she remembered what brought her to this empty time in her life. She couldn't recall a walk on a beach, a great vacation, or any person in her life whom she loved aside from her mom. *I'm to blame for this. It's all my fault.*

###

Steve woke up and forgot where he was for a moment. The sun spilled through the window and blinded him. The faint scent of coffee drifted into the room. Last night, he'd laid in bed staring at the ceiling, his head pounding like a sledgehammer. He loved his father and wanted nothing more than a real father-son relationship. For some reason, his father seemed to want to argue and second-guess him at every opportunity. So, Steve had prayed, and a sudden peace washed over him. Now he was ready to start over with his family, deal with his ex-wife, and change his poor attitude. He rolled over in bed and prayed for patience. It was Thanksgiving, and there was a lot to be thankful for.

After getting ready, he headed downstairs to the kitchen for breakfast. His mom was chopping celery and onions for the dressing. The turkey, already in the roaster, was ready to stuff. His father sat next to the fireplace, reading the paper. He didn't bother to glance up when Steve entered the room.

Steve searched the pantry for cereal and grabbed the milk. He passed the huge turkey on the way to the table.

His father turned the page. "Steve, what time are Brenda and Tyler coming?"

"Let's not forget about her boyfriend," he muttered as he sat down across from his father and poured the milk over his cereal.

His dad sneered. "What a dysfunctional family we've become. Boyfriends—exes, it's crazy!"

Steve swallowed a bite. "Divorce is messy. It changes everything." He shrugged. "I just want what's best for my son. If it includes boyfriends or a new husband down the road, so be it. She said they'd be here around one o'clock, but you know Brenda. She hates to be late. She'll probably pull up in the driveway at twelve-thirty." He finished his cereal, rinsed the bowl, and put them in the dishwasher. He watched his mother sauté the vegetables. "That smells good. Do you need help doing anything?"

"No, your dad can help me lift the turkey into the oven. Everything else is ready except for the gravy and the whipped potatoes. I've already prepared the green bean casserole and sweet potato pie." She added the onion and celery to the toasted bread cubes in the pot.

"If you don't need me, I think I'll take Boo out for a morning ride."

Two stables occupied the property: their family stable and the professional one. The professional barn held the horses that clients either trained for racing or just boarded. Both buildings were state of the art with nothing but the best in food, shelter, and trainers. As he walked toward the family stable, he smelled the faint fragrance of chrysanthemums lining the walkway and alfalfa hay's sweet aroma. The scents immediately brought him back to when he was a young boy and of the happier times when his father occasionally rode with him.

Unable to contain his excitement, he rushed past the other horses. "Hello, Boo. It's been a long time." The horse nuzzled him. Steve stroked his head. "You look good, ol' boy. Are you up for a morning ride?" Boo responded with a jerk of his head and a low snort.

Steve grabbed his saddle off the hook on the wall. "You're excited, aren't you, boy? I can tell by your eyes." He positioned the saddle, belted it tightly, and pulled the bridle over Boo. He stroked the horse's white mane. "I have an apple for you after our ride."

In one smooth motion, Steve was in the saddle, urging his horse forward. Boo's ears perked up when Steve made a clicking noise.

"Let's go. I have a feeling this will be the highlight of my day."

They sauntered down the lane. Acres of white split-rail fencing separated the pastures. Steve saw movement out of the corner of his eye. A magnificent looking silver-gray thoroughbred munched hay in the corral. Steve stopped to admire the filly. He heard the sound of water hitting the metal trough and called out, "Carl, is that you?"

The sound stopped. Carl hobbled around the corner. Boo pulled against the bit and eagerly responded as Steve guided him toward the fence. Carl tilted his cowboy hat in greeting and stroked

Boo's head. "Hello there, Beauregard. You're looking mighty fine. I took you out two days ago for a nice run, but today is special—you're goin' for a ride with your best friend."

Steve's father named the horse Beauregard and wanted Steve to call him Beau, but the horse's cream body and white mane looked more like a ghost in flight, so Steve called him Boo.

Steve had always admired Carl's natural ability to bond with horses. At first glance, it is evident that Carl limped like a feeble man but put him on a horse, and he looked like he and the animal were one.

"Happy Thanksgiving, Carl."

"Glad to see you made it home, Stevie." Carl's eyes sparkled.

Steve winced good-naturedly. "I guess if you can call Boo by his full name, you can get away with calling me, Stevie. But how is it that I keep getting older, yet you never seem to age?"

Carl laughed and rubbed under Boo's ear. "It's a combination of good, clean living and working around horses every wakin' minute."

Steve turned to watch the filly trot nervously around the corral, stopping at the trough. "I see we have a new beauty."

Carl's face lit up as he glanced over at her. "Your father may have found *the one*. It's still too early to tell, but look at her! She's a great looking piece of horseflesh—"

Steve interrupted. "How many times have I heard that before?"

Carl sighed. "You're right about that. We've been on the losing end as of late. But she's got a pretty good lineage with two strong bloodlines on both sides." The horse chomped while lifting her nose skyward and stared as if she knew they were talking about her. "I have a feeling about this one. Just you wait and see. Barring any injuries, she could be a winner."

From his perch atop the saddle, Steve could quickly scan the two-story stable that, with its opulence, could easily pass for a second home. Beyond the stable, the green grass in the pastures was turning brown with winter's approach. The vast amount of wealth his father had accumulated in his lifetime still surprised Steve. His father was always trying to get more—winning horses, more wealth, more prestige, working hour upon endless hour. Steve couldn't recall a conversation in the last ten years when his father had considered taking a morning off from work to ride.

No matter what it took, he wouldn't be a controlling, absent father to Tyler.

Carl seemed to read his mind. "Your father hasn't been around in quite a spell. I guess he's been busy traveling."

Steve stared at the filly. "I'm sure he's not too busy to hear about his newest investment. What's her name?"

"Corner Pocket. I've nicknamed her Kicker because she just loves to whack the stall. This little lady's got an ornery streak in her, though it don't surprise me none. She fought long and hard to be foaled."

Boo jerked his head and stomped. Steve stroked his mane. "Looks like you're more than ready to show me what you've got. Carl, will you join us for Thanksgiving?"

"Appreciate the invite, but I'm headed to my daughter's house. Mary organized a bunch of her friends to cook several turkeys and all the fixin's. I'm supposed to be at her house by noon. We're gonna box it all up and head over to the local food bank to dish it out."

"I can't think of a better way to spend the holiday. Tell Mary; I said hi."

Steve lightly tugged the reins and let Boo's instincts take over. Soon they were crossing the road into the forest preserve. The pebbled lane was vibrant with color, courtesy of the tree-lined path. Some of the oaks stubbornly held onto their leaves of red, gold, and brown. The only sounds were the crackle of leaves and the creak of the saddle.

Tension melted away. He relaxed as he listened to the slow, steady sound of hooves striking the ground. He breathed in the fresh air. Soon the path opened up into a field of long grass.

Steve's heart pounded in his chest. "Okay, Boo, you know what to do."

He tapped the reins and Boo's flanks. The horse surged forward at a fast trot. Another slight tap and Boo increased his speed to a full gallop. The cool air rushed around Steve, his face burned, and his eyes watered as the wind whipped past. For a brief moment, he thought of reining in, but a quick glance at Boo showed that he had no intention of slowing down.

Steve's need to feel the speed—the power—of the horse underneath him propelled him forward. His breath caught in his throat. Leaning in close to Boo's mane, Steve closed his eyes for a brief moment and relished this feeling of freedom—as if caught up in a good dream; he hoped to revisit again and again.

CHAPTER TWENTY

The odd thing about their home was how the cathedral ceilings carried sound throughout the house like a tolling church bell. His mother liked to joke that the house was an old busybody who couldn't keep a secret. His footsteps rang out all the way from the foyer, up the stairs, and into his room. He showered, dressed, and eased into being home again, looking through old albums and childhood treasures as the tantalizing aroma of the turkey roasting in the oven filled the house.

Steve heard Tyler's excited yell coming from downstairs. "Daddy, where are you?"

He hurried to the foyer. Tyler was jumping up and down, while Brenda and Antoine stood there looking somewhat stiff.

"Daddy! Happy Thanksgiving. I made you something!" He thrust out a black pilgrim hat at him. It was made out of construction paper and a paper plate and had a white belt buckle. "Put it on!"

Steve cracked a smile. "I remember making one just like this when I was your age." He put it on his head. It toppled to the ground.

Tyler laughed. "Daddy, you have a big head!"

"Are you calling me a fathead?" he teased. He placed the hat on Tyler's head. "I would love it if you'd wear it for me. Why don't you go show Me-ma?"

Tyler ran toward the kitchen, shouting, "Me-ma, look what I made."

Steve cleared his throat. "Hello, Brenda."

Brenda looked prim and proper as always. She was wearing a form-fitting red dress. Her light brown hair cascaded down her shoulders. Her green eyes darted away and back. "This is Antoine."

The man had a thin, athletic build and an angular face with dark eyes and dark hair.

Steve reached out to shake his hand. "Hello, Antoine,"

Brenda fidgeted with her scarf. "I tried to talk Tyler out of bringing that hat, but he insisted. It's a good thing it didn't fit; otherwise, you probably would've had to wear the silly thing the entire day."

"I would've worn it for Tyler, but I have to admit, I'm glad it didn't fit." Steve escorted his ex-wife and her boyfriend down the long hall to the kitchen. His father stood when they entered. "Hello, Brenda. It's been a while."

"Yes. The last time I was here, I dropped Ty off for a sleepover."

She hugged him and stepped away. "Preston, I'd like you to meet Antoine."

Although Steve was named after his dad and his grandfather, Steve's father preferred to be called by his middle name.

"Very nice to meet you," Preston said as he shook Antoine's hand.

Steve's mom was busy transferring the gravy into a tureen. She put down the bowl, and held her arms out to Brenda.

Brenda fell into her embrace. "Anne, you're amazing. I love coming here for the holidays with Tyler."

She shook Antoine's hand. "Welcome to our home."

"I brought you a little gift," Antoine spoke English but with a French accent. He held out a bottle of wine. "Thank you so much for inviting me. I've never been to a Thanksgiving meal before."

Anne nodded her appreciation, took the bottle, and set it on the counter. "I hope you enjoy our American tradition."

He sniffed the air. "In France, we don't eat much turkey. Is that what I smell?"

Brenda giggled. "It's a symphony of smells that all come together to make your mouth water and your stomach growl for hours before dinner."

Steve watched his mom laugh as she picked up the tray of unbaked rolls. "You're right about that." She placed it in the oven.

"Preston, can you get the drink orders? Why doesn't everyone find a seat? By the time we get settled, the rolls will be ready."

"Daddy, can I sit by you?"

Steve pulled out a chair for Tyler. "Come on, you little pilgrim, let's eat some turkey together."

Preston poured Chardonnay for the adults and sparkling cider for Tyler, then sat at the head of the table. Brenda and Antoine sat opposite Tyler and Steve.

After a few moments, his mother placed the gravy tureen and the basket of perfectly baked rolls on the table. She sat facing her husband across the long, laden table. "Steve, could you say grace, please."

Steve grasped Tyler's hand. Everyone took the cue and held hands while he prayed.

"Heavenly Father, I thank you for the blessings you've given us this year, and for the dinner that's been so lovingly prepared. I pray you give us another year of your grace and blessings so that we might make a difference in other's lives, Amen."

In addition to the gravy and rolls, there was sweet potato pie, green bean casserole, mashed potatoes, stuffing, and turkey. Steve could hardly wait to dig in. His father took some turkey and held the platter for his grandson. Tyler grabbed the drumstick. "I bet I can eat this whole thing."

As Steve reached out to accept the heavy plate full of turkey, his father said, through gritted teeth, "Are you sure you want to eat this, Steve, or do you want to make a difference and give it to the homeless or something?"

Steve glared at him and jerked the dish from his hand. *Why did I think Dad would take the gloves off for one day?* He stabbed at the meat, put it on his plate, and passed the dish to his mom. "Did you hear Carl and Mary are going to the local shelter to give out dinner?" he said stiffly.

"Yes," his mom said, "we helped support them by donating money to buy the turkeys."

His dad piped in. "Is that making a difference to you, Steve? Or would you rather I waited and gave more next year?"

Steve clanked his fork against his plate. "I didn't mean to imply that you don't give. Please don't take my prayer the wrong way."

His dad took a bite and swung his fork in the air. "It seems to me that ever since you became a 'born-again' Christian, you're more into other people and their problems than you are into making money for your family. You have responsibilities and a son to raise. Don't forget that."

Steve frowned. *Didn't God hear his prayer this morning? Was it too much to ask for a peaceful dinner with his father?* "Dad, this conversation is getting old. I know why you're acting like this. You want me to come back to work for you, but the answer is still no. You need to get over it."

Thankfully, the interrogation stopped long enough for everyone to eat in peace.

He tasted the stuffing and looked at his mom. "The dinner is delicious, Mom. Thanks for going to so much trouble."

Antoine swallowed a sip of wine, then said, "The dinner is so good; I think I may adopt America every November to eat turkey and all of this magnifique food."

Tyler poked fork holes in his potatoes. "If you think this is yummy, just wait for the dessert."

Steve finished the food on his plate. All he had left to worry about was getting through the pie and coffee.

He spied Brenda's arched brows. He knew that look. *Uh, oh. More trouble.*

Brenda's eyes narrowed to slits. "Preston, you should know by now that Steve will never come back to Chicago. Tyler says Steve loves Denver and his job. And they go to a church Steve likes. What else does your dad like, Tyler?"

Tyler's mouth was packed full of mashed potatoes, but he spoke anyway. "He likes his friend, Caitlynn."

Brenda glared at Tyler. "Don't talk with your mouth full." Then she turned to Steve, her eyes glimmering. "Oh! So now the truth comes out. You actually moved to Denver to hook up with your old girlfriend, didn't you?"

"Is this true, Steve?" his mother asked, "Caitlynn is there?"

Steve glowered at Brenda in anger. "Yes, Mom, she works with me." He stared into his mom's eyes. "Despite what you may think, I didn't take the job because she was there. I took it for a lot of reasons, that I don't need to justify."

Tyler's eyes flitted back and forth from Brenda to Steve. "Daddy, did I say something wrong?"

"Don't worry, son." He pressed Tyler's hand. "None of this is your fault."

Tyler took the napkin from his lap and tossed it on the table. "I'm done." He scooted back his chair and bumped into his glass of cider, knocking it over.

"Tyler, you're so clumsy," Brenda scolded. "You need to be more careful."

"It was an accident," Steve spoke harshly. He snatched Tyler's napkin and wiped up the mess.

His mother stood up. "It looks like everyone's finished. Why don't we bring our dishes to the sink and see about the dessert? Would anyone like coffee?"

Steve grabbed his plate plus Tyler's. "Mom, can we wait for a bit? I'm not ready for dessert just yet. Tyler, how about we play some football and then have Me-ma's famous pumpkin roll? Antoine, would you like to join us?"

Antoine rubbed his stomach. "I think I'll watch." He glanced at Brenda for assurance.

Brenda's lips thinned. Her eyes darted from Antoine to Steve. "Steve, can I talk to you for a moment . . . alone?"

"Ty, help Me-ma clear the table, I'll be back in a minute." He followed Brenda to the library. "What's so important it couldn't wait?" Steve huffed.

"I wanted you to know things are getting serious between Antoine and me."

He clenched his fist. "I'm happy for you. You have my blessing or whatever it is you want from me."

"I don't need your blessing." She tossed her hair back. "I want you to know that we might have to work out some additional custody issues. I want to go to France this summer, and I think it would be best if Tyler stayed with you."

Steve's jaw dropped. "You're kidding!" He took a step back. "You would leave Tyler for the whole summer? I have no problem keeping him, but how could you leave him that long?" *Was this some kind of trap?* "You need to think this through, Brenda. Really think about the impact it might have on our son." He pivoted and stalked out.

He pulled a football off the hall closet shelf and clenched it. His plan had been to stay at his parent's house until Sunday. But after his father's endless bantering, even on Thanksgiving…and now Brenda? He decided—he was leaving tomorrow.

CHAPTER TWENTY-ONE

Love is patient.
1 CORINTHIANS 13:4

Steve took the first flight to Denver Friday morning. Tyler was upset, but he assured Ty that they'd have double the fun on the next visit. Steve arrived home, took care of some quick errands, then stopped at the florist for flowers. With slow steps, he entered Saint Anthony's Hospital. The smell of alcohol and disinfectant assaulted him. It seemed every hospital shared the same nauseating odor. He wanted to gag.

After speaking to the woman at the information desk, he stepped into the elevator and punched the button to the third floor, room 322. He hustled past the nurses' station holding the vase of multicolored roses close to his chest, smelling their fragrant scent instead of the antiseptic. The door to Caitlynn's room was slightly ajar. Soft voices murmured within.

He took a step closer, cocking his ear toward the door, listening. Caitlynn wasn't expecting him, and he hated to barge in if she had someone with her. He nudged the door open a little more, hoping the movement wouldn't be detected.

A woman's soft voice said, "I know you're upset, Caitlynn. Please, don't cry . . . you'll make me start crying."

He raised a brow and took another small step.

Caitlynn sniffed. "It's all my fault this happened."

"You don't know that for sure. There could be any number of reasons."

"It said the chances for a hysterectomy increase." Caitlynn's voice shook. "Especially if there were complications."

Complications? From what? Steve leaned in further. Steve knew he shouldn't eavesdrop—the right thing to do would be to enter the room—but his legs froze and wouldn't budge.

She blew her nose. "I read an article on the subject. Endometriosis is a condition that could result—especially if an infection develops. This happened to me twelve years ago—my uterus was perforated, and I ended up with a fever and Pelvic Inflammatory Disease." Her voice wavered into more tears. "It took me weeks to recover."

"I'm so sorry this happened to you. Thank you for confiding in me—have you, um, discussed with your doctor this past medical history…what you went through after you had the abortion, all those years ago."

Steve closed his eyes, his stomach twisting into a tight knot. *Twelve years ago? Please, God, don't let this be true.* His legs turned to rubber; he braced himself with his free hand on the doorjamb. He wanted to collapse into the wall and melt onto the floor.

Caitlynn cried out. "No! Of course, he knows about my choice, even though I try hard to forget—every gynecological form I've ever filled out always asks *that* question."

The other woman spoke quietly, "You know I would do anything for you. You will have to take some time off before you can come back to volunteer. There's a course I think you should take through my church. They offer a post-abortion recovery class."

"I'm going through a tough time, Becky. That's all." Caitlynn snapped. "I can get through this. I don't need to go to some kind of twelve-step wannabe."

What have I done? Steve pushed away from the door, and in the process, knocked the vase against the wall. The women were suddenly silent. Panic seized him. I have to get out of here. He couldn't stay and pretend he hadn't overheard. He staggered down the hall, paused at the nurses' station, and forced a smile.

"Can I help you, sir?"

"Yes, could you please give these to Caitlynn Grant?"

The nurse's face lit up. "They're gorgeous! Why don't you give them to her? She's just down the hall."

Steve set the vase on the desk. "I would, but I just received a call I have to answer." He waved his phone at the nurse.

She turned the vase around slowly. "There's no card. If you tell me your name, I'll let her know you visited."

Steve frowned. "I'll tell her myself the next time I see her, but for now, let's keep this visit between us." His chest tightened, and his cheeks burned like they were on fire. "I've gotta go."

Breaking into a cold sweat. he hurried to the elevator, but his wobbly legs wouldn't move fast enough. Once outside the hospital, he gulped in big breaths of air to rid himself of the smothering feeling in his chest.

Somehow, he found his car and fell into the driver's seat. He slammed his hand into the steering wheel, and pain ran up his arm.

Twelve years ago. Having no reason to believe that he and Caitlynn weren't exclusive at that time, so... would he have had a child who was twelve by now? He bowed his head. His heart was like a stone in his chest. He sat in the cold car, with his eyes closed, heedless of time ticking away.

He wiped his eyes. *God, forgive me.* He started the car and drove mindlessly until he realized he was in the church parking lot. The lights in the church gym were on; several cars occupied the lot. One of them was Lee's. Steve grabbed his gym bag and stormed inside. He pulled out workout clothes and sneakers and changed. He entered the empty gymnasium, and then took a moment to read each scripture written on the walls, breathing deep.

One said, "I can do all things through Christ who strengthens me. Philippians 4:13." On the wall by the metal bleachers; "Not by might nor by power, but by My Spirit says the Lord Almighty. Zechariah 4:6." A picture of an eagle in flight was painted on the walls behind each net. "They will soar on wings like eagles; they will run and not grow weary, they will walk and not be faint. Isaiah 40:31."

He grabbed a basketball from a nearby bin and started shooting. The replay button in his mind wouldn't switch off. He missed an easy shot and dribbled to the half-court line. The events of the last few days fought for his attention. Should he have come back to Denver or stayed in Chicago to iron out his differences with his father? Typically, he couldn't spend three days without an argument. This trip, he only managed two nights.

He shot a basket, the ball hit the rim and bounced to the far left of the gym. Just like his thoughts. He ran to the ball in four giant strides, dribbled a few times, and tossed it high at the net. Lee caught it on the way down.

"I didn't hear you come in."

"I guess you were too busy running." Lee threw the basketball back to Steve. "Your aim is off. That means I might have a shot to win. Wanna play some one-on-one?"

"Bring it on!"

Lee grinned. "Give me a moment, and I'll go change."

Steve aimed and heard the satisfying swish of the ball through the net. He did this again and again until Lee returned.

"What are you doing here?" Lee asked. "I thought you went home for Thanksgiving?"

"Do you want to play, or do you want to talk?"

Lee's eyes widened. "Got it. How about a game of Twenty-One?" In three steps, Lee stole the ball from Steve and placed a well-aimed shot. "That's two. Only nineteen to go."

Steve covered him, but Lee made three more baskets before finally missing and lobbing the ball to Steve. Steve hit a three-pointer, dribbled inside the paint, and went for a layup. Lee blocked him, took a shot, and missed. Steve yanked the ball from him.

Lee's eyes narrowed, and he stood stock-still. "You're playing like you want to kill the ball. What's up, man?"

Steve sighed, his head pounding. "I left my parents' house early," he confided. "Got into another argument with my father. I just can't take his constant digs about my job, my life, or my faith."

"Whatever happened, it can't be that bad. He's your father. The Bible says to honor your father. It doesn't say you have to agree with him."

Steve held the ball. "I hear you, but that's not all. My ex-wife was there with her boyfriend, and decided Thanksgiving would be the perfect time to inform me of her plans to leave the country next summer with her boyfriend, Antoine—in France. Leaving Tyler with me."

"Doesn't she work?"

"She owns her own interior decorating business, but honestly, she doesn't need to work. She's an heir to the largest window manufacturer in the United States."

"So why is this upsetting you? I can't see why having Tyler for the entire summer is a bad thing. I agree it's not good for him to be without his mother, but you both seem willing to work things out."

"You call leaving your child and going to France for three months working it out?" Steve slammed the ball into the wall, and the sound ricocheted throughout the gym. "I call it irresponsible."

Lee chased the rolling ball and held it. "All these problems are serious, but not enough to bring you to the point of exploding. Or killing something." He pointed to the ball anchored against his side.

Steve walked to the nearest wall and sank to the floor. "You're right. But I don't know how to deal with this mess. I flew back this morning and went straight to the hospital to visit Caitlynn, bring her flowers and see for myself if she's doing okay."

He traced the grain of the wood floor with his finger. "She had a visitor. She was crying. I should've gone in, but I waited outside and . . ." His heart skipped wildly, and he swallowed hard. "Caitlynn told her friend that she thinks the hysterectomy was due to…well…a child she chose not to have."

"An abortion?" Lee frowned. "That's tough. What did you do?"

Steve looked into Lee's eyes. "I ran…just like I always do. I didn't know what to do, so I bolted."

Lee grabbed his shoulder. "I might've done the same thing. That's hard to hear."

"You don't understand." Steve's eyes were sandpaper from unshed tears. He swallowed hard. "Caitlynn and I have a history. We were in love twelve years ago, living together. We planned to get married."

Lee let out a sigh. "Whoa. She never told you she was pregnant?"

Steve shook his head. "This is all my fault." He leaned his head back against the wall. "We broke up twelve years ago, right after graduation."

"If you didn't know, why do you blame yourself?"

He covered his face with his hands. "Because I did know! Or at least I suspected she was pregnant, but I never bothered to ask. I ran, just like I did today." His voice fell to a whisper. "I didn't want to face the responsibility, so I bailed!"

Lee laid his hand on Steve's shoulder. "Steve, look at me, man. You have to go and talk to her. Don't you see? You've been given another chance, a chance to start over. You ran then, but now you know for sure you can face it head-on. You have to stop running." He raised his arm, pointing to the verse on the wall above them. "Look… 'I can do all things through Christ who strengthens me.' If there ever was a situation where you need strength, it's now."

Steve stood. "When I became a Christian two years ago, I thought it would be easy. All I could think about was how much I loved God and how much He loves me. It was such an amazing feeling. I thought grace, mercy, and love were all I needed."

Lee nodded. "You forgot forgiveness. Ephesians 4:32 says, 'Be kind and compassionate to one another, forgiving each other, just as in Christ God forgave you.' Christ forgave you so you must forgive others, and that also means the hardest of all—forgiving yourself."

They were silent as they headed into the locker room. "At the risk of sounding like a know-it-all, I wanna add one more thought," Lee said.

Steve scooped up his clothes. "So far, you've been the only person I can talk to."

"You have a great opportunity to ask for forgiveness from someone who isn't expecting it. I'm sure you can call your dad and ex-wife, air things out, and hopefully come to an understanding. I don't know how they will react, but I'm pretty sure Caitlynn will be a challenge because she won't be expecting what you have to say."

Steve nodded in agreement. "But I don't know what to say to her."

Lee squeezed Steve's shoulder. "I'll be praying that God gives you the right words."

CHAPTER TWENTY-TWO

Caitlynn shifted her weight in the hospital bed, trying desperately to come to terms with her results from the surgery. She gently touched her abdomen and groaned. Unfortunately, the operation was more complicated than even Dr. Plummer anticipated. The doctor turned out to be correct: the previous laparoscopic surgery did not help her endometriosis but instead had formed adhesions. The scar tissue had wrapped around her ovaries and obstructed her small intestine cutting off the blood supply to her bowel like poison ivy smothering their host plant—and damaging every place the endometriosis touched. Her uterus was removed, and unfortunately, her ovaries as well. The doc was optimistic that she'd be pain-free now. Complete recovery could take anywhere from three weeks to several months.

Out in the hall, a baby cried and the mother crooned soft words of comfort. Caitlynn didn't know what was worse: the pain from the procedure, or the hollow emptiness of loss. Like a fist, anger slammed into her heart, and for a brief moment, she grieved, longing so desperately for the chance to be like that mother in the hall comforting her baby. Then she closed off her mind from feeling. She couldn't go back and erase the past.

She shivered, pulled her covers tight and worried about the healing process taking a month or longer. In the hospital for three days, she was already antsy. All this time by herself, dwelling on what could never be, made her wish she could jump out of bed and do anything but lie here with her thoughts. She frowned and stared at her cell phone. Her mom called last night to wish her a Happy Thanksgiving and to find out how the surgery went. No doubt her mom would worry getting a call so soon, but Caitlynn wanted to hear her voice.

She scrolled to the number on her cell phone. "Hello, Mom. You're probably tired of me calling you all the time."

"Nonsense. Are you okay?" Her mother's voice lowered, "Is there a complication?"

"No, I'm fine. Just tired of being in pain and lying in a hospital bed."

"When do you leave?"

She closed her eyes. "Tomorrow. I can't wait to sleep in my own bed. I hired a home health care company. I don't know what I'm going to do about not working for a month. I think I might take the three weeks off, as planned, and ask my boss, Steve, if I can do some work from home."

"Steve? What happened to Russ? I didn't know you had a new boss. What's he like?" her mother asked.

"You know him." She paused. "Steven Carr."

Her mom's voice rose. "*The* Steve Carr. *No* wonder you didn't tell me. I could go over there right now and give him *what for*. The big jerk."

Caitlynn frowned as she thought about Steve and the disastrous ending to their dinner. "Don't worry about me, Mom. I can manage my own battles."

"He broke your heart, remember?" She spoke sharply. "Besides, I'm your mom, and I'll worry if I want to."

Caitlynn yawned. "He may be a jerk, but as a boss, he's been great. The station is being managed better than ever. Our newscast has held the number one spot for six weeks in a row."

"Don't defend him, honey."

"The feeling's mutual. I don't like that I'm forced to work with him." She scowled. If she had her way, it wouldn't be for much longer. "Oh, and he's a born-again Christian now. He likes to talk about how much he's changed, and he prays before meals."

"Humph. Those Christians! They're always inviting unbelievers to church."

Caitlynn's laugh turned to a moan. "Mom, I'm waiting for my pain pill to kick in. Don't make me laugh—it hurts. I bet he'll ask me to go to church with him and his son Tyler."

"He has a son?"

"Yeah, he's seven years old and cute as can be."

"Is Steve married?"

"No. He's divorced and shares custody with his ex. She lives in Chicago. I hope he moves back there as soon as possible." A yawn escaped. "Mom, I need to get off now." She yawned again. "The medication is working, finally. Hopefully, I'll be able to sleep. I can't wait to see you at Christmas. Love you."

Suddenly groggy, she struggled to find the off button. Deep loneliness spread through her like the pain radiating from her incision. She glanced out the window. The sky was dark, but large flakes as fluffy as cotton balls glittered under the parking lot's lights. *Was there really a God up there?* If so, why did she have to have a hysterectomy, and why couldn't she find someone to love her for her?

The doorknob clicked, and she watched it twist. Not another interruption! Just when she was finally about to sleep . . .

Her eyes were playing tricks on her. The pain meds were definitely working because Steve sidled into the room with a grim expression. He smiled slightly before sitting in the chair next to her.

"How are you feeling?" he asked.

She blinked, trying to focus. "I'm okay," she mumbled. A surge of adrenalin suddenly shot through her, taking with it the sleepy, relaxed feeling.

Why is he here? He was the last person in the world she wanted to see. When he quirked an eyebrow, she fished for something more to say. "The first day was brutal. I've never been in such agony in my entire life. My doctor says I'm recovering nicely, but this pain confirms why I avoided the surgery for so long." She sighed deeply.

He bit his lip. "When do you go home?"

"Tomorrow."

Steve's eyes darted around the room, never resting on anything for long. "This is a nice room, I guess." he paused, "But I still hate hospitals."

Uncomfortable that he was here, she nervously blurted out the first thought. "Me too. When I was a little girl, I wondered what I was going to do when I grew up because I didn't want to be a nurse or a teacher."

Steve chuckled. "I bet you were a cute little girl."

"I was an ornery little girl. Gave my mom all sorts of grief."

He slid to the edge of his chair. "I did too. What's the worst thing you ever did?"

Was he here to feel good about being the attentive boss visiting the sick? If she talked to him, maybe he'd feel he'd done his duty and leave.

"One time on April Fool's Day, I poured ketchup all over an old T-shirt, slumped over the fence, and screamed for my mom. She took one look at me, and I was sure she was going to have a heart attack. I burst out laughing when I saw the horrified look on her face. She got so mad; she didn't talk to me for the rest of the day. I felt terrible."

"Whoa. That's bad." He grinned. "I bet you never did anything like that again."

"You think so, huh? Well, you'd be wrong. I did all kinds of things to my mom."

He nodded his head. "Me too. When I was young, I buried my mom's jewelry box in my sandbox so I could pretend I was a sheriff catching a robber."

"Oh, no. What happened when she found out?"

"I'd forgotten all about my game. Eventually, Mom went to get something from the jewelry box, and it wasn't there. When I remembered what I'd done, I showed it to her. There was sand in every drawer. She had to send out her jewelry to be cleaned."

Caitlynn laughed then caught her breath so she wouldn't moan from the pain. "That's hilarious. I can just see you dressed up as a cowboy on your horse Boo."

"You remember him? He's still alive if you can believe it. We went for a ride while I was home." He held her gaze. "Just like old times."

She closed her eyes to shut out the pain. "Yes. I remember. We had a picture of you riding Boo hanging in—"

He sighed deeply. "Caitlynn, look at me. This is probably the wrong time to bring this up."

She struggled to keep her eyes open. The adrenaline surge from earlier was gone. She stared at him and stifled a yawn. "Then don't, Steve. Move back home. Go back to Chicago and be with your son."

Steve reached out and grasped her hand. "Caitlynn, I believe God doesn't do anything by coincidence. You and I are in each other's life again for a reason." He looked over at the vase of flowers sitting on the table. "Do you like the roses?"

"Yes. I've always loved roses." Caitlynn's eyes widened in surprise. "Did you send them?"

Steve squirmed; his voice raspy "I brought them to you yesterday. I would've come in, but you were talking—"

Caitlynn's cheeks flamed. Tears streamed down her face; she closed her eyes. She didn't have the energy to be angry. "You know," she whispered.

He brushed his finger lightly against her thumb. "I overheard . . . I should've come in, but I—" His face paled. He let go of her hand.

A deep pain tugged at her heart. Regret that she never told him about her pregnancy with his child slammed into her chest like a knife twisting her insides. She was silent for a moment, then she glared at him. "Go home. I'm stuck in this bed, in awful pain, and you show up and tell me you heard everything?" Caitlynn squeezed the blanket. "Go home."

Steve knelt by the bed. "Caitlynn, you're not the only to blame."

"What?" She shook her head in confusion.

Steve reached out for her hand. He swallowed hard; his eyes locked on hers. "Twelve years ago, I knew you were pregnant. I found your appointment reminder to Planned Parenthood."

Caitlynn closed her eyes. "Why are you telling me this now? She opened her eyes and jerked her hand away. "Are you feeling guilty because I can never have kids?" Her voice rose. "Ever."

Steve lowered his gaze. "Caitlynn, I'm telling you this because I'm as much to blame as you are. I loved you, and I left. I should've stayed." Anger filled his voice. "I left you pregnant, but I didn't care—I cared more about my career and what my dad thought of me—and I'm ashamed of what I did."

"Yeah, well, we all have our regrets, don't we?" Tears threatened. She squeezed her eyes shut, holding them back. Caitlynn slumped deeply against her pillow and crossed her arms, willing this conversation to end. "What do you want me to say? I'll say whatever you want me to if you'll just get out of here and leave me be."

"I'm sorry for everything I've done to you. I-I'm sorry I let my father get in the way of our love. I'm sorry I let him pressure me into breaking up with you." He sighed deeply. "I'm asking you to forgive me."

Caitlynn stared outside the window and tried to squelch her tears, but it was like trying to stop the snow. "Steve, please leave." She closed her eyes. "I forgive you if that's what you want to hear. But I need you to go. Now."

He rose from his knees. "Okay, I'll leave, but not before I say one last thing. Caitlynn, look at me."

She stared daggers at him.

"Your comment about never having kids? I don't know why this happened to you, but it's not up to me to question it, because I'm not God. But when I look at you, I see a woman God loves and a woman I once loved. I'll leave now, but I'm not going far. I'm driving you home whether you like it or not. And I'll take care of you." He gently brushed the tears from her cheeks. "See you tomorrow."

He left the room before she could tell him he was wasting his time. Why did he think she would accept help from him?

Caitlynn cried until she was numb. The medication once again relaxing her to the point where she fell into a deep slumber.

CHAPTER TWENTY-THREE

A bright light over her bed interrupted her sleep. A nurse she'd never seen came walking into the room.

Disoriented and sleepy, Caitlynn asked, "Who are you?"

"I'm Lena, and it's time for your meds."

"I've never seen you before. What happened to Cindy?"

"She had to work a different shift this week, so you're stuck with me, honey."

Caitlynn shielded her eyes with the cover. *I'm not your honey, so don't call me that.* She lowered the blanket and blinked rapidly. "Could you shut off this light, please, and put the desk light on instead?"

"Now, Ms. Grant, this should only take a minute."

Caitlynn scowled. The nurse spoke to her as if she were talking to a toddler.

"I want to make sure you take your medicine, and I can't see to do that in the dark, now can I?"

Caitlynn covered her eyes with her arm. "The light is hurting my eyes, and my head hurts." Irritated at this nurse's insensitive behavior, she spewed out, "Don't worry! I'll take the medicine—just turn off the light."

In a loud voice, nurse Lena said, "So sorry; no can do. Now here you go…hold out your hand, sugar."

Pushing her hand against the bed, Caitlynn tried to find a better position for swallowing the pills. "Can you help me sit up?"

"I'm sorry; I can't do that either. You need to do it on your own. Here, press this button, and your bed will come up to a sitting position."

"I know that." She spoke through gritted teeth, "My back hurts from being in the same position too long, and I want to stretch it out a bit."

"Oh, that's no problem, honey. I have a pillow right here." Lena raised the bed and jammed the pillow behind Caitlynn's back. "All you need to do is raise up a bit. You can do it." She smiled brightly.

Now her back ached and her incision hurt. "Just give me the drugs." She swallowed the pills and sank onto the pillow. "Please leave."

"Okay, sugar, I'll be gone in a jiffy." She scribbled in the chart and then reached to turn off the light overhead.

"Never mind. Just leave it on. I'm up now.

"Okay, honey, if you're sure now. I can see you've been crying." She patted Caitlynn's head. "You let me know if you need anything."

Through gritted teeth, Caitlynn said, "The only thing I need is for you to leave me alone."

Just then, there was another tap on the door. Caitlynn glanced at the clock. It was nine p.m. *When did my room turn into party central?* A priest poked his head into the room. He looked the part, complete with the white collar and friendly smile.

"Can I come in?"

Caitlynn was confused. *Why not add to the fun?* She muttered, "Yes, come in."

Nurse Lena smirked. "Hello, Father. I was just leaving." She turned to Caitlynn. "I'll be back in a little bit to recheck your vitals and see how you're doing."

The priest sat on the chair near her bed. "Your door was open when I walked by. I overheard your frustration, so I thought you might need rescuing."

She sighed in relief. "Yes, I did. Thank you."

"If you need to sit up, I can help you. I do it for many of the patients I see."

"I'd like that. My back is throbbing."

He skirted behind her. "Can you lean forward a fraction?"

Caitlynn did as instructed. He grabbed her gently under her arms and moved her up and toward the backrest. The pressure in her lower back instantly released.

"Do you want me to put a pillow between your lower back and the bed? Sometimes that helps."

"Please, but be careful. That's a tender area."

He folded a pillow in half lengthwise and slowly inserted it between her back and the bed. "I'm Father Mark, by the way, and I'm one of the chaplains here at the hospital."

"Hello, I'm Caitlynn Grant."

Father Mark walked to the chair and sat. "I know who you are. I've seen you on the ten o'clock news many times. I wanted to visit you and see if there's anything you need before you leave. I would be happy to say a prayer for your recovery."

Caitlynn winced. "Don't bother. I think God has better things to focus on than my problems."

"He can do the 'better things' you speak of and still have time for you, so don't worry about God. He's omnipotent." He winked; a smile spread across his face. "That means He invented the term multi-task—without the frenzy."

She liked his straightforward manner. "Okay, I guess I have a few questions I've been wondering about. I just had a hysterectomy." She wanted to cry, but there were no more tears left to shed. She rubbed her burning eyes. "Why is it that God can give children to parents who are so horrible that they abuse their kids, or they're drug addicts who neglect them altogether? And yet, I would love to have a family, but it will never be." Her voice faded to a whisper.

"Just a minute." He went over to the sink and tore off a paper towel splashing cold water on it. He squeezed out the excess. "I can tell you've been crying. It looks like your eyes are sore." He leaned over toward her. "Do you mind?"

She shook her head.

He laid the cool towel across her eyes. The burning ache in her eyes eased. "Close your eyes now and rest. I want to tell you a story."

"There once was a fair, good, and loyal king to the people in his kingdom. But some of the people in the land didn't feel the same way toward their king. They wanted what he had. They reasoned that it wasn't fair that the king should have as much as he did. The king heard their discontent and sent one of his esteemed leaders to reason with them. But instead of talking with the man, they killed him. The king sent another and another, and still, they killed them. Finally, the king thought, 'I know. I will send my son. Surely, they will respect him and honor him because he is my son, whom I love.' Well, the king sent his son—and they killed him too." He paused. "So, my question to you is this: if the king is God, and He loved His son, did He send His son to die for both the good and the evil people?"

"I guess so."

The priest removed the cloth and stared at her with kind brown eyes. "God loves you and wants what's best for you, but God's ways don't always make sense. Isaiah 55:9 says, 'As the heavens are higher than the earth, so are my ways higher than your ways and my thoughts than your thoughts.'"

He sat back down. "Don't try to figure it out. Trust me on this. If you spend your time wondering why bad things happen to good people, you're going to become bitter trying to play God. You're not God—and you have to trust that He knows what he's doing." He patted her hand. "Does that help at all?"

She wanted to tell him she understood what he was trying to say. But it still didn't make sense. How could God care so much if He sacrificed His own son? It gave her more reason to question God.

He stood and flashed a grin. "Caitlynn, like it or not, you're on my prayer list now. I'll pop by again and see if you're still around. If not, I'll watch you on the evening news." He squeezed her shoulder. "You take care now, and God bless you."

Her body ached—a desire to sleep swept in like a storm-tossed wave. First, the conversation with Steve and then the clergyman—her head was spinning.

Caitlynn fell into a deep sleep until a burning pain sliced through her abdomen. She glanced at the clock, 2:00 a.m. Throwing off the blanket, she moaned and hit the button to ring the nurse. Soon, her favorite nurse quietly entered the room.

"What can I do for you?" Cindy whispered.

"I feel awful. Both hot and cold."

"Let me take your temp." She quickly checked her vitals. "Your temperature is high;102 degrees. I'll be right back with some pain meds. The doctor will want to check on you. Do you hurt anywhere else?"

Caitlynn shivered and pointed to her incision. "Just here."

CHAPTER TWENTY-FOUR

Love is Kind.
1 CORINTHIANS 13:4

Squeezing the blanket until her knuckles turned white, she cried out, moaning in pain. The bedsheet clung to her body like an extra layer of skin. A chill ran up her spine, and goosebumps spread over her arms and legs. Beads of sweat dotted her forehead. She gritted her teeth, tossing side to side. Droplets ran down her face. Dizzy now, she tried in vain to shut out the memory twelve years ago, when another infection had ravaged her body. She whimpered as she tried to block out the memory, but it barged into her soul as the fever wreaked havoc on her flesh . . .

It was her graduation day at the University of Colorado. Caitlynn had made a checklist of everything she would need: camera, cap, gown, keys, makeup, and her speech. It would be just her luck to forget something and have to turn around in the traffic congestion. She'd checked off each item from her list with quick decisiveness—and triple-checked that her speech was in her handbag. In less than three minutes, she had the car loaded and drove on her way to Folsom Field.

Her stomach grumbled. She grabbed the package of saltines she had swiped from the restaurant last night and nibbled on one, barely managing to swallow before it threatened to come back up (along with the half-eaten toast she had choked down for breakfast). She was nauseous because she was responsible for the opening speech to the class of 1991, and though she'd practiced over and over in front of the mirror and at the rehearsal the day before, she couldn't help but worry that she'd flub somewhere along the way. The other reason for her nausea—she was five weeks pregnant.

Unable to keep food down lately, and overcome with fatigue so intense, she struggled to attend her morning class, and wondered when whatever virus she'd caught would subside. Then one morning she'd gone out to breakfast with Steve, and as they'd headed out to the car, she'd lost it all in the bushes nearby.

Steve had tried to comfort her. "Are you all right? Can I get you anything?"

She wiped her mouth with her sleeve. "No, I must have the flu . . . that's just what I need right before finals."

His brow had furrowed as he carefully brushed back her hair behind her ear and opened the door to help her into the car. He stepped away, staring at her with a funny look on his face, as if trying to figure her out. "Yeah, you're probably right. It must be going around."

But then she missed her period and began to suspect the worst. She made an appointment at Planned Parenthood. After filling out the necessary information and giving a urine sample, she'd sat in an exam room, unaware that her life would change forever.

A pleasant looking woman walked in and sat across the table. "Hi, I'm Sandy, and I'll be consulting with you today. I believe you're here because you think you may be pregnant." She reached out and touched Caitlynn's hand. "The test is positive. According to the dates you gave us for your last cycle, you're about five weeks along."

The world spun, making her dizzy. "I knew it," she'd said. Massaging her flat stomach, Caitlynn shook her head in disbelief. She was graduating from college with a bachelor of arts in journalism. She'd interviewed for a news station in Denver, and they were going to make her a job offer in a few days. She couldn't believe this was happening.

"We have plenty of options today for women in your situation," Sandy had said. "You can terminate the pregnancy while it's still early—right now it's just a bunch of cells that are multiplying fast." She leaned in close, her expression soft. "The procedure is relatively painless with just a small amount of discomfort, and side effects are rare. We provide everything for you, and you can be back to planning your future by next week."

A wave of panic had washed over Caitlynn. "What about my boyfriend? Don't you think I should tell him?"

"How long have you been together?"

"It's been about three years, but we've lived together for the past two years." She twirled a strand of her hair.

"I see." She removed her hand from Caitlynn's, and drummed her fingers on the table for a few seconds, and then said, "Of course, it's your choice, but I believe that when you walk in the door here, you are an individual, with choices that should be left to you and you alone. If you feel that it will make a difference in your situation, go ahead and tell him." She shrugged, "If not, that's fine too."

Caitlynn stammered, "I–I need some time to think. It's a huge decision, and if I tell my boyfriend, he may take the news better than I expect."

A smile split her face. "It's not like we haven't talked about the future and marriage. Initially the plan was to wait a few years to get our careers established, but maybe we could push the date up a little."

Sandy shuffled her papers and handed Caitlynn a business card. "Here's my name and the clinic phone number. You can take some time to think about it, but don't wait too long. Because if you do"—she glanced away— "let's just say the procedure becomes a bit more complicated."

If it hadn't been for the honking of a horn, Caitlynn would've run a stop sign on her way home. Shaking uncontrollably, she pulled the car over. She closed her eyes, willing herself not to cry. Her body had betrayed her by getting pregnant. She wasn't stupid; she had taken precautions. It had all seemed like more than she could handle—the long hours she'd spent studying, her commencement speech, final exams, job interviews . . . Everything piled one on top of each other, and when the tears spilled forth, she wondered if they would ever stop. And then she had done what she always did. She wiped away her tears, straightened her spine, and made a decision. She'd keep the secret to herself until after graduation.

Her fever raging, Caitlynn moaned. I don't want to remember any more...

On the morning of graduation, Caitlynn had been running late. Ever since she'd found out about her pregnancy, she was erratic and frantic. Even Steve noticed how distracted she'd been recently. Arriving a few minutes late, she'd spotted Steve with his parents.

"Hey! What took you so long? The ceremony is about to start," Steve grabbed her hand.

"Sorry...the traffic is nuts. Not everyone's father owns radio and television stations and can afford a limo," she'd teased. She quickly panned the crowd and grinned when she spotted her mom in the first row wildly waving. Caitlynn waved back and turned to Steve.

"No worries." Steve arched his brows. "I have a surprise for you."

She flashed a grin. "You do? I may have a surprise for you too—you never know."

He punched her arm playfully. "You can't keep a secret from me. You're too transparent."

Caitlynn laughed nervously and another wave of panic washed through her. *Did Steve know?* "Okay, fess up, what's your surprise?" she'd said nervously.

A wide smile broke across his face. "My father offered me a job at his Chicago news station as the weekend sports anchor. Isn't that awesome?"

Caitlynn flinched. "Are you accepting the job?"

"I'd be a fool not to. I know it's going to be tough for a while, but we'll work something out. You can come see me in Chicago, or I can visit you here in Denver. This is what we talked about—establishing our careers, making a place for ourselves as television news anchors, working hard to be the best at what we do."

Caitlynn's heart raced. A tiny voice whispered in her head. *Tell him.* The voice grew louder. *Tell him now!*

Steve pressed his lips together. "Caitlynn, you're too quiet. What's wrong?"

She'd pulled out the speech she'd written, "Overcoming Obstacles and Facing the Challenges Ahead." The warning bell sounded. The ceremony was about to begin.

Long distance relationships never work out. Her legs turned to rubber. She swayed. Steve grabbed her arm and led her to their seats. Teary-eyed, she kissed him softly on the cheek. "I couldn't be happier for you," she'd lied, breaking away from his embrace. She collapsed on the chair. *Why would he do this to me . . . to us?*

The ceremony opened with the chancellor's speech, which she pretended to listen to. Her stomach flipped and churned. *I thought he loved me.* The address ended in applause that sounded muffled to her ears. Tiny black dots floated past her eyes. *Please...I can't faint.* She exhaled deeply.

Steve patted her hand, smiling. "You'll be great. Go get 'em."

I can't tell him; my pride won't let me. Coming from the podium, she heard, "Please welcome, Caitlynn Grant."

Clutching tightly to her paper, her lips quivered into a fake smile. With her heart breaking into tiny pieces, she'd squared her shoulders, trudged up the steps to the podium, and with shaking fingers adjusted the microphone. "'You can have anything you want if you want it badly enough. You can be anything you want to be, do anything you set out to accomplish if you hold to that desire with singleness of purpose.' Abraham Lincoln penned these words…"

Suddenly someone was shaking her from her delirium. For a moment, Caitlynn didn't know where she was. Machines beeped. The scent of antiseptic filled her nose.

"Caitlynn, you're crying. What is your pain level?"

Caitlynn groaned. Her head pounded. "Nine," she muttered.

"Here…this will stop the pain." The nurse handed her a pill and a cup of water. "Is there anything else I can do for you?"

"Please." Caitlynn begged, "can I get a sleeping pill? My brain won't shut off, and my body is aching so badly, I don't think I'll be able to sleep."

The nurse hurried back a few moments later. "I need to get you out of your bedclothes now—you're drenched. Let's change your gown, and then you can take something to help you sleep."

Caitlynn grimaced in pain, thinking back to the week after college graduation—and the infection that had ravaged her body following the abortion—when her uterus was accidentally perforated... *Is there a pill that can numb my heart?*

CHAPTER TWENTY-FIVE

When Steve quietly entered Caitlynn's room, his breath caught in his throat. She lay as still as death with an IV in her arm. Medical devices surrounded the bed that weren't there previously. Her cheeks scarlet, her face a pasty white with dark under-eye circles. To further confuse him, a chaplain sat in a chair, head bowed with a rosary wrapped around his hand. He looked up.

He rushed to the side of the bed. "What happened?" Steve said in a panic.

The chaplain shook his head. "I stopped in to see her early this morning and was told she developed an infection. She's on a heavy dose of antibiotics, but she's going in and out of consciousness." He eyed Steve. "Are you her husband?"

"No." He pulled a chair over and fell into the seat. "Just an old friend."

He extended his arm. "I'm the chaplain here. Father Mark."

"Steven Carr." The two shook hands. "I also work with Caitlynn," he whispered.

"She's had it rough the past few days." Father Mark spoke low. "I visited yesterday, and we had a long chat."

Steve gnawed on his lower lip. "What can I do? I'm not family. They won't let me see her."

"I'm glad to help. Give me your phone number. I'll keep you updated." He nodded over at Caitlynn. "She's young and strong and looks to me to be a fighter." He looked thoughtful. "I bet she kicks this infection today and is home by tomorrow."

Steve pulled out his business card and handed him his information. "Thanks," he said, solemnly, "I appreciate this." He moved quietly to Caitlynn's side and gently brushed her hair back, smoothing it with his fingers. "I'll be back tomorrow."

Just then, the door swished open; the doctor strolled in, followed by a nurse. He extended his hand in greeting. "Hi, I'm Dr. Plummer."

Shaking hands, Steve barely managed to squeak out, "Is Caitlynn going to be okay?"

"Are you a family member?" the doctor asked.

"No." He stared into the doctor's eyes. "A friend. I, uh, I'm caring for her during her recovery."

He bobbed his head. "That's good. Unfortunately, I'm not allowed to talk to you about her condition. I hate to be the bearer of bad news but you're not allowed to stay if you aren't a family member."

Father Mark stepped forward. "I'll walk out with you."

At the elevator, the two stepped inside, and Steve punched the button for the first floor. He brushed his fingers nervously through his hair. "I wish I could do more to help."

"I'll check back later on Caitlynn and let you know if they plan to discharge her tomorrow." Father Mark squeezed his arm.

"Thanks. You know the comment you made about Caitlynn being a fighter? I'd better armor up because she and I will be battling it out tomorrow. She doesn't think she needs help. And, the last person she would want help from is me."

Father Mark grinned. "Then I'd better add you to my prayer list!"

It was all a fog. Everything ached; her head, her body, her back. Thankfully, she'd made it through the night, and her fever finally broke. She shifted in the bed and winced in pain. She was just so tired and wanted to be home.

A quick knock on the door caused her to perk up. "Come in," she said weakly.

Steve entered the room wearing a look of concern. "Good morning, Caitlynn. How are you feeling?"

"Why are you here?" Caitlynn glared. "Didn't I ask you to leave?"

Steve reached behind her gently and fluffed up the flattened pillow. "You thought you could get rid of me so easily? I told you! I'm going to care for you while you recover."

She sighed and melted into the pillow. "Wait a minute." She shook her head. "You think you can butter me up by fixing my pillow? I've hired help— experts at taking care of patients. I don't need your charity."

"Please let me help you." Steve said evenly.

Caitlynn looked away. She was so tired, and it hurt her head to think. As much as she didn't want to see him right now, he sounded genuine.

He touched her hand. "What happened, Caitlynn? You were supposed to leave today. You're not dressed."

She frowned. "I woke up around two a.m. with a fever. The doctor said I have an infection." Her eyes filled with tears. He reached over and pulled some tissues from the box.

"Is the antibiotic working?" he asked.

She dabbed at her eyes. "Yes. The fever finally broke. I'm waiting to see if the doctor discharges me today."

He dropped to the chair next to her. "I was here yesterday, but the doctor kicked me out. By the way, I met Father Mark. He was praying on your behalf. I like him." He drummed his fingers on his jeans. "I know you have someone picking you up, but please let me drive you home and help you during your recovery… it's the least I can do."

"Okay," she blurted. "I don't have the energy to argue." *Am I getting too soft? Maybe it's the meds talking.* Did she want Steve's help? She wasn't sure. The only thing she knew was that she wanted to be at home; *in her bed.*

"Good. It's settled then." He sighed in relief.

"I guess," she grumbled. "I'll let you help me on one condition: the second I want you gone—you are to leave."

"Deal," he said. He flipped on the television. "I guess you're stuck with me for the rest of the day." His goofy grin would melt a frozen candle on contact. "What do you wanna watch?"

###

By midafternoon, Caitlynn was released. Steve drove, while Caitlynn reclined in the front seat, a pillow rested over her abdomen, as she directed Steve to her townhome.

When they arrived, he hustled out of the vehicle and sprinted to the passenger side, just as Caitlynn opened her car door.

"Just a second! Don't get out." He grabbed her medicine and overnight bag from the backseat. "I'll help you." He held her arm firmly as she stepped out of his SUV. She cringed in pain, her face paling.

"I'm sorry, Caitlynn, I wish I had a car that wasn't so high off the ground." She held onto him as if he were a lifeline on a sinking boat. He grimaced as she clutched his arm, squeezing hard. He wrapped his arm around her shoulders and lifted her from the seat. "Try to walk. Just take it slow. I'm right here, and I'm not letting you go."

They made their way inside. The mirror in her foyer reflected him holding her tenderly as they walked toward the living room. He fought with a twinge of remorse. *What would've happened if he'd never left her?*

"Do you want to go to the couch or your bed?"

"I'm sick to death of being in a bed. Let's go to the couch."

Steve helped her into a comfortable position on the plum-colored couch, then panned the room. Her furniture was modern, sleek in style—more like a showroom than a place she actually lived in. Above the fireplace hung an abstract painting in shades of plum, black, white, and gray. Floor-to-ceiling shelves flanked the fireplace filled with brightly colored art objects and interesting looking books.

Watching Caitlynn in pain upset him. He wanted to help but instead felt helpless. "I'm going to get you some water."

In the kitchen, he quickly opened several cabinets until he found a glass, filled it with ice and water from the dispenser in the stainless-steel fridge and placed it on the coffee table. "Here you go."

Sleep. That's what she needs.

"Caitlynn, why don't you rest a bit? You look exhausted."

She closed her eyes. "Sounds good. What are you going to do?"

"I thought I'd go grocery shopping."

"I was going to buy food before my surgery but, uh, Wednesday turned out to be um—"

"—You don't need to explain." Brett's face flashed in his mind. "I get it. But if I'm gonna take care of you, I need to stock up on supplies."

"Do whatever you want. I'm too tired, and hurt too much to argue." She grimaced.

Steve chuckled, hoping to lighten the mood. "What? You're not gonna fight me? Get some rest. I'll be back soon." He swooped the throw off the back of the couch, spread it over her, and placed her cell phone within reach. "I need to get back before the online meal service arrives."

She gasped. "That was you? I got an email confirming the order, but they wouldn't give me any more information because it was a gift." She was silent for a few moments. "Thank you." Her shoulders softened. "That was very thoughtful."

###

Caitlynn closed her eyes, but couldn't sleep. The pain meds hadn't kicked in. She pulled the throw close and inhaled, appreciating the slight lavender scent over the medicinal smell of the hospital's blankets. Was it a moment of weakness that possessed her to let Steve help with her recovery? Did he hope to make up for the heartbreak he caused her all those years ago? And why, when this happened long ago, did she still hold so much anguish over the breakup and the abortion? Was it crazy to let him help at her most vulnerable time? It was important to stay in control—she'd let him do just enough to make it easier on her until she could manage on her own. The way it's always been. Her cell phone rang. Reaching for the phone, a sharp pain tore across her abdomen. She barely managed to say hello.

"Caitlynn, it's Jillian. I'm calling because I just left the doctor's office. They want to schedule an ultrasound next month. The doctor wants to check the baby's heart. I also get to find out if

I'm having a boy or a girl. I thought you might want to film the visit."

What she wanted was to sink into the couch like a turtle hiding in its shell. She could barely focus. "I like the idea of filming the results, but you called at a bad time."

"Oh, I'm sorry." Jillian's voice lilted in surprise. "I called your work number and they said you were out of the office. I figured you're probably on vacation with your boyfriend or something."

"No, it's nothing like that." Unbidden tears flowed. "I've…uh…I had…minor surgery—no big deal." *Except that it was.* She sighed. "I'll call you next week to arrange a meeting."

Jillian gasped. "I didn't know. I'm so sorry; I hope you get better soon."

Caitlynn frowned into the phone. "Thanks for calling. I'll talk to you soon." She ended the call.

A tiny giggle escaped at the irony of the call, and soon she was laughing loudly. Her stomach muscles contracted in pulsating pain with each outburst. Still, she couldn't stop. It was as if an unknown being possessed her emotions. *Am I losing my mind? Maybe I should pray. Where did that thought come from?* Was Steve rubbing off on her? She shook the idea away, snatched up the remote, and turned on the television.

Steve returned from the grocery store laden with bags. Soon the tantalizing aroma of garlic and onion filled her home. He hummed as he cooked. The comforting sounds helped her relax. She opened her eyes when she heard his footsteps.

"Here you go."

"You whipped this together?" Golden chicken rested on top of crisp salad greens, avocado, tomato, and red pepper in a raspberry vinaigrette dressing.

The combination of the food and the pain meds finally worked like magic, until she couldn't keep her eyes open.

"You didn't eat much." Steve set her plate next to his. "You look tired. Do you want to sleep on the couch or the bed?"

"I think I'll try the bed." She yawned wearily.

"Okay, I'll get you settled in and flip on the football game while I wait for the food delivery."

She yawned again, feeling defeated to rely on anyone—especially Steve. She surrendered begrudgingly for now, yet she held on tightly to his arm. "Just don't yell too loudly when the Broncos lose," she quipped. "I'm a light sleeper."

CHAPTER TWENTY-SIX

In the first week of Caitlynn's recovery, Steve dropped by every day before and after work tackling household chores and cooking duties, keeping her well-stocked in meals and snacks. She thought she'd bounce back within a few days, but the surgery had knocked the wind out of her sails, leaving her feeling drained to the core. After days of lying bedridden, she was allowed to shower and by sheer will, made her way into the bathroom.

She stood under the showerhead, allowing the water to stream down her body like a waterfall. It was so refreshing—as if the spray were washing away the pain, sending it down the drain. After changing into clean clothes, she didn't have the strength to blow dry her hair, so she applied a bit of makeup, styled her hair, and slowly walked out of the bathroom.

Steve sat at the table working on his laptop. Glancing up, his eyes widened. "Wow, Caitlynn. You clean up real good. Who knew?"

She giggled and said, "If it weren't for the fact that I'm too tired to walk across the room, I'd smack you."

"Honestly, you do look really good. You have color in your cheeks, and your eyes are bright again. I'd say you're finally on the mend."

His compliment had given her an unexpected rush, and for the next few days, his kind words sat in her mind like a Post-it Note. By the end of the week, she figured his visits would gradually taper off, then stop completely, but his usual pop-ins became the new routine. He'd stay for an hour or so, but on Saturdays, catered to her the entire day. Caitlynn realized, albeit reluctantly, that she enjoyed his company and even found herself looking forward to his visits. She remembered fondly one evening when Steve sat on the couch and watched an episode of *Touched by an Angel* with her, joking afterward that he'd have to detox with at least an hour of *Sports Center* after watching such a syrupy TV show. Steve seemed so positive and happy, even though she wondered why he wasn't depressed to be away from his son. He seemed to take the situation in stride.

She wished she were more optimistic like him. Instead, she dwelled over and over again on what the surgery meant. Deep down, she had always hoped to have a child, but the hysterectomy robbed her of that choice. Profound anger coupled with sadness impregnated her mind, refusing to lessen its hold. Why wasn't Steve angry and frustrated that he had a son he only saw twice a month?

A knock on the door interrupted her depressing thoughts. Steve was driving her to the doctor. She hastily brushed an errant tear from her cheek and opened the door. "Come in."

He walked inside. "Are you ready?"

"Yes, thanks for taking me to the doctor. I don't know why I can't drive. I'm perfectly fine," she scowled.

His eyes turned dark. "Hmm, I think it's going to be a bit tough for you to get into the car, let alone drive."

She bristled at his challenge. "Whatever. I could do it if I had to."

"I can tell you're feeling better—you're up to arguing," he teased. He slid his arm around her and led her across the threshold. "I know you're biting to get out of this house, so humor me on this. If the doctor gives you the go-ahead, I'll back off and let you drive home."

A half-hour later, Dr. Plummer carefully examined her incision, giving a slow nod. "The infection is gone, but you're healing slower than I'd like."

She winced when he gently pushed her scar.

"You need to take it easy for another week. Start by walking a little more, but at the same time, listen to your body. If you feel tired, rest. Don't push it."

She frowned. "That's what Steve says, but I'm sick of sitting on the couch. I feel fine. Let me go back to work," she pleaded.

"Caitlynn, I'm not releasing you to go back to work." He patted her hand. "You need to wait another week. As it is, only three weeks for recovery is pushing it. I'd like to see you again on Monday. No driving yet."

She twirled a strand of hair. "I feel like I'm a prisoner in my own home. Unfortunately, working from home isn't an option."

"I know this is rough." He studied her chart. "I'll need to do some bloodwork and then get your hormones balanced. I'm sure you've noticed your emotions are somewhat erratic?"

"Erratic?" A sarcastic smirk escaped. "More like borderline insanity! One minute I'm angry, and the next, I'm either laughing or crying."

"We had to remove your ovaries, so you're forced to go into induced menopause. I'll get you on the right hormones as soon as I review the lab report."

"Good." She smirked. "I'll let Steve know that help is on the way. Maybe he won't think I'm totally nuts."

"Is Steve your . . . significant other?" the doctor grinned.

"No. He's my boss. He just feels sorry for me. He thinks it's his Christian duty to help."

"Tell him thanks for me. I wondered how you were going to handle this alone." He touched her shoulder. "I'll have the nurse draw blood for the tests. I want to see you next Monday."

Caitlynn donned her clothes, headed to the lobby, and spotted Steve reading a copy of *Golf Digest*. He stood and entwined his arm into hers.

Suddenly exhausted, Caitlynn leaned heavily against his side. *I bet the patients in the waiting room think we're a couple.* Loneliness swept through her heart. Just for this moment, she walked beside him, pretending that they were just that—a loving couple.

He helped her into the car. "Tyler comes this weekend. I had planned to come over, but I think it might be too much for you. As you know, he's all boy, and I'm sure he'd be a handful. Do you think you can manage on your own?"

A flash of pain squeezed her chest at not being able to see Tyler. She was hoping he'd come and add some much-needed spark to her life as only kids can do. She missed holding the infants at the hospital. If she couldn't have children, at least she could enjoy their company, if only briefly. She spoke with her eyes shut. "You're right. Tyler would more than likely be bored out of his skull. I'm sure he'd hate to sit around the condo watching me sleep."

He sighed. "Caitlynn, don't be like this. I'm just trying to be practical. He's going to want you to play with him, and that can't happen. You're not ready for his kind of roughhousing."

"Don't worry about it. Believe it or not, I'll survive without you."

"Caitlynn." Frustration sounded in his voice. "Open your eyes—you're not fooling me. Tell me what the doctor said."

What did it matter? He'd go home this weekend and resume his life with Tyler. Who did she have to go back too? She watched the cars in the next lane speed past. "He wanted me to thank you for helping me during my recovery."

"What else did he say? You got bad news, didn't you?" He said softly, "How are you doing?"

She opened her eyes and stared out the side window. "The rest of the discussion is NOYB."

"You're wrong, Caitlynn." He squeezed her hand for a brief moment. "Believe it or not, I care about you. You don't have to tell me—it's your business—but it doesn't change how I feel about you."

Caitlynn stared out the window, refusing to look at him. "If you say so, Steve. Just drive me home so you can go off to work where you're needed."

###

Lord, give me strength. Steve prayed as he helped a grumpy Caitlynn onto the couch. She was definitely in a mood, but he didn't want to fight with her. He sympathized with her condition, her pain, but her nastiness was wearing thin.

He grabbed a cold bottle of water from the fridge, but when he went to open it, his hand slipped and water sloshed onto the carpet.

"Ugh," Caitlynn muttered.

Steve marched over and grabbed a paper towel to soak up the spill. He flung the wet towel into the trash, fighting to keep his temper under control. "I'm leaving now. If you want to pout because I'm not bringing Tyler over, that's your problem. But just remember, I'm doing it for you. Whether you know it or not, you don't need a rowdy seven-year-old around here."

She hit the button on the remote. "Yeah. I wouldn't know." Caitlynn spit out the words. "I'd be worthless around him anyway. Just go."

Steve stalked to the door. "Fine. Call me if you need anything."

"Don't bother coming back. I don't need you," she said.

Steve slammed the door.

Jogging to his car, he prayed silently, telling God he wanted to give up on Caitlynn. He couldn't take her negativity anymore. He was usually so positive, but her wild mood swings and yammering of "I don't need you anymore," and, "why are you here?" was getting the best of his resolve to help.

As Steve prayed, he felt the Lord tell him to stay strong. He didn't know how he could. The old Steve would have lashed out, blurting something cutting to get back at her for all the hurtful things she'd said. The new Steve was trying to listen to the Lord telling him to stay strong, except he couldn't help but wonder…what was the point?

CHAPTER TWENTY-SEVEN

Caitlynn twirled a strand of hair, anxious about what to do regarding Steve. Thinking about their fight, she could finally admit that she'd turned her anger at not being allowed to return to work on him. He didn't deserve her frustration when he went above and beyond to help in any way possible.

She rubbed her scars, feeling no pain. Dr. Plummer was correct too—she'd gained most of her strength back, and could now make breakfast and lunch with no problem. The ready-made dinners were a snap to thaw out, bake, and eat. Her only obstacle was that she couldn't drive. She had called on Monday and left Steve a message reminding him she was fine without his help.

The first few days on her own didn't bother her because she was still so distracted by her anger. But now it was Friday, the days and nights bled together into one big monotonous blur.

The pharmacy had called on Wednesday, reminding her to pick up the new hormone prescription. A brief thought about asking Steve flitted across her mind, but she didn't want to give him the satisfaction. Instead, she'd called Becky, who was happy to lend a helping hand.

Now, it was Friday evening, and she literally wanted to scream from boredom. She grabbed her phone and called Jillian. It went straight to voicemail. "Hi, this is Jillian. I can't come to the phone. You know what to do."

"Hi, Jillian, it's Caitlynn. I'm calling to confirm that I'll be back in the office this Tuesday. Let's connect so we can arrange the details to film the ultrasound appointment."

The icemaker rattled as it started plunking out ice, tossing several cubes into the bin. Other than that, the house was entirely too quiet. Any time Steve was there, she didn't notice the sounds.

He would talk about how Tyler was doing and ask how she felt and if she needed any help.

She snuggled into her blanket and pressed the button on the remote, turning up the volume to drown out the fact that the only living sound in her house was blaring out of her television.

On Saturday morning, it took her almost an hour to shower and dress. That small task zapped most of her energy. She looked at the unmade bed, knowing there was nothing left in her tank for housekeeping. If this was how she felt after doing such a small task, how would she ever manage work on Tuesday?

Should she do what the doctor suggested and take the full month off? *No.* She'd already taken off three whole weeks, which in her mind was more than she could handle.

She relaxed on the bedroom chair and closed her eyes, trying to muster up enough strength to blow-dry her hair. Without warning, her stomach churned. Nauseated from her medicine, she trudged to the kitchen, pulled out a package of instant oatmeal, and jumped at the sound of the doorbell. Annoyed at the interruption, she stalked to the foyer and opened the door.

Steve was standing there holding a paper bag from Panera Bread.

Caitlynn frowned. "The only reason I'm letting in you in is because of the bag you're holding. There better be a cinnamon crunch bagel in there. With some cream cheese."

Steve arched a brow. A cheeky grin split his face. "You won't know until I open the bag. You'll just have to take a chance."

Caitlynn swung the door wide, suppressing her smile. "Come in."

Steve was also holding a cardboard drink holder with what she hoped was coffee for him and tea for her, plus two orange juices. He placed the bag onto the table and pulled out two cinnamon crunch bagels. "I'm glad to see we at least have the same taste in bagels," he said.

She grabbed a knife off the counter and sliced a bagel in half. "Why are you here, Steve? Where's Tyler?"

"He's with a friend on a play date. I have to pick him up at noon." He took a bite.

"You don't need cream cheese?"

"What?" He looked aghast. "And ruin a perfectly good bagel? I don't think so."

She slathered a dollop of cream cheese on hers then took a bite. "Suit yourself."

Caitlynn watched Steve's eyes taking in her appearance. She wore yoga pants and a t-shirt, but her hair was still wet. He said, "You look tons better since Monday. How are you feeling?"

"Like my hair is wet. I need to go dry it."

"Caitlynn, it's me. I've seen you with wet hair before. Let's eat. You can finish your hair later."

Caitlynn was still nauseated—and to her surprise, hungry.

"It's good to see you're eating. Most of the time, you barely touch your food. He handed her a Panera cup. "I brought you tea."

"Thanks." She nodded in appreciation. "I know." She glanced away. "I'm trying to force myself to eat more. I'm too thin."

"That's good to hear," he said. "What other good things are you up too?"

"Let's see . . . I have a doctor's appointment on Monday. I'm sure he'll give me the green light to drive. I should be back to work on Tuesday."

"You're going to need a ride on Monday." He took a sip of his coffee. "I'll take you."

"You've done enough, Steve. You don't need to do this. Your Monday mornings are insane at work."

True, but I rescheduled my meetings. What time do I need to be here?"

"My appointment is at eight o'clock in the morning."

"I'll be here thirty minutes beforehand."

She wanted to stay angry with Steve, but the kindness he'd shown, yet again, had caught her completely off guard. Guilt over how she'd treated him and the rude way she'd talked to him tugged at her heart.

Caitlynn hurriedly finished her juice. "Okay." She glanced at him, suddenly nervous. "Thanks," and darted from the table. "I need to blow-dry my hair before it turns into a mini-version of Dolly Parton's."

Steve hummed a tune as he cleaned the counter off, stuffing the sack into the waste can. He grabbed the overflowing plastic bag out of the trash container. "I can empty the garbage. Be back in a jiffy."

Caitlynn giggled to herself on the way to the bathroom "Who says jiffy anymore?"

Steve felt lighter inside. His earlier prayers now confirmed not to give up on Caitlynn. She seemed to be pleased to see him and…if he were honest…he'd missed her too.

Everything about Caitlynn appealed to him. She had a special way about her that always kept him guessing, and he loved the challenge . . . well, most of the time.

He tossed the contents into the bin and headed back toward Caitlynn's. His phone rang from inside his pocket.

"Hello?" he asked.

"Hi, Steve, this is Abby," she said, in a high-pitched, frantic tone. "I think Tyler may have broken his arm. He was playing on the trampoline with Hunter, and landed wrong on his arm. He's holding it and crying. The closest emergency room is Littleton Adventist. I can get there in about ten minutes."

"Okay." His heart skipped a beat. *If I were with Ty, this would never have happened.* "I'll meet you there. I'm about thirty minutes away." His voice cracked. "I'm leaving now."

Steve's legs felt like he was running through quicksand to Caitlynn's door. Once inside, he heard the blow dryer, so he rushed into the bathroom. "Caitlynn! I have to go! Tyler may have broken his arm." He bolted out without waiting for a reply.

The drive was a blur as Steve weaved in and out of lanes, trying his best not to get a ticket. Approaching the hospital entrance, he grumbled in frustration as he tried to find parking. And just as he spotted a space far away, someone in the next lane pulled out. He quickly maneuvered his way in.

The emergency room double doors whooshed open. He spotted Tyler in the far corner, cradling his left arm, his face looked as pale as the white wall his head leaned against.

Abby had her arm around Tyler's shoulder. Hunter held his hand. Steve knelt in front of Tyler and brushed back his hair in a soft caress. "You don't look too hot, Tiger. Did you hurt your arm falling off the trampoline?"

Tyler sniffed as his eyes filled with tears. "Uh-huh. I tried to do a flip and fell on my arm."

Abby patted Tyler's shoulder. "He's been super brave waiting here for you. I checked him in, but they wouldn't see him without parental consent." She turned to Steve and pressed her lips together. "I'm so sorry he got hurt. I feel terrible."

"This wasn't your fault." *It's mine.* His mind berated him. I could've avoided the accident if I'd brought Tyler to Caitlynn's house. Instead, I controlled the whole dialog telling her why Tyler shouldn't come to her home. *Why didn't I listen to her?*

"It was an accident. I'm glad you were there to help Tyler. Thank you."

Abby stood. "Hunter, "Let's go tell the nurse that Tyler's father is here."

"That sounds good," Steve said with a nod. He wrapped his arm around his son's shoulder.

Two hours later, they departed with a cast on Tyler's forearm. The x-ray showed the ulna bone had cracked, but thankfully, not a complete fracture.

Steve helped Tyler into the SUV. "I bet you're hungry. Do you want to go to McDonalds?"

Tyler nodded. "I'm starving." He adjusted his sling and frowned. "How long do I have to wear this cast?"

"The doctor said for about three or four weeks. You should have it off the first week of the New Year."

Steve maneuvered the car into the drive-thru, placed their order, and leaned against the headrest, closing his eyes a brief moment while waiting in line. Guilt set in, making his stomach turn sour. Why did his time with Tyler have to involve illness or broken bones?

After they received their food, Steve pulled into the nearest parking spot. Dreading what he was about to do, he sighed deeply. "I need to call your mom and tell her what happened."

Brenda picked up on the first ring. He filled her in on the details. Hearing the anger in her voice, he pushed the phone close to his ear so Tyler couldn't overhear.

"I can't believe this!" she screeched. "Not only will I miss spending Christmas with Tyler because it's your turn, but now he's broken his arm?" Her voice caught.

He tried to think of how she might be feeling. Her little boy broke his arm. *On my watch*. "I know." He lowered his voice. "Look. I'll work something out with you, okay? I know you want to be here for him, and I'm sure he wishes you were here too. I'll make the flight arrangements back to Chicago for the 28th. That's a week earlier than normal. Will that work for you?" He held his breath. Or would she insist Ty fly back before Christmas?

The sound of silence hummed from the other end of the phone. Brenda sniffed. "That will work. I made plans for New Year's Eve, but I'll cancel. Tyler and I will ring in 2004 together."

"Thanks." Not realizing he'd been holding his breath, he exhaled deeply. "I'll call you later with the flight details. Here's Ty." He handed the phone to his son. "Your mom wants to make sure you're okay."

CHAPTER TWENTY-EIGHT

It does not envy
1 CORINTHIANS 13:4

Caitlynn woke before her alarm even buzzed. A huge smile split her face. *Finally, I can get back to what I love.*

Ready in record time, she backed out of her driveway—felt mild discomfort in her abdomen when she twisted—and pulled out onto the road. "I've missed you, Lulu," she said as she patted the steering wheel. "It's good to be back in the driver's seat."

She tightened her grip on the wheel and accelerated toward the highway, driving to work with a cheeky grin—overflowing with happiness. Caitlynn pulled into the parking lot, slid her employee key card through the feeder to open the gate to the parking garage. When she turned the corner, she slammed on the brakes. She pitched forward almost hitting her chest against the steering wheel. A sharp pain jabbed her insides. A black sedan occupied her parking spot. "Are you kidding me?" She shook her head and shrieked, "Tina!"

She whipped her car around to an abrupt stop. The parking area was packed. She jerked the door open, slammed it shut, and stormed into the building. A cold sweat overtook her, immediately followed by heat so intense that she didn't know if she should take her jacket off or pull it tighter around herself.

Wiping the moisture from her forehead, she yanked open the door to the building and stalked to the elevator, pressing the button multiple times as she tried to catch her breath. In the elevator, the overly annoying sound of Baroque music filtered through the hidden speaker. When the elevator dumped her onto the third floor, she marched down the hall to her office.

Her eyes narrowed; her pulse pounded. Papers sat scattered on her desk, along with a laptop and a cup of coffee. Her mouse pad, calendar, and photos piled willy-nilly into a box in the corner of the room. She flung her bag on the chair and left to find Tina—who had a lot of explaining to do.

She stomped over to the receptionist. "Deb, have you seen Tina?"

Deb looked up. "Hi, Caitlynn, I'm glad to see you're back. We missed you."

"Thanks."

Deb nervously shuffled papers on the counter, glancing away.

Caitlynn wondered what she looked like—with sweat dotting her brow and, most likely, a pained look on her face.

"Um, Tina's out on assignment. Why?" Deb asked.

"Her things are on my desk. I thought she knew I was coming back today?" Caitlynn folded her arms across her chest.

Deb's eyes darted nervously. "Caitlynn, um, you don't have an office anymore. You sit in the cubicle next to Tina's."

Digging her fingers into her forearm, she said. "Who authorized this—and why?"

Deb stammered. "I–if it makes you feel any better, that's not Tina's stuff on your desk. It's Carrie's."

"Carrie?" Her voice trembled.

"We've had a few changes recently. The company is trying to cut costs. We leased out the top three floors, and everyone who worked on the fourth floor moved. Carrie took your office since she works full-time as the marketing director. You get a cubicle since you're out of the office on assignment most of the time."

"I don't know what to say. Would have been nice if someone had notified me." Her stomach churned. "This is far from over."

"I'm sorry, Caitlynn." Deb blushed. "It must've been an oversight."

Caitlynn walked slowly back to her office, ignoring the sharp pain still twisting like a knife. She couldn't grab her box of belongings since lifting anything was off limits. She walked around the corner and spied the empty cubicle—barren except for an office chair and a phone. Four high walls separated her from the other cubicle. Sinking into the chair, she stared at the dull gray walls. The desk, ugly and uninviting. Why didn't anyone tell her that she didn't have an office?

She slid out of the chair. It was time to find Steve.

Steve was on the phone when Caitlynn barged into his office, looking worse for the wear. *Oh no.* She sat down opposite him. Her face was a mottled red, her arms crossed, and her foot tapped in triple time.

He quickly finished his conversation and hung up. "What's wrong? Are you ill?" He knew what was wrong, and he was dreading this moment.

She glared at him. "Why didn't you tell me I don't have an office anymore?"

"I'm sorry. I forgot to tell you." That was partly the truth. His motivation for not telling her might have been selfish in hindsight. Things were going well with them, something he didn't want to ruin. He realized now; he probably should have told her.

"Do you know how humiliating it is to come back to work after a difficult medical leave, only to find another person's *stuff* on your desk?" She clenched her jaw.

"I'm sorry, but it's only a desk. It's not as if you lost your job."

"I've had that office for six years," she snapped. "All of my stuff is thrown in a box like it's headed for the trash." Her eyes pooled. "I have an appointment with Jillian today that I need to prepare for." She blinked away her tears.

I blew it. Steve thought. *Why didn't I take five minutes to tell her the news?* "Caitlynn, I should've told you, and I'm sorry. You're not getting fired, and we all missed you—regardless of how this might look to you." Steve stood up. "Come on, let's go get your stuff."

"Why are you bothering now?" she said in an accusatory tone.

He held the door open and followed her out to the hallway. "I'll help you get settled, but I have to get back to work." He held her gaze. "You'd think you've been fired the way you're acting. An office is a place to work. You act like where you work is part of who you are."

She glared. "Of course, it is! If I don't have a job, I don't have any income."

In Caitlynn's former office, Steve picked up the box containing her belongings. "Where to?"

"Around the corner; second cubicle on the right."

He set the box on the desk. "You still have your title. Where you sit shouldn't matter. Besides, your job isn't your life; it's only a part of life." He looked into her eyes. "I can tell you from personal experience that if you let your job become your identity, you'll become self-centered and lose what really matters in life—loving others."

Her face paled. She rubbed her stomach and sat on the chair rather gingerly. A bead of sweat glistened on her forehead. She looked away. "I can really tell how much I'm loved around here."

He squeezed her shoulder softly. "You're right. I handled that poorly. Again, I'm sorry."

He knew she hated sympathy, but it was hard not to reach out when she looked so miserable. But nothing he could say would help. "Caitlynn, don't read too much into this. It's a cost-saving measure. You weren't the only one to lose your office." He glanced at his watch. "I've got to go. I'll see you at two for the staff meeting.

He walked hastily away, praying all the way back to his office. *Lord, show me what I need to do to help her through this—and help her see that there's more to life than her job.*

CHAPTER TWENTY-NINE

Caitlynn met Jillian and her mother at the doctor's office. She brought a small video camera, and whatever she filmed would be transferred to the system, spliced and edited. The nurse motioned Jillian into the exam room to change into a gown. A few minutes later they were escorted inside. Caitlynn pressed the record button on the camera; the red light flashed on, instantly she pushed down her own personal anguish over this tender scene, seemingly tearing her insides to shreds, wondering all over again why she ever agreed to this story in the first place—and went to work.

Jillian rubbed her belly. "Just think, Mom, in a few minutes you'll know if you have a granddaughter or grandson."

Dr. Fischer whisked into the room, followed by his medical assistant, Lena, who closed the door. "Hello, Jillian." He shook her hand. "It's good to see you again." He walked to the sink. The soap he washed his hands with smelled like oranges. His gloves made a smacking noise when he inserted his hands inside. The ultrasound machine hummed quietly. Dr. Fisher rubbed gel on Jillian's belly and picked up the ultrasound wand.

Jillian giggled. "That gel is warm. It feels good."

"We aim to please around here. Let's see what you're having." He pointed at the screen. "There's the heartbeat." He watched the baby on the screen then moved the wand around.

I can't stand the suspense," Jillian cried. "What do you see, Doctor? Is it a boy or a girl?"

"You're having a girl. Everything checks out. The heart looks good—she has a strong heartbeat."

Caitlynn had never before seen a baby in utero. The ultrasound view showed the perfectly formed little one looking quite content. She willed her mind to focus on the task at hand and not her erratic emotions dwelling on what she'd never experience. Instead, she panned the camera for a close up of Jillian.

"I'm so happy, Jillian gushed. "I wanted a little girl to dress up in pretty clothes."

"There's a little more than that to having a baby, Jillian," her mother frowned.

Jillian rolled her eyes. "I know, Mom. Could you just let me enjoy my moment?"

Dr. Fisher interrupted. "Congratulations, Jillian. You can get dressed now, and I'll have the nurse get you a copy of your ultrasound." They hurried out of the room.

Jillian rubbed her baby bump. "Hello, my little Skylar."

Caitlynn stood in the corner, filming. She focused in on Jillian's face; she looked peaceful, almost angelic, as she rubbed her belly. And as hard as Caitlynn tried, she couldn't stop a tear from running down her cheek. Quickly, she brushed it away. She'd never experienced this kind of wonderment. Shutting the camera off, she padded to the door.

Jillian looked up, her face glowing "Mom, I think I feel Skylar moving? I feel this fluttering sensation."

Brushing another tear away, Caitlynn looked over at Peggy and Jillian, thankful that they were both staring at Jillian's belly. "I'm so happy for you. Congratulations. I got some good shots of you both."

Jillian stepped down from the table. "Can you come with us now, Caitlynn? I want to go to Red Robin and celebrate. Plus, I'm craving a burger."

Peggy, bit her nail and looked as if she would rather swim with a shark than celebrate with her daughter.

Caitlynn's heart ached for this unborn child. "Thanks for inviting me. I'd love to come. This baby needs to be celebrated."

"I can't," Peggy sighed, "I took off work to come here and I need to get back. Can you do me a favor and take Jillian home?"

"Mom, it won't take that long." Jillian rolled her eyes. "It's not like they're going to fire you if you don't get back right away.

Don't you want to celebrate? You have a little granddaughter on the way."

Peggy picked lint from her sleeve. "Honestly, I don't know how to feel about any of this. But I know one thing; I can't take advantage of my boss's kindness by returning two hours later than I anticipated."

Caitlynn intervened. "I would love to take Jillian home." She turned to Jillian and said, "Why don't you get dressed. I'll meet you in the waiting room."

Caitlynn followed Peggy out.

"I hope you know that I only want what's best for my daughter," Peggy blurted. "She's at the age where she doesn't consider the impact of her decisions. She thinks the world exists only for her. I'm trying to get her to understand that with choices come consequences. It isn't just about her."

Caitlynn paused. "It's hard at her age. I don't think I learned that lesson until much later."

Peggy's eyes clouded over. "She's going to have a baby, and the only thing she can think about is cute clothes? Why can't she see how much her life will change? She thinks it's all going to stay the same—and no matter how hard I try; I can't seem to convince her of how tough it's going to be with a baby." Peggy blinked back tears as she buttoned up her jacket. "I have to go." She hurried out.

A birthday party was in full swing at Red Robin, kids laughing and screaming all over the place. Caitlynn could feel the start of a headache. "Can you take us to a seat that's not so noisy?" she asked the hostess.

The hostess sat them in a booth tucked in a back corner.

Jillian pointed to the birthday. "Pretty soon, I'll be bringing my daughter to a party here."

Caitlynn grabbed the menu and looked it over. "What's good here?"

Jillian's eyes widened. "You've never been here before?"

"No. This looks to be a family restaurant—not a place I'm likely to frequent."

"You have to try the Red Robin specialty. It's got a fried egg on top of a hamburger. It's delicious."

"Sounds perfectly awful."

"They have strawberry lemonade that's endless. It comes in a pretty goblet. It's so good."

"I think I'll stick to the salad and soup combo and water."

Jillian carefully studied the menu. "I'm staying with my original order: The Red Robin Burger and a chocolate shake."

After they ordered their meals, Caitlynn asked, "What are you going to do after the baby is born?"

"I'm lucky because Skylar is due in May. I graduate that same month, and then I have the summer to spend with her before I start class in the fall."

"What do you plan to major in?"

"I have a full ride to Denver University. I planned to be a lawyer, but instead, I'll go to a vocation school and become a court reporter. I have to decline their offer by July first."

"I'm sorry you have to pass up on the scholarship, but I can see how difficult that would be to care for an infant. Are you going to live with your mom?"

Jillian looked out the window with a dreamy expression. "I'm sure my boyfriend Marcus will come around once he sees the baby. He broke up with me when he found out I was pregnant, but I know he'll reconsider once he sees her…we'll probably get a place. He can go to college and I'll go to work and take classes at night."

Caitlynn listened. Jillian really was living in a fantasyland. In Caitlynn's experience, males did no such thing. She had no doubt this was going to end badly, and she felt sad about it all. "What about Skylar? Who will take care of her while you attend school?"

"I have it all figured out. I'm sure my mom will babysit, or Marcus can watch her." She shrugged. "I'm not worried."

Caitlynn focused on the server placing their food on the table, thankful for the distraction. Peggy was right—her daughter had her head in the clouds.

A mother walked by holding an infant. Jillian twisted to look. "I can't wait to hold my baby," she said.

The familiar pain wrenched at her heart. A thought surfaced out of nowhere—if only she'd made a different choice, she, too, could've had a child. Now she seemed to be the only woman in Denver who would never have a child! "It won't be long. Five more months?"

Jillian took a bite of her burger and swallowed. "If I go full term, it will be the end of May."

"What do your friends think of your pregnancy?"

"Oh, they're so supportive." She smiled wide. "They plan to throw me a baby shower and can hardly wait to babysit!"

Caitlynn took a bite of her chicken tortilla soup, skeptical that any of the plans Jillian was making would come to pass. Still, she wanted to sound supportive. "You seem to have it all under control. When do you want to meet again?"

"I hope we can get together soon. Come to my baby shower." Her eyes sparkled. "I really like you…you accept me for who I am. Please say you'll come?"

Although touched by Jillian's kindness, the last thing she wanted to do was go to a baby shower with a bunch of over zealous high school girls. "I'm not sure, Jillian. That's a long way off. Can I let you know when it gets closer to the day?"

Jillian sighed. "I guess." She slurped her chocolate shake. "I hope you say yes. I told a few of my friends that you and I are friends now. They think it's so cool."

Caitlynn chuckled. She had forgotten how transparent teenagers were. Sometimes they could be a refreshing change.

CHAPTER THIRTY

Steve picked Tyler up from Hunter's house, and they headed to Whole Foods to shop for groceries to make the belated Thanksgiving dinner for Caitlynn.

"What if she says no?" Tyler threw two cans of green beans in the cart.

Steve shrugged. "Then I guess we eat turkey for a week."

Tyler picked up a small cellophane-wrapped package. "Daddy, let's get some mistletoe."

"You do know what you're supposed to do when you stand under mistletoe?" Steve wiggled his brows.

Tyler's cheeks turned pink. "Yep. You kiss." He cracked a smile.

Steve threw it into the cart. "I think I'd better keep an eye on you. What a flirt!"

Tyler giggled. "Mom bought some. Sometimes she stands under the mistletoe for a long time waiting for me to figure it out just so she can get a kiss. It's so funny."

"That sounds fun. I suppose dads can kiss their sons under the mistletoe too…"

"No. Just moms and girlfriends."

He pretended to look disappointed. "Okay, what's next on the list?"

"The stuff for sweet potato pie."

They bought the rest of the items on the list and loaded the groceries into the car. As they drove, Steve said, "Caitlynn will be shocked when she finds out our plan. Tyler, what are you going to say when you call?"

"I'm gonna remind her we were supposed to eat chili cheese dogs but then I got sick. I'm gonna ask her if it would be okay if I make her dinner."

"What will you say you're having?"

"Pizza. My second favorite food."

"That sounds like a great diversion tactic."

Tyler bounced in his seat. "Yeah, and then she'll come over, and we can surprise her with a turkey dinner."

Steve chuckled as he called Caitlynn and handed over his son the phone. When Caitlynn answered, Tyler was so excited to ask her to dinner, Steve said a silent prayer she wouldn't have any plans for Saturday. Tyler beamed. "She's coming. She said she couldn't make it until four o'clock because she has to buy some baby clothes. Is she having a baby?"

Steve stiffened. "Nope. She's on assignment, taping a segment for a news program."

"On babies? How boring. My friend has a baby brother, and he says all the baby does is cry and sleep and poo."

"You're hilarious." He ruffled his son's hair. "Let's hope it's a bit more exciting than that."

"Did you get the Christmas tree and the decorations out of storage?" Tyler asked.

"Yeah! We're going to be busy this weekend. You up for this?"

Tyler's entire body wriggled, exclaiming, "I can't wait!"

Earlier Saturday, Steve hung the mistletoe by the front door and helped Tyler decorate the tree. The stockings hung from the fireplace mantel. A fire blazed in the hearth, warming the living room, as Christmas music played softly in the background. The scent of roasted turkey filled the air and mingled with the intoxicating aroma of cherry and pumpkin pie baking in the oven. Every dish they ate on Thanksgiving Day was prepared, from the green bean casserole to the sweet potato pie and warm, flaky rolls.

Four o'clock rolled around, and Caitlynn was right on time. She pulled into the circular drive and parked.

"She's here!" Tyler raced outside to the porch. Steve watched from the foyer. She was carrying a small package and a white poinsettia. "Hi, Ms. Caitlynn, can I carry that for you?"

"What a little gentleman! Thanks!" she said with a smile.

Tyler escorted her inside as Steve stepped back allowing them space.

"Daddy!" Tyler giggled and pointed. "You're under the mistletoe!"

Caitlynn glanced up and laughed nervously. "We can pretend it's not there..."

"Oh, no!" Tyler's cheeks flamed. "You have to kiss her—it's the rules."

Steve quirked a brow and looked at Caitlynn. Her face turned as bright as the red cellophane covering the flowerpot. A light dusting of snow clung to her hair and cream-colored coat. She looked like an enchanting snow queen in the soft light. All he had to do was bend down and . . .

"Tyler, how about you give Caitlynn a kiss instead?"

Caitlynn stooped low and said, "Tyler, I would love a kiss from you." He blushed a redder hue and landed a quick peck on her cheek.

She smiled, squeezing his shoulder. "How sweet of you." She stood and said, "That's not pizza I smell."

Tyler jumped up and down, and the poinsettia leaves bounced wildly. "Surprise!"

Steve took the plant before his son caused any more damage. Tyler continued in a singsong voice, "I was sad that you were in the hospital on Thanksgiving, so I asked my dad if we could make you a surprise dinner.

"This is the most thoughtful gesture I've ever received, Tyler. I don't know what to say." She handed her gift to him. "This is for you, but you have to wait until Christmas."

Tyler ran to the tree and placed the package on top of the gold-trimmed tree skirt. "Thanks, Ms. Caitlynn! I can't wait!"

She pointed her finger at him pretending to be serious. "No peeking or shaking!"

Steve helped her out of her jacket, brushing his hands over her shoulders, his heart beat erratically. He steadied his breath, hung it up, discreetly appreciating the way her dark wash jeans hugged every curve as did the crème-colored sweater. He hurried to control his racing heart as he ushered them toward the kitchen.

They passed the living room. Steve watched Caitlynn admiring the Christmas stockings, then her gaze cut to the painting of a majestic Mountain Range with a cowboy riding a horse in the distance above the fireplace, "I see you still like horses. Your home looks like a lodge."

Tyler piped up. "He has a picture of his horse, Boo, on the wall. Do you want to see him?"

Steve intervened. "Let's go to the kitchen. Dinner's ready."

Tyler charged ahead. "Okay! Last one to the table has to do the dishes!"

To Steve's surprise, Caitlynn ran, trying to beat Tyler. She scurried into a chair, but Tyler was a step ahead and sat seconds before her. "I won!" he shouted.

Caitlynn's laughter bubbled out. "No fair! You had a head start."

Steve lagged behind. "No fair! I was carrying the plant."

"Sorry Dad," Tyler teased. "Dish duty!"

"Ty, can you put the poinsettia on the hearth, but not too close to the fire?" Ty hopped out of his seat and grabbed the plant.

Steve pulled the tray of rolls from the oven and turned on the stove to warm the pan filled with gravy. "Dinner should be ready in just a few minutes."

He saw the look of wonder on Caitlynn's face as she stared at the dining room table set with china, glowing amidst the soft candlelight. Goblets of water sparkled, shimmering softly. Steve put the potholders on the counter. He could feel her eyes on him.

"I don't know what to say," she said. "No one has been this kind to me in a very long time. To think that you wanted to make up for the fact that I didn't get a Thanksgiving dinner—"

His heart skipped another beat. "I'd like to take the credit, but to be honest, it was Tyler's idea. He wanted to make this for you. I just provided the opportunity and the know-how." He stared into her eyes.

Tyler galloped into the kitchen. "I know what you got me. I can tell."

Steve stirred the gravy and wondered what would've happened if Tyler hadn't come into the kitchen right then.

"Okay, Mr. Smarty-pants," Caitlynn said, "if you guess it, I'll let you open it."

"It's a video game!"

"Could be," she shrugged, "but I'm the best ever at keeping a secret, and I'm not spilling the beans."

Steve placed the rolls into a wooden bowl. "Let's figure out your gift after we eat. I bet you're starving."

Tyler rushed to the dining table and plopped onto a chair. "I am. Let's eat."

Dish by dish, Steve pulled the turkey, the stuffing, the green bean casserole, and the sweet potato pie out of the oven and set them on the table.

"What can I do?" Caitlynn asked. She stood next to him.

Steve breathed in the scent of her flowery perfume, which smelled better to him than the meal he'd prepared. "You can help me carry all this to the buffet in the dining room." He nodded at the rolls. "Can you grab those?"

She reached for the rolls just as he grabbed the crock of mashed potatoes. His arm brushed against hers. A current coursed through his body, and his breath stilled as he gazed into her eyes and stayed there. Her face glowed like that of an angel on the top of the Christmas tree. Her perfume lingered in the air, and he inhaled deeply. Everything about tonight was perfect, and—miracle of miracles—she seemed to genuinely like Tyler. He couldn't tear his eyes away from her, and for a brief moment, he wished it could be the three of them at the table for more than just this meal.

Steve stepped away quickly. "It's time to eat."

Caitlynn seemed content to ignore his touch. Walking over to the table, she asked, "Ty, how long will you be here?"

"I get two weeks off for Christmas!"

"What are you going to do?"

"Hang out with Hunter," He said as he snatched a roll from the basket.

Steve finished bringing the food to the table and glanced around. "Everything looks like it's ready." He sat down.

Tyler grabbed his hand. "Take Ms. Caitlynn's hand so we can pray."

Steve wasn't so sure. Could she tell his feelings for her were in turmoil? Tyler already had his eyes closed, and his head bowed. Steve glanced at Caitlynn, then reached across the table. Her small hand enclosed softly around his. A tingle moved from his fingers to his heart just as it had years ago. He prayed. "Dear Jesus, thank you for all the blessings in my life. I'm thankful for my son, my job, and that we can share this wonderful meal with Caitlynn—and we pray that she grows stronger with each new day." He bushed his thumb over her palm. "Amen."

###

Caitlynn closed her eyes for a moment—desperately trying to control the spark that threatened to burn out of control when Steve held her hand. *What is happening?*

She picked up her fork, savoring a few bites. "This is all so delicious, Steve."

"Thanks. It's my pleasure. By the way, what are your plans for Christmas?

"I'm going to Scottsdale to see my mom. She retired there about six years ago. She heard the dry heat might be better for her arthritis, but so far it hasn't worked."

"Can't she have surgery and get better just like you?" Tyler took a bite of his roll.

"Not with arthritis, sweetie." Caitlynn quickly changed the subject. "Do you like to ski?"

"No, I don't like to ski—I love it! Dad, remember when we were skiing around the trees, and some guy hit you from behind?"

Steve nodded. "How could I forget? I was so thankful he didn't hit you, or I would probably have gone to jail for assault."

"Dad was so mad! He hunted that guy down at the lodge and told him he had no business tree-skiing if he couldn't stay in control."

Whoa! What did he say?"

Steve scooped a forkful of stuffing. "He apologized. I hope he took my advice. Do you still ski?"

She tried to think of an answer to such a simple question—except it wasn't so simple because she'd rather not ski at all than ski alone. During their junior year, she and Steve would take weekend trips during the ski season, and she had very fond memories of skiing down the mountain then turning right back around to do it all over again. There was nothing quite like skiing in Colorado. "Yes, but I don't go as often as I'd like."

Tyler grabbed a turkey leg and took a giant bite. "Why don't you come with us?" he said with a mouthful of turkey.

She was touched by his generosity to include other people in his fun. "Thanks, Tyler, but I can't hit the slopes for a while. I have to get better, remember?"

"When are you going to be better?"

"In a couple of months."

Tyler counted with his fingers. "December January February. You're going to be better by February." He grinned ear to ear. "Hey, Dad—can we go skiing with Caitlynn in February?"

Steve pointed his fork at him. "First of all, don't talk with your mouth full. Secondly, how do you know Caitlynn wants to go with us?"

Tyler's smile was so contagious that she couldn't say no. "You're very nice to invite me. Let's see what happens as we get closer to the date, shall we?"

Tyler waved his turkey leg in the air. "Okay, but you probably won't be able to keep up with me."

"Oh yeah, I think I can hang with you. I'm a pretty good skier."

"Whatever." His eyes twinkled mischievously. "You might be good . . . for a girl."

Caitlynn laughed and turned to Steve. "What are you teaching this kid?"

"Sorry, I can't take any credit...just stating the facts."

"Okay, okay. I get it." She bantered back. "You're issuing me a challenge. I can see that." She teased. "I guess we're going skiing in February."

After dinner, Caitlynn helped clear the table. Steve refused her offer to wash dishes, as he and Tyler loaded the dishwasher. When they finished, Tyler said, "Can I open Ms. Caitlynn's gift? Please?" he pleaded.

"It's not up to me."

Tyler jumped up and down in excitement. "Is it okay, Ms. Caitlynn?"

She squeezed his shoulder. "It's fine with me."

Tyler ran into the living room and slid on the wood floor all the way to the tree.

Steve called out, "Wait for us. We're going to get some pumpkin pie first. Then we will watch you open your gift."

"Daddy, I ate too many rolls," he yelled. "I'm full."

Steve placed a slice of pie on a plate. "Here you go." He offered her the plate as he picked up the can of whipped cream.

She rubbed her stomach. "I'm so full; I don't think I can eat any more."

"I watched you eat your dinner, and as usual, you ate like a bird." He looked at her with concern. "Please try a few bites."

Caitlynn took the plate from him. "Okay, but no whipped cream."

Steve dispensed a pile of whipped cream onto his pie. "Okay, more for me."

"That has to be four or five inches high." Caitlynn chuckled. "It looks like you want a little pumpkin pie with your whipped cream!"

"Hmm," he joked. "Exactly right!"

They sat on the sofa in the living room. Tyler already had his gift in his hand. He looked at his dad, pleading.

Steve nodded. "Let her rip."

Tyler tore the paper in the blink of an eye. "Awesome! It's the newest game for Wii."

Steve raised his brow. "How did you get your hands on that game? It's been sold out for weeks."

Caitlynn flashed a smile. "I have a connection. Before you came, I did a story on a video game inventor. He knew someone who knew somebody else, you know..."

"Can we play it now? Please?" Tyler begged.

"You go ahead, and we'll watch while we eat."

Caitlynn took a few small bites. The pie had the perfect balance of cinnamon and nutmeg. "Did you make the pie, Steve?"

"Hardly. I bought them from Whole Foods."

She glanced at the fire in the hearth. Two merry-looking snowman hangers on the mantle held their red-and-white stockings. The tree lights twinkled next to the bay window. Tyler sat playing his video game while Steve relaxed on the couch eating his pie.

Her heart ached as she set her plate on the table. Sitting here was like watching actors perform on stage while she waited, stuck behind the velvet curtain, wishing to be part of the cast. It was always her and her mother. Her father was out of the picture by the time she was nine years old. No Dad, no siblings, no extended family. Holidays were spent with her mother; nothing like the big family gatherings she watched on Christmas movies.

"I have to go." She stood.

"Already?" Tyler asked without taking his eyes off the TV. "I wanted to show you my room and all my toys."

Her breath caught in her throat. *If I stay any longer, I'm never going to want to leave.* She walked quickly toward the door. "I need a rain check on that. I, um, I'm getting tired."

Steve and Tyler walked her to the door. Tyler giggled, "Look, you and Ms. Caitlynn are under the mistletoe again."

Steve looked up. "You're right."

Before she had a chance to protest, Steve gently wrapped his arms around her and kissed her on the cheek. Caitlynn's heart raced wildly, and she knew without looking that her cheeks were scarlet. His kiss left a lingering caress behind. She wanted to lash out and say something to break the moment, but her mind shut off at the warmth of his touch. He released her. She swallowed and stuttered, "Th–thanks for dinner. It was a great surprise. I loved it."

Caitlynn swooped down and hugged Tyler. He hugged her back tightly. His hair smelled as fresh as the air after a summer rain. It filled her senses, leaning in for a few seconds before holding him at arm's length. "I'll see you in February. Make sure you practice. I don't want to see you cry when I beat you down the mountain."

Tyler nodded. "Okay. I'll surprise you by how good I am. You just wait."

Steve held her coat. Her arms trembled as she eased into the sleeves. She didn't button the jacket so they wouldn't know her fingers were shaking.

When Caitlynn returned home, cold and alone, she flipped on every light and collapsed on the couch under the throw. No red-and-white Christmas stockings were gracing the mantel. She never bothered much with the traditions of Christmas. It was such a hassle to put it up and then pack it all away again afterward. Besides, it wasn't practical to have a tree when she went to her mother's every year for Christmas.

Steve's house decked out—festive and bright. Tyler bragged about how he practically trimmed the tree all by himself. It wasn't hard to see how happy they were together. And Tyler had orchestrated the idea for dinner. He was such a great kid.

Steve seemed to be on his best behavior . . . except for the kiss. She touched her cheek and glanced around the room again. Nothing Christmassy about her home—more like barren, dull, and ordinary. She could go shopping and decorate, but why bother? There was no one to share it with. She recalled Tyler's cute giggle at one of his silly jokes. The only sound she heard now was the furnace fan kicking on in the hallway.

She traced the outline of her scar through her sweater, closed her eyes and imagined a tree in the corner decorated with twinkling lights and shiny ornaments, filled underneath with brightly wrapped presents for her child.

She bit her lip. No child. No loving relationship she could lavish with gifts. Her scar still ached if she pressed. She opened her eyes and grabbed the prescription bottle sitting on the coffee table and took a pain pill.

The plan had been to ignore Steve. Why didn't she say no to dinner? And whatever possessed her to say she would go skiing? She wrapped the throw around her shoulders and broke the silence. "What was I thinking? I should've thanked them for dinner and bolted without a backward glance." Now she knew what it would be like to have her own family, and it broke her to pieces.

CHAPTER THIRTY-ONE

Jillian stuck a red bow on the last of the presents. A pile of brightly colored boxes and bags surrounded her on the couch, the result of all the cutting, taping and wrapping. Her mom's CD played softly in the background as the familiar tune of, White Christmas, filled the living room.

The Christmas tree in the corner sparkled with multi-colored lights and festive ornaments. Her mother helped her make some of the older ornaments when she was in grade school. Jillian marveled at her first-grade picture enclosed in a green felt, bell-shaped ornament, complete with sparkly brick-a-brack. She remembered making it in art class and proudly giving it to her mom.

Back then, it was important to have her mother's approval. She loved her mom. But what she thought regarding her and the baby didn't matter. Rubbing her tummy, she caught her breath. *Is that Skylar's fist or a foot?* "Hey, you! Settle down." She tenderly poked the baby.

The door opened, and her mother rushed in from the cold, balancing plastic bags full of groceries in each hand. She shut the door with the back of her foot, hurried to the counter, dropped the bags down, and shook her fingers. "Ow! I don't know why I think I can carry so many at once."

Jillian sprang from the couch. "I didn't know you were shopping. I would've put a few more items on the list."

"I know." Her mom teased, "That's exactly why I didn't tell you."

Jillian rooted through one of the bags and pulled out some BBQ potato chips. "Yum. Did you get any other good stuff?"

"Hey!" No peeking in the bags... a few stocking stuffers may be in there for you."

"All right, I'll go—but I'm taking the bag of chips." Jillian pulled a bottle of water out of the fridge, plopped down on the couch, tore open the bag, and watched her mom. "What are we having tomorrow for Christmas Eve dinner?"

"The store had a great sale on prime rib, so I splurged and bought one. We can have a nice dinner on Christmas Eve, and I'll make French Dip sandwiches for Christmas Day!"

"That sounds so good. We haven't had a dinner like that in a long time."

Her mom put away the last of the refrigerated items, joined Jillian on the couch, and grabbed a handful of chips. "I know. It's been a tough time for both of us." Her mom's eyes held hers. "I want to have a nice Christmas with you and Nana." She munched on a chip and slowly swallowed. "What do you think? Can we get along for the next 48 hours without arguing?"

"Mom, I wish you would just be happy for me. I have everything under control. Once Marcus sees our baby, he'll take one look at Skylar and realize he's made a huge mistake. He'll come back. We'll make it work. You just wait and see."

Her mom gently stroked Jillian's hair. "I'm serious about wanting peace in our life for two days. It's Christmas and I don't want to fight. I'm not going to say a thing. If that's what you think about Marcus, it's your prerogative."

Jillian couldn't remember the last time her mom played with her hair. She stared at the ornament that held her picture. Would Skylar look like her? *Will I play with my daughter's hair?* Jillian smiled, "Okay, I'll try if you will. She stood. "My shift tonight at the dry cleaner is only a few hours from 4:00-7:00, so I have to get ready—but six months from now make sure you apologize to me when everything works out just like I planned." She gave her mom a quick hug.

###

On Christmas Eve morning, Jillian woke up, showered and dressed, then padded into the kitchen to make her morning bowl of oatmeal. Oatmeal seemed to be the only food she could stomach after swallowing the horse pill her doctor called prenatal vitamins. She made the instant oatmeal and poured the milk, cinnamon, and sugar over the top. Sitting at the table, she peeked outside. *No snow.*

Part of her wanted a white Christmas, but on the other hand, the roads were clear, which helped with her busy day delivering gifts to her friends. Traditionally, they exchanged gifts the day school ended for Christmas break, but this year, she'd had to wait until the next pay period to buy presents. Her last paycheck had gone to purchase maternity clothes—since at four months, she could no longer fit into her jeans and skin-tight T-shirts.

Her mom shuffled into the kitchen in her worn-out slippers, and frayed pink terry robe that looked like it needed to find a new home in the rag bag. She grabbed a mug out of the cabinet and filled her cup from the coffee maker she religiously programmed each night. Sitting down next to Jillian, she took a sip and said, "You're already dressed to go out—what's on your agenda today?"

"I'm delivering what I bought to my friends. It'll probably take most of the day."

"How about an early dinner and afterward watch a video?"

"That's fine, but we still have to open one gift on Christmas Eve…it's tradition!"

"I thought you might've outgrown that by now?" Her mom picked up her cup about to take a sip.

"Never!" Jillian grabbed her bowl and spoon, rinsed them off, and set them in the sink.

"This is going to be a great day. I love giving to my friends."

She darted over to her mom and kissed her silky-soft cheek. "See you later."

###

Jillian rang the bell at Sasha's, their dog barked like he was going to tear her into tiny pieces. The door opened. Sasha's mom held their giant black lab, Roscoe, by the collar. "Hey, Jillian! Come in out of the cold."

"Thanks, Mrs. Kane. Is Sasha here?"

Sasha's mom crunched her brows together. "No, I'm sorry. She was called into work this morning. She was supposed to be off today, but one of the kids at Wendy's was a no-show. She gets home at five tonight. You could try coming back later."

"I can't. My mom and I have plans." Annoyed that Sasha didn't bother to call to say she wouldn't be home—Jillian handed the brightly wrapped box to Sasha's mom and faked a smile. "That's okay. Can you give this to her?"

"How nice of you to do this, Jilly. Of course, I will. I'm sure my daughter will call you later." Her eyes honed in on Jillian's stomach. "You're finally starting to show. I think you're going to be one of those who don't get very big until the last month of pregnancy. You take care and have a Merry Christmas."

"You too, Mrs. Kane. She turned and walked quickly to the car, hustled inside, and turned the key to start the engine.

Super irritated that Sasha was working, she frowned. She'd bought Sasha her favorite perfume. Every time they went to the mall, Sasha went to the perfume counter at Dillard's and then sprayed *Angel* all over herself until you could hardly stand near her. She had wanted to watch Sasha open it.

Trying hard not to be upset, Jillian put the car in drive and headed down the street toward Cassie's. Twenty minutes later, she knocked at Cassie's front door.

Jillian heard loud footsteps race down the stairs, and the door burst open.

Cassie wore a bright orange top, only a shade or two lighter than her shoulder-length red hair. Her jeans had rips strategically placed above the knee by the designer.

Cassie's green eyes widened. "Hi, Jillian! I've been waiting for you all morning. What took you so long?" Cassie ushered her up the stairs. "Let's go to my room."

Jillian giggled, holding Cassie's package and following her friend's lead. "I came as soon as I could."

Cassie opened the door and plunked down at the head of the bed. Jillian took her usual spot at the foot, then stretched out her arm to hand over the present.

"Here you go, Cassie. I can't wait another second. You have to open it now."

In less than three seconds, Christmas wrap was torn open. "You got me the M.A.C lip-gloss set! Oh, you're sneaky. You saw me ooh and ahh over it when we went shopping two weeks ago."

"Yes." Jillian smiled ear to ear. "Surprise!"

"Thanks, but you shouldn't have." Cassie stared at Jillian's bulging belly. "You have enough to worry about right now without buying me a gift."

Jillian turned her head to hide her disappointment. She'd first met Sasha, Cassie, and Tori in the seventh grade, and they had always exchanged something at Christmas. Did they forget this year? So far, she hadn't gotten a single present in return. Of course, she knew it was better to give than receive, but geez…why didn't they tell her that nobody was exchanging gifts this year?

Cassie leaned toward Jillian and rubbed her tummy with a quick stroke. "You're getting big. It's as hard as a rock." Her eyes opened wide. "You won't be able to hide being preggers when break is over. The whole school is going to stare at you."

Jillian shrugged. "Who cares? They've already been gawking at me like they've never seen a pregnant girl before. Did they forget about Marty?"

"Who?" Cassie had a blank look in her eyes. "Oh, yeah… that was last year."

"Let them talk. I don't care." Jillian placed her hand across her stomach. "I can't wait for Skylar to be born. We're going to be inseparable—except when my mom babysits so I can go to school and work."

Cassie grabbed her cell phone off her bedside table, looked at the display, and frowned. "I've waited the last two hours for Logan to wake up and call me. We're supposed to talk about what he plans to wear to the Snowflake Dance in January."

Jillian grimaced. She had gone last year with Marcus. She'd danced until her feet hurt and then flung her shoes to the side of the gym and danced some more. "You're going to have a great time. I remember—"

"You wanna see my dress?" Cassie bounced off the bed and opened her closet door. A beautiful winter-white formal shimmered with translucent beads sewn across the front, the princess-cut gown was covered with a layer of flowing chiffon. "Isn't it money?"

Jillian walked over to caress the silky fabric. She brushed her hand lightly across the beads. "Money? Are you kidding? It's the most beautiful gown I've ever seen. Honestly, it looks like you could get married in something like this."

Cassie laughed. "You say the craziest things. I'm going to a formal, not getting married. I don't want to settle down for a long time. I plan to make something of—" her words trailed off.

"What? You don't think I plan to make something of myself?" Jillian crossed her arms. "I will. Just because I'm having a baby doesn't mean I've ruined my future."

Cassie touched her shoulder. "I didn't mean it that way. Of course, you'll be fine."

Jillian could feel her eyes burning. *Don't cry.* "Skylar and I will be more than fine."

"Come on, Jilly." Cassie's eyes darted from her dress to Jillian's. "I didn't mean it. Why don't we talk about the baby shower coming up?" Her forced smile didn't reach her eyes.

"Let's talk about it another time." Jillian grabbed her keys. "You need to talk to Logan anyway. I have to go." She flung the door wide open.

"Okay." Cassie followed. "But don't be mad at me. I know things will work out for you. I just have a lot on my mind right now with Christmas and the dance." Cassie gave Jillian a quick hug. "Merry Christmas, Jillian, and thanks for the lip-gloss set."

The car heater blasted warmth as she drove to her best friend Tori's house. She wanted to scream. What had happened to her friends? They were supposed to be on her side. All they seemed to care about was this stupid formal coming up. And why did Sasha go to work? She knew they were meeting today. There was no reason why she had to work. Did she do it on purpose?

The heater suffocated Jillian until she could barely breathe. She flipped off the fan, pulling the gloves from her hands and unbuttoning her coat. Beads of sweat formed on her brow. *Tori won't be like Sasha and Cassie.* She stopped in Tori's driveway, grabbed the last gift, and slammed the car door shut.

Jillian rapped her knuckles on the door twice—so they knew it was her—and stepped inside.

"There you are." Tori gave her a quick hug and rubbed her belly. "I think you've grown bigger since I saw you last week."

Nausea came so fast, Jillian held on to the doorjamb as a wave of dizziness hit her.

Tori held her arm. "Are you okay? Your face is turning as white as Scooter's fur." Hearing his name, her snowy-white Bichon Frise ran and jumped on Jillian's leg."

"No, Scooter." Tori scooped him up. She guided Jillian to the nearest chair. "Come sit down. Mom! Come quick and bring Jillian some water!"

Jillian faintly heard the faucet turn on. Tori's mom ran over with a glass of water, sloshing some over the side. "What's wrong?"

Tori's mom and her best friend gaped at her like she might not survive the next few seconds. Prickly heat started at her chest and spread to her face. Part of it was from the pregnancy, no doubt, but most of it was from deep embarrassment. If there was one thing she avoided at all costs, it was making a scene.

Tori's mom held the glass out. "Take a drink, Jilly, you'll feel better."

Dutifully, Jillian drank. "Thanks, Mrs. Butler. I just stood up too quickly when I got out of the car, that's all."

Mrs. Butler's eyes bored into hers. "Jilly, if this keeps happening you need to tell your doctor. Okay?"

Jillian took another sip and nodded. "Don't worry; I'm fine now." She handed the glass back. "Thanks."

"I'm baking cookies. If you need me, just holler." Mrs. Butler bent down and picked up Scooter. "Come on, little guy, you can keep me company." She made her way to the kitchen.

Tori's eyes were as round as CD's. "Wow, Jilly, you scared me to death. I thought you were going to keel over."

"Sorry." Jillian held out the gift to her friend. "Merry Christmas."

Tori grinned, pulling the tape off the Santa Paper ever so slowly before sliding out the box. Snapping the lid open, she stared at the sterling silver chain and heart-shaped charm. "I can't believe you remembered! We must've looked at this, what, four months ago?"

Jillian's eyes widened. "I bought one too, so we both have one. It says, best friends, on the back of the heart."

Tori carefully removed the necklace, barely glancing at the inscription, she unfastened the latch, placed the chain around her neck, and beamed. "What do you think? I bet it will go perfectly with my dress for the dance."

Jillian's voice faded. "It will look great." Her glance darted over to the tree where, stacked underneath, lay beautifully wrapped gifts adorned with fancy ribbons and bows.

Tori stood quickly. "Just a minute, I'll be right back." She skipped down the hall.

Jillian waited; her breath caught in her throat. Hopefully, it was the latest CD from The Red Hot Chili Peppers, sold out when they'd gone together to Best Buy.

Her friend came running back, carrying a paper plate wrapped in plastic wrap. "Here you go. My mom made some Christmas cookies. Merry Christmas!"

###

At home again, Jillian slammed the door, trudged over to the counter, and flung the plate of cookies down. She ripped open the plastic wrap, yanked out a green, tree-shaped Spritz cookie, and popped the entire thing in her mouth.

"How was your gift-giving?" her mom asked, "Did you have a good time?"

"Let's see…" Jillian grabbed another cookie and gestured in the air. "If you count a no-show, a friend who has no clue, and no gifts from anyone in return as fun, then yes, it was loads of fun." She bit into the cookie and willed away her tears.

"Oh, sweetie, I'm so sorry. Come sit." Her mom's eyes softened. "I was just going to make some hot cocoa. Let's talk, okay?"

Jillian scooted out of the barstool and sank into a chair. "I'm not sure I have friends anymore." Another stupid tear rolled down her cheek.

Her mom handed her a mug of cocoa and sat next to her. "Why do you say that? You always have a great time with your friends."

"I used to, but now all they can talk about is the stupid dance. Why are they so self-centered? They have no clue how *I* might be feeling." She took a sip. "It's not like I'm going to the dance." She shook her head in disgust. "They're so insensitive. All they can think of is themselves."

"They're just excited, that's all. They still love you." She patted Jillian's arm.

"Oh yeah?" She sniffed; fresh tears rolled down her cheeks. "We've bought each other something for Christmas since seventh grade. If they love me so much, why didn't they buy me anything this year?"

"You said it yourself. The Winter Formal's coming up. It's January 15th, isn't it?"

"Yeah, so?" Jillian grabbed a tissue and wiped away tears.

Her mom took a drink. "How can they afford to when the winter formal is in three weeks?"

Jillian stared into the cup, inhaling the sweet smell of chocolate. "I guess you're right," she mumbled.

"Honey, I don't want you to get mad, but I have to say this. You don't buy for your friends expecting gifts in return—and you should never buy a gift hoping to buy friendship."

Jillian rolled her eyes. "I know, Mom." She glanced away. "I just wanted it to be like last Christmas. We had so much fun, but now it seems as if we're all going separate directions. At least they seem to be excited about the baby shower. It's a long way off, but I know that will bring us together again." She wrapped her hands around her mug, excited. "I can't wait! And then when the baby comes, they'll have so much fun helping me with Skylar."

###

Jillian laid her napkin next to her plate. "Mom, that was yumm-o. I hope I can cook as good as you someday."

"I'm glad you liked it. Help me with the dishes—then we'll open a gift."

"You don't have to ask me twice!" Jillian grabbed her plate, utensils, and glass, bolted out of her chair, and turned quickly to the sink. "Ouch!"

Jillian dropped the dishes on the counter, scattering the silverware as she put her hand on her lower back.

Her mom rushed over. "What's wrong?"

"Ow! A terrible pain goes from my back all the way down my leg."

"Here, hold on to me, and I'll help you to the couch."

Jillian clung tightly to her mom, then slowly sank into the cushions. "What is this?"

"You've hurt your sciatic nerve. You have to be careful when you're pregnant. Your joints get loose from all the extra hormones. When I was pregnant with you, I bent down to pick up a sock and threw my back out for a week."

Her mom walked to the kitchen and filled a Ziplock bag with ice. "Here, honey. Put this where it hurts. I'll go start a warm bath for you—but not too hot; you don't want to cook the baby!"

"Mom…" Jillian rolled her eyes.

"Sorry," her mom hid a smile. "I couldn't resist. I just think it's so funny what pregnant women can and cannot eat or do. The list is so long these days. Being pregnant is stressful enough, but all these rules add fuel to the fire." She squeezed Jillian's shoulder softly. "I'll get the bath started and clean up the kitchen. You take care of your back."

An hour later, Jillian sat on the couch, still pressing a bag of ice to her back. She called down the hall. "Mom, are you ready to open your present?"

Her mom bustled into the living room with a huge smile on her face. She was holding a large bright red gift bag that was overflowing with dark green tissue paper. She sat next to Jillian. "I sure am."

"Here." Jillian said eagerly. "You, first!"

As her mom unveiled the item, she asked, "When did you have time to do this?" Her eyes glistened.

Jillian pasted a mischievous grin on her face. "Tori and I went together to get our senior portraits done back in August."

The look of appreciation on her mom's face made Jillian's heart warm.

"It's beautiful." The photo of Jillian's senior picture also had an inset of her 1st-grade picture. She set the frame on the side table. "How did you get the two pictures in the same photo?"

"That was easy. My friend, Kyle, is in PhotoShop at school, so I asked him to do this for me. He's a wiz at all this technical computer stuff."

"Thank you, Jilly. I couldn't ask for anything more!" Peggy hugged her daughter tightly. "Your turn!"

The loving warmth of her mom's embrace still lingered. "Jillian pulled out one sheet of tissue after another. "Is there anything in here?"

"Yes, keep going." Her mom flashed a smile.

"Do I need to dig to China?" Jillian's hand struck a hard object. "Got it."

She lifted the surprise out of the bag. "You got me a digital camera!"

"I thought you might want to use it tomorrow—and you'll definitely need a nice camera in a few months." She looked directly at Jillian's baby bump.

"Oh, Mom. This is great! It's small enough to fit in my backpack."

"Uh-huh. And I got one that's supposed to be shock-absorbent. Hopefully, it will last and take quality pictures."

Happiness flooded her soul. This was so much better than the hostility these last few months. Jillian leaned in, "Thanks, Mom," and kissed her cheek.

"You're welcome. "Do you want to watch a video now? I bought us, The Lord of the Rings: The Fellowship of the Ring."

The next morning, Jillian sat next to her mother and grandmother, amazed at all the great Christmas gifts she had received. She was still in shock over the camera—until she opened the iPod and gasped. She knew how much they were. Where did her mom get the money for such an expensive item? She gave her mom and Nana huge hugs and kisses. "Thanks!"

She held up her new camera. "Say 'Merry Christmas!'"

Both her mom and her grandmother groaned and said, in unison, "No more pictures."

"Okay, but I had to take a picture of Mom with her new duds. This is a big moment for us. No more old raggedy robe and slippers."

Her mom wrapped the baby-blue robe close around herself. "I love them, Jillian! Thanks!"

"Believe me when I tell you, I love them too," she joked back.

Nana chimed in. "Speaking of love, I love my new sweater, Jilly. Thank you."

Jillian munched a Spritz. "You're welcome, Nana. I'm going to check out my iPod. Let me know when the sandwiches are ready." She rubbed her abdomen. "Ouch! I think Skylar is going to be a kickboxer the way she's pelting me."

CHAPTER THIRTY-TWO

Steve threw the ball into play, ran to midcourt, and made a three-point shot.

Lee said, "You're in the zone, man."

"Things are good. Tyler comes home for Presidents' Day in two weeks. I have the station running the way I want it, and I love living in Denver."

Forty minutes later, they sat in the bleachers and toweled off.

Lee asked, "Whatever came of your conversation with Caitlynn at the hospital?"

Steve stared at his gym shoes. "I talked to her, but let's just say she isn't willing to forgive me. Our relationship—if you can call it that—is so complicated." He swiped his hand through his hair. "I can tell she's fond of Tyler. She only tolerates me."

Stuffing his towel into his duffel bag, Steve continued. "Tyler made her a surprise dinner. He called her and set up the whole thing. I bet she wouldn't have come if I had done the invite. It was the week before Christmas. She seemed to enjoy the evening." He glanced at the mural of the eagle on the wall and blew out a breath. "But toward the end, she seemed to draw into herself. She watched Tyler play the video game she bought him for a few minutes and then made an excuse to leave."

"Did Tyler sense anything was wrong?"

"No" He shook his head. "In fact, things seemed to be going great." He grimaced. "Tyler asked me to buy mistletoe and we hung it over the door. That night, Ty pointed out that Caitlynn and I were directly underneath. I kissed her on the cheek. I probably shouldn't be telling you this, but between you and me, I wanted to kiss her. Really kiss her, not just a soft peck." He glanced at Lee. "I think I'm falling for her again, and I'm not sure if that's wise."

"You hurt her once." Lee zipped his bag and held Steve's gaze. "As a pastor, I'm telling you to go slow and pray for guidance. With what you've shared, I don't think Caitlynn is ready to offer you a second chance."

"So, you think I should avoid her? Treat her more like a work associate than the woman I care about?"

"You have to consider her perspective—she isn't exactly putting out the welcome mat for you."

Steve walked out of the building with Lee. "You're right. I should keep our relationship professional. I don't want to see her hurt. I care for her too much. If she doesn't want me around, I won't push it."

###

Steve rubbed his eyes and focused on his computer monitor. The ceiling vent blasted warm air, yet he shivered. He and Tyler had a quiet weekend. Tyler wasn't feeling good—complaining of a runny nose and sore throat—so they laid low and watched too much TV. Tyler left yesterday, but by then, it was too late. Waking up this morning, Steve felt like death warmed over. Now, sitting in his office, he was shivering, his throat sore. He sucked on a throat lozenge. Sweat beaded his forehead. Was he feverish? Just then, his cell rang. It was Brenda.

"Do you remember Kelly and Greg Long, my clients in the Gold Coast area?" she asked.

"Yes…" Steve answered. "Both pretentious and snobby, he thought.

"Well, they bought a home in Aspen, and they want me to decorate. They asked if I could fly out next weekend. I wanted to see if Tyler could stay with you."

A quick glance at the calendar told him it was the weekend before Presidents Day. "Of course," Steve answered.

"Thanks," she said. "I owe you one. We'll talk soon."

Steve leaned back in his chair and closed his eyes, trying to quiet the pounding in his head. He was excited to see Tyler, but he hoped he felt better soon. Maybe they could go skiing . . . with Caitlynn.

A tap on his office door was like thunder. "Come in," he managed to squeak out.

Caitlynn rushed in and sat on the edge of the chair across from him. "Hi, I wanted to talk to you about—" She paused and stared. "Are you okay? You look flushed."

Steve cleared his throat. "I must've caught Tyler's virus. He had a sore throat, and now I guess it's my turn."

"That's how it always goes." She smirked. "I bet Tyler's fine now that you're sick."

"Actually, he wasn't a hundred percent, but I put him on the plane. He's back at school today, so I guess he's okay." Is she asking to be polite, or does she genuinely care? "What do you need?"

"I wanted to talk to you about my next meeting with Jillian."

"She's due in May, right?" He pressed his temple.

"Her due date is May 20th. I see her tomorrow, so I'm going to have to miss the Tuesday afternoon staff meeting. I wanted to let you know."

Why does she perch on the edge of the seat, ready to bolt out of here any second? He swallowed and grimaced. "You can't change it to another day?"

"No. The only doctor's appointment she could get was on Tuesday at three-thirty. I plan to meet her there and film some footage."

"How many more meetings are left?"

"Let's see." She raised her index finger. "There's tomorrow." The next finger followed. "Her baby shower in April." The third and fourth fingers followed as she rattled off her checklist. "And after the baby is born, we'll film her bringing Skylar home, and then one week later, her taking care of the baby. So, I guess I have four meetings left."

"Sounds like you have a handle on the timeline." A blast of dizziness hit. "Just think…three months from now, you'll be finished with this story."

She stared at him for a few moments, a frown crossed her face "You're right. But right now, three months seems like a long way off."

"I bet Jillian is thinking the same way. The last trimester when Brenda was pregnant, she constantly complained of heartburn and couldn't find a comfortable—" He looked at her face. Regret instantly surfaced. He ran his fingers through his hair. "I'm sorry, Caitlynn. That was an insensitive thing to say."

She stared into his eyes as if she were seeing him for the first time. "You really have changed, Steve. A long time ago, you would've never apologized for saying the wrong thing. Apology accepted." Her lips trembled. "I hope you feel better soon." As she left, she shut the door quietly behind her.

He banged his hand on the desk. *I'm an idiot.*

###

Tuesday afternoon, Caitlynn sat with Jillian in a booth at Reggie's Pizza Parlor. "How do you know about this place?" she asked.

"A lot of the kids from my school come here after the football game on Friday nights." She scanned the room.

"It's a change from your usual burger craving."

Jillian scrunched her nose. "I think I've overdosed on those. They sound terrible. All I want now is cheese pizza, but once I eat it, I get terrible heartburn, so I have to have strawberry ice cream to stop the pain."

Caitlynn shook her head, amazed. "The way you eat, I can't believe you've only gained 20 pounds so far."

Jillian took a bite of pizza but stopped mid-chew. Her face turned so red that Caitlynn worried she might go out like a light. She touched Jillian's hand. "What's wrong?"

"Marcus just walked in."

Caitlynn slowly turned. Marcus stood about six-foot-three and was as skinny as he was tall. His nickname could've been, Slim. He had on a letter jacket; his light brown hair skimmed the collar. He looked like any shaggy, baby-faced kid. His friend was almost as tall but stocky, with the same jeans, T-shirt, letter jacket, and tennis shoes. Marcus said something to his friend, who had slid into a booth across the room, then he strutted over to Caitlynn and Jillian. On closer inspection, he was wearing a track and field jacket with an icon of a runner and the words "cross country."

His dark brown eyes flashed. "What are you doing here, Jillian?"

Jillian smiled broadly, and her face lit up. "I thought you might be here. I wanted to introduce you to Caitlynn. She's doing a news story about me for Channel 12. Just wait until you see—"

Caitlynn tugged a strand of hair until it hurt. Jillian was acting like a little kid begging for attention. Her wide eyes looked up at Marcus as if he was some kind of Greek god.

Marcus looked pointedly at Jillian's stomach in disgust. "You look like a horse. Why are you embarrassing me by showing up at school? Every time I walk down the hall, someone snickers at me. Isn't there an alternative high school for girls like you?"

Jillian's smile faded. "What are you talking about? I'm having *your* baby. Or did you forget your part in this? You were never embarrassed when we were going out!" Her face was blotched the color of the red-checkered tablecloth.

He smirked. "It's your fault you got pregnant. You're such a liar—you said you were on the pill." His words dripped with disgust.

Caitlynn wanted to plug her ears. She closed her eyes as old memories piled atop one another like a crashed cargo train of crushed dreams. Are all males the same? Is it only about sex with them? She wasn't sure she could trust herself not to lash out and interfere where she didn't belong.

Jillian's eyes misted and threatened to overflow. "I was." She sniffled. "I know it's not what we planned, but we could make this work..."

"I'm not ready to be a father. I can't take that kind of responsibility. I want to finish school, go to college, have fun—"

Jillian jerked her napkin from her lap and wiped her eyes. "You seemed game for all sorts of fun when we were dating, but now that the fun is over, you want to pretend it never happened?" Her voice shook.

Marcus glanced at his friend and scowled. "I've got to go. Trevor is waiting. My mom says you should put the baby up for adoption. It's better that way. It'll be better for you, too." He rushed away, said a few words to his friend, and they bolted out the door.

Jillian crumbled into a heap, crying softly, her tears staining the tablecloth.

Caitlynn sighed deeply. *I wish I could fix her broken heart.* She scooted out of her side of the booth and sat next to Jillian. She wrapped an arm around her shoulder.

"I'm sorry you had to witness that," Jillian whimpered. Fresh tears erupted.

"If you knew he might be here, why did you come?" Caitlynn asked tenderly.

"He's on a different track than I am at school, so I don't see him." She wiped her nose with her napkin. "We met last spring. We were both on the cross-country team then." Her breath caught. "I was sure he would change his mind and want us to get back together once he saw me." She traced one of the squares on the tablecloth. "He acted like it was my fault I got pregnant." She took a drink of water and dried her tears. "I'm so mad right now, I don't know what to do. Why doesn't he want to have our baby? What's wrong with him?"

Knowing firsthand just how Jillian's heart was feeling right now, Caitlynn pressed her lips together, and her chest tightened. "I can't answer that question."

"But I'll tell you one thing." Jillian pointed her finger like she was a prosecuting attorney accusing the plaintiff of perjury. "He's never going to see Skylar. Ever. I don't care if I ever lay eyes on him again. What did I even see in him?" She choked back her tears.

Caitlynn softly squeezed Jillian's hand. "Let's go. You're so upset; I'm afraid you're going to go into premature labor."

Ten minutes later, they were driving toward Jillian's house. Caitlynn turned on the radio, switching from talk radio to the soft rock station, anything to help Jillian calm down. They drove without speaking. She listened to the music and Jillian's occasional sniffles. Jillian's eyes were closed, and her blonde hair fell across her cheeks.

Caitlynn's first instinct was to reach out and comfort her. She pulled up to the curb outside Jillian's home and touched her lightly. "Are you okay? I can come in if you'd like."

Jillian shook her head. "No, I want to be alone. I have stomach cramps. I think the pizza made me sick, and I'm so tired, I want to take a nap."

"Look, Jillian, you need to know that I would never hurt you. None of what just went on today will be in the story." She stared into Jillian's puffy eyes. "You have my word."

Jillian opened her car door. Her face was still so red and mottled from crying that Caitlynn's heart ached.

Jillian softly stroked her belly. Honestly, I think you're the only true friend I have…the only one who accepts me for who I am."

She shut the door, and Caitlynn watched Jillian amble slowly across the grass with her shoulders slumped and her head bowed.

CHAPTER THIRTY-THREE

It is not proud.
1 CORINTHIANS 13:4

Steve punched the snooze button for the second time and closed his eyes. He coughed and rubbed his throat to ease the burn. Every muscle in his body ached. All he wanted to do was burrow under the covers and sleep all day…sleep until all this pain eased. He could count on one hand the number of times he had missed work because of illness. He said a quick prayer for strength, slowly walked to the bathroom and looked in the mirror. *Is that a rash on my neck and chest?*

Twenty minutes later, he was showered, dressed, and slumped in a kitchen chair. He wiped a drop of sweat from his brow. His cheeks were feverish. *The flu?* All week he'd struggled through phone calls and various meetings with Ed and his staff—and he'd purposely avoided Caitlynn so she wouldn't get sick. What if he gave this to her, and she unknowingly gave it to Jillian? Besides, he wanted to follow Lee's advice and give Caitlynn space. Because Lee was right—she'd never given him any indication that she cared for him in any other capacity but professionally.

He looked at the kitchen clock and frowned. Seven-thirty. *I'm going to be late.* He reached up and pressed his throbbing temple. Every evening this week he felt sure he'd wake up the following morning feeling fine, which is why he'd never called Brenda with the news that he was sick. He needed to be at the airport by 5 p.m. to pick up Tyler—but first, he had to get through this day. Maybe a pain reliever would help.

He stood to take his coffee mug to the sink but stopped when all he could see were tiny black dots. He staggered over to the counter, dropping the cup. Breaking glass sounded. Everything went dark as he crumbled to the floor.

A light drizzle blurred the windshield. Turning up the heat, Caitlynn shivered in time with the swish of the wiper blades. She put one hand over the air vent to warm her fingers. "Lulu, I wish I were home sleeping under a pile of warm blankets instead of driving to work this morning."

Monday's were never easy, but add a gloomy rainy morning to the mix, and a mad dash from the parking lot to the building made it all the more difficult.

First thing on the agenda—update Steve regarding Jillian. She parked, grabbed her things, and sprinted from the car. Steve's reserved parking spot appeared vacant. *That's odd?*

After dropping off her belongings, she walked to Steve's door. The room dark and vacant. *Where's Steve?* She rounded the corner looking for his administrator. "Hey, Paula. Have you seen the boss?"

Her eyes widened. "He's home." She shook her head. "You won't believe what happened. He caught chickenpox from his son. In fact, he's so sick, he passed out and hit his head! Thankfully, he came to and was able to call a friend.

"Really?" Her voice rose. "Is Steve okay?"

He has a high fever and can hardly move. The doctor has him on a fever reducer and anti-viral drugs. In fact, both of them are at the house."

"What about Tyler?" she exclaimed.

"Tyler is doing fine with the Calamine lotion and pain reliever."

Caitlynn exhaled in relief. "Thanks for letting me know." She walked to her office and sank slowly onto her desk chair.

She doodled on a legal pad thinking of Steve and all the help he had provided during her recovery—warming the food he'd bought from the online meal service, watching television with her while she recovered from her surgery—not to mention the number of times he took her to the doctor when she couldn't drive.

There was no choice. Steve had helped her with no strings attached, and now she had to reciprocate and help him through his illness. From the depths of her heart, she wanted to help in any way possible…but it might prove awkward. This wasn't in her plan, but how could she stand by and not help Tyler? And…

She gasped. *What if I expose Jillian and the baby to the chickenpox?* She quickly searched the internet to see if being around a pregnant woman would be an issue. She exhaled. From what she read, if Jillian already had the chickenpox, she would be in the clear.

She quickly called Jillian. "Hi, Jillian, I know you have to be in class in a few minutes, but I have a question. Have you had the chickenpox?"

Jillian's soft laugh sounded in Caitlynn's ear. "You ask the strangest questions. Let's just say that I had the worst case my doctor had ever seen from my neck to in-between my toes. Why?"

"I want to help someone out who caught the virus, but I didn't want to jeopardize your baby's health."

"No worries. I've got to get to class now. Later."

A wave of relief swept through her. She would stop and get a DVD of the latest Disney movie for Tyler, even though she had no idea what that was. And she'd pick up this month's *Sports Illustrated* and the current edition of *Newsweek* for Steve. Chicken noodle soup always tasted good when someone was sick. She'd buy several cans—saltine crackers too.

She cracked a smile. *I can give back by making lunch for them and watching the movie with Tyler.* If she hurried through the critical things that needed to be finished at work today, she could get to their house by lunch.

In record time, she finished her work and dashed out of the building into the rain. By noon, she'd purchased the items she wanted and was on her way to Steve's house. The gate to the driveway stood open. Parking her car in the circle drive, she grabbed the groceries, ran to the covered porch, and rang the bell.

Thinking maybe she should've called first, she was about to leave the bag on the doormat and walk away when the door opened.

"Yes?" A slender woman dressed in black skinny jeans, ballerina flats, and a cream-colored cowl-necked sweater stood at the door with a look of curiosity. She was beautiful, with shoulder-length golden-brown hair and green eyes with tiny flecks of gold.

Hi . . . Steve and I . . . we work together. I heard he was sick," Caitlynn stuttered.

The woman opened the door wider "The rain is really cold. Please come inside."

Is this his girlfriend? Caitlynn stepped inside and lifted the bag. "I brought a few things I thought Ty and Steve might like."

"Aren't you sweet?" She took the bag, then flashed a fake smile. "I'm headed to the kitchen."

Caitlynn followed a few steps behind and sniffed appreciatively as her mouth watered.

The woman plunked the bag down on the kitchen table. "I'm Brenda. Tyler's mom."

Caitlynn gave a quick nod. Of course, this was Brenda. She and Tyler had the same shaped eyes and mouth. She suddenly felt self-conscious about being there and wondered how much Brenda knew of her and Steve's past...

The smell of chicken noodle soup permeated the air. A large pot simmered on the burner with what looked like thick homemade noodles in a creamy broth with chunks of chicken, carrots, and celery. *Do I smell baking bread?* The kitchen gleamed, soup bubbled, bread baked.

Obviously, things were well under control here. Clearly, no help was needed in caring for Steve and Tyler. She wanted to hide her pathetic attempt to be helpful by bringing five cans of soup. "I'm Caitlynn Grant." She extended her hand. "I've met Tyler a few times. He's such a great kid."

Brenda shook her hand, lightly touching Caitlynn's like a butterfly alighting for a brief second before leaving for a better option, then rubbed her hands up and down on her jeans a few times, before opening the bag. "Thanks. I was supposed to fly from Denver to Aspen on business, but I couldn't leave with Tyler and his father so sick."

Brenda pulled out the DVD Caitlynn had brought. "Ty will love this. Thank you." Pulling out the magazines, she stacked them in a pile next to the movie. Thankfully, she left the soup cans and the crackers in the bag. "Do you want to take these upstairs to Steve and Ty?"

Caitlynn clenched her fist for a moment before she reached out for the items. She wanted to turn tail and run out the door as fast as her legs could carry her. Why did she rush over here to help? Why had she thought she'd be needed in their lives? That returning the favor he'd done for her recovery would be invaluable to Steve and his son, and somehow, they couldn't get along without her?

"I'll just pop in for a few minutes. I don't want to intrude."

Brenda pressed her lips together in a thin smile. "I'm sure they'd love the company." Her voice sounded aloof. "Tyler's room is the first door on the right. Steve's is at the end of the hallway." The buzzer sounded. She donned an oven mitt and pulled out a loaf of golden-brown bread.

Caitlynn whirled out of the kitchen as quickly as she could and escaped up the stairs. She rapped on Tyler's door.

"Come in."

"Hey there, Tyler. I thought I'd visit the patient." She smiled and stopped in the middle of the room.

Tyler was sitting on the bed and bounced up and down, excited, his cover tucked around his chest. "Come sit on my bed. I can't believe I finally get to show you my room!" His laughter filled the air.

Caitlynn moved a toy fighter jet out of the way and took its place at the foot of the bed. She glanced around; her eyes wide. "You must really like the Chicago Cubs."

He wriggled under the blanket. "I like them so much! This is exactly what my room looks like in Chicago."

On one wall was a three-sided replica of the Chicago Cubs dugout, complete with blue paint, red letters, and the bed in the center. On each side of the bed there were lockers and cubbies crammed with toys. The white baseball-shaped rug on the floor read Chicago Cubs. The words were written in red with blue stitching for the seams on the ball. Pennants and posters decorated the rest of the walls.

She squeezed his hand, affectionately. "I'm so glad I got to see your room. I love it." She held out her gift. "I guess you probably own this already. I had no idea you were such a baseball fan."

"This is great! *The Rookie.* No, I don't have it. I can't wait to watch it!" He put the movie on his lap.

"How are you feeling? Are you itchy?"

"Not when my mom gives me medicine and rubs calamine lotion on me. But I scratch like crazy when it wears off." He pushed away the covers and lifted his shirt. "See?"

Tiny raised red dots covered his torso, from his neck to the waist

"Hmm, you've a pretty good case! I bet you hurt." She smoothed out a wrinkle on the bed cover. "How's your dad doing?"

Tyler bit his lip. "He's very sick, and it's all my fault. If I hadn't gotten chickenpox from my friend, Dad wouldn't be sick." Tears filled his eyes.

Caitlynn wanted to wrap her arms around him to comfort him. What could she say to encourage him? "Tyler, have you ever rough-housed with your dad and hurt him by accident? Maybe you hit your head on his mouth and gave him a big fat lip?"

Tyler chuckled and pointed to his eye. "Yeah, he likes to tell me how, when I was two years old, I gave him a black eye because I head-bumped him when he leaned over to pick me up."

"This was an accident too, Ty. You didn't mean to give your dad the chickenpox, just like you didn't mean to give your dad a black eye." She patted his leg. "Your dad is strong. I'm sure he'll be better soon. Don't worry."

Tyler's face lit up as if she'd just said there was a closet full of candy in the next room.

"Thanks for coming to see me." He gave her a quick hug.

"Anytime, Tyler. I'll check on you again in a couple of days." She patted his hand. "I hope you feel better soon," and quietly closed the door.

Caitlynn found Steve's room and knocked. She heard coughing, then in a hoarse voice, he said, "Come in."

She could barely see his outline—almost as if he'd been swallowed into a dark hole in the middle of his bed. Muffled sounds emanated from the TV nestled in the armoire across from his bed. The room had the same feel as the rest of his home—similar to a rustic lodge in the Rocky Mountains.

She pasted a smile on her face. His ashen complexion shocked her, and she quickly looked away to the window. A cloud moved across the window and darkened the room. She had to squint to see the light rain pelting the pane.

Steve was the first to speak. "Hey, I guess it's your turn to check on a sick patient."

She held out the magazines. "I brought you these. I'll just put these on the nightstand." She glanced around for a place to sit. A chair stood in the corner of the room. She dragged it close to his bed and sat. "You don't look so good." A light sheen of sweat covered his forehead.

He wheezed and coughed into his hand. "Two days ago, I thought I'd be good as new in a few days, but now it seems I've taken a turn for the worse." He shivered. His eyes wandered to the sound of the rain, tapping lightly against the windowpane.

"Caitlynn?" He turned his gaze on her. "Do you still like to walk in the rain?"

She drew her brows together. "I haven't done that in a while, but yes, I do."

"Do you remember our long walks in the rain discussing classes and the professors we liked or disliked?" He closed his eyes.

Why was he talking about rain? Could he be delirious? She scooted forward, nervously brushing a loose strand of hair behind her ear. She raised her voice. "Are you okay?" She put her hand to his forehead. "Steve, you're burning up." She brought her ear to his chest, and her heart hammered uncontrollably when their eyes met. His lungs sounded like a baby swinging a noisy rattle.

She jumped out of her seat. "Steve, I think you have pneumonia. You sound just like my mom when she was diagnosed. You need to go to the hospital. I'm getting Brenda." She rushed to the door.

"Caitlynn?" he gasped.

"Hmm?" Her stomach lurched each time he wheezed like he was sucking air through a straw.

"I'd like to take a walk in the rain with you again."

He wasn't thinking straight. The fever must be causing him to say crazy things. "Okay, Steve." Her voice softened. "We'll go sometime." Then her voice caught in her throat, and she squeaked out, "Let me get help."

She rushed downstairs to the kitchen. "Steve is very sick. I think he has pneumonia. He isn't breathing right, and he's talking crazy." She talked so fast she could hardly spit the words out.

Brenda dropped the slice of bread she was holding and rushed up the stairs with Caitlynn following close behind her.

Steve lay trembling, drenched in sweat. "He didn't look like this earlier." She brought her hand to his head and stared into his eyes. "Steve, I'm not equipped to handle this kind of sickness. I agree with Caitlynn: you need to be admitted to the hospital. I'm calling an ambulance."

Tyler stood in the doorway, whimpering. "Mommy? What's happening? Why are you calling an ambulance?"

Hurrying to him, Brenda knelt down and gently grabbed his shoulders. "Ty, I think your dad needs to go to the hospital. He's having trouble breathing, and I want to make sure he gets help."

Tyler twisted away from his mother and ran to his father's side. "Daddy? Are you okay?" He held his dad's hand.

Steve attempted a smile. "Ty, I hate to admit this, but I think your mom and Caitlynn are right. If I go to the hospital, I bet I'll be better before you know it." He squeezed Tyler's hand.

"Caitlynn, please phone 911." Brenda frowned. "I'm going to take Tyler downstairs and wait for the ambulance. You stay with Steve." She gently pushed Tyler out the door.

Caitlynn's voice cracked with nerves as she described the necessary details to the emergency operator. "What? You won't transport a patient if they have pneumonia?" She clenched her fist and looked over at Steve, who was watching her with an astonished expression.

She hung up and sat as close to him as she could without touching him. "They won't take you, Steve. I guess I'm driving you to the hospital. Brenda doesn't know where it is, and anyway, Tyler needs his mom."

He stared into her eyes. "I bet you wish right about now that you'd stayed at work today."

"What? And leave all this drama for someone else to experience?" She tried to joke.

He laughed and then coughed into his sleeve. "Don't make me laugh. It hurts." He closed his eyes.

She glanced at his sweat-soaked T-shirt. Was that a good sign? Did it mean the fever was breaking?

His eyes fluttered open. "Caitlynn?" he gasped. "Will you do me a favor?"

She nodded.

"The second drawer is where I keep my shirts. Can you get one for me so I can change into a dry one before we go?" He coughed into his sleeve again.

In a flash, she ruffled through the drawer and found a navy-blue shirt. He struggled to sit up. Her heart pounded in fear. He swayed as if a faint breeze would knock him over. *Please don't pass out.* His face paled as he struggled to slowly peel his shirt off.

"Umm, do you need help?"

"Would you mind?" His eyes darkened. "I'm so dizzy, it's ridiculous," he said in frustration. His body shivered. Weak and frail, like a sick little boy in his parent's bed.

She worked swiftly—exchanging the damp for the dry. She sucked in a breath at the sight of his chest, stomach and back covered entirely with chickenpox. She pretended to act as if red welts on the skin, and changing a man's shirt was no big deal, but what she really wanted to do was hold his hand and reassure him that everything would be okay. "There you are." She grinned to break the tension. "I bet you feel better."

He collapsed against the pillows and closed his eyes as if that small amount of effort sucked away all energy. "Thanks, Caitlynn. I'm glad you're here."

"Can you stand? I'll help you down the stairs."

He nodded. "There are some sweatpants in the bottom drawer. Please get them for me. I'll change and call you when I'm ready."

Ten minutes later, Caitlynn wrapped her arm lightly around his waist and helped him down the stairs. "The ambulance won't come. I'm going to drive him to Littleton Adventist."

"You said my daddy was going to be okay!" Tyler cried.

Caitlynn was shocked. "Tyler . . . I'm—"

Brenda rushed over, grabbed Steve's other arm, and said, "Tyler, hold the door open. I'll help Caitlynn get your dad to the car." She glanced at Steve. "Do you have your wallet and cell phone?"

"Yes" He barely nodded "I'll have Caitlynn drop me off at the emergency department and help with admittance, if necessary." Sweat dripped from his forehead.

Brenda glanced at the hall closet. "Steve, you better get a coat on. It's freezing outside."

"Why?" He arched his brow? "You afraid I might catch pneumonia?" He teased.

Brenda helped him into his coat and grimaced. "It's just like you to make a joke out of this."

Caitlynn stifled a smile and shrugged into her jacket.

"Don't worry, Son." He leaned over and hugged him. "I'm going to be fine. Are you feeling better?"

Tyler pulled up his pajama top. "Most of the bumps are scabbed over already."

"Good. That's what I want to hear." He kissed Tyler on the forehead. "I'll call you tonight."

Tyler opened the door. "I love you, Dad."

Rain mixed with snowflakes covered the driveway. Brenda helped Caitlynn get Steve into the passenger seat, and then she joined Tyler on the porch. Tyler brushed away his tears and glared at her. Guilt tore at Caitlynn's heart. It was clear Tyler was angry for his expression looked as if he'd never forgive her for telling him his father was going to be okay.

CHAPTER THIRTY-FOUR

It is not rude.
1 CORINTHIANS 13:5

Caitlynn checked her watch and sighed. *Three-thirty*. Forty-five minutes ago, she'd had no choice but to violate Steve's privacy when she rummaged through his wallet, flipping past a picture of him with Tyler, a considerable amount of cash and several credit cards to try to find his insurance card and driver's license. She'd handed the necessary information to the clerk and waited impatiently for the admittance papers. The minute they'd arrived, they rushed Steve into the emergency room for treatment. Finally, with the required paperwork in hand, she approached the desk.

"Can you tell me the room number for Steven Carr?"

The nurse eyed her up and down. "Are you his wife?"

The badge on the nurse's uniform said, *Nadine*. "No, Nadine, I'm not. He isn't married. He's my boss. I drove him to the hospital." She set the paperwork on the counter. "Here are his admittance papers."

The nurse scooped them off the counter and glanced briefly at the documents. "It's hospital policy only to allow immediate family to stay with the patient," she said, warmly. "But I guess I can make an exception since you're the responsible party. We've transferred him to the second floor, room 204."

After all the trouble she went through to help Steve, it never crossed her mind that they might not let her see him. Her stomach churned from hunger, and she could feel a headache lurking. "Thank you."

"Wait," the nurse said. "Mr. Carr is considered contagious. Is there a chance you might be pregnant?"

Caitlynn stiffened. "No." She walked away.

She hesitantly entered the room. It was dimly lit, with machines beeping and buzzing. Steve was asleep. His breathing still sounded like a freight train wheezing up a steep incline. Sitting in the chair next to him felt like an eternity watching him labor for each breath. She stood up and took a step back. This was all so surreal. She paced back and forth like a tiger trapped in a cage. She twirled a strand of hair, brushed it behind her ear, and tiptoed to the side of his bed.

Her stomach grumbled, head pounding, as a wave of dizziness reminded her she hadn't eaten since breakfast.

He moaned and thrashed his head side to side. Should she shake him awake? He was able to breathe, *right?* Oxygen entered through clear plastic tubing attached to a machine and flowed through to the vented oxygen mask covering his mouth and nose. Clear fluid dripped from an IV bag into a vein, as a machine flashed neon green numbers. What did the numbers mean?

His eyes darted from the machines, then over to her, like *he* was the one trapped in a cage. He looked outside the window that brought light but no fresh air to the sterile room. "I have to get out of here," he mumbled.

She could barely make out what he said because the mask muffled his words, but she was relieved that he was awake and speaking. She wished she could wipe the anxious look from his eyes. She leaned in. "You'll be able to get out of here once you get to breathing on your own. You have pneumonia."

Steve closed his eyes and whispered, "Who gets pneumonia from chickenpox? I thought I was stronger." He opened his eyes and scowled. "Tyler must think I'm about to die."

She couldn't forget the look of fear on Tyler's face. She tried to ease his worry. "I'm sure you're motivated to get better quickly so you can hang out with your son."

A doctor entered, nodding slightly at Caitlynn, and then at Steve. "Hello, Mr. Carr, I'm Dr. Acton, the attending physician on duty." He scanned the readings on the machine. "I understand you have a severe case of varicella with pneumonia? I don't see this often…"

He looked at Caitlynn. "And you must be Mrs. Carr. You must not be pregnant because you're not wearing a mask."

Caitlynn held back a sharp retort. Was there something on her forehead that said she'd be stupid enough to enter a room with a placard posted outside the door that read "Chickenpox" with a picture of a pregnant woman in a red circle with a line through it?

She plopped down on the chair in the corner and folded her arms. "No, I'm not Mrs. Carr. I work for Mr. Carr. He permitted me to be here. And no, I'm not pregnant." She pressed hard against her temple.

Dr. Acton tilted his head slightly to the side. "Then I guess you have nothing to worry about."

He turned to Steve. "I need you to lean over a bit and breathe as deep as you can. I want to listen to your lungs." He put his stethoscope to his ear. The doctor finished his chest exam and studied Steve's chart. "It looks like the Emergency physician started you on the right course of treatment." He eyed the whiteboard. His name, plus the nurse-on-duty's name, *Crystal*, written in blue. "You're lucky. Crystal is one of our best. You're in good hands." He scribbled on the chart and slipped it in the slot near the bed. "You should be improving in the next day or so. If you recover as quickly as I hope you could be home in the next few days. Do you have any questions?"

Steve's eyes narrowed. "No, just do whatever you need to do so I can get out of here. Pronto."

He patted Steve on the shoulder and turned to Caitlynn. "I'll return later this evening." He shut the door on his way out.

Steve stared out the window. "It's snowing so hard it's sticking to the window."

He ogled the monitors. "God? Why is this happening? I should be playing with Tyler out in the snow."

He kicked his feet free of the sheet. "I hate this." He leaned back with a defeated look on his face. "If I have my way, I'll be with my son by the end of the week."

Caitlynn didn't know what to say. That he was lying in a hospital bed with a helpless look on his face crushed her soul. She walked over to his bed and held his hand.

The door opened, and Brenda entered, holding the magazines Caitlynn had bought. She discreetly tried to pull her hand from his grip, but Steve squeezed tighter and brushed his thumb across the top of her hand. A feeling like butterflies fluttering soared straight to her heart.

He spoke first. "Why aren't you with Ty?"

"I called Hunter's mom to see if she could come over and watch him while I came and checked on you." She glanced at Caitlynn and Steve holding hands and arched her perfectly shaped brow. "Hunter's already had the virus. They're watching *The Rookie*." She waltzed over to the bed.

Caitlynn slipped her hand away and stepped back. Her hand still tingled from Steve's grasp, and she felt the telltale sign that her cheeks were practically on fire.

Brenda gaped at Caitlynn. Then turned to Steve and grinned. "The oxygen—" she tilted her head toward Caitlynn— "and the personal attention must be helping. You look like your color's coming back." She set the magazines on the table. "Don't you dare die on me," she teased. "I don't want to raise Tyler without a father."

Steve crossed his arms. "I don't plan on dying anytime soon." His expression darkened.

Caitlynn took another step back. They looked so good together—Steve's dark brown hair and eyes the color of the sky just before sunset, and Brenda's perfect olive-colored skin with those beautiful green eyes and light brown hair—it was clear to Caitlynn that she didn't belong. They both had a flawless complexion while she had freckles that she tried in vain to hide with makeup. She felt out of place with her strawberry-blonde hair and her freckles across her nose and cheeks must surely be beyond beet red. *I need to get out of here.* She cleared her throat. "Steve? I'm gonna head home now."

Brenda stared at Caitlynn. "Thanks for everything you've done today." She turned to Steve and slowly smirked. "As Caitlynn's boss—I really think you should give her a raise—for everything she's done for you today."

Caitlynn couldn't decide if she wanted to wipe the fake grin off Brenda's face or simply laugh?

She shrugged. "He helped me through a tough time last fall, so this is the least I could do." She made sure to paste on the practiced smile she flashed at the end of a live television interview and focused in on Steve. "I hope you're better and back to work soon."

He scowled, but before he could speak, she made her escape, bolting to the elevator and pushing the button for the first floor. As the door closed, the familiar feeling of solitude enveloped her. *I should've left hours ago.* She reminded herself that she was only helping Steve for Tyler's sake. The last time she saw Tyler, he looked so frightened, with his eyes as round as dinner plates, clinging to his mother's side as if he would never let her go.

The door opened, and she rushed outside. With every step, the mix of freezing rain and snow pelted her cheeks and stung her eyes until they burned and went blurry. She fooled herself into believing the weather was the reason for the tears, and finally, she sought shelter in the safety of her car. All she could think about was the way her body betrayed her when long-forgotten butterflies fluttered in her stomach and the tingle that spread from her hand to her heart when Steve brushed his thumb across hers.

CHAPTER THIRTY-FIVE

Steve rested his head on his desk. His head pounded to a thump-thump-thump he couldn't stop if he tried. Two weeks since his illness, and he still wasn't back one hundred percent. Chickenpox seemed like such a wimpy disease to make him this weak! In January, he'd signed himself and Tyler up for the church ski trip Lee was organizing during spring break, but now it was less than a week away, and he didn't have the strength to ski down the driveway, much less down a mountain nine thousand feet high in oxygen-depleted air.

Returning to work was supposed to get his mind off his painfully slow recovery. His eyes watered as he stared at the screen, and his head ached. He leaned heavily against the chairback and shut his eyes to stop the burn.

Pondering the last few weeks, he shook his head in frustration. Caitlynn had been such a help to him when he was admitted to the hospital. It was so hard to get her to reveal any type of emotion regarding their relationship, so seeing the worried look on her face as he lay in the hospital bed had confirmed two things.

First, buried deep inside her, was a heart that cared. He knew she did, of course, by how she acted around Tyler and how much she loved volunteering at the Children's Hospital. But when it came to her feelings for him, he was certain they were nonexistent . . . until he saw the look of worry on her face, when she stood by his hospital bed, gazing at him with an expression of tenderness and concern that displayed more than any outward action.

Secondly, he was miserable trying to ignore his feelings for Caitlynn. Even though Lee had advised him to maintain distance and keep his interaction purely professional—he could do so no longer. He was falling for her all over again. And if he were honest, admit that he'd never stopped loving her. He'd thought he loved Brenda and married her, but they'd both married one another for so many wrong reasons—including trying to please their families.

Caitlynn, his heart raced out of control. He wanted more. A real relationship. How could he show her he'd changed—that no matter what, he wouldn't run as he did years ago? And that he'd always be there for her no matter what.

Right now, he should be thinking about work, not Caitlynn. *God, can you help me here? If you want me to pursue Caitlynn, can you give me some direction? If not, please let me know, and I'll back down. Whatever your will is, I want to walk in it. Amen.*

The day dragged on and on. And, with his head still pounding, he decided to finally call it a day. Driving home, Tyler weighing heavily on his mind, he thought about the ski trip. The Olympian snowboarder Cory Powers, planned to perform an exhibition, and Tyler was so excited. He sighed heavily and grabbed his phone to call Lee and cancel.

An idea formed. *What about Caitlynn?* He knew from past experience she was an excellent skier. Maybe she would take Tyler...he swallowed his pride. Tyler is what matters, and placed the call.

"Hi, Caitlynn. Uh, got something to ask… before my illness, I signed up Tyler to participate in the ski trip at Winter Park. It's this Saturday. Ty has been so excited about it. The problem is, I'm not ready to tromp up and down a mountain on skis. So, I'm wondering…would you be willing to go in my place?"

Several seconds of silence elapsed. He held his breath.

"Um . . . can I think about it and call you back tonight?"

He'd hoped she would've been ready with a quick reply of yes, but that was probably wishful thinking. "Of course, you can."

"I'll talk to you soon."

"Sounds good." He hung up and threw the phone onto the passenger seat. Anger flooded his mind as his head continued to throb in triple time. Why did he have to get sick in the first place? All he wanted to do was take Tyler skiing, and now he had to rely on someone else to do his job.

One by one, his past failures with his son scattered across his mind like ominous storm clouds rolling in from a distance. The divorce, moving to Denver, losing Tyler while hiking, leaving early on Thanksgiving, Ty's broken arm—*on my watch, chickenpox*—and now, still so weak, he couldn't ski. He shook his head in disgust. All those failures pointed to one conclusion: his attempts at controlling his circumstances had backfired. He had about as much control over his life as telling the stars not to shine.

Once home, he swallowed two pain relievers and plopped on the couch. *Lord, I'm sorry I tried to put my plans before yours. Help me to stop controlling and start surrendering. Help me to see that you know more about what I need than I do.*

His call with Caitlynn was still fresh. *If Tyler isn't supposed to go with Caitlynn, or ski at all, for that matter, I'll accept it as your Sovereign will.* Several minutes later, the peace of the Spirit flooded deep into his soul.

His phone jolted his eyes open. He was pleasantly surprised. Either the pills had started working or releasing his concerns to the Lord had done it, but either way, his headache was gone. He liked thinking it was the Lord's doing. Picking up his phone, he saw Caitlynn's number flash across the screen, and he answered.

"I've had a chance to think about your request . . . I have Saturday off, so I can take Tyler on the ski trip."

She sounded so nervous that his first impulse was to try to make her comfortable. "It's okay, I know I'm asking a lot from you…or anyone for that matter."

She whispered something he couldn't quite catch. *Is she cursing?*

"I want to take him. Ty shouldn't have to miss out just because you can't take him. The problem is . . . can you come with us? You could sit in the lodge and read." She poured the words out in a rush. "I'm not comfortable going with Tyler and a bunch of people I don't know. What if Ty got hurt?"

Touched that she cared so deeply for Tyler's well-being, he said, "I never thought of that. Blurting out before she changed her mind. "Tyler would love it if we were there. We can eat lunch together."

"What time should I arrive at your house?"

"6 a.m. We leave from the church at six-thirty."

"Phew, that's early. You're asking a lot on my day off." She teased.

Steve chuckled. "I know." His voice lowered. "Caitlynn? Thanks for doing this. I'll call Tyler and let him know the plan."

"No problem. See you Saturday."

Steve sat for a few minutes in stunned silence. He'd given her an out so she wouldn't have to spend the day with him. But here she was asking him to go too. Was God answering his prayer about Caitlynn already? He called Tyler.

"Guess what, Ty? You and I have a date…"

An hour later Steve woke up from a nap feeling groggy, but rested. He sat on the couch, just about to turn on the TV when his phone vibrated—shocked to see it was his father calling.

"Hello, Father," he said.

"Son." That one word carried a lot of intensity, and Steve's stomach dropped.

"What's wrong?" Steve cried out. "Did something happen to Mom?"

"No, she's fine—or as fine as she can be under the circumstances." His voice faded to a whisper.

Relief swept through him that his mother was okay, but he was still gut wrenched. Squeezing the phone, he asked. "What happened?"

His father choked back a sob. "She died. The filly died this morning."

Steve shook his head in disbelief, "What?" He shot off the couch and paced. *Corner Pocket—dead.*

"She caught a virus. It's been going around the horse community. More than two dozen horses have died so far in the county, and it's spread across the state line into Indiana."

Steve sighed into the phone. "Oh, Dad, I'm so sorry."

"She was strong and from a great bloodline." He choked back sobs. "I'm never going to have a horse with those qualities again."

"How's Mom taking it?" Steve asked as he pulled his fingers through his hair.

"She's in her room, bawling her eyes out. We're all crying like babies." His voice cracked with emotion.

"Dad, I wish I was there. How is Carl?"

"Carl resigned today." His father's voice hardened. "He blames himself for Corner Pocket's death. He said it was a sign that he was too old to work with horses. I agree with him. He needs to retire out in the pasture where he belongs."

"Dad!" Steve's voice rose. "You can't mean that! Carl's been with us since I was in kindergarten. He's practically family."

"I trusted him to raise a healthy mare, and he let me down." His voice fell to a whisper. "Maybe it's time for us to call it quits."

"You can't do that. Mom loves her job managing the horses." Steve rushed on, "You're in shock right now. Don't make any decisions for a few weeks." He didn't know what made him angrier—hearing that his father had allowed Carl to resign, or hearing his father's defeated attitude.

"Steve?"

Steve had to press the phone close to his ear to hear his father's soft tone.

"This mess has made me think about a lot of things. I've given you a hard time over your faith in the last few years. I can see now that I was wrong. I'm sorry." He breathed heavily.

Steve swallowed a lump away. *My father, apologizing?* Steve wanted to tell him how much this meant, but he knew his dad would just brush it off as nonsense. So he said, "Dad, I understand. Call Carl and ask him to come back. Do it for Mom. Please," He paused a moment. "And Dad? I'm praying that God will take this terrible tragedy and make something good come from it."

"Okay, son. You do that." His father cleared his throat. "I never called you when you were ill. I left it up to your mother to see how you were recovering. I'm glad you're back on your feet again," he said, soon ending the call.

Steve's mind ached as if pummeled by a punching bag. First, his father called to say Corner Pocket had died, and by the end of the call, he was saying he was sorry and wanted prayer? Was his father's heart softening? Or was this just temporary because of the pain he was suffering? Either way, it showed a side of his father that Steve never knew existed.

He told his father he would pray. Usually, he'd pray sitting on the couch. But for some reason, he was compelled to do it differently. He knelt on the floor, folded his hands on the cushion, and bowed his head.

CHAPTER THIRTY-SIX

It is not self-seeking
1 CORINTHIANS 13:5

Caitlynn squeezed the steering wheel, as she turned her car into the parking lot of Vista View Church. Her stomach lurched. "Lulu, I hope this isn't a waste of a great ski day." She counted five cars with at least four people per vehicle. She looked at their smiling faces. "At least they look happy."

She spotted Steve's SUV—how could she miss it—and parked next to him. Tyler ran to her door and waited for her to step out of the car. He spoke in a rush, "Ms. Caitlynn, this is my friend Hunter."

The boy was six inches taller than Tyler with a scattering of freckles across his cheeks. Hunter smiled shyly.

"Hello, Hunter. Are you ready to ski?" Caitlynn asked.

Tyler tackled her with a bear hug. "I'm so glad you're taking me skiing!"

Lee sauntered over with a clipboard in one hand and patted Steve on the shoulder. "Glad to see you, man. I've missed you at our basketball games."

"Me too. Lee, this is Caitlynn. Caitlynn, this is Lee Yamigucci, our children's pastor—and the guy who runs me into the ground at our drop-in games."

"Hi, Caitlynn." He shook her hand and then knelt eye-level with Hunter and Tyler. "Hey, you two! Don't be showing me up on the bunny hill." He checked their names off the list on the clipboard.

Tyler and Hunter chortled in unison. "The bunny hill? The last time I was on the bunny hill, I was five years old," Tyler said.

Hunter nodded like a bobblehead. "Yeah, we don't do bunny hills."

"Oh…okay. I was just making sure." Lee pretended to write on the clipboard. "Ty and Hunter don't do bunny hills. Prefer to ski the Double Black Diamond expert slopes."

Tyler high-fived Hunter, "Oh, Yeah!"

Lee shouted: "Gather round. Each child's assigned to an adult chaperone. No child is to ski alone. Take a minute to join up with the adult you're paired with." Tyler squeezed Caitlynn's hand.

"The plan is to ski until eleven-thirty," Lee said. "Then eat lunch together in the group dining room. We will have forty-five minutes for lunch. At twelve-fifteen, we will go as a group to the half-pipe park where Cory Powers will treat us to an exhibition. You must check-in with me before you go home. Otherwise, I will assume the worse and have the ski patrol out searching for you!"

Caitlynn whispered to Steve, "Why would Cory agree to this for a church?"

"I'm told his family attended our church since he was a baby," Steve answered.

"Still, he didn't have to say yes." She tried to keep the shock from her voice. "That's so kind of him."

"Let's pray before we head to the slopes." Lee clasped hands with the kids on either side of him. The rest followed, all holding hands.

Lee's voice rang out, "Lord, thank you that we can gather together. We ask for safety. Let us get to know each other better through this experience. We appreciate this outing, and acknowledge and delight in the fact that every good and perfect gift comes from you. Amen."

Steve squeezed Caitlynn's hand slightly before loosening his grip. A spark like a ray of sunlight breaking through the clouds warmed her soul, and her body tingled. Was it the prayer or Steve's touch? Asking God to be a part of the day's activities seemed so natural to Lee and Steve. Did God hear all prayers? She wasn't sure, but she liked the peace and the warmth inside her soul when the prayer ended. It was as if giving thanks to God meant something.

The group piled into cars. During the commotion, Steve consented when Tyler begged to ride with Hunter.

Her heart raced. *Alone with Steve on a two-hour drive?* A few months ago, the idea of a car ride with him for even ten minutes would've put her into a state of panic. Now, it didn't seem altogether awful—and she was helping Tyler at the same time. She stole a quick glance. He still looked pale, and had yet to regain the weight he'd lost during his illness.

Would this be too much for him? "You know, if you find you're too tired when it's time to go, I can drive us home."

"Thanks!" Steve replied. They followed the car in front. "Let me see how I feel. I may take you up on the suggestion."

"Is Tyler a good skier?"

"Once he gets his ski legs under him again, he'll haul down the mountain full of confidence. But until then, he's just doesn't care how slow he goes; he's content to figure it out first."

"Good to know!" A chuckle escaped. "We'll go on a green run first—but not a bunny hill—before we get to the blue runs."

"I'm sure he'll appreciate that." He confirmed with a brief nod.

"What about Hunter and his father? Will they hang out with us?"

"More than likely. I bet Lee will too. He brought Blake with him. Tyler, Hunter, and Blake are good friends."

"Does Lee have kids?"

His eyes darkened. "I heard that a few months before we started attending, his wife, Carly, was pregnant with their first child. The baby was stillborn. They're still in the process of coping with the grief."

"How awful! You can tell how much he loves kids. It just bubbles out like a fountain. I bet he'd be a great dad."

"Hopefully, when they're ready, they'll try again."

The snow-covered hills against the backdrop of the pine trees looked like a scene from a postcard. Lee and his wife's sorrow shocked her to the core. Earlier, watching Lee full of energy and enthusiasm as he interacted with the children, she'd been positive that his life was perfect and that he lacked for nothing. Even his prayer was all about giving thanks. How could he thank God when he suffered so much? She traced the scar from her hysterectomy. Why would God do this to them . . . to her? Father Mark had said, "Bad things happen to good people because we live in a fallen world." Maybe this wasn't what God had originally planned. But he allowed all of this hurt in the world. Didn't he?

"Steve?" She stared at him as he drove. "Why would God let so much pain and suffering go on in this world? Doesn't he care?"

"He cares." He was silent a moment. "It may not always appear that way. We report the news. It's our job, and more times than not, the news is distressing." He paused a moment.

"The good news is that we have a choice about how we handle our disappointments. We can run away from God and blame Him for all the terrible things that have ever happened in our lives, or we can run to Him and accept that whatever happens, He has a plan, and He can bring good out of awful circumstances."

"How is that possible?" She clenched her fist.

"John 16:33 says, 'In this world you will have trouble. But take heart! I have overcome the world.'"

"Hmm…" She honed in the majestic mountain peaks.

"Put's things in perspective, doesn't it?" He reached over with the other hand and softly unclenched her fists.

Her hand relaxed in his for a brief moment before she pulled away. "I guess so." Caitlynn closed her eyes willing her heart to slow it's erratic pounding.

Later, the group stood at the base of the resort. Lee pointed out where they were to meet for lunch. Steve headed to the lodge. Caitlynn followed Tyler, Hunter, and Hunter's dad, Westin, to the ski lift.

Lee and his ski buddy, Blake, were in the chair behind them. When the chairs dropped the group off, they skied to the head of the green run and stopped.

Lee teased Tyler, "Your dad went to great lengths to get out of skiing, didn't he?"

"Yeah." He giggled. "I'm going to tell Dad that a girl ski's better than him."

Caitlynn laughed. "That'll go over great, I'm sure."

Hunter yelled, "Hey, Tyler, last one down is a rotten egg," and started down the slope.

Tyler slowly carved a wide serpentine from one side of the slope to the other. She followed close behind. "You're doing great, Ty! Keep going!" True to Steve's prediction, Tyler took his time, unfazed by Hunter's challenge.

Eventually, they met the group at the bottom. Hunter tapped Tyler's pole lightly. "I beat you. You're the rotten egg."

Westin glared at his son. "Hunter! It's going to be a long day if you plan to keep teasing Tyler like this. Let's just have fun and quit trying to make it a competition, okay?"

Tyler shrugged. "It's okay. I won't be the rotten egg for long. Let's go on a blue run next."

On the next chair lift, Blake and Tyler sat side by side, while Lee and Caitlynn sat together.

"It's great that you were able to do this for Tyler," Lee said.

"No problem. I'm glad I could help."

"When Tyler first came to our church, he gave Steve a hard time. He didn't want to come because he didn't know anyone." Lee looked on as Blake and Tyler were cutting up. "Now, look at him."

Tyler threw his head back and cackled. It warmed her heart, so much so that soon she was grinning just as big. "He's a great kid."

At some point during the next run, Tyler gained his confidence and raced beside Hunter and Blake as if they were trying to outrun an avalanche. It was all she could do to keep up with Westin and Lee.

She slalomed in delight, her skis crunching through the snow with each and every turn, the wind whisking. She breathed in the fresh scent of the thin air mixed with pine, reveling in pure pleasure the ability to be healthy enough to ski.

Four months ago, she was recovering in a hospital bed. Now, no more doubling over from the debilitating pain—and she was having fun with Tyler, an adorable kid so full of life. Too bad Steve had to be part of the package, but even he didn't seem to grate on her nerves as much anymore.

Her mind darted to her goal. She still wanted Steve out of her life. *Didn't she?* But if he left, that would mean Tyler would go too. None of it mattered right now, though; this day was Tyler's. She stopped next to him, standing with his group of friends.

"Hey, Blake, do you recognize Ms. Caitlynn?" Tyler said.

He shook his head. "No. Should I? Is she famous?"

"Sorta. She's on television. She's a reporter for Channel 12."

Both Blake and Hunter stared at her as if she'd just stepped out of a television screen. "Wow. I guess I do kinda recognize you," Hunter said.

Blake stared wide-eyed. "I can't wait to tell my mom."

Ty yelled, "Hey, there's your dad and Lee." The boys took off.

When it was time for lunch, they raced to the lodge. Once there, Lee said, "Caitlynn, would you mind taking Blake? I'm going to wait here a few more minutes for the rest of the gang."

"Sure. Come on, you two. Tyler, let's go find your dad." She clomped up the stairs, best she could in clunky ski boots. Tyler held open the door.

A warm fire crackled in the massive stone fireplace. She spotted Steve motioning them to a lunch table. The kids ran over with Westin following behind.

Tyler's eyes twinkled with mischief. "Daddy, Caitlynn is way better than you. You should take a lesson."

"Is that so?" He grinned. "I'm glad she wasn't too slow for you. I was worried—her being a girl and all."

"Whoa," Caitlynn fired back. "You're talking pretty big, considering you're the one sittin' in this lodge."

Tyler, Blake, and Hunter laughed so hard Caitlynn thought they were going to fall out of their chairs.

"Touché. If I had my gear with me, I'd ski the rest of the day just to prove to you I can."

She retorted, "Oh, I know you can, but Westin and Lee might show you a thing or two."

Caitlynn was having so much fun; she almost forgot she was with a bunch of religious people. They all seemed so real and had such a calm demeanor about them. She glanced around the table. The kids giggled, and the men were smiling, teasing one another.

Two workers brought out bowls of chili for the adults, chicken nuggets, and fries for the kids, plus water and hot chocolate. Laughter rang out again. She looked across at Steve, and for the first time in a long while, she smiled at him, happy to share this moment. He sat up straighter, picked up his drink, and stared into her eyes as he took a sip. *What if his hand was warming hers instead of the cup?* She shook the thought away.

After lunch, they headed to the half-pipe to watch Cory Powers. He executed his trademark move so flawlessly it was hard to count all the flips and twists in the air. The kids oohed and aahed and screamed, "Pow-er Surge! Pow-er Surge!" until their voices were hoarse. Cory signed a T-shirt for each child, which they all promptly put on over their ski jackets and vowed not to take off until their moms made them.

Lee shouted, "Huddle up! The lunch and exhibition took longer than expected, but I think you all had a great time, didn't you?"

The kids squealed out their approval. "Co-ry, Co-ry!"

Lee made a cut gesture with his hand to hush the kids, then glanced at his watch. "We have enough time for one last run before we head home. Let's meet back here in forty-five minutes."

Caitlynn's thighs still burned from the last run—and their short break to eat lunch and watch Cory had only confirmed to her tired, aching muscles that she was ready to go home and soak in a hot tub.

Thankfully, they finished the last run, and once again at the base of Winter Park. Lee verified that everyone was accounted for before anyone left. He shook Caitlynn's hand. "Thanks for coming. It was great to meet you finally. I can see why Steve—"

"Lee?" Westin interrupted. "I can give Blake a ride home if you'd like."

Lee released her hand, turned to Westin. "Thanks, man, but I promised his mother I would look after him. She's meeting me at church."

Caitlynn loosened her boots. *What was Lee going to say about Steve?*

Steve carried Caitlynn and Tyler's equipment as the group headed to the parking lot. Her legs ached and felt like she walked on two sticks of rubber. The car didn't seem this far away from the ski resort this morning, but now she was positive they'd walked at least a mile. Steve unlocked his SUV and stowed the skis and other gear, shutting the tailgate, as Tyler and Caitlynn collapsed in their seats.

She rubbed her aching thighs. "Tyler, you officially managed to wear me out."

Tyler yawned. "I'm tired too." He leaned over and gave her a peck on the cheek. "Thanks for taking me. I had so much fun."

"You're welcome." The kiss still warmed her cheek. "I had a great time too." She patted his knee.

Steve started the engine. "Did you two have fun?"

"Yes," they said in unison, but Tyler's answer was a very sleepy-sounding affirmation.

"I'm glad. Let's go home."

###

Caitlynn melted into the couch like she was a rag doll. Every muscle in her body ached from chasing Tyler down the mountain. As tired as she was, she couldn't stop thinking about her day. The innocent peck on the cheek from Tyler; and the smile she shared with Steve during lunch. Watching Lee interact with all the kids. Her discussion with Steve about God. *Does God care about me? If so, how could God possibly make anything good out of me never being able to conceive? Or the horrible news Steve confided to me about Lee and his wife's baby dying at birth?*

The way Steve gazed into her eyes and spoke her name—almost like a caress—made her wonder if he wanted more than just a work relationship. That day in the hospital when he wouldn't let go of her hand . . . today, his eyes locking in on her as if he was the happiest man on the planet that she was there with him.

His church group was another surprise. She'd assumed they'd be self-righteous, thinking that they were better than her because they were Christians. But nothing could have been further from the truth; they had all seemed like ordinary people with the same struggles she had—except they also appeared to have some sort of inner peace. How? Was it because of their faith?

She jumped slightly, startled at the chime of the doorbell. She peered through the peephole; saw a delivery guy who looked barely old enough to drive, holding a beautiful bouquet of pink and white roses. She opened the door.

"Are you Ms. Grant?"

"Yes."

He thrust out the container holding the cut flowers. "These are for you!"

Caitlynn grabbed the vase. "Thank you!" He had such a bright smile that she couldn't help but do the same.

"Hold on a second." She quickly closed the door, placed the flowers on the table, and grabbed a ten-dollar bill from her wallet. Rushing back, she opened the door. "Here you go. Thanks again."

She walked slowly toward the table, admiring the roses, so beautifully arranged. *Who would send me flowers?* She snatched the card. *It might be from Jake trying to weasel his way back.* She opened the card.

Caitlynn,

Thanks for helping me out today. Tyler and I had a great time, and I hope that we can all ski together soon.

Fondly,

Steve

I knew it. All the attention he kept paying her lately was for a reason. In her experience, a guy only sent flowers to impress her with his thoughtfulness. And that only happened if he wanted more from the relationship. And based on the guys she'd dated—like Jake, more meant sex.

She walked to the garbage but stopped when the delightful fragrance drifted toward her. She inhaled in appreciation. *Why waste a perfectly beautiful bouquet?* She placed the vase on the dining room table, admiring how the flowers added instant beauty to the room. Like a spark on dry kindling, her temper flared. Arrows of doubt pelted her mind. She spoke aloud, breaking the silence once more. "This is not in my plan." The tantalizing aroma filled the room. "You're wasting your time. People don't change."

CHAPTER THIRTY-SEVEN

On his drive to work, Steve wondered if Caitlynn received the flowers. Should he say anything about them, or wait for Caitlynn to speak up first? The last time he bought flowers turned out disastrous. The dating scene seemed more complicated than when he was younger—but the one thing that never changed was the sting of rejection a guy felt when he drummed up the courage, and then heard *no* for an answer. Asking Caitlynn out would probably be like banging his head against a brick wall. He switched the radio station to sports talk and raised the volume.

This is ridiculous. Uncertainty taxed his brain, putting him in a foul mood. He needed to focus on work, not on flowers or women. He pulled into his reserved spot and entered the building. On the short elevator ride to his office, he refocused his thoughts onto the meeting with Ed. He walked down the hall at a fast clip, determined to get ready for the early morning meeting. When he turned the corner, he stopped abruptly. Caitlynn stood waiting at his door, twirling a strand of her hair with a frown on her face. *God, help me. I'm not ready to deal with this right now.*

He reached into his pocket for his office keys. "Good morning." He opened the door and gestured for her to enter. "Have a seat."

"I'll stand. What I have to say won't take long."

His first impulse was to lash out against what he knew was coming. But as he stared, her little girl trait of twisting her hair and the very adult look of irritation he read in her eyes brought a thought to his mind so completely foreign to him that he knew it had to be from the Lord. *Give her grace.*

He stopped an arm's distance away. "I know why you're here. You don't have to say a thing. I'm sorry I sent the flowers to you. I thought you might take it the wrong way but I couldn't help myself. I hoped you might view it as a kind gesture for all you've done for Tyler…and myself." He looked deep into her eyes. "Let's just forget it ever happened, okay?"

She took a step back, stopped twirling her hair, and gasped. "You're sorry?" She stepped to the right and looked around him. "Where is the old Steve? The one who never apologized for anything?"

"I've told you this before." Shaking his head. "I wish you'd believe me. I'm not the same person I used to be." He mumbled under his breath. "Thank God."

Caitlynn slumped into a chair as if her balloon had suddenly popped. "I geared up for a fight for nothing."

Steve took his time walking to his chair. He sat and smiled slyly. "We can still fight if you want, but I warn you, I've never backed down from a good battle."

"No." She fumbled nervously. "I'm good. Let's just call a truce, okay?"

As she opened the door, Steve couldn't help it. He had to say what was on his mind. "Caitlynn, I want to get one thing straight." He stared into her eyes. "I'm apologizing for sending the flowers…but I'm not one bit sorry about why I sent them."

A look of shock crossed her features; her cheeks turned bright pink. She practically flew out the door. He chuckled to himself and shook his head in amazement. Now look who's running—again.

For Steve, work dragged by, one slow day after another, as Caitlynn did her best to avoid contact. The only time he caught a glimpse of her was during the Tuesday morning staff meeting. The rest of the week, she headed out in the field. From a professional standpoint, he should be glad to see her either hunting up stories or interviewing Jillian. Still, he knew her real motivation—stay as far from him as possible. By Friday afternoon, his black mood returned as he drove from work to play basketball. Three guys were taking turns shooting baskets when Steve entered the gym.

Lee was dribbling the ball down the court. Steve stole it and made a shot. "I'm ready to play, so bring it!" An hour and thirty minutes later, Steve and Lee sagged against the gym wall.

Lee snatched up a towel and mopped his forehead. "I'm glad you brought Caitlynn skiing. I wanted to meet her."

"Yeah, I wanted you to meet her too so you could see why it's so hard for me to keep our relationship strictly professional." He wiped the sweat from his brow.

"Y'know, sometimes it takes an outsider looking in to read what you may not be able to see clearly."

Steve sighed. "See clearly? If you mean Caitlynn going out of her way to avoid seeing me, unless it involves Tyler, then yes, I'd say I'm in the dark."

Lee looked thoughtful. He paused a moment. "Has she ever flat-out refused you when you asked her to go somewhere with you and Tyler?"

Steve shook his head. "No, but she makes it very clear that the only reason why she's going in the first place is because she loves Ty so much."

"Uh, huh." Lee punched Steve's shoulder lightly. "You're as clueless as I was when I met my Carly. She says dense didn't even describe me when it came to my ability to see the signs she was throwing my way." He took a sip from his water bottle. "I'm changing my tune here, Steve. I told you to stay away from her because of her anger over your past. I didn't want to see you both heading down a dead-end street. I was wrong."

"I want to get to know her again on a personal level." Steve groaned. "I just sent her flowers, thinking that would be a great start, but apparently, she felt threatened. I told her on the note I wanted to invite her skiing, and I'd love to—but asking her out would be like falling head first into a retaining wall."

He gave Steve's shoulder a squeeze. "I think somewhere, buried deep inside, she cares for you." He shrugged. "I mean, she adores your son. There's no way she'd want to be around Ty if she truly hated you."

CHAPTER THIRTY-EIGHT

Four inches of snow covered the ground on the day of the shower. Caitlynn heard the familiar scraping sound of a snow shovel and turned to see Jillian's next-door neighbor clearing the drive. Caitlynn rang the bell and waited.

The door opened. "Come in." Peggy rubbed her furrowed brow. She looked so stressed, Caitlynn wished she knew her better so she could say or do something to help.

Stepping through the door, Caitlynn immediately understood Peggy's anxiety. Twenty teenage girls crammed the small living room and dining room, all talking nonstop. Occasionally, a loud burst of laughter rang out. A few moms with dazed expressions sat clustered on the couch watching their teenagers carry on.

Jillian reigned in a chair; a bouquet of balloons tied to the back. Clearly enjoying the lavished attention from all the adoring guests. Tori, her best friend and hostess, sat next to her.

Caitlynn spied an empty chair in the living room and sat down, holding her gift in her lap. A discreet glance at her watch showed five minutes past eleven. The invitation read that the shower would end at two, but that wouldn't happen by the look of things. Peggy handed a glass of punch to Caitlynn and then rushed back into the kitchen. The smell of barbecue filled the air, but the frown on Peggy's face, along with her frantic stirring, suggested that she had a bit more to do before serving lunch.

I better get this over with. Caitlynn set her present on the table next to the cake and sauntered over to Jillian. She got the camera ready. Conversation stopped abruptly.

Jillian's smile reflected in her eyes. "Everybody, this is Caitlynn. Do you remember when I told you about the story, she's doing about me…and the baby." she beamed. "I'm so glad you came, Caitlynn."

Every girl turned and stared, mouth agape, as if she'd just materialized from thin air. Caitlynn faked a smile. *This is going to be a long day.* A stabbing ache started above her left temple. "Do you mind if I film?"

"Go right ahead." Jillian and all her friends giggled in unison.

Caitlynn brought the camera up and pressed the record button. "It's nice to finally meet your friends, Jillian. You've told me how they all plan to help you babysit once the baby comes."

Tori piped up. "I can't wait to hang out with the baby. It'll be so much fun to hold her. I'm going to spoil her rotten."

One girl across the room said, "I'm going to be there every day." or "I love babies!" Another blurted, "I can come after work to help."

Jillian glowed as brightly as the sun reflecting off the snow outside, and said to Caitlynn, "See what great friends I have?" Then Jillian turned toward a pimple-faced brunette and whispered.

She shut the recording off. Whatever they were saying, was off-limits to the camera. She quickly returned to her chair, and gazed over at the mothers—all whom seemed to be wearing identical expressions of misery having to be at a baby shower. But also, relief, that *their* daughter wasn't the one pregnant. One of them glanced at her watch and sighed. Tori's mom glared at her daughter. Tori shrugged a shoulder in dismissal and continued to chat.

At noon, Peggy finished cooking and finally served lunch. Tori brought a plate of food to the guest of honor, and the rest stood in line for the barbecued pork sandwiches, coleslaw, and fruit salad. For the next hour, Caitlynn picked at her food as the girls ate and continued their constant blabbering. She wondered what they could possibly still have to say. *Was I ever like this?*

Eventually, Tori stood, passed out pens and paper, and chirped, "It's time to play a few games now."

Caitlynn pressed her fingers over her temple and groaned inwardly. Jars of unlabeled baby food passed around among the girls, as they all tried to guess the contents. Then, a tray filled with about 20 commonly used baby items were quickly shown. They each had one minute to jot down what they remembered. Finally, each person tore off the number of squares from a roll of toilet tissue that they guessed would fit around Jillian's belly. Tori flashed a huge grin and deliberately tore off 15 squares, just to tease Jillian. More laughter followed.

What am I doing here? A celebration like this is for family and close friends. Why didn't she just give Jillian her gift at another time? Jillian was happy. Her friends were having fun giving her this party. Caitlynn hid a frown. She'd never have a baby shower—ever. *No baby, no shower.* She sipped her drink, wishing for something more potent than orange and pineapple juice with lemon-lime soda and floating mounds of sherbet ice cream.

Tori's mom stood like she wanted to move things along. "Tori?" she said. "Jillian has a huge number of gifts." Her lips curved into a thin smile. "Why don't you cut the cake and I'll help you pass it out. We can all eat while we watch Jillian open presents."

Tori's eyes narrowed. "I guess that will be okay. Come over here, Jillian, and I'll take a picture with your camera of you with the cake."

Jillian waddled over. "This is such a cute cake." The round, three-layer white-frosted cake had strawberries circling around the sides. A pair of baby booties, frosted in a sunny yellow, decorated the top. "My mom bought my favorite—fresh strawberry cake. Wait till you taste this. It's de-lish." She posed for the camera and then sat on the chair next to the pile.

Jillian opened her first one—a frilly newborn-size pink and white polka dot dress with matching booties. One of the girls grinned. "I had to buy that for Skylar. She's going to look so cute."

More newborn dresses followed. One friend bought a sleeper in pastel colors and a couple of receiving blankets, but most of the gifts were rattles, baby bottles, disposable diapers, or tiny shoes.

Caitlynn hid a smile, knowing that Jillian would love the items she had bought. Finally, Jillian opened Caitlynn's gift—and gently rubbed her fingers across the silver picture frame engraved with

Skylar in block letters. Next, she unwrapped a stuffed white baby lamb. It had several buttons on its belly; when pressed, you'd hear the sound of the ocean or spring showers, a mother's heartbeat, or whale sounds.

"Oh...I've read about this!" Jillian, hugged it close. "It's supposed to help the baby sleep."

It was almost four by the time the last two gifts were opened from her mom. As Jillian unwrapped them, she cried out in delight, "You bought the car seat and the baby swing! Her mouth dropped open. Thanks!"

Peggy replied, "You're welcome. Nana wanted to be here, but she's sick with a nasty cold. She bought you the crib you wanted."

Jillian gasped in surprise. "That's awesome!" She held one of the tiny dresses. "My daughter is going to be the best-dressed baby on the planet." Her eyes glistened. "Thanks so much for all the gifts, everyone!"

Caitlynn stood to leave. The mothers said hasty goodbyes, and when it was Caitlynn's turn, she said, "Thanks for inviting me. I'll talk to you in a few days."

"I'm so happy you weren't a no-show." Jillian pressed Caitlynn's hand. "My friends didn't believe me when I said you were coming." She glanced at her friends, who were standing in a circle and chatting. "Things are working out. My mom might not want to help Skylar and me, but my friends are all about it! They can't wait until I have Skylar so they can be near her."

"You seem to be in good company." The constant chatter and giggling, the gifts, the games, the lunch, the cake, and small talk— it all made her want to run out of the house screaming. Instead, she gently squeezed Jillian's shoulder. "Talk to you in a few days." Then she escaped to the quiet confines of her car.

CHAPTER THIRTY-NINE

It is not easily angered
1CORINTHIANS 13:5

On Sunday afternoon, bag in hand, Steve knocked on Caitlynn's door. He raked his fingers through his hair and gripped the bag's plastic handle as if he were holding on to a lifeline.

She opened the door, her brows arched. "What are you doing here?" Her voice lilted in surprise.

"I come bearing gifts." He shook the bag and hoped his expression looked suitably mysterious. "Care to see what's inside?"

Caitlynn's soft laugh in response held promise. *Good. She hasn't slammed the door in my face.*

She waved her hand over her attire. Wearing a long-sleeved black T-shirt, baggy sweatpants, and her purple fuzzy slippers. She opened the door wider. "I bet Brenda never dressed like this." She took a step off to the side. "Come in. I was just watching a movie—definitely wasn't expecting company."

"I would've called first, but I didn't want to take the chance." He walked over to the kitchen counter and deposited the bag on the table.

"That I'd say no?"

He ignored her comment. A Ford truck commercial blared from the other room. "What movie are you watching?"

Caitlynn's eyes held a dreamy look. "Sleepless in Seattle."

He moaned. "I'm glad I brought refreshments. I'll need them if I'm going to watch this movie with you."

She gave a half shrug. "Like I said, I wasn't expecting company. Besides, it's almost over."

He pulled out the Frito corn chips. Next came a can of refried bean dip and a bag of microwave popcorn. "At least I've got some man food to eat while I watch a chick flick."

Caitlynn stared at the dip and chips. "You've got to be kidding. The last time I ate junk of this caliber was in college."

"Don't pretend you don't like it." He said, knowingly. "We ate this practically every weekend while the Broncos played." He pulled out a six-pack of Mountain Dew and reached into the bag once more. "I got this for you." Out came a six-pack of Diet Dr. Pepper.

Tom Hank's voice interrupted her response. "I don't have time to argue," she said. "You're lucky the movie's on. Bring your junk food over and try not to crunch too loud." She plunked down on the couch, propped her feet on the coffee table, and turned up the sound.

"Okay. Be right there." A minute later, the smell of popcorn filled the air. Steve laid the food out on the coffee table and sat close to her. Scooping a chip into the dip, he popped it into his mouth. "There's one more item in the bag to show you, but I'll wait until the movie's over."

"Shh." Caitlynn opened a can of Diet Dr. Pepper. "Let's talk at the next commercial."

"When did you get to be such a romantic? You're not going to cry when they meet at the top of the Empire State Building, are you?"

Caitlynn rolled her eyes at him. "I don't cry at movies. And I've always liked stories with happy endings." She scooped up a handful of popcorn. "Now, please be quiet. We're getting to the best part."

This time it was his turn to roll his eyes, but then did as he was told, content to sit quietly next to Caitlynn. He scooted close to her, pretending to reach for the bean dip. He watched in amusement as she dipped her chips into the dip. A few minutes later, she absently went back for more and then moved over, widening the gap. He gritted his teeth and watched the movie to the bitter end.

"I never tire of that movie." She sighed happily, grinning ear to ear.

"Geez, I wish I could get a smile like that from you. What do I have to do? Star in a Hollywood romance?"

She gave a playful smirk. "Leave town, for starters."

"I'm ignoring that last remark. Go look in the bag and see what I brought."

Jumping from the couch, Caitlynn walked over to the table, reached into the bag, and nodded in disbelief. "Are you regressing?"

"We used to play this every day. I know you love it."

"Backgammon? What are we going to do next? Walk the campus of the University of Colorado?"

"No. We're going to play this game. Open it, and I'll help you set it up."

She huffed. "Okay. Just so you know, I can still play this game. I hope you're ready for a beat down."

"Just so you know, Tyler and I play this when I can wrestle the video game controller from him."

"I'm not Ty," she said as she spread out the game board.

Steve's gaze swept from her eyes to her lips and stayed there. "So, I see."

Her cheeks pinked. In the soft light, her hair glowed, and her eyes sparkled—an ethereal essence. For just a moment, he caught a glimpse of the Caitlynn he fell in love with back in college. He sucked in a breath. *This was the woman he used to know*—lovely and so full of life he could barely keep up with her high spirits. Reminded once again of all the reasons he cared for her: how she acted around children, especially his son. How hard she worked at her job and never complained. He even loved it when she twirled her hair when she was nervous and wasn't afraid to say what was on her mind.

Did he love her? His heart hammered in his chest. *Yes.* Beating so loudly he was sure she could hear, he wanted to reach over the coffee table and kiss her. She turned an even deeper hue as he turned his attention back to her eyes. "Roll the dice."

They played five games. He lost the last game. "I think you cheated. I want a rematch."

"I told you—I'm not Tyler," she teased. "Besides, why would I give you another chance?"

Reluctantly, Steve rose from the chair. "It's getting late." He held her gaze. "Thanks for humoring me today with the trip down memory lane. I had a great time."

Caitlynn followed him to the door. "Steve? I know what you're trying to do—"

He put his finger to her lips. "Shh. Let's end the evening on a good note. This is what I should've done at Christmas." Then tenderly, he kissed her soft lips. As if he'd just stepped on a high voltage tripwire, a jolt spread throughout his body. He stared into her eyes and saw confusion. He gently traced her lips with his finger. "Goodbye, Caitlynn. See you tomorrow." He walked out— and winced when the door slammed shut, all the while grinning in amusement, because he knew the door slam was a sure thing. *At least she didn't slap me.*

Caitlynn's lips still felt his lingering kiss. The warmth of his lips only magnified the betrayal of her body's response, as if her life force somehow never forgot the deep intimacy they had once shared. She leaned back on the couch and shut her eyes. When he had traced her mouth with his finger, tiny sparks of pleasure had sent shivers through her body. She took a few deep breaths to calm her still-racing pulse. Her lips still tingled, tormenting her with a reaction to his kiss that she'd much rather ignore.

She had vowed to get him out of her life, and force him back to Chicago. Skiing with Tyler flashed through her mind. The memory of driving home together and talking about the day's events, just like any typical family. The way Steve went out of his way to help her recover after surgery. His apology. She had tried to keep as much space as possible between them. Why did he think she cared for him?

Jake's accusations haunted her. *Am I sending out the wrong signal?*

Kissing her, whether she wanted him to or not, was more like the old Steve, selfish—taking without a second thought. She still wanted to make him pay for the way things had turned out between them. Didn't she?

In so many ways, his actions had shown, how much he'd changed. But it was too late. To trust him once more after the hurt he'd caused her so many years ago seemed impossible.

His kindness, and limitless help, during these last few months only made it that much harder to do what needed to be done. Her stomach twisted into a hard knot. If she was going to drive Steve out of her life, she needed to do it now—before their relationship grew even more complicated. He obviously wanted more from the relationship than she was ready for. *He's going to hurt me, just like before.* Hot anger pulsed through her veins. *The only difference is; I can't get pregnant now. Who does he think he is? And why does he think he deserves a second chance?*

She picked up the phone and made a call. An image of Tyler's soft peck on her cheek and his heartfelt thanks for taking him skiing emerged out of nowhere, but she managed to push those feelings deep into the shadows of her heart.

"Caitlynn? What a nice surprise."

"Hi, Brett, I hope I didn't call too late."

"Are you serious? It's only ten o'clock. In New Orleans time, that's early."

"I wanted to ask if you had a chance to talk to your friend." She bit her lip.

"I only need your go-ahead, and the dirty deed is done."

Caitlynn stammered. "Wh—what's involved?" She twisted her hair.

"He'll provide you a CD loaded with the pornography of adult women. Once downloaded, it will imbed into his C-drive. The IT department will pick up on it and flag it down." Brett laughed mercilessly. "So much for Steve and his loftier-than-thou image. He should be fired by the end of the week. You have no idea how many men get fired for this very thing. It's practically an epidemic if you ask me." Brett's voice slurred, "And even if he is the *bosh*, there's zero tolerance for pornography at the station."

"I want him back in Chicago. He doesn't realize it would be better for all of us…but I do." Steve was a threat to her—at the very least, he could fire her, but worse still, he could break her heart all over again…and that was never going to happen—ever. Ignoring the tiny voice that whispered for her to stop, she gripped the phone until her knuckles turned white. "What if we get caught?"

"Caitlynn." He hiccoughed. "Don't be shilly. Wear gloves if you're that concerned, and destroy the evidence so that nothing can be traced. You're worrying for nothing. Look, it's going to cost you five hundred dollars. You send me the money. I'll give it to my guy and mail you the CD. You can figure out the right time—and if you've got the guts to do it or not."

"Brett, give me your address before I change my mind." Her fingers shook as she jotted down the details.

"Look, Caitlynn, whatever the dude did, he deserves to be ruined. If I were there, I'd do it," he snarled. "This station is a far cry from Denver, and it's all his fault. I don't know why he harped on me about being negative. Who'd he find to replace me? Another goody-two-shoes, I bet." His voice tapered off.

Caitlynn shivered. Brett's voice dripped with hatred, a poisonous snake striking at its target. "Um, thanks—I'll mail the money tomorrow." She hung up and wiped her clammy hands. Just talking about it made her so nervous she could feel the hair on the back of her neck rise.

CHAPTER FORTY

Steve stared blankly at the computer monitor. His lack of attention deepened his bad mood. Today was Wednesday—and Easter was four days away. Tyler would be here in two days for the holiday. He should be excited, but all he could focus on was Caitlynn and her disappearing act.

What did she think I would do? Rush in on Monday morning declaring her undying love for him? Ignoring him seemed to be her favorite mode of communication. Maybe he scared her off with his kiss, but he wanted her to know his true feelings. Had he ever stopped loving her?

His father had never liked Caitlynn, and he'd made it clear to Steve how she didn't measure up. "No father in the picture, raised by a single mom. All she's after is your money, son; trust me on this," his father had said.

The pressure to marry someone like Brenda—wealthy and with the right family connections—seemed so right at the time, and there were qualities Brenda possessed that he admired. But from the start, their relationship had been two people playing tug-of-war. With Caitlynn, it had never been difficult. When they were in college, their friends would tease them and say they were so much alike; they completed each other's sentences.

Steve knew God didn't make mistakes, and thankfully, Tyler had resulted from his marriage—Tyler, who was the best thing that had ever happened to him. For his entire life, he had to be in control and make decisions on his own terms and conditions. But God kept showing him, time and again, that he needed to surrender the control he clung to so desperately. God knew the right decisions, and all he had to do was let go and let God. Then why did it seem so hard? Why did he give a problem to God only to take it back again? Over and over. Was this part of maturing as a Christian? Did Lee struggle with this ping-pong back and forth with God?

The shrill sound of the phone interrupted. It was his mother. "This is a nice surprise," he said, his spirit lifting. "You don't usually call me at work."

"I wanted to ask a favor." Her voice sounded anxious.

He held his breath. "What is it?"

"Ever since Corner Pocket died, your father either mopes around the house or works until midnight, to the point where he's sleeping in his office."

"It's a tough loss. Dad was banking on that horse. He was sure he had a winner."

"We all were. But you can't pin your hopes on an animal." She sighed. "Why don't you come out for Easter? It would do your father good. And I know I could use some time with you too."

Steve wanted to kick himself for not thinking about going there in the first place. He was so wrapped up in his own problems; he hadn't even considered helping his parents through their pain. "Of course, I'll come. Let me call Brenda and tell her my change of plans. If it's okay with her and Ty, I'll be there on Friday evening and stay until Monday morning. Ty can go to the service at Willow Creek with me—"

"Steve?"

"Yeah?"

"Let's have brunch at the club after service, and if it's okay with you, your dad and I would like to go to church with you and Ty."

"You're kidding?" There was no way to keep the shock out of his voice. "That's great, Mom! I'll see you in a few days." He spent the rest of the day smiling.

###

Early Sunday evening, tired from the full day of celebrating Easter—and stuffed from the brunch—Steve lounged on a loveseat, enjoying the heat from the fireplace, listening as the wood crackled and popped. His parents sat on the couch across from him. The occasional snapping sound when the wood hit an air pocket and the smell of the smoke wafting up the chimney, mesmerized him into a peaceful, relaxed state. The chandelier lights were dimmed low, and the glow from the fireplace cast shadows across his parents' faces.

Two days ago, when he first saw his father, he took a double-take. Dad's hair jutted out at right angles. Usually an immaculate dresser, he wore a baggy pair of dingy brown sweatpants and a faded black T-shirt—something he'd typically only be caught wearing in the gym. To make matters worse, the corners of his mouth drooped as if he'd aged ten years.

Now, here they were. His mother paged through a magazine, regal as always. His father folded his hands in his lap and closed his eyes. Thankfully, his grimace was gone, but it didn't keep Steve from being concerned. He asked, "How did you two like the Easter service?"

His father opened his eyes and scooted up a bit taller in the cushions. "All this time, I had wondered what kind of church you attended when you lived here. I don't know what I was expecting, but I must say, I liked the music, and the pastor was excellent. I may even go again."

His mother's jaw dropped, but she quickly snapped it closed. "I liked it too. When everyone was singing, I got goosebumps—and the message about God's grace…."

"Yes, the Grace." Silence ensued. The two of them taking in the moment.

Steve continued. "Ty had a great time too. He saw some of his old friends. If you go again, maybe you can take Ty. He would love it." He turned to his father. "How's Carl doing? I went down to the barn and introduced myself to the new guy, Chandler."

His father's scowl deepened. "I apologized to Carl—told him I wanted to start over—but he declined to return." He closed his eyes again. "He said it was his cue to retire."

"That's too bad." Steve drummed his fingers on the armchair. "How does Boo like Chandler?"

His mom laughed lightly. "He seems determined to show Chandler how it's done in the stable. The first day, Chandler was an hour late feeding Boo. Boo whinnied for an hour, stomped his hoof over and over, and nudged him with his nose." She giggled again. "Now, Chandler makes sure Boo gets fed on time."

"Are you planning to buy another thoroughbred?"

"Nope. Not ready yet. I put my heart and soul into each one of my horses."

"I know, Mom. Take your time. I'm sure you'll find the right horse out there when you're ready."

His father piped up. "I don't know. Maybe, Carl is right. Maybe, we should retire from the racing business."

"Are you serious?" Steve said in disbelief. "What would you do?"

His mom interrupted. "Sell the place—move to Denver. There's actually nothing keeping us here except for Tyler, and your father can work anywhere as long as there's an airport nearby."

In stunned silence, Steve searched to find the right words. "You sound as if you've been thinking about this for some time." His gaze darted from his father to his mother.

"We've discussed it at length." Her voice rose, and she said excitedly, "We would see you and Tyler more than we do now. This horse farm is more work than I want to tackle at this stage in my life. I want to travel with your father, and it's just not possible living here."

Steve shook his head. "I'm in shock. If you're happy, then I think it's great. I guess you could both use a change in your life."

His father's eyes bored into Steve's. "I hope you still think it's great when we're nosing in on your personal space." His upbeat tone filled the room. "Having us so close to you could take some getting used to, son."

Steve tried to stay positive, and he truly was happy for his parents—but the question that kept surfacing in his mind was…what would happen to Boo?

CHAPTER FORTY-ONE

Adrenalin surged, instantly awake, as she scooted across the bed to her cell phone on the nightstand. "Hello?" she said frantically.

"It's Peggy . . . sorry to bother you, but you wanted to know when the baby was coming. Well, the contractions started an hour ago, and we're on our way to Swedish Hospital."

"Oh Wow!" Caitlynn gasped. "Jillian's a month early?"

Peggy chuckled nervously. "I guess Skylar's eager to see the world."

Caitlynn shot out of bed, relieved it wasn't bad news about her mother. "I'm on my way."

An hour later, she tapped on the door to Jillian's room and stepped inside. This was the first time Caitlynn had ever been in a maternity ward. She didn't know what to expect—but somehow, this seemed luxurious. Soft lighting overhead bathed the room. The bed centered the room with gleaming white built-in shelves on either side, plus an oversized chair and a rocker. A sink with dark marble countertops and white cabinets lined one side of the wall. A vase with fresh flowers graced the windowsill. *Coffee?* Her nose twitched at the rich aroma. The room looked like it could be in an urban-style hotel. Jillian lounged in bed, rubbing her belly, while Peggy sat in the chair with a book in her lap.

"You two look way too relaxed," Caitlynn commented as she leaned over and hugged Jillian. "Are you okay?"

"So far, so good!" Jillian exclaimed. "A few contractions hurt, but they go away and come back a few minutes later. It's not that bad."

Peggy shook her head. "Not yet, but it's coming like a freight train. Just remember to breathe."

Jillian rolled her eyes. Caitlynn now knew as Jillian's trademark response. "Whatever."

Caitlynn looked at Peggy. "How far apart are they?"

"Three minutes. She's around four centimeters dilated."

She glanced back at Jillian. "Are you going to have an epidural?" she asked.

"Why?" I told you I'm fine. They don't hurt that much."

"Um, maybe not now," Caitlynn agreed. "But you'll really feel it once the contractions come closer together and they last longer. Then there's the transition, and that's when it's quite painful."

"How do you know so much about this? Did you have a baby?"

"No." Caitlynn closed her eyes briefly, willing the stabbing pain in her heart to go away. "I did a story on a midwife once."

"My mom and I went to birthing classes, and I plan to have a natural childbirth."

"I took similar classes when I had Jillian." Peggy scanned the room. "Barring any complications, the birth will be here. I can tell you, the delivery room I had was a far cry from this one!"

"When I followed the midwife, the mother stayed in her home. I didn't hang around for the delivery, for privacy reasons."

"I want you here, with me, Caitlynn." Jillian pleaded. "Please say you'll stay!"

A contraction hit just then. Caitlynn looked at the monitor as Jillian breathed through the pain.

"Whoa. That one hurt more than the last one."

Peggy took a sip from her mug and picked up her book. "Jillian, you should get the epidural."

Jillian rolled her eyes and rubbed her tummy. Caitlynn brushed a strand of hair from Jillian's face. "I won't leave if that's what you want. Ryan's coming with the camera. He won't film the birth. He's just going to take a few shots and leave, and then continue filming for a few more minutes once the baby is born."

A nurse hustled into the room. Her nametag said, Cherrie. "Hello there, Mommy. How are you feeling?"

"I feel some pain, but most of all, it's just a squeezing pressure that starts in my back and goes all the way around to my stomach."

"If you feel you can manage, walking sometimes speeds things along."

"How long should I walk for?"

"Play it by how you feel. Your body will let you know."

Jillian pushed the covers away. "I'm sick of being in this bed anyway. I've been here since four this morning, and it's already seven o'clock. This baby needs to come!"

"Did you forget everything you were taught?" Peggy sighed. "You could be here all day and night delivering that baby."

"There's no way that's happening. I haven't eaten since last night's dinner, and the nurse said the only thing I can have is ice chips. Caitlynn, walk with me down the hall and back. Let's get this party started."

Ryan walked into the room, lugging the camera. "What party? Where?" He grinned at Caitlynn and Jillian.

"Great timing, Ryan." Caitlynn smiled in return. "We were just going to walk for a few minutes. I would love for you to take some shots of Jillian walking in the hallway."

Two hours later, Jillian lay on the bed moaning in pain. "Mom, make the pain go away."

Her mom tenderly wiped the sweat from Jillian's forehead. "It's too late now for an epidural. You're too far along. I know you're sick of hearing this, but focus and breathe."

Caitlynn sat on the other side of Jillian and held her hand. "I feel so helpless. Is there anything I can do?"

"You're doing enough just by being here." Jillian squeezed Caitlynn's fingers.

Ryan took one final shot of Jillian, her face wrinkled in pain, her lips pursed, breathing out in tiny gasps. He kept the camera trained on Jillian's face. Her lips were turning blue.

Peggy looked nervous. "I pressed the call button five minutes ago. Can you run and get the nurse?"

Caitlynn barreled out the door and around the corner to the nurses' station. "You need to come. Jillian's lips are blue."

Caitlynn followed Nurse Cherrie into the room. The nurse strode to Jillian's side and watched her breathing, fast and shallow.

"Sweetie, you're hyperventilating. Look at me."

"I'm going to throw up." She held her hand to her mouth.

Caitlynn rushed over with the plastic container. "Here." She pulled Jillian's hair back as she retched.

Peggy whispered, "I'll be back in a minute." She fled out the door.

The nurse handed Jillian a glass of water. "Here, rinse your mouth out."

Jillian swished and spit, then lay against the pillow and moaned.

"My mom can't take it when someone vomits. I come from a long line of weak stomachs. We all puke if we see someone puking. Even talking about it can make my grandmother hurl. Mom will be back in a few minutes."

Ryan turned off the camera. "I'm outta here." He looked a bit green. "I got some good footage. Caitlynn, call me when the baby's born." He stumbled out the door.

Nurse Cherrie soaked a washcloth with cold water at the sink, squeezed out the excess, and carefully wiped Jillian's face. After rechecking Jillian's cervix, Cherrie said, "You're doing great, Jillian. You're eight centimeters dilated now, so I'm going to get the doctor. This baby is close. I bet your little girl will be born within the hour." She moved to the door. "Be back in a minute."

Caitlynn gently rubbed Jillian's cheek with the cool cloth. "Center in on breathing out. Pretend you're blowing out a flame on a candle that won't stop glowing."

Jillian cried out as the pain started again. Her cheeks flamed bright red and she gritted her teeth.

"Don't hold your breath. You'll hyperventilate again." Caitlynn grabbed Jillian's shoulders. "You can do this, Jillian. You're strong! I know you are! Fight through the pain. Focus."

"That's easy for you to say. You're not the one having a baby," Jillian shouted angrily.

Caitlynn frowned. She had to reach Jillian. She shouted back, "I'd give anything to trade places with you, Jillian! I'll never have the experience you're having now. I long for a child of my own but I can't have children. Ever!" She stared into Jillian's eyes. "Now, you're doing this! You hear me? You're going to get through this delivery, and you're going to have a beautiful daughter to show for your effort."

Jillian squeezed her eyes shut. Tears flowed, dripping onto her hospital gown. "I'm so mad at you. Stop yelling at me." Her eyes flitted open, and if looks could inflict pain, Caitlynn would be in a world of hurt. She arched her back with a grunt. "Okay. I get it. I'm a baby whining over the pain."

Caitlynn realized she was holding her breath when another contraction hit. It was hard to watch Jillian's low moan turn into a guttural cry. Jillian wrapped her hands around the bedrail and squeezed. "Come on, breathe, Jillian. Let's do it together. Show me."

Jillian took a deep breath and exhaled while saying, "He, he, he, who," through the contraction.

Caitlynn mimicked every sound and breath, relieved when Jillian inhaled a deep, cleansing breath and exhaled when the contraction ended. "You did it!"

Jillian's eyes bored into hers. "I can feel another one coming, and I feel pressure." Then she screamed.

Peggy entered the room and rushed over. "The doctor is coming right behind me." She held Jillian's hand. "Nana is on her way. She should be here soon."

Dr. Fischer entered and examined Jillian himself. When he finished, he looked at Jillian. "You're about nine centimeters." He studied the monitor as the next contraction came. "I'm going to call in the rest of my team. You should have your baby soon." Walking over to the phone, he dialed, said a few words, then hung up. In less than two minutes, four additional nurses filed into the room.

Jillian held onto Peggy's hand. "Mom, I'm scared," she whimpered.

Caitlynn turned to leave, but Jillian grabbed for her hand frantically. "Please don't go." She turned her head. "Mom, if anything happens to me, I want Caitlynn—"

"Hush now. Don't think like that. You're going to be fine." She caressed Jillian's cheek.

The doctor stared at the monitor with a look of concern. "The baby's heart rate is dropping. In the next few contractions, you're going to feel like pushing, but I want you to fight that urge. I'm sure the umbilical cord is wrapped around your baby's neck." He stared into Jillian's eyes. "Don't get nervous. This happens in about twenty-five percent of all births."

The next contraction started. "Mom, I want to push! What do I do?"

Peggy's face was tense. "Think about what the doctor is doing. He's helping Skylar right now. Focus on what's happening with him instead of the urge to push."

Tears ran down Jillian's cheeks as she again squeezed her mother and Caitlynn's hands.

Caitlynn could hardly believe she would actually witness a birth. It was all so surreal and a bit nerve-wracking.

Dr. Fischer rolled his stool closer and said, "Okay, Jillian, I'm going to put my finger between the cord and the baby's neck so she can breathe. Go ahead and push, but when I tell you to stop, don't bear down." He looked at the monitor.

Jillian nodded. "I'll try." A few seconds later, her eyes grew big, and she croaked out, "I have to push."

"Not yet," Dr. Fischer said sharply.

Peggy gripped Jillian's chin and turned her face toward her. "Look at me. If you push now, the baby is going to be in trouble. You can do this. I know you can." She brushed back a strand of Jillian's hair.

"The head is crowning. Go ahead and push."

Caitlynn had never seen a face turn purple before, but Jillian's was proof that it could happen.

"Stop!" the doctor commanded. "I see the problem." He quickly unwound the cord.

"Okay, Jillian, go ahead and push again. Let's get her shoulders out and greet your baby girl."

Tears threatened to fall. Caitlynn quickly wiped them away. A feeling of both awe and amazement welled up inside—for the first time, she understood the miracle of birth.

The doctor squinted and honed in on guiding the baby through the delivery. "Come on, baby girl, you're almost there."

Jillian screamed and grabbed her mother's forearm as she pushed. Beads of sweat trickled down her face.

Peggy wiped Jillian's brow. "You're doing it, Jillian!"

There was one final push, and then the room filled with the sounds of a baby's wail. The doctor held on tightly to the slippery baby and gently placed her on Jillian's stomach. "She looks healthy. I just cleared her mouth and lungs of any fluid. She's nice and pink." He turned to a nurse. "Let me clip this cord that gave us so much trouble."

Watching Jillian stare at her tiny, perfectly formed baby, Caitlynn's tears flowed. She couldn't stop, even if she wanted too.

Jillian whispered, "Welcome to the world, Skylar."

Nurse Cherrie said, "We need to get her vitals, Jillian—we'll bring her right back to you." She carefully lifted the baby, snuggled the infant into her arms, and walked over to the scale in the corner of the room with another nurse. Then they left the room.

"Congratulations," Dr. Fischer said. "Now, one more push and we'll be just about done. You've torn a bit, so I'm going to have to stitch you up. You're going to feel some tugging."

Caitlynn hastily brushed away her tears. "I don't know what to say. Congratulations seem so anti-climactic."

Jillian's face glistened. "I know what you mean. I feel like I just went through a warzone and came out alive." She grinned in triumph.

Peggy was beaming. "Dr. Fischer, where is the baby? Can I go see her?"

Concentrating on his task, the doctor spoke without glancing up, "Go down the hall to the viewing area." His eyes darted briefly to Jillian. "You're lucky. Skylar's lung functions are normal. Most preterm babies have low oxygen levels."

Peggy kissed her daughter's forehead. "I'm so proud of you." She turned toward Caitlynn. "Do you want to come?"

"You go ahead. I'll stay here with Jillian."

Dr. Fischer removed the drape and stood. "I'm done here. I'll be back to check on you soon." He patted her arm, then turned and closed the door behind him.

"Are you going to call Ryan?" Peggy asked.

Caught up in the magic of the moment, Caitlynn had forgotten all about her job. "Um . . . yes," she stuttered. "I'll have him come back in about an hour."

Peggy kissed Jillian's cheek. "I love you. You did great." She hugged her. Her cell phone buzzed. "It's Nana . . . I'm going to take this outside." She quickly left the room.

After the commotion of the birth with all the nurses and the doctor, the quiet room seemed comforting somehow. "Your mom is right. You did great! I've never been part of an actual birth. I'm so amazed, I can't find the words. You look tired, but also amped up. Is that how you feel?"

"I feel like I'm on a cloud," Jillian said. "Sort of a dreamy sensation, wondering if I actually had a baby. I don't think it's sunk in yet."

A knock sounded on the door, and a nurse carted in the clear plastic crib where the baby slept peacefully. "Here she is! All cleaned up and ready to see you, Mommy!"

Jillian exclaimed in awe. "She's so tiny. I want to hold her, but I'm afraid I'll hurt her."

Nurse Cherrie chuckled and scooped Skylar gently up from the bassinet. "Hold out your arms, Jillian."

Jillian opened her arms to receive her sleepy daughter.

"You always want to support her head. Very gently but firmly when you pick her up, hold her neck and head, and support them like this." She carefully laid Skylar in the crook of Jillian's arm.

"Now wrap your lower arm around Skylar's little legs. You got it, I'm going now, but I'll be back soon to check on you." She left the room.

Jillian was glowing with the bundle in her arms. "Let's unwrap her and see what she looks like." With her free hand, she carefully peeled back the blanket. "Look at those perfect fingers and toes, and her legs and arms are so tiny."

"Watch." Caitlynn stretched her finger over to Skylar's tiny hand and touched it lightly. Instinctively, Skylar wrapped her hand around Caitlynn's finger. She brushed the top of Skylar's hand with her thumb. "I love babies. I volunteer twice a month on Saturdays in the NICU at the children's hospital. My role is to love and comfort the babies by rocking them. I always look forward to going."

Jillian's eyebrows shot up in surprise. "You've been such a great friend to me, and you're so nice, I guess I just assumed you'd be married . . . with children." Jillian removed the pink cotton hat from Skylar's head and caressed her feather-soft blonde locks. "I had no idea. I'm sorry I never thought to ask before."

With one last caress, Caitlynn gently pulled her hand away from Skylar's grasp. Frowning, she felt a wave of self-pity prick her soul like a sudden bee sting. Tears threatened to fall, and that was the last thing she needed. *Don't think—focus on Jillian.* "No, I'm not married, and I don't have any children, but you don't need to apologize."

She stood. "I'm going to go call Ryan to come back in and film you and Skylar." As she turned away, her stomach growled, a reminder that—in the excitement of the birth—she hadn't eaten since last night. "I'll be back in a few minutes, Jillian."

"Don't leave me alone!" Jillian's voice rose in panic.

Caitlynn pasted on the brightest camera-ready smile she could muster. "Jillian, you're not alone." She gazed longingly at the baby. "Hold Skylar. Your mom and Nana are on their way, remember?" She shut the door behind her.

Striding quickly, her footsteps rang hollow in the empty hallway. She stepped into the vacant elevator, punched the button, leaned back, and closed her eyes. She was used to feeling lonely, but this was so much more—it was also a deep sense of loss. Experiencing Skylar's birth had brought back every emotion she had tried so hard to push down over the years, only to rise to the surface again--like a giant wave crashing on the shore breaking her heart into the tiniest of pieces. How did one stop a wave?

As she stepped out of the elevator, she spied Peggy and Nana entering the next elevator over. She ran out the front door of the hospital and gulped in deep breaths of fresh air. A wave of dizziness hit her. Rummaging through her handbag, she pulled out a food bar, then called Ryan.

"It's Caitlynn." She ripped the food bar packaging open as she paced in front of the hospital entrance, battling another dizzy spell.

"I guess you're calling to tell me Jillian had her baby? I'm sorry I bailed. I had to get out of there." He laughed nervously. "Having a baby is beyond intense. I could tell that filming the moment was the last thing she needed."

"Very true. Not to worry. We have enough footage." Caitlynn focused on what was left. She had to film Skylar and Jillian. Then there was the home visit a week later. "How fast can you get back?" On the one hand, she wanted to get the filming over with, but on the other hand, she dreaded going back into the room with all the smiling faces celebrating something she would never experience.

"I'm on my way," Ryan assured her.

She hung up and looked west toward the mountains. Suddenly feeling that this story would never end—because even after filming the last shot, she still had to put the story together, finish editing, and then air the program, before she could finally bury it in the archives, along with all the painful emotions flooding her mind like a sudden thunderstorm on a summer day.

CHAPTER FORTY-TWO

It keeps no records of wrong
1 CORINTHIANS 13:5

Like the warm chinook winds of spring that mimic a wind tunnel in intensity and then just as quickly move on, the week flew by—and suddenly, it was Caitlynn's day to visit Jillian for the last time. Caitlynn clenched her fist and briefly closed her eyes, willing the emptiness she carried within; as well as the envy she knew would rise like smoke from ashes to remain in check. Taking a deep breath, she knocked.

Peggy opened the door wide and greeted Caitlynn and Ryan. "Come in." Deep, dark circles under her eyes, showcased her exhaustion. Peggy yawned behind her hand. "Excuse me. We've had a tough time. Skylar doesn't want to sleep—or eat much either. Jillian's with her, and I'm pretty sure she's in her room crying."

They walked into the living room. Baby shower gifts lay scattered along with other miscellaneous baby items covering the couch and the kitchen counter.

"We've spent a small fortune trying all these brands of formula, and so far, none of them have worked," Peggy said. "Skylar can't seem to tolerate any of them. She pulls her little legs up to her tummy and cries and cries, and it makes Jillian so upset that we all end up a tearful mess."

Caitlynn looked at the cans of infant formula lined up like birds on a wire. "It sounds like she has colic. I volunteer at Children's Hospital, and some of the parents have their babies on a formula specially designed for babies with sensitive stomachs. It says 'colic' somewhere on the label."

"At this point, if someone said I should stand on my head to help Skylar, I would." Peggy sighed. "It's Saturday, and we don't see the doctor until Monday. If you don't mind, I'm going to run out and find this colic formula. Would you stay with Jillian and the baby until I get back?"

Caitlynn turned to Ryan. "What do you think? Are you okay with staying?"

Ryan shrugged. "Fine with me, but before she leaves, let's get a shot with Skylar, Jillian, and her mom—"

"Caitlynn?" Peggy interrupted. "You come with me? Ryan, you wait here. I'll come get you after we look in on Jillian and the baby."

He set his camera on the floor by the door and sank into the couch. "Works for me."

They walked down the hall together. Peggy tapped on the door and they stepped inside. A white bassinet stood next to a full-size bed—a bed, almost unrecognizable, with baby dresses strung from one end to the other. Jillian lay in the middle. Tears streamed down her cheeks. Skylar slept peacefully in her arms. "I just got her to sleep." She quickly wiped the tears away. "I think the only reason she fell asleep is from pure exhaustion."

Peggy swept up the discarded baby items and crammed them into a drawer. "Let me tidy up some before Ryan comes. Jillian, why don't you hand Skylar to Caitlynn and go change." She eyed her daughter still in her nightclothes. "You haven't left the bed all morning. Your hair's a mess, and you need to put on something decent."

Jillian handed Skylar to Caitlynn. The baby stirred for a moment and then fell back asleep.

"Phew." Jillian blew out a pent-up breath. "For a moment there, I thought she might wake up." She shook her arms. "It's amazing how heavy a tiny baby can be." The closet door was wide open. "Why doesn't anyone tell you that you won't fit into your clothes after you have a baby? And why do the movie stars all seem to be rail thin after they have a baby?" Shrugging her shoulders, she sighed. "I guess I'll wear this again." She frowned as she pulled out a white T-shirt and a pair of black sweatpants. "Be right back."

Caitlynn rocked Skylar in her arms and slowly inhaled her fresh newborn scent. "Hello, sweet baby Skylar. Why are you giving your mommy such a hard time? Don't you know you're supposed to eat?"

Peggy stopped in her tracks and stared. "You're amazing with her. Look how she lifts her eyebrows when you speak to her."

"That's because she can feel I'm not nervous." Caitlynn looked up at Peggy. "I've been around a lot of babies. If you act nervous around them, they sense it and start fussing." She ambled from one end of the bedroom to the other. "Now, Skylar, are you gonna eat and stop your complaining?"

With her eyes still closed, Skylar raised an eyebrow and grinned lopsidedly. Caitlynn's heart ached, and Peggy burst out giggling.

"She knows we're talking about her!" Peggy exclaimed. Perched on the edge of Jillian's bed, her mood sobered. "It feels good to laugh. I forgot how much a baby changes your life. Jillian has the baby blues and cries constantly. She can't get Skyler to eat without crying immediately after, plus she feels guilty for not nursing her. Cry, cry, cry—that's all I've heard for the past week."

Peggy sighed deeply. "I wish I could do more. I've tried to find the right baby formula, and I've taken my turns holding Skylar so Jillian could get some desperately needed sleep. But I'm worried. I have to go back to work on Monday."

"What about Nana? Can she come over to help?" Skylar stirred in Caitlynn's arms.

"Yes. She's coming over Monday to go with Jillian to the doctor." Worry deepened the frown lines on her brow. "My mom isn't retired yet. She's only sixty."

"What about Jillian's friends? They said at the shower they would be there for her."

"Ha! What a joke! Their idea of helping is to come over for 20 minutes, coo over the baby, and leave." Peggy shook her head, and her eyes clouded with concern. "I think that's part of why Jillian is so depressed. One by one, her friends are ditching her."

The conversation stopped when Jillian entered. "I can't believe she's still sleeping! Should we wake her? What about her clothes? I have all these adorable dresses . . ."

"No to all of your questions." Caitlynn caressed Skylar's arm, admiring her dusty-rose-colored sleeper with tiny white bows woven into the fabric. A tiny barrette shaped in a bow held back a lock of blonde hair. Caitlynn's heart squeezed tight. *Don't you dare cry.* "She's perfect just the way she is," she whispered.

She handed Skylar to Jillian. "Here you go, Mommy. I'll get Ryan. We will film the three of you, and then Ryan and I will interview you while your mom goes to the store to look for the colic formula." She fled out the door and down the hall.

"Ryan? Are you ready?"

"What's wrong?" He snatched the camera up. "You look upset."

"Nothing, I'm just anxious to get this story wrapped up."

Caitlynn tried to convince herself that this was the truth. The real truth was—she never wanted to let Skylar out of her arms. She'd held plenty of babies at the hospital. *Why Skylar?* As she walked back to the bedroom, she brushed her abdomen. *Because Jillian and I share a similar story, but with a very different ending. Jillian kept hers—but I.... utterly heartbroken chose my career over my child.* A hollow emptiness twisted like a knife into her soul.

Ryan filmed Skylar napping in her bassinet and then panned the camera lens wide as Jillian and Peggy looked lovingly at her.

"Let's finish the rest of the interview on the couch," Caitlynn choked out. She led the way to the living room, where Ryan filmed Peggy tenderly cradling Skylar.

Caitlynn turned to Peggy. "We've got enough of you with Skylar now, so why don't you purchase the baby formula?

Peggy kissed Skylar on the cheek. "Sounds good." She handed the baby to Jillian. "I'll be back soon." A minute later, she waved and was out the door. The screen door banged closed.

"Go ahead and take a seat next to me." Caitlynn attached the tiny microphone onto Jillian's shirt. "Are you comfortable with this?"

"Are you kidding? I've always wanted to be on television!" Jillian cuddled Skylar tight to her chest. The baby stirred in her mother's arms and opened her almond-shaped dark blue eyes.

Caitlynn signaled to Ryan, and he pressed record on the camera. The red light blinked on. She began, "Jillian, you're seventeen and according to United States government data, you are one of about 4000 teenage girls who will have a baby this year."

"That's why I agreed to tell my side of the story," Jillian responded, and then she paused. "I didn't plan for this. I guess I thought it would never happen to me."

Caitlynn softened her tone. "You're an honor roll student, with a scholarship to Denver University, with plans to become an attorney. You graduate next month. Do you still plan to go to college?"

Skylar whimpered. "No, uh . . . I plan to go to night school and be a court reporter." Jillian jostled Skylar nervously. "Shh."

"What's been the biggest challenge you've faced during pregnancy and birth?"

"I suppose I should say the delivery—it was definitely the most physical pain I've ever endured." She paused a moment and stared into the camera. "I missed prom, and I'll miss my graduation. And in years to come, I won't look back on the fun of my senior year. That's been tough. But to me, the biggest challenge was dealing with all the disappointed looks I've gotten from my classmates."

"Can you explain?"

"I'm not an idiot." She looked over at Skylar. "I took precautions—but it didn't work." Once I found out I was pregnant . . ." Jillian paused, then continued carefully, "I knew that keeping my baby was the only choice I'd be comfortable with."

Caitlynn glanced lovingly at Skyler. Her heart burned in her chest. *What if I would've made a different choice?* She brushed the thought away. "Is there anything you want to tell your peers about your experience?"

Looking into the camera, Jillian's lips became a thin line, and her eyes narrowed. "If there's anything I can say to the girl out there who thinks getting pregnant won't happen to her—don't believe it. I have a close friend who took a pledge of abstinence until she gets married. Her dad even gave her a special ring for it. At the time, I thought it was such a stupid idea."

Skylar squirmed in Jillian's arms. Jillian turned the baby around and held her softly against her shoulder. "No contraception out there is 100 percent fail-proof." Skylar whimpered again, and then began to cry softly. "But abstinence is."

"We met at an adoption center—"

Jillian scowled and interrupted. "My mom made me go there." She stuttered and looked away. "I—I'm keeping my baby." In three seconds, Skylar's whimpering went from a cry to a piercing wail.

###

On her way home, Caitlynn stopped at the large silver box that housed her mail and pulled out the contents. A small package fell to the ground. She picked it up and tore open the padded envelope. Inside the clear plastic case was a CD. Embedded on the front was a hologram of a dragon. *It's here.* Her hands shook slightly as she peeked inside, looking for a note. There was none.

Butterflies swirled in her stomach as if they were a swarm of killer bees. *Steve.* He was the reason for her heartache. Why hadn't he loved her enough to stay? She would've told him about the baby. It was his fault she could never have kids. An aching pain pierced her heart. What would her life be like if she had told Steve about the pregnancy? Her thoughts raced faster and faster. *Would I have had a boy or a girl?*

Dark clouds blocked the sun's rays, darkening the sky. She pulled into her garage, hurried inside, and sank onto the couch, twirling the silver disc. Her head pounded, her stomach ached, and butterflies swarmed. Her heart drumming to the beat of her throbbing head.

Before Steve came back, her life made sense. There was no confusion. She worked hard, took her lumps climbing up the proverbial ladder, and spent any free time volunteering at Children's Hospital. Happiness wasn't something she expected in life, or in love, for that matter. Ending one bad relationship after another had left a few regrettable scars but what made up for all the heartache was her job.

Not anymore. Once again, it was his fault. If she would've never met him, there wouldn't have been an abortion. No infection. No endometriosis. And no hysterectomy. He had to go. Not only leave but the desire to get back at him for everything—the pain of the abortion, the hysterectomy, the emptiness of her life. All of that was bad enough, but to have to face him every day as her boss? That was too much. Her first idea to get him to leave was to rattle his faith. Dressing in that skintight black dress like a street girl on the prowl—with Tyler at the table no less! She still felt the sting of embarrassment when Steve had laughed at her that night.

Then she tried to make him jealous by going out with Brett. And what did Steve say? He warned her to stay away from Brett for her protection. At least there was something to show for that complete waste of time. Her plan to avoid him didn't really fix the problem. She scowled at the memories and stared at the disc containing illicit images.

The sound of ringing startled her. She rummaged through her bag and pulled out her phone. It was the Children's Hospital.

"Hi, it's Becky. I know you're not supposed to volunteer today, but Sara canceled, and I need your help. Can you come?"

Usually, Caitlynn loved to help out, but after today's interview, the ache in her heart was too painful. It was as if an old wound had ripped open, and her lifeblood was gushing out like an old-fashioned water pump. The last place she wanted to be was with more babies, but there was no way Caitlynn could desert her friend. "Be right there."

She quickly freshened up, took two Tylenol for her pounding headache, and drove mindlessly toward the hospital. At the first opportunity on Monday, she would download the CD onto Steve's computer. Human Resources would flag the pornography, forcing him to resign. He was part-owner of the station, but he still had to report to a board of directors. They'd probably buy his ownership and boot him out on the street.

Her stomach lurched, the painful throbbing in her head pulsated. Light rain pattered the windshield. The soothing sound brought with it a long-forgotten memory of how much she loved walking in the rain with Steve. He must have loved it too because he brought it up when he was in the hospital. She shook away the unwanted image. *Don't romanticize about long walks in the rain.* Quit thinking about him and stay focused on what matters. Soon he'll be a thing of the past, and she could get back to her old way of life.

CHAPTER FORTY-THREE

Spring in Colorado was nothing short of magical. The ground was hard from winter, the trees bare, but the sun shone every day. The temperatures gradually rose until there was an explosion of warmth. Buds on trees, flowers poking from the ground, the grass turning green. Steve was amazed at how fast the seasons changed. In Chicago, the winter seemed to drag on forever.

He had just finished an at-home workout and was cooling off when his phone vibrated. He grimaced when he saw it was Brenda. He knew this call would come, but he hoped she might've changed her mind.

"Hello, Steve," she said curtly. "Tyler's last day of school is three weeks away, and I would like to spend that time with him before he leaves to your house for the summer, and I head off to France."

"You're still going? Don't you think traipsing off with a boyfriend who races throughout Europe impulsive?"

"Stop." She paused. "You don't understand. It's serious between us."

Anger seeped into his voice. "Serious? Are you kidding me? What are you saying? You're going to marry this guy and live happily ever after and take Tyler with you?" He mumbled under his breath, "I'm never going to let that happen."

"You left Chicago, didn't you, Steve?" Her voice shook. "You have no problem asking Tyler to take a plane to your house—"

The idea of Tyler living in France with his ex and her new husband shook him to the core. "This isn't the same, and you know it!"

Brenda let out a breath. "You're right, of course. I don't know what's going to happen between Antoine and me. But I do know

I'm not going to take Tyler away from you or uproot us to France. Give me a chance to figure this out."

"I've never told you this before…" He squeezed his hand into a fist. "When Tyler stayed with me last summer… he missed you so much, he cried. But now…even if I wanted to send him back early—I don't have that option if you're in France."

Brenda sniffed and whimpered, "I bought the ticket. I'm going with Antoine. I have to see for myself if this is going to work out between us. It's a month away." Her voice hardened. "That gives you plenty of time to arrange daycare and prepare for Tyler to stay with you for the summer."

"Fine." He was exhausted, as if he'd just completed a half marathon. "Talk to you soon."

"Steve?" she pleaded.

He willed himself not to hang up and imagined, instead, how satisfying it would be to hurl the phone across the room, "What?" he snapped.

"I'd appreciate it if you'd try to be positive around Tyler. Please assure him I'll be fine in France."

"I'll do my best." He pressed the end button and slammed the phone on the couch. He'd be upbeat around his son, but he'd never understood why Brenda would want to follow some race car driver around the European Grand Prix circuit as if she were part of his gypsy caravan?

What if Antoine asked her to marry him? He couldn't control his ex-wife, but he had a say-so in Tyler's life. He closed his eyes. "Please, God. Nothing good can come of this if she marries Antoine. I don't want to fight another custody battle for Tyler."

With heavy steps, he climbed the stairs and flopped on Tyler's bed. He and Tyler had built this dug-out together; twice. The first time had been three years ago right before the divorce, in Brenda's house. They'd made it again when he moved to Denver so Tyler would feel at home.

For one fleeting moment, he thought about work—and that meant Caitlynn, which quickly moved from a tiny flicker to a towering flame. Three long weeks since he'd kissed her. He groaned. Felt more like three years. He stared at the blue paint with the Chicago Cub's emblem.

At first, giving Caitlynn some space seemed wise—but three weeks? He refused to wait any longer. *I love her.* This morning, he prayed asking God again for help in figuring out what to do regarding her. The only word that came to his mind—that kept coming to him—was *wait.* Why should he wait? He desired a relationship with her. More than anything, he longed to show Caitlynn how much she mattered…to spend time with her. Was there something wrong with that?

He pressed his lips together. *I have to tell her what a fool I was to leave the first time.* On the nightstand stood a photo of him and Tyler at a Cubs game. Being a success in work had trumped any of the relationships he'd ever cared for…Caitlynn, Brenda, his son. Only after inviting Jesus Christ into his messed-up life did he finally realize there was more to existence than money and success. A relationship built on love was more important than his career.

Caitlynn. He loved her. Hadn't he waited long enough, God? He wasn't going to run, and he wasn't going to let her walk away without a fight, even when her actions showed a lack of interest. Trying to figure out Caitlynn was like analyzing the two sides of a theatre mask—comedy and tragedy.

Outwardly, she might have slammed the door behind him, but she couldn't hide the spark he had seen in those gorgeous blue eyes when they kissed—not the first time, under the mistletoe; definitely not three weeks ago at her house.

All he needed to do was free her from the mask she wore and show her how much he cared. It was the ninth inning, the bases were loaded, and he was at bat. He needed to score.

She might be uncomfortable dating him when they both worked together, especially since he was her boss—but he couldn't care less what anyone at work might think. It was time. First thing Monday morning he'd step up his game, and he wouldn't take no for an answer. By day's end, there would be no doubt in Caitlynn's mind, and he would win her over.

CHAPTER FORTY-FOUR

Love does not delight in evil but rejoices with the truth
1CORINTHIANS, 13:6

The sun sparkled, not a cloud in sight, and the temperature held promise of a warm spring day, so why did chills run down Caitlynn's spine? Was this a sign she was going to get caught? If so, she'd go to jail for sure. She picked the disc off the passenger seat, tucking it into the zipper compartment of her purse. The toughest part of the plan would be finding the right opportunity to sneak into Steve's office and do the deed. At some point he'd have to leave. That way, she could slip in, burn the disc, get out quick. Job done. Just thinking about it made her hands shake. To calm herself, she gripped the steering wheel and drove.

Somehow her plan would work out, but first, she needed to finish the edits on Jillian's story. Part of her was sad not to be involved in Jillian and Skylar's life. They'd become friends over the last five months. But regularly watching Jillian with Skylar would be like yanking her heart out and crushing it into a pulp.

She flipped on the lights to her office and settled in her chair. Bile rose in her stomach and flipped like an acrobat in a circus. *An omen?* A few seconds later, Ryan rushed through the door. "Hi, Caitlynn." He stared for a few seconds. "Are you feeling okay? You look a bit piqued?"

Is my nervousness that obvious? "I'm fine." She forced a smile. "Are you ready to complete the edits for our story on Jillian?"

"Yes. It will probably take all day. We have all the footage for the past five months, plus the birth and Saturday's film."

"Let me look over a few emails, and I'll meet you in fifteen minutes. Hopefully, we have enough to run a three-day story. Originally, the storyline was to explore why teenagers keep their babies, but I also want the piece to be an eye-opener to really convey how tough it is to be pregnant as a teenager and a mom."

"I think it's going to be amazing." He said, confidently.

They spent the day editing until both were satisfied with the final product. Ryan's name would be credited as the photojournalist and Caitlynn's as the journalist. They watched the finished piece. The first segment focused on Jillian and why keeping the baby was important to her. The second day of footage showed Jillian studying her homework, working at her part-time job, and going to her doctor visits over the months. Caitlynn relived all over again the moment when Jillian found out she was having a girl. The third day covered the baby shower, the delivery, and ended with the last interview at her house.

Ryan clasped his hands. "I think this is our best work ever."

"It turned out so much better than I imagined. I bet the ratings shoot sky high during the three days the story airs."

He looked at the clock on the wall. It was four-thirty. "Let's ask Steve to come see this before he goes to the five o'clock broadcast. I bet he places it in the lineup this week."

She stiffened. *While Steve and Ryan view the story, I can download the disc.* "Would you mind showing him without me? I—I've got work to catch up on."

"Sure. But don't get mad if I take all the credit." He joked.

A few minutes later, Caitlynn hurried to her office, grabbed the disc, and walked casually down the hall. She jumped in surprise. Steve was still there! He hung up the phone and stood.

When he saw Caitlynn through the glass, his eyes brightened. He quickly held the door open. "I told Ryan I had to finish a call first; then I'd come right over. I don't need to be at the five o'clock show because I'm staying for the ten o'clock."

In a rush, Caitlynn said, "I won't be joining you two. It took all day to edit the piece, and I have something I've been putting off that can't wait any longer."

"I don't want to stand in the way of whatever you need to do." His eyes sparkled to a deeper shade. "If it's important to you, then it's important to me." He looked at the disc. "What's in your hand?"

Caitlynn's legs weakened to a rubbery mess. She drummed up a lie. "It's, uh…pictures I took of Tyler and me skiing. I thought I might download them onto your computer . . ."

"Thanks. I'd love that. But you don't need to do this for me—you have something urgent to finish." He motioned to the desk. "Go ahead and leave it. I'll download the photos and return the disc to you tomorrow."

"Uh, you're right—I need to go." She clenched the disc tightly to stop her trembling hand. "You know what? I think I'll write down a list of who is in each picture. I'll bring it back tomorrow."

He tilted his head to the side in confusion and shrugged. "Whatever you say." His tone softened. "On that note, there's something I've wanted to say to you for a long time now. Why don't you come by at lunch tomorrow? We can eat in the cafeteria, and talk then. Afterward, let's download the pictures."

Riddled with anxiety, she managed to squeak out, "Okay, see you then," before she raced out the door. *Did I just agree to eat lunch with him?* She couldn't meet him for lunch! The longer she had this disc, the bigger the risk of getting caught. She rushed to her office and collapsed into her chair, stuffing the disc deeper into her handbag.

The rest of the day passed in a blur. Caitlynn was so distracted she could hardly focus. She barely remembered getting home and making dinner. That evening, Brett called. She cursed under her breath. She didn't want to talk to him, plus he was calling after ten.

"Hello?" she snapped.

"I wasn't sure if you were at work or not, so I waited till after the ten o'clock sh-news."

"Brett, are you drunk?"

"I've had a few, but I'm fine." He belched into the phone. "'Scuse me."

"What do you want? I don't like talking to drunks."

"Don't use that high-and-mighty tone with me. I called to shee if you got the disc and if Steve's fired."

"It came, and no, he's not. You got the money. That's all you should care about."

"Look, Caitlynn," he whined. "I'm shorry. Let me start over. It's been so lonely here and I miss you. I feel bad about the way our date turned out. I hate this place. And I hate Shteve."

Every time he said the word *hate,* his voice hardened. A chill went straight through to her heart. She changed her tactic. "Brett? You really should try to control your drinking before it controls you. You could lose your job."

"Ha!" he screeched. "Are you kidding me? This place is so lax they just did a story on people who think they're vampires." He laughed harder. "Try convincing Mr.Goody-two-shoes to do a shtory like that."

"Brett?" She hoped her tone sounded sincere. "Don't take this the wrong way. I don't have any hard feelings toward you, but under the circumstances, I don't think it's wise for you to call me." Her voice lowered. "I hope it doesn't come to this, but if I'm investigated, the authorities could ask you questions you may not want to answer."

"Whoa, whoa, whoa!" he shouted. "Don't pin this on me. All I did was p-provide the source to you. My shands are clean. I'm not going to lose sleep over this. Shteve fired me."

Poisonous venom practically dripped off each word he spoke. Caitlynn suddenly felt filthy inside. "Brett, please don't call me anymore." She shivered. "I have to go." She ended the call.

All night, Caitlynn tossed and turned, remembering the myriad reasons she needed Steve out of her life once and for all. Her mind wouldn't blank out the flashbacks; how much she'd loved him, the painful sting of rejection, and her heartache when he dumped her.

The way she'd hardened her heart so she could do what she did next... The clinic told her the cluster of cells inside of her weren't really a life yet. She'd believed it all. Lying on a cot afterward, she'd shivered under a thin blanket while her mind recoiled. Because it was at that point, she realized she'd just made the biggest mistake of her life, and there was nothing she could do to set things right.

Guilt, shame, and regret flooded her entire being. She remembered closing her eyes and feeling darkness so deep and loneliness so vast it was as if it were tangible; something she could reach out and touch. Tears had fallen from her eyes as she stared at the tile ceiling and counted all the tiny holes. Looking up from the cot, she'd pretended the holes on the ceiling tiles were the holes in her heart, and one by one, she plugged them up and imagined her future. She would work hard and become great at her job. Her career would be more important than anything life had to offer. After all, love was only found in fairytales . . .

Years later, all that was true—except for the one hole that she could never figure out how to plug. *Children.* She loved kids. She had no way of knowing, all those years ago, just how much.

Her pillow soaked with tears of grief, she flipped it over and laid her head on the pillowcase's coolness. The ache of sorrow hurt her heart deeply; she stilled her breath to calm the erratic pounding. The only way she could ever love a child of her own would be if she adopted. There was a three-year waiting list for a baby. If she put in the paperwork right away, she'd be 35 by the time she held her baby in her arms. *I bet adoption agencies look for married couples first before a single parent.*

Anger consumed her. The only thing that mattered was making Steve pay. If she'd never met him, never fallen in love, never had the abortion, she would've never needed the hysterectomy. Working with Steve made her crazy. He brought out the painful past she tried so hard to bury. Tomorrow would be the last day he would be in her life. She had to separate herself from him at all costs. It was the only way to free herself from this pain.

###

She lucked out. The next day Caitlynn heard that Steve and Ed had a board meeting blocked off for two hours in the conference room; no one was to interrupt. She snuck into Steve's unlocked office, closed the blinds, and stared at the monitor. All she had to do was stick the disc into the drive and burn the disc. Her hands were clammy. She guided the condemning CD in the slot, wiped her hands, and looked around the room. She'd never been in his office without him and had certainly never sat in his chair.

A silver-framed photograph of Tyler smiling, happy in his father's embrace, sat next to the monitor. Tyler's smile was so pure and innocent. That's what she loved about children—their honesty and the sheer joy they showed in everything they did—even hugging.

Her tears blurred Tyler's smile out of focus, and one by one, like a photo album on display, her mind recalled the first time she'd met Tyler on the hike. She shivered, thinking of the gruesome sight of the dead deer Tyler witnessed. Another image of Tyler and Steve helping her during her recovery…the turkey dinner he'd surprised her with, and his huge smile that he'd pulled it all off. Then skiing together…

Tyler. The photo faded further until all she could make out was Steve and Tyler merging into one image. Steve was behind all the kindness shown to her. He'd demonstrated with his actions how much he cared for her—and what did she do? Fight his every move. Why? Did she really hate him so much? No! She might even . . .

A chill cut through her, sending shivers down her spine like tiny slivers of ice. *I can't do this. Not to Steve or Tyler.* Tyler had to stay innocent and pure. It wasn't going to be by her hand that Steve would get fired, and Tyler would experience this level of hatred—for her. In one swift move, she pulled out the CD with a jerk.

Her breath came in short puffs. All at once, she felt dizzy, sick to her stomach, and trapped. The sense of feeling trapped when she first set eyes on Steve in November was nothing compared to how suffocated and powerless she felt now.

It was clear—she had only one option.

CHAPTER FORTY-FIVE

Steve passed the break room, appreciating the fragrant aroma of fresh coffee. He could use a cup. Sleep had eluded him last night. All night long he'd tossed from side to side, trying to shut his mind off about what he wanted to say to Caitlynn. Even now, he still wasn't sure about how to handle the situation.

As usual, there was a load of work that needed his attention before meeting her for lunch. He realized during his sleepless night that what needed saying to Caitlynn required privacy. Telling her his deepest feelings in front of the entire news station cafeteria would be awkward, to say the least. He'd ask her to lunch someplace nice.

He poured himself a cup of coffee and headed toward his office. The real problem was her disappearing act. She was a real pro at avoiding him, especially after the kiss. *Why was she so fearful?* He had to reach her. God gave him a second chance—a new beginning. Now he would ask Caitlynn for a second chance. And while he was at it—ask her out. She liked to hike; that was a good starting point. He'd take her to Garden of the Gods in Colorado Springs.

Thankfully, he wasn't the same person she knew all those years ago. Back then, he didn't have the patience to work through complicated relationships, nor the wisdom. Otherwise, he would've had enough sense to have her go with him to Chicago. Or he could've stayed in Denver and worked with her—but more importantly—they would've had a child…their child. This time, he wasn't going to cave into anyone. All he needed to do was continue to show Caitlynn the same forgiveness, grace, and mercy that God had shown him. He'd tell her how much he cared for her and hope for the best.

When he reached his office, he stopped cold. *Why are the blinds closed?* He turned the doorknob.

Caitlynn's eyes were so round they looked like they might explode from out of their sockets. "Oh, no," she moaned.

Surprised to see her and shocked she would come into his empty office; he did a double-take. *What's going on?* And why is her face so red and blotchy from tears? "Why are you sitting in my chair? And why are the blinds closed?"

"I'm sorry, Steve." She sniffled and seemed hardly able to look at him.

He set his cup on top of the desk and looked at her in confusion. "You snuck into my office like some kind of hood on the street. What were you doing?"

"This." She held out a disc.

Still confused, he grabbed it and sighed with relief. "Pictures of the ski trip? Then why the tears?"

She stood and backed away from the chair. "No . . . not exactly," she whispered.

He stopped a few feet from her. The tiny hairs on the back of his neck issued a warning.

Help, God.

"There's an etching of a dragon? What is this?"

Caitlynn sank into the chair opposite his desk and closed her eyes. "I wanted to hurt you. The way you hurt me." She wiped an eye. "And get you to leave once and for all...back to Chicago—"

Steve stepped back as if the wind had just been kicked out of him. "What did you do?"

"It's more like what I didn't—what I couldn't do..." Her voice caught.

"Spit it out, Caitlynn. I'm losing patience here. What do you mean?"

In a rush, she continued, "Like I said, I wanted revenge, you know? So, I got someone to download...something horrible—

illegal images, onto this, and I was going to infect your computer." She stared at her feet.

"You mean Porn?" He tossed back his head like he'd just been sucker-punched. Anger swirled through him. "You knew there's a zero-tolerance policy on pornography and I'd get fired . . ." He sank into his chair.

"Yes." Her face turned blood red, tears fell in swift succession. She rushed on. "I couldn't go through with it." She focused in on her hands. "It was too high a price. I couldn't ruin your career, or have you fired…and then I started thinking about Tyler and how much I care about him, and I've decided—"

Crack.

Her head shot up at the sharp sounding noise. She looked incredulous. "You broke it?"

"Yes,"

"Why would you do that? Why aren't you escorting me to Human Resources? Didn't you hear a thing I just said? What I tried to do to you?"

"Caitlynn, stop." He glared at the two broken pieces in each hand and then looked at her. "I get it. I know what I did to you was wrong, and I wish I could change it." He frowned and then mumbled, "It's difficult to forgive when the hurts of the past stand in the way of happiness."

He stared into her eyes. The truth he planned to profess—the plans to invite her to lunch, ask her on an actual date. All gone. He lowered his voice. "I can't force you to forgive me. I get it now."

"I was so bent on making you pay for everything wrong in my life." She stuttered, "I-I can't go on like this. I'm resigning, effective immediately."

"Resigning is a very serious step." His chair made a rolling sound when he stood quickly and flung the damaged goods in the trash. "I don't accept." He grabbed a few tissues from the credenza and held out his hand. "Here."

He paced back and forth behind his desk. "I could turn you in for this. Or get you fired, maybe even arrested. But that will never happen. Not by me." He jerked his head toward the garbage. "Besides, I destroyed the evidence. Remember?"

He stopped dead and stared at her, trying to come up with a compromise. "I think the best thing for you"—he paused and closed his eyes briefly, trying to control the hurt inside— and for me—is to give you some space, some time to think. I'll authorize a four-month leave of absence. I hope you have some money saved?"

She wiped her tears. "I'll take the leave of absence." She stared at him with an expression of shock. "You really aren't the same person, are you? I expected to get crushed, yet you're worried if I have enough money? The only thing I have of any value in my life is money." She stood to leave and whispered, "And it's not much."

"Caitlynn, don't leave yet." *God, give me your words because right now, I feel like throwing in the towel. Give up. I don't want to be that person again.*

He took two steps closer. His heart pounded like a jackhammer. "Caitlynn, a little over two years ago, I experienced forgiveness." He paused, "I hope someday you can find it in your heart to forgive me for what I did to you. I know I don't deserve it, and I'll understand if it never happens because I know what I did to you was wrong on so many levels. And the price—"

"That's just it." Her voice wavered. "How can I forgive you… when I can't forgive myself?" She flung the door open and fled down the hall.

###

Caitlynn burst through the door of the ladies' room. A glance in the mirror quickly turned to shock. Bloodshot and swollen eyes, puffy lips, and tear-stained cheeks told the pathetic story. As best as she could, she rinsed away the damning evidence.

She hurried to her cubicle. First, she packed the awards she'd won over the years, her personal papers, and other items she'd brought to work. Then she downloaded important files she wanted to save onto a thumb drive as she glanced around at the bare walls. It took fifteen minutes and one medium-sized box to pack what she'd accomplished over the years.

Thankfully, she didn't bump into anyone on the way out. She stepped outside into the warmth of the sun and breathed deeply. The trapped feeling she tried so hard to ignore wouldn't loosen its grip. *I finally have Steve out of my life. Why do I feel this heavy darkness?* Depositing the box in her trunk, she slid into the driver's seat, opened the convertible top, and drove out of the parking garage.

The entire way home, she inhaled and exhaled, trying to calm her racing heart. Returning home didn't feel right—in the middle of the day. The house had a foreign, empty, feel—like it wanted to be alone with no intrusions. She flipped on the television. There, now there's some noise. She walked the short distance to her bedroom and collapsed on the bed, her mind spinning.

What just happened? She couldn't go through with her plan. Steve should've fired her. She should be apologizing to him; instead, he asked her to forgive him? Why? *He really has changed...and for the better.* It was as if she'd just been given amnesty. Where did this forgiveness come from? Did he get it from God? *If I had it in my heart, I would forgive him, but it's just not there.* Her heart felt hollow, numb and broken.

Right now, she needed someone to love her even though she didn't love herself. Were love and forgiveness like two sides of a coin? If you love, do you also forgive? Does that mean Steve loves me? If he did, she was sure he wouldn't now, not after what she had tried to do. Her handbag was on the bed. She took out her phone and called the one person she knew loved her.

"Hello?"

Hearing her mother's voice brought instant comfort. "Hi, Mom." Her voice quivered.

"Why are you calling me at this time of the day? Shouldn't you be at work?"

"I won't be going to work for a while. I . . . um . . . took a leave of absence," she whispered.

"Caitlynn? What happened?"

"Mom, do you remember Steve? I told you I work for him?"

"Yes. I remember. I remember a lot of things about you and Steve. I always liked him. That is until he decided to break your heart." Her voice faded. "Why?"

The tears wouldn't stop. "I did something I'm horribly ashamed of." She sobbed.

"Oh, honey, it must be serious if you're no longer working."

"It is. I tried to get him fired by downloading, um, something illicit, onto his computer. But I couldn't go through with the act. He found me at his desk, and—"

"Caitlynn Rose!" Her mother's tone deepened. "Whatever happened between you two all those years ago is your business. I think I know, but I'm keeping my thoughts to myself until you tell me when you're ready. But this is serious. What you did is reprehensible!"

"I know," she said in a shaky voice. "Mom, he gave me a second chance. I was going to resign, but he insisted I take a leave of absence." She wiped her tears.

"Caitlynn, you know I don't like to beat around the bush, so I'm just going to say it straight. You need counseling. This is irrational behavior, and it started when Steve came back in your life. Somehow his return triggered this need for revenge."

Caitlynn sighed.

Her mom's tone softened. "Listen to me, sweetie—I love you, and I could've told you that you'd never go through with such a devious plan. But the fact that you allowed this to go from a thought to a near action concerns me. Go to a counselor, and deal with this behavior."

Swiping a tear, Caitlynn agreed. "You're right. I'm ripped up inside. I'll ask around for a good therapist." Suddenly exhausted, she closed her eyes and laid her head on the pillow. "Mom?"

"Yes?"

"I'm sorry." She hung up the phone and surrendered to a night of restless sleep.

CHAPTER FORTY-SIX

Steve threw the ball and watched in satisfaction as it swished through the net. Standing underneath, Lee caught the ball, then chucked it back to Steve and said, "I'm glad you're here. I've been praying for you and Caitlynn. How are things going?"

Steve glanced away, bounced the ball a few times, and went up for a lay-up, which bounced off the rim. "If the events in my life were on a graph, this week would show a line plummeting from the highest to the lowest in one blow." He one-hopped the ball to Lee.

"What happened?" Lee caught it and jogged over.

"Let's start with the high points. I finally made up my mind to ask Caitlynn out. I had the whole thing planned." He shook his head in dismay. "I was going to suggest a hike and tell her how much I cared for her."

Lee's eyes narrowed. "Why do I have a feeling this didn't go well?"

Steve stretched his palms out in front of him as if to motion Lee to stop. "Just wait—there's more. I'm not sure if you've watched our newscast the last few days, but Caitlynn did a story on a teenager who ended up getting pregnant—"

"Yep, you're talking about Jillian. Carly and I have watched it both nights. It wraps up tonight. I can't help but think what a huge problem this is for our society. I feel so sorry for that girl."

"Yes…we'll, we had a rating sweep," Steve spoke in a monotone voice. "The highest the station has ever had. Caitlynn and Ryan will probably win an award for this story."

Lee cocked his head. "Let's get out of here." He lobbed the ball to the corner of the gym. "Come on."

Steve followed Lee to the other end of the church. They walked around the large reception area and stepped into a hallway with offices on both sides. Lee opened the first door on the right.

Steve glanced around, impressed. Three bookcases, filled with books, lined one side of the room. There was a modern-looking desk and a large, sleek, black leather couch as well as a glass coffee table. A colorful mosaic lamp graced a glass end table. Pillows matching the colors in the lamp—red, orange, lime green, and bright blue—lined the sofa.

"I like your office better than I like mine," Steve observed, taking a seat.

"Thanks. Remnants from home, but it works." Lee sat a comfortable distance from Steve on the couch. His eyes darkened with concern. "Do you feel like talking?"

"What about the pick-up game?" Steve glanced at his watch. "It starts in a few minutes."

"No matter." Lee shrugged. "They can warm up and we'll join the game later."

Steve leaned forward; hands clasped. "Let's just say, I know what rejection feels like now more than ever before." He paused. "Caitlynn hates me so much she attempted to get me fired by downloading porn... of, ah, women... onto my work computer."

"Whoa." Lee gasped. "Attempted?"

"I caught her in my office," he mumbled. "She said she thought of Tyler and couldn't bring herself to do it—and that I didn't deserve to pay so high a price for what I did to her." He sighed. "This was all about revenge, and the sad part is, I probably do deserve it."

"Did you turn her in?"

"No. In a way, I feel as if I was protected from a potentially destructive situation. I don't know . . . maybe God put thoughts of Tyler in Caitlynn's mind so she would reconsider. I just don't know." He shook his head, bewildered. "She wanted to resign, but I told her to take a four-month leave of absence to try and get her head straight."

"This is about the past, isn't it?" Lee said, somberly. "Didn't you tell her you were sorry and ask her to forgive you when she was in the hospital?"

"I did, but apparently, her reply was just lip service to get me out."

"Or could be she spoke the words, but they have yet to travel the eighteen inches from her head to her heart."

"Maybe." Steve grimaced. "And apparently, I have fallen in love with her all over again, but this time, she's the one hurting me."

Lee studied him a few moments. "What about you? Have you ever asked God to forgive you for the role you played in Caitlynn's pregnancy?"

Frowning, Steve looked over at a picture of Lee and his wife with their two Yorkies. "I never really singled out that particular sin. I asked Jesus to forgive me of my sins when I invited Him into my heart."

Lee said, "Let's dig a bit deeper. Caitlynn needs our prayers, and she needs serious help. But right now, so do you. Let's ask Jesus to forgive you and free you of this. I bet that, eventually, you'll be able to do the same with Caitlynn."

"Right before she ran out of my office, she said she couldn't forgive me because she can't forgive herself." Steve shook his head and looked down. "I know what she means."

Lee asked softly, "Will you let me pray for you?"

"Yes," he replied, closing his eyes.

Lee bowed his head. "Father, we cannot change the sorrows of the past, nor predict the future. We only have today, and today we're asking you to forgive Steve regarding the abortion. But more than that, we pray for freedom from the chains that bind us, Jesus.

Psalm 86:5 says, 'You, Lord, are forgiving and good, abounding in love to all who call to you.' Lord, I pray that you will flood Steve's heart with the power of forgiveness, and show him your deep abiding love for him that covers all rejection like deep snow blanketing the ground. Amen."

A peace—gentle and as calm as a light breeze, appeared suddenly out of nowhere. Instantly, heat starting in his heart filled his entire body, overflowing with forgiveness and an intense love he couldn't explain.

All the shame harbored in his soul; instantly wiped clean, leaving behind a weightless sensation of freedom. "Jesus," Steve prayed, "I am sorry for my part in the pregnancy and abortion, and for the pain it's caused Caitlynn all these years. Please forgive me. Forgive me for skipping out on her and bowing down to the pressures from my family over the love I had for Caitlynn." He whispered, "Lord, I still love her, and I surrender her to you. Amen."

Lee looked up at Steve. A smile lit his face. "That was powerful, man! How do you feel?"

"A hundred times lighter." He chuckled. "I think I could probably run sprints up and down the court."

Lee stood. "What's stopping you? Let's go see if the rest of the guys are here." He reached across and quickly squeezed Steve's shoulder. "I'm really glad we prayed together. Thanks for confiding in me."

All Steve could manage was a nod. He swallowed the lump in his throat.

They walked over to the gym. "What are you doing next week?" Lee asked. "Why don't you come for dinner?"

###

On the drive home, Steve felt like the burdens he'd been carrying had been lifted off his back and given to someone else—which, in a way, they were—to Jesus Christ. He'd dragged through the past week as if deep cuts had ripped his heart into ribbons. On Wednesday, he'd prepared for the upcoming board meeting and notified Nora authorizing Caitlynn's leave of absence. So upset about Caitlynn, he cared little about the rating spike, unable to shut off all the negative images circling around and around in his mind. But now, like water down a drain, all of it had disappeared with one prayer. How blessed he was to have found this church and to have met Lee.

His heart felt so light and free and whole again. Free from the sorrow and the hurt he'd caused Caitlynn. Even the pain he had suffered from what she attempted to do seemed to lessen. Tyler was coming soon for the summer, though he still questioned Brenda's actions, he had a feeling it would work out fine.

The bottom line was that he needed to trust God more; quit trying to control his own little world—like he could, anyway. He maneuvered his car into the garage. Once inside, he took out a piece of paper from his desk and wrote, "More of YOU and less of ME" and taped it onto his computer. That way, he'd remember to go to God first, instead of trying to fix everything himself, only to screw everything up before finally asking God for help after he'd already made a big mess of things. Just like a little kid who didn't learn, disciplined for the same thing over and over.

CHAPTER FORTY-SEVEN

It took ten days for Caitlynn to step away from the couch. The first several days were pure misery, especially when she watched the three-night special about Jillian and Skylar. It turned out exactly the way they'd planned. Ryan's video shots were amazing. The way he zoomed in on Skylar revealed how Jillian stressed over every tiny detail-and it showed Peggy's exhaustion. He made it seem so personal, capturing every nuance.

Ryan called her immediately following the last show on Friday.

"Ryan, you're amazing!" She tried to make her voice light.

"We're a great team. The emotions you brought out when you asked all the tough questions was the hard part. It made my job so much easier."

"Thanks, Ryan."

"Caitlynn, are you okay?" He lowered his voice. "I've heard rumors."

"Only believe half of what you hear." She laughed sarcastically. "Actually, you might want to believe it all. It might be true."

"Whatever…I'm not buying it," he sighed. "I think the rest will do you good. Although, you could use some meat on your bones."

"I think that's your way of saying you care. Ah, Ryan, you shouldn't have," she teased.

"Caitlynn, I'm serious." He hesitated. "I want you to come back, but only when you're ready. Okay?"

Tears stung her eyes. "Roger that, Ryan. Don't worry about me. I'll be fine. I just need to take some time to, um, heal."

"How long will you be gone? Tina took over your cubicle already. I could kick her bootie out—"

"No." She closed her eyes. "Thanks, though. I'm glad you have my back. I have a four-month leave of absence."

"Okay, Caitlynn, see you then." He paused. "You take care."

"Thanks, Ryan." She squeezed the phone. "Talk to you soon."

The next call came from Jillian on Saturday. "Caitlynn! Thanks! That was so great!" She giggled. "My phone hasn't stopped ringing. I knew I'd be back on the A list after my friends saw me on television. None of them can believe I supported abstinence. Oh! And Tori! She was the friend who signed the abstinence pledge. She's an instant celebrity now, thanks to me. All the girls at school ask her about her ring, where her father bought it, and what paper she signed. Ha! I bet the guys aren't too happy!"

"I'm glad your life is getting back to normal, Jillian. Sorry I haven't called lately. I've been,"—she hesitated— "busy."

"I totally understand. This is the first bit of excitement I've had since Skylar was born. I wanted to tell you thanks for the advice about the colic formula. She seems to tolerate the milk, and the doctor visit helped too. She gave me some tips to help Skylar's tummy issues. There's this warm wrap I put around her tummy that helps her fall asleep instantly. Your little lamb seems to work too. Skylar likes the whale sound."

Caitlynn ached to hold Skylar. *Why does this baby have such an effect on me?* "I'm glad it's all working out for you, Jillian," she murmured.

"I hope I'm not crowding your space, but I wondered if you'd like to stay friends." She paused. "I really like you. You were there for me when all my friends deserted me, and Skylar likes you, too."

Touched by Jillian's bravery to step out on a limb, Caitlynn didn't want to reject her. Jillian was like the little sister she'd always wanted. But could she handle being around the baby? She bit her lip. "Of course. But it may be a few days or even a week before I get back to you . . . I'm working through something right now."

"That's fine. Skylar isn't feeling well. I took her with me to the Gap today, so I could buy some jeans that fit. I'm so sick of sweatpants. I'm not sure if that's why, but since we got home, all she's done is sleep."

Caitlynn twisted a strand of hair. "That's not like her. Is she running a fever?"

"I'll check her when she wakes up. I'm sure she's fine." As if on cue, Skylar wailed in the background. "She's awake. I'll talk to you later."

###

Two weeks later, Caitlynn finally found a counselor she could trust. Last November, Dr. Plummer had told her to think about therapy to help her deal with the hysterectomy. She finally called his office, and he referred her to Michelle D'Amo, a professional therapist who worked exclusively with women suffering from anxiety and depression. Her mother would be proud of her for going; she'd call her this weekend to update how it went.

The office building, located in a historic brick building that the city of Denver had recently restored, stood directly across from the Cherry Creek Mall. Under normal circumstances, being so close to the mall would've resulted in a shopping trip which housed some of her favorite stores. But shopping held little appeal now. All she wanted was to sleep and watch reruns on television. She found a parking spot and sat for a moment listening to cars whizzing by and birds singing in a shade tree next to the sidewalk. *What if I'm making a big mistake? Can I really trust her to help me?* She closed her eyes and leaned back.

Think of this as research. If you were doing a story about counselor's, you'd walk right in with authority. She grabbed her purse, jumped out of the car, and slammed the door shut. On her way up the sidewalk, tears filled her eyes. *I can't live like this. I have to get help.* She threw her shoulders back. *If I don't do it now, I never will.* She headed inside.

The office decorated in the era of the Victorian era was like turning back in time. Dark oak paneled wainscoting stood halfway up the walls. Above the paneling, a cream-colored wallpaper with wide vertical stripes made the room inviting. Stepping further inside, she stared at a stunning painting of a wrought-iron-gated garden full of blooming rose bushes, with petals ranging from deep to varying shades of pink to the purest white. A pink climbing rose bush reached up and around the outside of the gate, inviting the viewer to step into the secret garden. From there, a path led to a beautiful three-tiered marble water fountain in the center of the garden. A tiny yellow finch perched on the edge of the fountain. The trail continued, circling the fountain and ending at a gazebo. The image was so serene and beautiful that Caitlynn instantly relaxed. There was no receptionist waiting, just a small sign that read: "Please be seated. I'll be with you in a moment."

Caitlynn sank into the Victorian-style overstuffed royal blue couch. Two ivory-colored high wingback chairs sat opposite. In the center of the grouping was a beautiful oak coffee table with cherubs carved into the sides. A medium-sized white crystal chandelier centered the room, casting a warm glow. The matching ivory-colored curtains were light and airy, letting in as much light as possible. Caitlynn settled on the sofa. There were no magazines, just a coffee-table-sized book of famous paintings and another book about Colorado's history.

Two minutes later, Michelle opened the door to her office. She was carrying a clipboard with some papers.

"Hi! You must be Caitlynn." She smiled warmly. "I'm glad you're here." She reached out and shook Caitlynn's outstretched hand.

Caitlynn sized Michelle up in an instant. There was no way Michelle could deny her Italian heritage. Shoulder-length jet-black hair, beautiful olive-colored skin, heart-shaped face, and large almond-shaped brown eyes told the story. She wore black dress pants with a simple teal silk blouse and expensive-looking pumps. But more than all that, she looked like she was good at her job.

"Thanks for seeing me," Caitlynn responded. She panned the area. "I love this room."

"Thanks. I believe that privacy is critical. You will never see the client before you or after you, and vice versa. My appointments are 50 minutes long so my clients won't overlap with each other."

"I like that." She breathed a sigh of relief.

"For that reason, I would ask that you arrive no more than five minutes before your appointment time, and when we're finished, you'll leave from a door in my office."

She nodded her consent.

"You have two options. We can either go to my office or sit here."

"I feel comfortable here."

Michelle tapped the clipboard with the pen. "There are three forms here. One is a privacy contract stating that everything you tell me is in confidence." She flipped to the second page. "This is a consent form giving me your permission for counseling services. The next form is the intake form. Basically, I'm asking for a brief history and why you are seeking counseling." She handed over the clipboard and the pen. "I'll give you a few minutes to fill these out. When finished, knock on my door." She stepped into her office.

Caitlynn began filling out the necessary paperwork. When she got to the question, "Why are you here?" she paused. *What do I write? I tried to get my old boyfriend fired? Or my plan for revenge backfired? Do I mention my eating disorder and tell her the real reason I'm here? No.* She couldn't do that until she was sure Michelle could be trusted. She wrote, "Relationship issues."

CHAPTER FORTY-EIGHT

Jillian yawned, took a sip of her soda, and tossed the letter on the coffee table. The last five weeks were a blur and to top it off, for three days in a row now; she'd sacrificed precious sleep in order to arrive before classes started just so her mom could watch Skylar before work so Jillian could take her exams. Tomorrow. Saturday, May 29th. Graduation Day. The last place she wanted to be was walking with her class only to be singled out as the girl who had "the kid."

Her friends rarely came around, but at least they were cool about Skylar. It was the stares she'd endure from the rest of her classmates that bothered her. No way would she succumb to that kind of torture. She wasn't going.

Besides, Marcus would be there. Her stomach knotted into a hard ball. She looked at Skylar sleeping with her elbows bent and her arms relaxed at her sides. Why did she think once the baby was born, he'd come running back? *Stupid, stupid, stupid.*

Skylar's bottom lip trembled, a split second later she let out a shriek. Jillian lifted her from the infant carrier and held her close. "What's wrong now?" She shut her eyes and sank into the sofa, gently bouncing Skylar. "I just fed you and changed you. Are you tired?"

Skylar squirmed.

Jillian sprang from the couch and paced from the living room to the kitchen.

Skylar cried louder. Tears glistened against her soft skin.

"Shh, please don't cry." Jillian transferred her baby to the crook of her arm and caressed her cheek. If only Caitlynn were here, she'd know what to do. Jillian felt a twinge of guilt. She'd pretended everything was great when she talked to Caitlynn, but really only told her half of the truth.

No. She didn't even tell Caitlynn that much. The honest truth? Skylar tolerated the formula, and she was sleeping better—but the harsh reality was that if Skylar wasn't sleeping or eating, she was crying. Caitlynn said babies could feel anxiety, but no matter how hard Jillian tried to relax, Skylar's little body would tense up, and a few minutes later, the wailing would start.

After pacing back and forth for almost ten minutes, patting Skylar on the back and listening to her whimpers, the muscles in Jillian's arms burned. Once she lay Skylar down, Jillian's arms would hang like limp rags from the pain.

Finally, her tiny body relaxed and surrendered to sleep. Jillian kissed her cheek, walked down the hall, and gently placed her in the crib. Her tiny lashes fanned out against her lower lids. Jillian watched her baby sleeping peacefully with her little hands curled into fists. Now it was Jillian's turn to cry, but for very different reasons. She wiped away the tears, shut the door, and tip-toed down the hall. She picked up the letter again and read the salutation.

Dear Jillian,

Welcome!

The University of Denver is pleased to offer you a full academic scholarship…

The words on the page blurred together. She'd received the letter the day before Skylar was born, reading it multiple times these past five weeks, explaining the scholarship's details, and stating the deadline for her response. At this point, she had one week left to sign the papers and send in her final acceptance letter for the fall semester. If the school didn't get her documents by the end of next week, they'd terminate the scholarship.

A cry escaped her lips. She stretched out on the couch and closed her eyes. Her head pounded like a Reggae band had taken occupancy, and her stomach twisted into more knots as she finally faced the cold, hard, truth. *My mom is right. I'm not ready to be a mother. Like she said, I'm not mature enough to handle being a parent.*

Marcus had never even bothered to call. All the plans I hoped for—that Marcus would realize how much he loved me and would want our baby, that he would work while I went to school, that we'd all live happily ever after. What was I thinking? She crumbled the letter and hurled it across the room.

Do I just go from one poorly made decision to another? Tears streamed down her cheeks. *Am I strong enough?* Jillian heard her mom's key slide into the front door lock.

A few seconds later, Peggy entered, took one look at Jillian, dropped her handbag on the floor, and rushed over to her side. "What's wrong?"

"Mom, we need to talk."

Peggy glanced at Jillian for a split second. "Sweetie, sit up." She sat close to her daughter on the couch. "What's going on?"

"Mom, you were right. I can't raise my baby this way." Tears ran down her cheek. "I want so much more for Skylar than I can offer right now. If I keep her, what kind of life can I give her? I love my child, but she needs more than I can offer. I'm not ready for motherhood." Jillian sobbed into her hands.

Peggy's eyes welled up. "Oh, sweetheart." She reached out and held her daughter.

"If," she stuttered, "…if I give Skylar up, she'll have love, but she'll also be provided for in all the ways I can't."

Peggy released her embrace and held Jillian's hand. "You know I'm here for you, Jilly. I hate to see you suffering." She wiped a teardrop from Jillian's cheek. "Skylar is special to me, and I love her…but I also love you." She held Jillian's gaze. "I want you to follow what's in your heart, no matter how difficult."

Jillian's gaze darted to the floor. "I want to go to college and graduate and make something of myself." Her voice quaked. "Hopefully, one day, I can be a wife to someone who loves me and bring another child into this world; I can support financially and emotionally." Her breath caught.

"Do you know what kind of sacrifice you'd be making? Are you prepared to never see Skylar again?"

"No," Jillian crossed her arms, eyes locked on her mother. "I can't do that." She shook her head. "I won't. I need to stay in contact." Fresh tears formed.

"I don't think I could do it either." She stood, pacing. "I want to know how my granddaughter is doing."

"Mom? I want to give my baby to someone who doesn't mind if I'm partially in the picture—and you too."

"You mean like an open adoption?"

"Yes." Jillian looked lovingly into her mother's eyes. "Mom? I've never told you this before, but I appreciate everything you've done."

"Oh, Jilly."

"I mean it, Mom." She sniffed.

Her mom's eyes glistened. "What do you plan to do?"

Jillian stood and picked up the letter. Careful not to damage it further, she straightened it out. "Sign the acceptance letter and go love on Skylar until I figure out the next step."

###

Caitlynn's sat in her all-time favorite position at Children's Hospital; rocking an infant in her arms and felt warmth spread throughout her. No matter her mood—holding a baby always made her melt.

Becky took advantage of the moment and checked the infant's temperature as Caitlynn rocked him.

She grinned. "It's been a while since you've volunteered, Caitlynn. I've been worried about you. Are you okay?"

"I am." Caitlynn hugged tight the little one she was holding. "I started counseling, and I really like the therapist. She's very professional, and I have no problem talking to her. She asks the type of questions I can answer honestly."

"Do you think you'll go back to your job?"

"You mean, face Steve?"

Becky nodded. "Tell me to shut up if I'm stepping out of line."

"That's what I love about you, Becky." Caitlynn giggled. "You're so refreshingly real."

"Uh-huh. That's a polite way of telling me to mind my own beeswax."

"Actually, I have a little less than three months left to decide. Caitlynn continued, "My counselor thinks I'm experiencing anxious depression. I've told her bits and pieces, just to see if I could trust her."

"Are you going to tell her everything?"

"Eventually." She tenderly caressed the baby.

Becky turned to face Caitlynn. "Here I go, butting in where I don't belong, but there's a program at my church you might want to think about."

"What is it?"

"It's a program that helps women heal their emotional scars from abortion."

Caitlynn brushed her finger across the baby's brow. The child fluttered her eyelids before closing them again to sleep. "Becky, please never stop caring. It's what I like best about you." She paused. "I don't think I'm ready for that yet. I'm going to give counseling a try first, but I'll keep it in mind."

Becky checked the patient's pulse. "I watched the story on Jillian. She's lucky her baby was only one month early. I'd say a quarter of our preemies in neonatal ICU are from teenage moms. That story made me wonder. Jillian said she plans to raise Skylar, but have you ever considered adopting a child?"

"Are you kidding? I fantasize about it all the time. Half the time I'm here, I pretend the little one I'm rocking is mine."

"Why don't you adopt?"

"I was holding out for the all-American dream: a man, marriage, a baby, and a cute house with a white picket fence." She glanced away.

"Well, you have the house." Becky chuckled.

She cracked a smile. "You mean townhome. I don't know why, but I instantly bonded with Skylar."

"Probably because you were there from the time the baby was first in Jillian's womb. You were at the delivery and with her afterward. It was like you were the adoptive parent going through the events leading up to the birth with the birth mom. You couldn't help it; you fell in love."

Caitlynn stood and walked to a crib. "I guess so." She placed the sleeping child within. "I received a call from Jillian. Mommy and baby are doing great. She wants me to remain friends with her." Caitlynn walked over to the next baby and carefully lifted an infant girl and rocked softly. "I hope she means what she says. At first, I wasn't sure I could handle being the odd one out, but I adore Skylar… Jillian is great."

"Everyone could use more friends." Becky stared intently. "Especially a girl in Jillian's situation. I have to finish the rest of my rounds. Are you good here? Do you need anything?"

"No. I'm good." The baby she was holding looked up at her with such trust in his eyes; Caitlynn was sure her heart would burst. She held tight to her tiny hand and whispered, "I'm good," and hummed a lullaby.

It was dark by the time Caitlynn finished volunteering. Quickly shuffling across the parking lot, she unlocked her car. Once inside, she checked her phone for missed messages and saw a voicemail from Jillian and Tyler

Her heart quickened. Both messages sounded vague. *Is Ty okay?* She quickly called Steve's cell phone. Tyler answered on the second ring. "Hi, Tyler, it's Caitlynn. Your message asked me to call. What's up?"

"Uh, I'm staying with my dad for the summer."

"Are you having fun?"

"I guess," he mumbled, "but I miss my mommy."

Caitlynn grimaced. *It must be so hard on him.* "Where's your dad?"

"He's downstairs working out. He left the phone for me in case you called so I could talk to you." Tyler cleared his throat. "Ms. Caitlynn? Can you come over and hang out with me sometime?"

Her heart squeezed until she could barely breathe. "Sweetie, I would love to but—"

"We could go out for ice cream. Dad said you were taking a break from work right now, and you might be too busy to see me."

A spark of anger flashed. Steve said that just to make her so mad, she wouldn't back down—and it worked. "Ty, I am never too busy for you. When do you want to go?"

"Tomorrow is Sunday. We go to church in the morning, but I don't think we have any plans afterward."

"I'll tell you what. You tell your dad that I'm coming over tomorrow at two o'clock. I'll pull up front and honk my horn when I get there." Hopefully, she could avoid Steve until she was ready to face him. Her stomach lurched at her shame. It was still so raw she had no choice but to push the memory aside.

"Okay," Tyler agreed.

"Oh, and Tyler? Just you and me—no dads allowed."

He giggled. "Yeah!"

"See you tomorrow." Before she could say goodbye, he hung up.

Next, she called Jillian. "Hey, Jillian, how it's going? Is everything okay?"

"You didn't listen to the message?" she said.

"I did . . . so what do you want to talk about?"

"I don't want to discuss this over the phone."

Her voice was so serious. Caitlynn bit her lip. "Are you okay?" *She's going to tell me she's changed her mind about us staying friends.* She held her breath.

"Sort of." Jillian sighed. "Actually, no…I'm not." She sighed again. "Can you come over tomorrow?"

"I could come in the morning, but I have to be somewhere at later in the day."

"Why don't you come over around eleven? My mom cooks brunch on Sunday. You can eat with us, and we can talk."

"Sounds good. I'll see you tomorrow. But everything is okay with Skylar, right?"

"Oh yes, Skylar is more than fine," Jillian responded, and that was all Caitlynn needed to hear.

Once home, she felt dizzy with emotion. The conversation with Becky forced her to take a hard look at her life. She'd read it was at least a three-year wait to adopt a baby. *What am I waiting for?* Always in the back of her mind, she'd held on to this fantasy that she'd be lucky enough to conceive a child with her husband, but she couldn't seem to find Mr. Right. Longing year after year for love to find her had been a waste of time—and now, thanks to the hysterectomy, it was impossible for her to ever get pregnant anyway. She rubbed her stomach absentmindedly.

When Jillian called to say she wanted to remain friends, Caitlynn couldn't believe her good fortune. What a coincidence, because, deep down, that was exactly what she desired—to stay close to Jillian and Skylar. She even liked Peggy and her "say it like it is" style of parenting. It reminded her of her own mother.

An idea emerged, and she grinned. She'd go to breakfast tomorrow and tell Jillian she wanted to be more than a friend. She wanted to be like an aunt to Skylar—to be part of her life and love on her and help babysit and spoil her, just like a family member. The loneliness that frequently smothered her like a heavy blanket wrapped around her body on a hot summer day, lifted briefly; and for a fleeting moment, she felt lighter, as if she could breathe for the first time in a very long time.

CHAPTER FORTY-NINE

It always protects, always trusts, always hopes, always perseveres
1 CORINTHIANS 13:7

Caitlynn hummed a tune, happy to have a reason to wake up early for the first time since she left her job. Today she would see two of her favorite people: Skylar and Tyler. The clock read seven-thirty. She picked up her phone and called.

"Hi, Mom. I knew you'd be awake."

"You're up early. How are you doing today?"

"I'm getting there. I found a great counselor, and I started volunteering again."

"That's wonderful, honey."

She could practically see her mom's smile. "Mom? There's something I've been mulling over for some time now. What would you think if I adopted a baby?" She held her breath.

"I'm sure you've gone over all the pros and cons of adopting. If there's one thing I know about you, you'll research this until you know everything there is to know and then some."

Caitlynn laughed nervously. "That's true."

"You know me, Caitlynn. The apple doesn't fall far—I love kids, too. But isn't there a long waiting list?"

"Yes." Caitlynn sighed. "I interviewed a woman at an adoption agency for a story I just did. I could talk to her and start the process. I–I'm just not sure."

"Why? You love children. I've never met a child who doesn't immediately want to play with you the moment they set eyes on you."

"I just feel so awful about what I've done," she whispered. "Do I even deserve happiness?"

"Caitlynn, you stop this nonsense right now!"

She was a teenager the last time she'd heard her mom yell like that.

Her mom continued, "The way I see it, you have two choices. You either accept what you've done and learn from it, or you can go to Steve and apologize. Personally, I think you should do both. And while I'm at it, why shouldn't you adopt? I think it would do you some good. Sacrifice and motherhood are cut from the same cloth."

"Okay, Mom." She chuckled into the phone. "Wow, I haven't heard you get this riled up in a long time." She paused. "I'll keep you posted, okay? And I'll think about your suggestion regarding Steve."

"Great." Her mother let out a breath. "I'll change the subject. What are your plans today?"

"Jillian called and wants me to have brunch with her and her mom, and then I'm going to see Tyler and take him out for ice cream. He's staying with Steve for the summer, and missing his mom, so I'm trying to help."

God, if you're up there, please help me to see Tyler and not Steve today. I just don't think I can face him.

"Sounds like a wonderful Sunday."

"Mom, I wish you lived closer." She frowned. "Arizona is too far away."

"I know. I miss you too. But the warm weather helps my arthritis."

"Mom, you know what? I've just decided. I'm coming down there." Her stomach fluttered in excitement. "I have time off now, and I haven't seen you since Christmas."

"I would love that, honey," her mom said with a lilt in her voice.

The sweet sound of her mother's voice soothed the raveled edges of her mind. "I'll look into flight times and dates and get back with you." She paused. "I love you, Mom."

"I love you, too, Caitlynn. Have a great day."

Knowing that she'd see her mom soon, filled her with a renewed spirit. Caitlynn threw on some running clothes, drank a glass of water, and headed out to her favorite jogging trail, carefree and light as a feather.

###

The aroma of waffles grilling, bacon sizzling, and eggs cooking wafted in the air. Peggy was in the kitchen pouring batter in the waffle iron. "I hope you're hungry," she said.

"I am," Caitlynn replied. Jillian's baby lay sleeping comfortably in a baby swing. She couldn't resist. She walked over and kneeled, "Hello, little angel," she said. "You've grown since I last saw you."

Jillian looked like she'd been crying. Probably lack of sleep, Caitlynn reasoned. The sleep-deprived teen leaned over and kissed her child lightly on the cheek. *Why does it look like Jillian was doing all she could just to hold herself together?*

"Breakfast is ready," Peggy announced. "Caitlynn, since you're our guest, you go first. It's pretty casual around here. We're serving buffet-style." She handed out the plates. "There's OJ and water at the table. Would you like a cup of coffee?"

"Orange juice is fine, thanks." She took a portion of waffles, bacon, and eggs. Then took a seat at the table and waited as they filled their plates and sat.

"Thanks for having me," Caitlynn said. She poured syrup on her waffle. "I haven't had a home-cooked breakfast in a long time."

"I'm glad you could join us. It's nice to see you again." Peggy took a bite of egg.

The waffle was delicious and reminded her of being a little kid on a Sunday morning. She glanced at Jillian. "Are you feeling okay? You're not eating."

Jillian picked up a slice of bacon and then set it back down. "I'm sorry. I can't eat right now." She took a sip of water. "I . . . um . . . asked you over for a reason. Why don't you and Mom eat while I talk?"

A sinking feeling came over her. Setting down her fork, she asked. "What's going on?

"I invited you over because I wasn't completely honest with you on the phone the other day."

"Okay," Caitlynn answered cautiously. "What do you mean?"

"I've misled you this whole time. Things aren't going as well as I've led you to believe." She started to cry. "It's just . . . so hard. It's . . ."

Caitlynn reached across the table and gently placed her hand over Jillian's. "It's okay, sweetie. Take your time." The poor girl was exhausted and overwhelmed.

Jillian blew her nose and sniffed to stop crying. Caitlynn squeezed Jillian's hand, hoping it offered a small measure of comfort.

She took a deep breath, then sobbed out. "I'm reconsidering my decision to keep Skylar." She blotted a stray tear with her napkin.

The world stopped. The room started to spin. Caitlynn wasn't sure she'd heard correctly. *Did she just say . . .?* She glanced over at Peggy, who was also tearing up. "Wh–what are you saying?" she exclaimed, her voice rising. "What do you mean?"

"Mom," Jillian cried, "help me."

"Jillian," Peggy said tenderly, "you have to be the one to tell her. I'm not going to put words in your mouth. You can do this."

Caitlynn tried to swallow the lump in her throat, but it felt stuck. Her heart pounded in her ears.

Very slowly, Jillian said, "I've come to the realization that I'm not ready to be a parent."

Caitlynn gasped. "What?" She released Jillian's hand.

"I don't know how to say this, so I'm just going to bare my soul." Jillian swiped the tears from her eyes. "I want Skylar to have so much more than I can give her. She deserves to be loved and cared for by a responsible and established mother, with a good job who can give her everything I just can't be for her right now." She dabbed her eyes.

Stunned, Caitlynn leaned back heavily against the chair. "Jillian, I'm sure you've thought this through, but are you positive you want to do this? You'd be giving up your rights as a birth-parent."

"This has been the hardest month of my life. I love Skylar with all of my heart, which is why I have to do this."

Caitlynn was stunned speechless. She wanted to scream and tell them the mistake she'd made so long ago, how much she ached to hold her own child in her arms, how she always questioned what would have been.

"You can't," Caitlynn blurted. "I–I mean . . . trust me; I know how difficult this is. I . . . you love Skylar . . ."

Jillian sighed. "I've done nothing but think about this for weeks. Mom and I have discussed it again and again. I don't want to give my child up to a stranger. I've gotten to know you for the last five months, and you were always there for me. I remember what you told me in the hospital…how you long for a child. You can't have children…"

Caitlynn closed her eyes, reliving all over again the pain of her choice and the subsequent hysterectomy.

Jillian continued. "I want an open adoption where I can get updates and pictures and maybe even visit at Christmas and birthdays." Jillian stared at her with a serious expression Caitlynn had never seen before.

Jillian grasped her hand. "Caitlynn . . .I'd like you to raise Skylar." She paused. "As her mother."

Is this a dream I'm going to wake up from? "Did you just say what I think you said?" Caitlynn whispered.

"Yes." Jillian bit her lip. "What do you think?"

A joyous feeling started from the lowest depths of her soul, bubbled up and spilled out like nothing she'd ever experienced. "You're serious?" A smile tugged. Me? Skylar's mom?

Jillian nodded. "I am—"

"Jillian, never in my wildest dreams would I have imagined a moment as special as this. I think I need to confide in you both…" Her voice shook, her lip trembled. "A few months ago, I could've never confessed what I am going to say now, but, uh, I was a few years older than you when I made a very difficult decision to terminate my pregnancy. One day later, I ended up getting a raging fever and infection that caused long term reproductive complications. Last November—I underwent a hysterectomy."

Jillian sucked in a breath. "I'm sorry."

Her mind couldn't wrap around this moment. It seemed so healing to feel such joy instead of the guilt and shame forever locked tight around her heart.

"My heart is bursting with happiness; I've never in my life felt like this." She blinked a tear away and tried to keep her voice from shaking. "I would be honored to raise Skylar as my daughter."

She reached out and grabbed Peggy's hand. The three of them held hands as if they were of one mind, a circle of three, and they all turned and watched Skylar slumbering peacefully.

"What happens now?" Caitlynn asked. *God? I think you might be up there after all. Please don't let me wake up. Let this actually be happening.*

"You know I plan to be a lawyer someday, so I'm sure this won't surprise you." Jillian cleared her throat. "I've already contacted an adoption attorney, the best in the state. I'm not taking any chances with something going wrong during the process. In Colorado, we can expedite terminating the birth-parents' rights and have it completed within about ten days. The adoption would then be finalized six months afterward."

Jillian sounded like she'd memorized her last paragraph word for word from the adoption attorney. "All right," Caitlynn said, "When do you want to meet with the lawyer to start the process?"

"Is tomorrow too soon? I don't want to wait any longer than I have to. I think it's the best to do this quickly."

Skylar stirred in the swing and opened her eyes.

"May I hold her?" Caitlynn asked.

Walking over to Skylar Jillian picked her up. She held her close, kissing her. "Yes."

Caitlynn's eyes pooled with unshed tears. She held out her arms in welcome. A surge of warmth like the sun shining after a downpour drenched every cell in her body until all she felt was a love so profound, she couldn't speak. She carefully placed her in the center of the blanket.

They all sat on the floor surrounding Skylar. Caitlynn shook a bunny-shaped rattle and watched the baby's smile light up the room, following it with her eyes. "How observant!"

"I know!" Peggy said. "Jillian was just like that when she was a baby. You couldn't put anything past her."

Caitlynn held Skylar's hand for a brief moment then stood. "I have to leave," She took one last look. "'ll see you tomorrow…what time?"

Jillian walked with her to the front door. "I made an appointment for three-thirty. Why don't you meet me here and we can go together? Nana said she'd watch Skylar. Mom plans to leave early from work to meet us there."

"I'll be there." She hugged Jillian. "Thank you. I won't let you down."

Jillian hugged her back and looked somberly into her eyes. "I know. This is what I want for my daughter. I'll see you tomorrow."

Caitlynn had to be on a cloud. The joy she felt earlier kept building with such ferocity she didn't know if she wanted to laugh or cry. The day had started out great, but this stunning surprise had surpassed all her expectations.

Then she stopped—would Jillian back out? What if she changed her mind?

She shook the horrible thought away. She must remember to take one day at a time—better yet, one hour at a time. She couldn't wrap her head around it all, and she didn't fully understand what had happened in there, but right now, she had an outing with Tyler. She practically collapsed in her car and sat trying to recover from pure shock. She still had a few minutes before she had to get on the road…she tilted her head back on the seat, closed her eyes, and burst into tears.

CHAPTER FIFTY

From the hallway, Steve glanced at the living room with its huge stone-covered fireplace, cold and empty, waiting for winter to return—and the large sun-kissed kitchen that had somehow seemed lifeless without Tyler. To have his son for the summer was the highlight of his year. At least then he had a reason to come home in the evenings. He'd pick Tyler up from daycare after work and enjoyed every minute until he put him to bed. Everything he did was for his son, but still, it wasn't enough. Tyler needed his mother. Brenda had called and talked to Tyler last night. After Steve put Tyler to bed, he listened at the door and heard him crying. The sound tore at his heart.

With a glass of iced tea in hand, Steve headed out onto the patio and sank into a chaise lounge, lost deep in thought. In so many ways he'd tried to right the wrongs of his past—his marriage, divorce, now Tyler just about living out of a suitcase, volleying from parent to parent. And then there was Caitlynn.

Surprisingly, when she drove up, she practically radiated happiness. He'd never seen her look like that before. Was that how she looked before he was back in her life? Was this glow from the break from work, *from him?*

When he approached her, she glanced away, but not before he saw the guilty look in her eyes. He wanted to walk right up to her car window and tell her . . . what? He understood her pain? All the wrong decisions he'd made along the way, trying in vain to control the outcome, only to have it all come crashing down like a house of cards? He lived with a big pile of guilt too. It was time to relinquish control once and for all and accept the grace given to him. The prayer with Lee had been so powerful—and releasing; he finally knew complete freedom from all the sins in his past. It was time to God-up and man-down.

The clouds drifting past were as scattered as the images that popped into his mind about Caitlynn. In the first week, any mention of her, flooded him with anger. It took the rest of the month to finally come to terms with what must have driven her to do it.

Revenge was her motivation. Without God in her life, she'd decided it was up to her to make sure he'd pay for his mistakes. What she didn't know was that God already paid the price by sending Jesus. Revenge wasn't hers to inflict.

The image of her hugging Tyler like he was the most important person in her life made him smile. Deep down, there was a part of Caitlynn; he'd never stop loving. Just as he knew it was time to let her go. If he was going to give God control, it also meant giving everything up—even Caitlynn. *Lord, show Caitlynn how much you love her.*

If she wanted to resign, it was up to her. *And Lord, help her to have it in her heart someday to forgive.* His heart tightened as if it might burst at the thought of never seeing her again. He took a sip from his drink. He was grateful to Caitlynn for taking Tyler out. His son missed his mother so much. Hopefully, Caitlynn and Tyler would have a great time today and would meet often. If the only time he ever saw Caitlynn was when he waved to her from his front porch, then so be it. And if she never came back to see Tyler, he would continue to do whatever he could.

His cellphone rang, and he groaned. *Brenda.* Her voice sounded strained. He made a quick calculation. "It's late in France, isn't it?"

She laughed nervously. "You're right. I wanted to let you know that I'm leaving tomorrow for Chicago."

"You are?" He couldn't keep the surprise from his voice. "Why?"

"It's not what I expected it to be like with Antoine on his summer circuit. I never see him." She cleared her throat. "I thought traveling to Europe would help me take my mind off Tyler being at your house, but instead, all I can think about is missing him."

"What does Antoine think?"

"We're breaking it off. It's best for both of us. Coming here has opened my eyes," she said softly. "He's not ready to be a husband or...," she mumbled, . . . "a stepfather."

"Have you bought the ticket yet?" He drummed his fingers nervously.

"No. I'm going to the airport in the morning. Is Tyler there?"

"I'm sorry. He went out for ice cream with a friend. I have an idea. Why don't you connect through Denver and stay for a few days? You can hang out with Tyler before you head back to Chicago."

"Really?" Excitement flooded her voice. "I can stay with my friend Lily if she's in town or find a hotel nearby."

"Let me know when you'll be arriving. We can surprise Tyler." He chuckled into the phone. "He will love seeing you."

And just like that, things were working out.

CHAPTER FIFTY-ONE

You have a beautiful home," Jillian stood while holding Skylar in Caitlynn's living room. The baby swing with a soft fleece covering and fuzzy animal-shaped mobile stood out in stark contrast to the glass dining table and modern furnishing.

"I'll show you the rest of the house."

Caitlynn's bedroom—a French Country vibe, looked amazingly cozy, but didn't fit the sleek modern look of her living room. "This looks like a room a queen would sleep in." Jillian laid Skylar on top of the fluffy soft ivory comforter. "You're a princess now." She smiled at Skylar and kissed her cheek.

"Do you want to see the nursery?"

"Yeah. I want to see how the crib and the changing table I gave you looks in the room." She picked Skylar up and followed Caitlynn down the hallway.

When Caitlynn opened the door, Jillian gasped. "This is beautiful. When did you have time to do all this?"

The room—decorated to look like a carousel with three four-foot high, three-dimensional carousel horses, giraffes, and zebras in pastel colors painted on the wall. A sparling gold chandelier dipped down from the center of the high ceiling. Pastel colors of silk fabric cascaded down from the light and stopped where the ceiling met the walls.

"Do you like it?" Caitlynn beamed. She brushed her hand across the crib sheet. "I know it's only been two weeks since you and I started expediting the process with the lawyer, but I've been too excited to sleep, so I've gotten a lot finished."

"I love it! This room looks like it came straight from the pages of Pottery Barn for Kids."

A plush rocking chair sat in the corner. There was a violet pillow with a gold embroidered crown and Skylar's name written underneath.

Jillian walked over to the rocking chair and sat down, grinning at Skylar. "You're going to love your room." Excitement filled her voice. "I love this room. Skylar loves to rock. We don't have a rocking chair, so I rocked her in my arms."

"Thanks for telling me. I'll try to do what Skylar is used to." Caitlynn paused a moment. "Jillian, the judge turned over the parenting rights to me today, but I want you to know, this isn't goodbye. You take your time figuring out how involved you want to be in Skylar's life."

"I know what I'd like. The final say is up to you, though." Her breath seemed caught in her throat. "You're Skylar's mom now."

"How do you see this relationship working between us?" Caitlynn's eyes darkened.

"Um . . . I'd like to be like a family member. Maybe I could be like a cousin to you? I'd like to pop in every once in a while. I'd like to see her at Christmas and on her birthday and get pictures of her as she grows up."

"Do you want Skylar to know you're her birth mom?" Caitlynn twirled a strand of hair.

"I'm not sure." Jillian rocked Skylar softly. "Not right now. I think that might confuse her." She stared into Caitlynn's eyes. "You're her mom, and we'll get advice about that when the timing is right."

Caitlynn let out a huge sigh. "Okay. I like that arrangement. I'm sure to most people this might seem like an unusual way to handle an adoption, but to me, you're more like my little sister than a cousin."

Jillian said, brightly. "This isn't so unusual."

"Why do you say that?"

"When I was a little girl, I went to church with Tori, and I still remember Moses' story. For some reason, Pharaoh wanted to kill all the Jewish baby boys, so Moses's mother went to the river and put him in a basket in the water. She sent Moses's sister to watch as it floated down the river. One of the Pharaoh's daughters found the basket floating in the water. She rescued baby Moses and raised him as her own. When Moses's sister sees that the princess decides to keep the child, out comes the sister from her hiding place by the river and says she knows of a woman who will nurse the child . . . Moses's own mother."

"That's a remarkable story! I love it!" Caitlynn exclaimed. "The baby is saved, his mother is in his life as much as possible, and he ends up becoming a great leader if I remember correctly. I wonder if the princess knew the nursemaid was Moses's mom?"

"Probably," Jillian said.

Even if she tried, Caitlynn couldn't contain the way her heart overflowed with joy. The judge ordered Jillian's birthrights relinquished, but there was a six-month interim period before it would be permanent. Jillian could still change her mind and take the baby back, but Caitlynn hoped for the best. Jillian caressed a lock of Skylar's hair and traced her head as if memorizing the softness.

"It's pretty amazing when you think about it," Jillian whispered.

Caitlynn said, "I bought some formula and diapers. I'm going to get them from the car and put some things away. I'll be back in a few minutes."

"Go ahead." Jillian settled comfortably. "We'll be fine."

Caitlynn stepped out of the room and stood still. She took a deep breath, gathering herself; otherwise, she thought she might faint. She peeked in the room and saw Jillian holding Skylar, and she did everything in her power not to cry at the sight.

Suddenly, she felt something powerful—otherworldly—come over her, and she couldn't move. It was as if something was holding her to this exact spot. Her heart was full and sad all at once as she watched Jillian speak loving words to her daughter.

"You have no idea what's happening, little one," Jillian whispered. "I'm going to leave you in good hands."

Tears flowed down Jillian's cheek. "You're going to have a mommy who will take good care of you, love you, and give you so much more than I can right now. Whatever happens, please don't feel like I've abandoned you."

She snuggled Skylar close. "There won't be a day that goes by that I won't think of you. I love you so much." She caressed her baby's cheek. "I'm going to go to college and become a successful lawyer, and one day down the road, I hope to have a family. When I do, I hope someday you'll want to be a part of my life."

She tenderly stroked Skylar's hair. "Never think I'll love my other children more than I love you because it simply won't be true. When the time comes for you to know me as your birth mom, I hope you'll understand that I gave you up because I love you, and your happiness is worth more to me than my desire to keep you."

She kissed both of Skylar's cheeks and sobbed, "This isn't goodbye. It's more like I'll be watching over you...from a distance."

She held Skylar's hand and lovingly stroked each tiny finger. She hugged her close again, basking in the warm embrace of her child, memorizing the feeling, as her tears fell onto the blanket Skylar was snuggled in. Back and forth, Jillian rocked. Her voice quivered as she quietly sang, *"Hush Little Baby,"* one last time.

Caitlynn silently wept. Jillian's words caressed her ears and her heart, and she never wanted to forget this moment . . . a tender, beautiful moment between a mother and a daughter, a bond so strong it would be forever.

After she was able to pull herself together, she entered the room. Jillian stood and held out Skylar for Caitlynn.

"She likes to be facing out, looking at where she's going. If you put her over your shoulder, she'll start to cry, thinking you're trying to get her to sleep."

Caitlynn's eyes glimmered. "Smart girl."

"Here. You try." Jillian handed her over. "Also, Skylar needs to be burped halfway through her bottle. And, she loves to stare at the bunny rattle when you shake it! I think she's trying to figure out why I keep shaking it in her face. Her very favorite blanket is the one the hospital gave her."

The doorbell chimed. Skylar stirred.

"My mom's here. Do you want me to get the door?" Jillian asked.

Caitlynn nodded and followed close behind. Peggy stood on the landing; her eyes bloodshot and puffy, holding two plastic grocery bags.

She grimaced a lopsided grin. "I brought a few more things for Skylar."

"Come in." Caitlynn bit her lower lip.

"I found a couple of bottles and some bath stuff."

"That was thoughtful of you," Caitlynn whispered. "Thank you, Peggy."

"Mom, I was just showing Caitlynn how Skylar likes to be held."

It was clear Peggy cried the entire way over. "Caitlynn, would it be okay if my mom held her?" Jillian asked.

"Of course." Her voice shook. "Please do."

Peggy nodded and held out her arms to receive Skylar. She turned to Jillian. "Honey, there's a camera in one of the bags. Will you take our picture?"

Jillian rummaged through the bag and found the camera. Then she took a couple of snap shots.

"Let me take a picture of both of you with Skylar," Caitlynn said. Snapping the picture, her eyes misted. "I-I can see how difficult this sacrifice is that you're both making." Her voice shook. "I can never thank you enough, nor can I find the words to express what I feel in my heart."

Peggy kissed Skylar's cheek. "I'm going to miss you, angel." Her breath caught. "I know we've made the right decision, but this is harder than I ever imagined." She looked helplessly at Caitlynn.

"Mom, take a picture of me holding Skylar."

Peggy gently transferred Skylar to Jillian's arms and took a picture of Jillian and Skylar cheek to cheek.

"Do you have tissue?" Peggy asked Caitlynn.

"In the bathroom, first door on the right." She came out of the bathroom, dabbing her eyes.

Caitlynn nodded toward the sofa. "I have to show you how much this child means to me. Please take a seat." She sat, and Jillian took the next cushion over while Peggy sank into the chair.

Caitlynn looked at Skylar lying comfortably in Jillian's arms. "I'm not sure I can tell you what's in my heart."

But I will try "I know how much you love Skylar, and I want you to know that I will do everything I can to be the best parent possible. I love her so much already." Caitlynn touched her heart. "I know the love I have is going to grow deeper still. I feel like I'm on the top of an iceberg—only the tip shows above the ocean, but underneath the waves is a love so deep it reaches far below the surface, just waiting for me to discover more."

"I know." Jillian nodded. "That's exactly why I picked you. Besides my mom, you're the only one who stuck with me. At first, I thought the only reason was that you wanted to finish your story." She glanced down at her lap. "Remember when we went out for pizza? I knew you were for real when you stayed by my side during that pathetic scene with Marcus. You were so worried about me, and you asked if I wanted company when you dropped me off." She tilted her head slightly. "That did it for me."

"I had no idea!" Peggy's brow furrowed. "Marcus!" she spat. "I hope I never see him!" She stared at Caitlynn as if really seeing her for the first time. "Thank you for being there for Jillian."

"I would do it all again."

Skylar stirred in Jillian's arms and opened her eyes. "Mom? Caitlynn and I talked, and she said we could see Skylar at Christmas."

Peggy's eyes sparkled; a smile lit her face. "You've made me so happy." Her sigh sounded like one of great relief. "Now we have something to look forward too."

"We should go." Jillian tenderly kissed Skylar on both cheeks. Then, with outstretched arms, she surrendered her daughter to Caitlynn. "Here you go." Her eyes pooled. "Please take good care of her." Her breath caught. "I know you will."

Peggy stood. She leaned over and kissed Skylar on the cheek and then kissed Caitlynn. "Take care of my angel. I know you'll be a terrific mother. I'll see you at Christmas."

Caitlynn choked up, "Thank you," she murmured. She snuggled Skylar as the tears fell. "I'll see you then."

Jillian's reached for her mother's hand and walked out. She turned to get one last look before Caitlynn closed the door.

Caitlynn hugged Skylar close to her chest every beat pumping wildly. She tenderly kissed Skylar on the forehead and said softly to her new daughter, "Welcome home, my love."

CHAPTER FIFTY-TWO

As Caitlynn sat in the rocker feeding Skylar the remaining few ounces of formula, she reflected on the past several weeks. So much had changed in that short time. It was as if she were on a roller coaster, inching up a steep incline, terrified, but also excited about what she'd experience next.

She only knew a few sacred hours of sleep at a time, between feedings and changing diapers. Pacing the floor as Skylar cried, her little face wrinkled in pain from colic. All of it was new to Caitlynn, and her heart melted with every smile and every tear. If she had to choose, her very favorite was naptime. She'd lay Skylar on her chest and fall asleep, feeling the warmth of her baby's tiny body. Each little breath was like a soft feather caressing Caitlynn's skin.

In three weeks, the leave of absence was over, and Caitlynn was busy finding full-time childcare. She'd interviewed several prospective babysitters before finally deciding to go with Sara, a young woman who lived nearby with her husband, a physical therapist, and their two young children. Caitlynn had connected with her instantly.

Today, they'd arranged a trial run to leave Skylar for a few hours with Sara, so Caitlynn could meet with her counselor.

"There you go. You're all finished with your bottle." She patted her baby's back. "Are you going to burp?"

Skylar, wearing her pretty powder-blue sundress and tiny matching socks, looked up and cooed, then gave a little belch. Caitlynn smiled in satisfaction. "Does this mean your tummy is getting better? In two weeks, you'll be four months old. "I sure hope by then this colic will be a thing of the past."

Standing up, she changed Skylar's diaper, grabbed the baby bag, and headed to the car, gently strapping her into the infant car seat. A few minutes later, Caitlynn was inside Sara's house giving last minute instructions. "If there's any problem, give me a call. I'll hurry back."

"You sound like a first-time mommy." Sara chuckled. "There won't be a problem. We're going to get along just fine."

"Okay, but just so you know, Skylar has colic and can be fussy."

"No worries. I have no problem holding this little one while she cries. Both of my kids suffered with it too. She'll outgrow it, just like they did."

"I'm looking forward to the day," Caitlynn admitted. "For now, though, I should be back in about two hours. Thanks."

Sara held Skylar and lifted the baby's arm as if she were waving good-bye. "See you later Mommy."

Caitlynn's shook her head, amazed. She still couldn't believe she could now be called "Mommy."

Caitlynn sank into the comfy couch, glad to have a few minutes to rest while she waited for Michelle. A few moments later, Michelle walked in and took a seat in the wingback chair.

"Hi, Caitlynn." She smiled. "How is it going with your new baby?"

Caitlynn wanted to pinch herself. "It's amazing. I-I can't explain it," she stuttered. "For the first time in my life, I feel like I'm doing what I was meant to do."

Michelle's eyes widened. "Why is that?"

"I've always loved my job, but it never satisfied me. I've always known something was missing. I volunteered at the Children's Hospital in neonatal, and I loved that too, but it was like being thirsty for a big glass of water, and all I got was a sip."

"And now you can drink as much as you want."

"Yes. I finally feel satisfied."

Michelle tilted her head and stared at Caitlynn. "You seem different. When you first came to see me, you were in such pain. Now you look serene."

"I don't feel like the same person." She looked down at the rug. "I'm going to try to explain how I'm feeling. Steve . . . he was the reason I came to counseling, but Skylar is the biggest reason I've changed." Tears pricked her eyes. "Before she came, I felt as if a ten-foot brick wall surrounded my heart." She stared into Michelle's eyes. "Skylar's like a wrecking ball that smashed the bricks into a million little pieces and exposed my heart to what it feels like to love."

"Brick by brick, you had protected yourself from ever being hurt again. But it also stopped you from truly loving yourself and from fully loving others."

Caitlynn could only nod, too torn up to speak.

"You told me when you first came that you had a four-month leave of absence. It's almost over. Have you decided what you're going to do?"

"Coming here has helped me realize that I'm not the horrible person I thought I was. You showed me that when I lashed out at Steve, it was to protect myself from ever getting hurt by him again. My job was the most important part of my life, and my need to protect what I loved propelled me to seek revenge. I just couldn't adjust to him coming back into my life."

"And in the end?" Michelle took a tissue from the box and handed it to Caitlynn.

"In the end . . . I couldn't go through with it. The thought of Tyler, Steve's son, hating me, stopped me from pushing the button."

"Was there any other motivation?" She leaned forward and waited.

"Yes," Caitlynn whispered. "I loved Steve. We met in college. We fell in love and lived together for two years. I was positive we were going to get married."

"What happened to change that?"

"He's from a wealthy family. Maybe you've heard of them? Carr Broadcast Communications?"

Michelle nodded. "I have."

"His father did his best to break us up," Caitlynn said coldly. "He offered Steve a job in Chicago that he couldn't pass up."

"That's not true, though. He had a choice—he could've said no."

"That's pretty much what Steve said when he apologized to me."

Michelle raised her brows in surprise. "When was this?"

Caitlynn sighed deeply. "I know what you're thinking. He apologized, and I still went after him."

"Why don't you tell me the rest of the story?"

Caitlynn wiped away a tear. "As I said, we were in love, and I had our whole life planned. We'd get married, both find jobs working together at a station in Denver, and then I'd tell him I was pregnant."

"But that never happened." Michelle reached over and tenderly squeezed Caitlynn's shoulder.

"No," Caitlynn whispered. "I took the job in Denver, scheduled an abortion, and tried to forget." Her shoulders shook. She looked down to the floor and sobbed.

"I see." Michelle handed over the box of tissue and waited for Caitlynn to stop crying.

"The whole thing with Steve…the baby—it broke my heart."

"And halted your heart from love—that's when you started building the fortress around your heart, isn't it."

"Yes…I never wanted to experience again how much it hurts when you lose the only relationship that truly matters."

"And now?"

Caitlynn beamed through her tears. "And now there's Skylar. She's my wrecking ball. My new beginning."

"I'm so happy for you." Michelle squeezed Caitlynn's hand a brief moment. "I want to help you through the next few weeks. You have to decide if you can forgive Steve. If you can't do that, then you have to figure out if you can work with him, or if it's time to find different employment."

Caitlynn gasped. "That's exactly what my mom said! You've helped me realize how wrong I was to have so much anger and blame placed squarely on Steve's shoulders. What I…almost did is reprehensible. I feel so guilty."

"The first step was listening to your mom. You're on the right track. Guilt sometimes can be a great motivator to change. Shame, on the other hand, is never a constructive feeling." She grinned. "I bet your mother is a wise woman."

"She is. My mom is the reason why I'm here." Caitlynn's voice rose with excitement. "I plan to visit her next week so she can meet her new granddaughter. She's only seen pictures."

"That's wonderful!" Michelle exclaimed. "I'm sure you'll have a great time." She stood and said, "Let's schedule a time to meet in two weeks."

Caitlynn practically skipped to her car, feeling as if a heavy weight had been flung from her shoulders and hurled into space. Her heart; free now, from the pain she'd held onto—overflowing with love. Not loss. She couldn't wait to see Skylar. She sat in her car and pulled down the visor mirror to see the damage her crying had caused. She cleaned her face with a tissue and applied fresh lipstick. Was it her imagination, or did her face look like it glowed? She smiled at the reflection in the mirror, and for the first time in over twelve years, she liked what she saw.

###

Becky held Skylar. "Oh, just look at her! She's got the bluest eyes I've ever seen." She turned and studied Caitlynn's features. "The second bluest I've ever seen. Your eyes remind me of the color of the Caribbean Sea. Skylar's are more the color of the sky."

"I know. Doesn't she look as if she could've been my child?"

"She is your child."

"Well, you know what I mean."

"Do you know how lucky you are? Most people have to wait years to adopt." Becky caressed Skylar's fingers. "You're a blessing, that's what you are." Looking up, she spoke again, "She's a miracle if you ask me."

Caitlynn grinned so wide her cheeks hurt. "I know."

Becky stared thoughtfully at Caitlynn. "You've changed. You glow like a woman on her wedding day. Do you know that?"

"I'm happy." Caitlynn glanced at her daughter.

"I get that. But there's more. You've gained some weight." She eyed Caitlynn up and down. "You look lovely. I'm probably speaking out of turn—"

"Go ahead." Caitlynn interrupted. "You're gonna say what's on your mind anyway." She giggled.

"Your smile reaches your eyes now."

Caitlynn twisted a strand of hair. "Thank you. I have so many positive changes…I'm working on my eating habits—or lack thereof." Through therapy, she'd learned that one of the long-term struggles for women who've had abortions is eating disorders.

"I can't explain—I guess it's because I love Skylar so much. She's melting my heart more and more each day. I feel different…as if I can love again." The faint patter of rain hit the window.

Becky briefly watched it drip against the window and then smiled. "That must be it. I'm happy for you."

"Put Skylar on the baby blanket. I want to show you what she can do."

Becky placed Skylar on her tummy in the middle of the blanket and waited. A few seconds passed. Skylar rose up on her hands, leaned to one side, and rolled.

"Look!" Caitlynn softly clapped with pride. She was sure her child had to be the smartest baby on the planet.

Becky giggled. "That's great. She's totally looking around the room like she's just itchin' to explore."

"I know. She also loves lights. They mesmerize her. And she likes music."

"Have you talked to Jillian?"

"Yes. I sent her the latest photos. She meets her new roommate this week and registers for classes."

"When do you go back to work?"

Caitlynn bit her lip. "I found a sitter…I have to be back in three weeks."

"What about Steve? Do you think you can work with him?"

"That's the elephant in the room, isn't it?"

"What worries you the most when you think about seeing him?"

"My heart," Caitlynn whispered.

"Huh?" Becky tilted her head. She was silent for a moment; then her eyes popped open. She looked up to heaven. "Oh! Dear Lord, I don't believe it!" She hit the side of her head. "All the plotting and scheming, the fuming that he was back in your life. You still love him! Everything you did was to protect yourself from hurting again."

"Yes." She stared into Becky's eyes. "I do…I thought for sure he was a phony. He kept saying, 'I'm different, I've changed; I'm not the same person I used to be.' He talked about God and how important his faith is to him now. He asked me to give him a second chance . . ."

Caitlynn spoke softly. "I didn't believe him. I couldn't figure out how someone could change from the most self-centered person I've ever known to someone who thinks about others so selflessly." She shook her head. "I thought it had to be an act."

"And now?"

"*People can change.* I-I can change." She looked lovingly at Skylar. "She's taught me to love. Unconditionally. The loneliness, the broken relationships… all of it is fading like an old photograph. Something's different." She brought her hand to her heart. "I can't explain."

"You might not be able to explain it, but I can, girl! You gotta go tell Steve what you just told me!"

"What do I say? When I think of what I've done, I'm wracked with guilt."

"That's a good start. It's not like you have to go to him declaring your undying love! Just tell him you're sorry. See where it goes from there."

Caitlynn glanced away. *Could she do it?* What was stopping her? Rejection? Pride? "Becky, can you watch Skylar for me? I'd like to go now before I chicken out."

Becky lifted her hand for a high five. They smacked palms. "You've got guts! I love it."

"I either have guts or no common sense. The diapers are upstairs in Skylar's room, and there's formula on the counter." She gave Becky a peck on the cheek, snatched her rain jacket from the closet, and slid into it. "Thanks. I owe you. Wish me luck."

Becky nudged her to the door. "I'll do one better. I'll send up a prayer."

The windshield wipers swished every few seconds, clearing away the scattered drops that fell from the sky. On the way to Steve's house, Caitlynn recalled everything he'd done to show her that he'd changed, from helping her through her recovery to making dinner for her at Christmas. She touched her lips, remembering his kisses.

Then there was the hike when he had told her he'd changed, that he was a Christian, and that Jesus Christ had given him a second chance at doing life the right way. He'd come to the hospital and apologized for his part of the pain she was in. But none of it had registered. It was as if her heart was a chunk of ice, and her eyes had blinders on, and the only thing she felt or saw was her pain.

You were there when Steve had the chickenpox. You helped Tyler adjust to the turmoil in his life: bought him gifts, took him skiing, and made him feel important.

The thoughts surprised her. They didn't come from her. The only thing she thought about was how she managed to be so bitterly wrong about everything.

God? Is that you? She pulled into the beginning of Steve's long drive and slammed on the brakes. Butterflies flitted in her gut. The security gate was closed.

She parked her car and stepped out. The early evening shower touched her skin like tiny drops of dew. She lifted her face to the sky for more and breathed in the fresh scent of the damp grass. Assessing the situation took about ten seconds. *I guess I'm hopping a fence.*

Check the gate.

She hurried over and pushed it easily to the side. It must've blown shut during the storm.

The winding road was about 300 feet from the house, but the only way she could see his home is if she stood on her tiptoes and looked through the branches of some cottonwood trees. *I'm not backing out now. I'll walk. That way he won't see the headlights from the car.*

The closer she got, the slower she trudged. A hodgepodge of images raced through her mind: Steve praying at his meals, the warmth of Steve's hand in hers, his kiss, how much she cared for Tyler, and the miracle of her baby. *Miracle!* The most wonderful gift of love ever given to her, could only come from one source. *God? You were there all along. I see it now!*

Her hot, salty tears mixed with the coolness of the raindrops and flowed to the ground. She let out a cry and dropped to her knees. *You brought her into my life so I could feel your unconditional love.* She looked up at the gray sky and thought about Skylar. *And you brought her to me so I could figure out how to love. Jesus, I'm sorry. Please, please forgive me.*

Warmth spread through her being, filling her with such love and a sense of forgiveness, so deep, that she was on fire. The raindrops fell like they were coming straight from heaven, cleansing her. She lifted her head, tears falling faster, and soaked her heart with the deepest love and the most amazing peace she'd ever known. A powerful presence like an electric current penetrated deep into her spirit. But she wasn't afraid as it filled every empty crevice in her soul, all the way to her innermost being. All the shame and guilt vaporized like steam, and an unspeakable joy flooded her heart. Giddy, she laughed, as she felt higher and lighter, as if she could dance on a cloud. Looking through her tears, she could almost see God smiling.

A still small voice in her spirit uttered three words: *I love you.*

CHAPTER FIFTY-THREE

Love never fails
1CORINTHIANS. 13:8

Steve closed his eyes and listened to the rain hitting the windows. Tyler was spending the night. at Hunter's. The icemaker plunked out ice, and the fan hummed from the air conditioning.

Baseball was over next week. The following week they were going camping, and then fly to Chicago so Tyler could get ready for school. He drummed his fingertips on the couch cushion in double time. Not only would he drop Tyler off, but he'd also get to see Boo one last time before his parents moved to Denver. They had sold the horse farm, and next month, they'd be moving into their new home in Cherry Creek Hills, only twenty minutes away from him.

He stared at the painting of Boo. Some of his favorite memories were of riding his horse. Leaving Boo would be hard, but he found a small measure of comfort in knowing that Boo had a job. The woman who bought the property ran a business teaching kids with disabilities how to ride. She'd fallen in love with Boo and asked if he could stay.

So much change was coming in the next few weeks. How would he get through it? He would miss Tyler's immeasurable energy. And then there was Caitlynn. Ever since he'd given Caitlynn over to God, he sensed a feeling of peace deep in his soul. He had had to let go, once and for all, and let God do his will. No matter how hard it was, he would wait and see what happened. Three weeks wasn't long. Would she resign? Would finding another job away from him help her? If so, he'd help out in any way possible. He had connections in the industry and could get her a job somewhere—even if it meant he'd never see her again. Her happiness meant more to him.

During the last three months, all he had thought about was what he could've done differently with Caitlynn. Deep down, he knew the answer. Nothing. He wouldn't have changed a thing. He had tried to show her that he'd changed, hoping that through his actions, she'd see; he loved her, but it backfired.

He had no choice now but to accept whatever the future would bring and pray that somehow Caitlynn would be okay. His mouth quirked. He could have told her that she'd never go through with her act of revenge. *She's hurt. I am too, but for a different reason. You put her back in my life. Why? So, I could see how much I love her, just to let her go? Tell her I'm sorry? Lord, help.*

The doorbell rang, and he jumped slightly in surprise. He wasn't expecting anyone. Opening the door, his jaw dropped. There stood Caitlynn, smiling and crying at the same time, her face radiating joy. She glowed from the top of her soaking wet hair to the bottom of her muddy tennis shoes.

"Hey…I bet you're surprised to see me." Her voice shook.

He stepped out onto the porch next to Caitlynn and closed the door. A few feet away, the rain fell. Puddles formed on the driveway, but on the landing, they were dry.

He spoke softly, "What are you doing here, Caitlynn?"

She radiated brighter still. "I . . . have a baby—"

"What?" he responded. That was the last thing he thought would come out of her mouth.

"Yes, I have a baby . . . Skylar. After a long, hard decision, Jillian said she couldn't—"

"That's amazing…I-I'm happy for you," he said and took a step closer. He shook his head in wonder. It sounded like a God-thing to him.

"Th-thanks." She gazed into his eyes and took a step back. "I came to see you because—"

He took another step toward her. "Are we going to keep doing this two-step?" He grinned at her muddy shoes. "If so, we both need dancing shoes."

She giggled. "Don't make me laugh. I'm serious. I'm trying to tell you that I'm sorry . . . so very, very sorry. I honestly have no words about what I've done . . ." She rushed on. "But I've changed. Skylar, her love. No, it's more than that. It's the love I have for her. It's God. He's real! I've realized . . . so much." She sighed deeply. "I'm so sorry, Steve, I get it now. Remember when you asked me to forgive you?"

She bridged the gap between them by stepping so close to him; he couldn't tear his eyes away.

"Will you please forgive me?" Her mouth trembled.

"Yes, I forgive you." He smiled joyfully. *This is the Caitlynn I fell in love with.*

"I-I . . ." she stuttered, "I want to prove to you I've changed. Everything I did to you was to protect my heart from feeling hurt again because I never stopped . . . I've always loved you." Her lips quivered. "How can I win your trust back?" Her voice shook. "We can take it slowly." Her lashes glistened from unshed tears.

"Shh." He broke into another smile. Overcome with happiness, his heart skipping just like it had the very first time they met, he placed his finger on her lips, lingering. "Caitlynn, you don't need to say a word. "I can see it written on your face…and in your eyes. You smile from the heart now." He softly brushed her cheek. "Your face glows like you've swallowed the sun."

He looked out. The rain was slowing to a soft drizzle. The dark clouds were breaking up; soon, the storm would stop and give way to the blue sky, fresh and new. He held out his hand. "Walk with me."

Caitlynn leaned in, clasped his hand, and replied. "In the rain."

ACKNOWLEDGEMENTS

I came to this writing journey with a story idea God placed in my heart many years ago. Like a blank page staring me in the face, I had no idea where to begin. Word, by, word, the story unfolded and I can say without a doubt that this novel is the result of staying obedient and never giving up!

A colossal thanks to my friends and family who have read the book and given helpful feedback.

To my critique group; Debbie (writing as Anna Wise) author of **Mercy Me**, Sondra Umberger, author of **Unrivaled-Rewoven** suspense series—they've been through multiple revisions and kept the faith that this manuscript would morph into the novel it is today and I couldn't have done it without their support and encouragement along the way.

I want to thank my cover designer, Keno McCloskey, for her amazing artistry and creative suggestions during the design process.

And finally, a very special thanks to my husband, John. He is an invaluable critique partner, beta reader, and encourager. Spiritually and emotionally, he continues to stand by me every step of the way with unconditional love and support. He truly believes in me and I find that incredibly motivating.

BOOK CLUB QUESTIONS

Have you ever wanted to enact revenge? If so, what was the consequence?

Caitlynn doesn't come across as a likable person or someone you would want to get to know personally. Discuss why?

Caitlynn's character slowly evolves from cold and calculating revenge to loving those around her and desiring forgiveness. What plot points in the story helped Caitlynn to make these changes?

How did the interaction with Steve and other believers help her to question what she believed about God? Was there ever a time in your life when the message of Salvation through Jesus Christ was shared?

Abortion is a painful topic for most women; how can you help those who are affected by this difficult decision? How does God's forgiveness play a role in helping women on both sides of the spectrum?

Steve tries to show Caitlynn he is not the man he used to be—and is trying his best to show her by his actions—that God loves her. Have you ever tried to share Christ with someone you love, but have been rejected by them? How does prayer help you to overcome the hurt and not give up?

Steve fails over and over again because he thinks he has to make decisions happen on his terms. God shows him throughout that he needs to rely more on Him and trust that the outcome is in God's hands. What areas in your life do you find hard to relinquish as you, "let go and let God?"

Jillian gave her child up for adoption. Adoption is a tender topic that takes many viewpoints. This book relates to the adoption story of baby Moses' by the daughter of Pharaoh. Jesus told of the landowner who sent his son to collect what was due. However, the evil farmers killed his son, symbolizing Jesus Christ's death for our sins. (Mathew 21:33-36) Both accounts reflect a deep love and selflessness, mirroring the sacrifice it took for Jillian to give up Skylar. What was difficult for you to grasp? And did it give you another perspective regarding adoption?

If you, a loved one, have had, or know of, those affected by abortion, or considering adoption there are many agencies to contact for help.

www.nationaladoptionhotline.org
Nationwide adoption center both for those who are thinking of placing their baby for adoption, and for those who have turned to adoption as the result of infertility.

Hope After Abortion.com. www.hopeafterabortion.com.
It's normal to grieve a pregnancy loss, including the loss of a child by abortion. It can form a hole in one's heart, a hole so deep that sometimes it seems nothing can fill the emptiness. You are not alone.

***

Finally, if you need God's forgiveness for any painful decisions in your past, it's a gift for you—and only requires that you pray and ask Jesus to forgive you of your sins. If you sincerely believe in your heart and mind that Jesus is the Son of God—you are forgiven! Jesus asks in return that you follow him and seek him with all your heart, mind, soul, and strength. My prayers are with you as you journey in this life with love only found in Jesus Christ; truly forgiven and truly free!

***

Thank You for reading my novel. You can follow me on social media as well as my website—www.genevrabonati.com, to find out when my next release is available, blog posts, and giveaways.

My desire is to write inspirational romance novels that bring light to the struggles in our society today by offering hope that can only be experienced through faith in Jesus Christ.

I welcome your emails and look forward to hearing from you!

Genevra Bonati is published in Chicken Soup for the Soul, The One Year Devotional of Joy and Laughter and has multiple articles published.

It is through her experience of being loved and forgiven by her Savior, Jesus Christ, that inspires her to write of true freedom.

Email: **genevra.bonati@gmail.com** or **www.genevrabonati.com**

Genevra Bonati

Where romance and relevance unite!